JAMIE C★LLINS

THE Secrets & Stilettos SERIES

★

BLONDE Up!

BLONDE UP!
Copyright © 2015 by Jamie Collins
All rights reserved.

1980585628

Cover Design & Interior Format by The Killion Group
www.thekilliongroupinc.com

BOOKS BY
JAMIE COLLINS

★ ★ ★

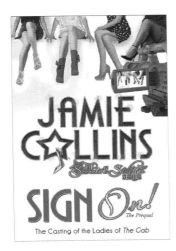

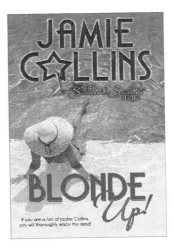

DEDICATION

★ ★ ★

To my Stilettos, the best Reader Group any author could ask for. Thank you for being the best part of the journey. Happy reading!

~ Jamie

PROLOGUE

★ ★ ★

"The idea came to me as I was standing in line at the grocery store," explains producer Bumpy Friedman, of the creation of Global Network's all-woman talkfest, scheduled to air next month. The groundbreaking show will feature four female hosts with definite star power. A spokesperson for the network says, "We aren't afraid to be intelligent as well as controversial." Friedman, the thirty-five-year veteran, goes on to add, "What could be better than Oprah, Ellen, and The View—on steroids? Daytime snooze-talk goes Real Housewives, TMZ-style. We will offer viral topics with headline-worthy guests on multimedia platforms to meet the current appetite for hot and unscripted gossip served up by the best celebrity hosts in the business. So, in simple terms... that's how The Gab was born."

—Media Magazine 2015

CHAPTER 1

★ ★ ★

GLOBAL STUDIOS. NEW YORK CITY
FALL 2015

BUMPY FRIEDMAN HAD A VISION. It kept him up at night, and it fueled him throughout the day.

The elevator doors snapped open, and a push of briefcases, overcoats, and power ties scattered in all directions.

There were important matters at hand. Deals to be won. Viewers to capture. Market shares to be claimed. Station executives bent over smartphones streaming with appointments, contacts, opportunities, all wore it—the same indelible look: the Game Face. Impervious to fear, this was a powerful weapon in the volatile jungle of network television programming. It was the first day of fall Sweeps, and that translated to one simple collective mission: *survival*.

Time was money, and money was the name of the game. That, of course, and ratings, without which, heads would roll. It was as simple as that.

Bumpy Friedman had been here before. The pressure fazed him little. He knew to trust his gut instincts. And today, his gut said victory.

He burst through the mammoth plate glass doors, customarily late, his Rolex still on Central Standard Time. Couldn't get the damn thing to reset since the last business trip to Chicago, so he just left it that way. Did the math, give or take the Daylight Savings factor. It was going on five months now, and it was really beginning to become a royal pain in the ass.

The executive offices of Global Studios were a stunning testament to the TV station's long-standing position of first place. Portraits of network legends, beloved celebrities, and corporate aristocracy enshrined in chrome frames lined the walls of the sterile gray corridors high above Fifth Avenue. Each revered icon a mainstay, and due in large part to the verisimilitude of Bumpy's genius.

This was where it all happened. The colossal Global Studios logo glistening above the marble and granite reception desk said so. This was it—the magic place. Disney-*freaking*-land!

"Good morning, Mr. Friedman."

The devastatingly beautiful ice princess perched at the reception desk didn't look up. She was the new skirt from the agency and was, not incidentally, amazingly stacked. He approved of the way she looked sitting behind the big desk and, moreover, the sure way she provided a rock-solid hard-on in his pants every time he saw her.

"It is, isn't it?"

One glance was all it took.

He missed nothing—of course, ask him her name and he would have to use a lifeline. Bumpy was the type of guy who only paid attention to the things that mattered, to him. Today, she was sporting a fuzzy pink sweater the color of cotton candy, an ass-hugging leather skirt, and dark-chocolate suede boots. *Not a bad way to start the goddamn day!* He decided that he would have to hire her on full time if this kept up.

Next, Bumpy rounded the corner, past a current of har-

ried production assistants and office personnel. An endless
whir of schedule logs, traffic orders, storyboards, and script
revisions were deftly being stacked, shuffled, and carted
from in-basket to in-basket like a meticulous symphony.
Christ! But he loved it all! The excitement, the hectic
pace... every inch of his empire was humming with energy.
All this and it was only six—make that—*seven* thirty in the
morning!

He realized that today, he even loved the derisive and
ever present scowl on the cleaning woman's face as she
wheeled past him. She, along with her janitorial cart, was
yet another hallowed fixture in the halls of the station's
ninth-floor executive offices for as far back as he could
remember; just as she had been when he first started working for the network, snot-nosed and stupid over thirty-five
years ago, there in the very same building. The job was a
favor from his uncle, who wrote a semi-regular column for
the *New York Times* back when Bumpy himself was just an
amateur reporter, struggling to follow his dreams with a
young wife and infant child; eager then to do whatever it
would take to secure a job with any major network. Sort-
ing shipments in the mailroom back then suited him just
fine at the time, although it, along with hustling appliances
at a side job in sales, barely kept him and his new family
fed during those "ground zero years," as he liked to refer
to them.

"Morning, Violet!"

No response. She wasn't a fan.

Come to think of it, she despised him back then too.
Only, now, she did it *slower.*

Her base expression was tempting to contest, as was his
usual practice, but today, rendered impervious by his blissful mood. He would not be swayed.

"Why, thank you... and you have a great day yourself,
Gorgeous!" He chuckled to himself, grinning in his wake.

Bumpy loved his job. Mostly, he loved the challenge

of living up to his own legacy—a proven track record of notable successes that had earned him the position of Chief Executive Producer for Global's daytime program roster for the past seventeen of his thirty-five-year tenure. He loved the rush of adrenaline that never seemed to stop flowing; day after day, book after ratings book. He particularly loved the thrill of signing on new blood when he was lucky enough to strike pay dirt—like today.

This morning's meeting was about to score him, along with the rest of his executive and programming team, the "boys with the golden balls," big-time points with the corporate heavies. Bumpy knew that he was just moments from sealing what would most likely be the biggest deal of his entire career, and the high was positively incredible. One thing was for certain, with retirement looming on the not-so-distant horizon, nothing was going to stand in his way. Nothing. He was determined to go out with a bang.

He rounded a sharp left into the break room. LeMaster, from marketing, was waiting and headed him off at the pink doughnut box.

"They're here!"

"Excellent." Bumpy nodded, peering beneath the lid.

"Hey, who took all the jelly-filled?" He sneered. "Is one goddamn strawberry roll too much to ask for? Vultures!"

"Here... have the fritter," LeMaster said, sliding from the chair to his feet. He watched as Bumpy helped himself to a coconut cream instead and then, all thumbs and fumbles, retrieve a warm Diet Coke from deep within the crumpled paper sack he carried in lieu of a briefcase. The bag contained exactly five more sodas. It was common knowledge that this, along with a pack and a half of Marlboro's, would pretty much round out Bumpy's diet of champions before the day was over.

Bumpy was a second heart attack waiting to happen, the recipient of a recent triple bypass already the previous year. He was breathing heavily and already beginning to break a sweat. No surprise. He was terribly out of shape, bow-legged, stocky, and at an unhealthy one hundred ninety pounds. LeMaster often joked in private that his boss looked like a cross between a bloated chimp and a lepre-chaun. Bumpy's ruddy face registered distraction, which was standard issue regardless of the occasion, thus caus-ing him to appear every bit the absentminded professor; a persona that he lived up to with tireless verve. He had remarkable eyes, though. Shark blue, that shrank to beady dots behind his Harry Caray pop bottle specs that were forever sliding forward on his stub nose. LeMaster fidgeted as he waited for his boss to devour several pastries before coming up for air.

"What time did they get here?" Bumpy asked.

"The first three at around a quarter to seven... one by one. Two of them arrived in limos, one in a Rolls—caused quite a scene out in front. They've been sitting down in the conference room with Conrad. We're still waiting for the last one to arrive."

"Good." Bumpy grinned, licking his pudgy fingers clean.

"I've been here since five thirty going over some of the numbers with Mike," LeMaster reported. "Apparently, things are—"

"You are taking care of them, right?" Bumpy asked in between breathy swallows of the fizzy soda.

LeMaster balked. Bumpy had a way of always question-ing his staff's competency.

"You've got to be kidding, right?" LeMaster threw him-self into the response, arms flailing and eyes popping about. "Everyone's goin' freakin' nuts! Shirley's been taking their orders for lattes and cappuccinos and shit, and running back and forth to Starbucks like some awestruck groupie!"

"Well, great, then. Perfect!" Bumpy's smile widened as he grabbed another doughnut and scooped up his bag of sodas, inadvertently wiping a sticky hand across the back of his suit pants in the process. "Barry should be on his way as we speak."

LeMaster's face blanched at the sight of Bumpy using a two-thousand-dollar Armani suit as a napkin. He then raked hard through his movie star hair with disgust. "Yeah—okay, great."

They were all a bit edgy.

Bumpy liked the fact that LeMaster was on top of things. That was what he paid him for. Even though the guy was a bit of a *putz*, overall, he was right to trust his instincts with that one. Bumpy knew that LeMaster despised him, but that if the guy had aspirations of ever rising from the trenches of marketing hell to the revered ranks of program development, production, and beyond, then so be it. He would have to kiss Bumpy's ass. It was the way things were done. If he had any brains beneath that perfect head of hair he had, he would know to leach every ounce of brilliance he could from the best, and ride Bumpy's for as long and as far as possible.

Bumpy could make people do things. It was all about selling when you came right down to it. "Put the right package in front of people and they'll buy anything," he'd always say. And if anyone on Earth had the power to make it happen, it was Bumpy Friedman. While many didn't always agree with Bumpy's methods, no one could deny the fact that he did make the numbers, which translated to millions in profits for the station's bottom line—or used to. Now it was time for him to prove it once again. With ratings dangerously slipping due to much-needed changes in the daytime lineup, everyone had to wonder if it could be done—everyone except Bumpy. He was sure as shit.

LeMaster, along with the production staff, regional program managers, and Willard Conrad himself—the highest cheese on the network ladder, all had to have faith that Bumpy Friedman's newest vision would keep them out on top. And, moreover, Bumpy had to have faith that the four women he was about to hire, waiting down in Conference

Room B, could deliver.

LeMaster rubbed his hands together briskly. "Ready, then? Shall we do this thing?"

Bumpy belched unreservedly. It was enough said. He was ready.

CHAPTER 2

★ ★ ★

BORN ON JUNE 12TH, 1947 in Edmond, Oklahoma, Aloysius Theodore Friedman was an awkward child. The name *Bumpy* was a moniker from childhood that explained a host of scrapes and bruises that he incurred at the hands of his ill-fated doom—chronic clumsiness. Being branded with a name like Bumpy played a lot smoother in his adolescent-day run as a fullback for the high school football team. Then, when anyone made mention of bumps or bruises, they were most likely *caused* by number thirty-seven—Bumpy, "The Obviator," Friedman. But true habits are tough to break. Bumpy was a walking casualty, everywhere except on the playing field. Hence, the name stuck into adulthood.

In high school, Bumpy was an A student in spite of holding the record for truancy. He played football until a knee injury took him out late in the last season. At nineteen, he opted for the Army over college and enlisted in 1966. He arrived in Vietnam on Christmas Eve, in Pleiku. He was then quickly deployed to a base camp in An Khe, where he served for eighteen months, first training and then working in radio communications. He was responsible for reporting conflicts and firefights to headquarters, which, in turn, would provide air or ground troop response. He endured the direct hit of mortars and ammunition on the depot at An Khe in November of 1967, with explosions that lasted for days. The rest of his time was spent counting the minutes until he could return home, after which, he promptly willed himself to forget what he deemed the darkest three years of his life.

At twenty-two, he returned home to live with his parents. Bumpy took odd jobs and helped with the family farm, all the while dreaming of brighter horizons far beyond Oklahoma. His father, Howard Friedman, was a Christian-Jew who worked the night shift in an iron mill and ran a small pig farm with the unwavering devotion of Job. His mother, Adele, was a Sunday School teacher. She grew gardens of seasonal vegetables for canning and taught bible school weeknights at the church. In spite of his parents' religious fervor and much to their shock and disappointment, Aloysius was a professed agnostic and much preferred the wonders of the secular world. Namely, he was fascinated with television.

He couldn't get enough of it. The Westerns: *Gunsmoke, Wagon Train, Bonanza;* variety shows with Ed Sullivan, and Danny Thomas, and Red Skelton; sitcoms like *I Love Lucy* and *The Honeymooners*; heart-stopping dramas, such as *Perry Mason, The Twilight Zone,* and Hitchcock. His other favorites included *Father Knows Best, 77 Sunset Strip,* and *Bandstand.* He often recalled marveling at having seen Edward R. Murrow reporting on CBS's *See It Now* with cigarette smoke swirling around him, looking suave and in charge. And David Garroway's signature sign-off at the news desk of NBC's *Today Show:* "Peace" was, to Bumpy, sheer genius.

Seeing the world through the fish-eye glass of the family's Ecko television receiver that had the VHF channel selector and made that great clicking sound when you turned the knob brought a fast-changing world into full view. Television had power—real power to reach people—and Bumpy knew that in no time, every household in every corner of the nation would benefit from its seemingly infinite reach, from space to Spokane. Television was capable of taking one anywhere, including him. The very concept excited Bumpy. He wanted nothing more than to fuel his growing passion; to learn how this phenomenon worked and to somehow, someday, be a part of it. Only, he had no idea how he would accomplish that.

The answer finally came one day when the family television set just stopped working. Bumpy blindly attempted to fix it himself, and to its detriment, destroyed the set beyond repair in the process. When his father had indicated that he had no intention of replacing it, citing the heap of ray tubes and wires as being, "The Devil's toy box anyway," Bumpy knew it was time for him to leave. He had been back home for only a year, but knew that much had changed, and that the time had come for him to move on and claim his place in a world where opportunity and the future beckoned.

CHAPTER 3

★ ★ ★

ONCE HE HAD SAVED UP enough money, Bumpy moved to New York City to live with his Uncle EJ, certain he could find an exciting job in media waiting for him. Emmitt Jackson Friedman was his father's only sibling and had long been estranged from the family due to a dispute that left neither brother speaking and caused EJ to trade his inheritance for aspirations of being a writer in New York City. Making the decision to leave despite emotional pleas from Bumpy's mother to reconcile with his father before doing so, played out in vain. Howard Friedman's stoic detached silence confirmed that it was time. Bumpy left and never looked back.

Bumpy and his Uncle EJ shared a drippy cold-water basement flat in Queens. EJ wrote freelance columns on occasion for the *New York Times,* along with shorts for a literary magazine in the burrow. He drank himself into oblivion most days, and somehow managed to teach English language classes at night.

Persistence and luck eventually landed Bumpy a job with a local newspaper, first selling subscriptions, and then taking a desk on the office floor as a research assistant, where he trudged in the trenches of obscurity for the next eighteen months before being promoted to assistant copy editor for a columnist named Hank Whitman. Hank was a crusty war veteran with one arm, who wrote cutting barbs about the world's sorry state of affairs from a squeaky chair. He chain-smoked Winstons and typed adequately enough with his one hand. He taught Bumpy everything he needed to know. "You have a great potential, *Hickseed*," he would jab, bullying the gawky kid from Oklahoma with the girl-length hair and dumb ambition burning in his eyes, saying, "Why dont'cha use that genius head of yours and get me a story lead off of the *Today Show*." Stealing a gem from Frank Blair's news reports was Hank's idea of solid research.

Bumpy complied. Hank was resourceful, for sure. He had three televisions cranking at all times. "Windows of opportunity," he called them.

Bumpy's lesson in journalism further entailed cleaning up Hank's rat-hole of an office, starting with the filthy commode, fetching his bourbon and cigarettes when he ordered him to, and placing off-track bets on the ponies for him, by meeting with a bookie named Smitty, just off the back dock every Thursday. Occasionally, Hank would have young Bumpy retype his hen-pecked drafts, and frequent edits—in triplicate. He didn't believe in carbon paper's usefulness in the least, which kept Bumpy chained to a prehistoric Underwood that was no less the size of a small piano (and about as heavy), pounding out his mentor's brilliant editorials on the sticky manual keys, as the gray television screens glowed behind him, stacked like crows on a line along the windowsill.

In 1973, at age 26, Bumpy met Hylda Strom, a towering German beauty with a quarter-mix Italian and Cherokee that gave her an exotic mane of jet-black hair that did nicely to set off the bluest eyes he had ever seen. She wore her hair up in a tightly wound chignon like a librarian. Hylda didn't give him the time of day for the first two

long years that he wished she would. She was a clerk at
the Five & Dime where Bumpy stopped regularly to buy
Hank's supply of typewriter ribbon and No. 2 pencils. He
attempted to tell her more than once that he was a feature columnist for *The Regal*, and that seeing her beautiful
smile made him "happy as a dead pig in the sunshine." She
didn't understand half of what he said, due to his Okie
dialect, nor did she believe for a minute that feature col-
umnists bought their own pencils, but she figured that the
clumsy Southern boy with the sweet, senseless expressions
couldn't be all that bad. As he was often fond of saying,
"Even a blind hog finds an acorn now and then." And she
was his. Eventually, she fell for his charm and the two were
married.

By that time, Bumpy had finally worked his way onto
the page, writing occasional by-lines and fill-ins in for
the Obituary department whenever they were short a
copywriter. But his primary duty, much to his chagrin,
remained assisting Hank Whitman.

Hank's retirement in 1978 marked the end of the column and was all the incentive Bumpy needed to rekindle
his dream to find television work, so he moved his new
wife and then-infant daughter, Daphene, uptown in search
of brighter horizons, namely, a sunny two-bedroom garden apartment with southern exposures, hissing steam
radiators, at a hefty eighty-dollars-a-month rent.

A few weeks later, he had walked through the door of
Global Network's television station touting a few of Hank's
columns, passing them off as his own. Morey Grafton, then
General Manager of Global Network, and former Oklaho-
man himself, was impressed with Bumpy's ambition, even
though he saw through his bald-faced ploy. Hell, Grafton
had been reading Hank Whitman's column religiously for
years, and as he was so fond of saying, "You can't hide
manure from a *bull-shitter!*" Nonetheless, he liked gump-
tion when he saw it, and gave thirty-one-year-old Bumpy

the only position he had available—mailroom runner. The job paid less than dirt, but Bumpy figured that he would earn his keep and work his way up the ranks to prove his worth. He had to. It was his dream. So, in addition to his mailroom duties, he took a weekend job at Al's Appliance World, which sold everything from washing machines, phonographs, and new-fangled vacuums, to console TVs. He was in television all right, and the first time he switched on a brand new Zenith on the showroom floor and saw the grainy image come into view in "living color," his heart positively skipped a beat. The future, it seemed, looked bright indeed.

CHAPTER 4

★ ★ ★

I T WAS HYLDA WHO HELPED Bumpy to eventually find religion and, later, to take some business classes at the university and to lay off the booze just after their second-born, Jerry, entered high school; when things at work began to change, and the demands to produce in a highly competitive market heated up. Hylda had threatened to leave him if he didn't change his ways. It was his loving wife, all right, who finally set him straight, a move that didn't hurt his career in the least.

Finally, in the early nineties, he was appointed as a production executive at Global, eventually heading up the entire division, going on to have a hand in creating some of the network's top-rated shows, including two long-running daytime dramas, four game-show premieres, and an early morning news-magazine program, called *Sunrise Today*. Soon after, Bumpy was named director of daytime program development, East Coast, making Global Network *the* place to be mornings to mid-afternoons, Monday through Friday. Again, the pressure was on to perform, and without fail, Bumpy delivered.

Still happily married, he now had four grown children. Daphene was an accomplished artist; Jerry a real estate lawyer; Tommy a studio musician; and Irene, the youngest, a student pursuing a graduate degree in TV production at UCLA. He couldn't have been prouder, or more grateful for his good fortune. By the spring of 2010, he and Hylda were empty nesters—finally, with two German Shepherds, three Boxers, and a Toy Poodle that had more ribbons than a maypole. It was Hylda's passion to breed and show dogs. He and Hylda had been married for thirty-five somewhat tumultuous, but loving years. They lived in a sprawling house in Dix Hills just outside of Manhattan. Bumpy also had a small apartment in the city, but rarely used it. Mostly, Tommy crashed there whenever he was in town to record or pick up a gig.

Life was good. Every day, Bumpy would get up before daybreak and drive into the newly awakening city in his vintage Dodge pickup. A ritual, he said that kept him humble to his early roots. He was not in the least concerned with what other people thought about him. Propelled through life by his quick mind, Southern wit, natural business sense, and the good graces of his tolerant and saintly wife, Bumpy broke rules and hurled through obstacles with graceless abandon. But he made good television programming and, in the end, that was all that mattered. With even more time and a little luck from his new-found Almighty, he was certain, before it was all over, he could do even more, and possibly make a real mark on the world.

Five years later, when viewership had started to wane to anemic proportions and the numbers for his division began to spiral into deplorable depths— a trend then nearly three straight quarters running—Bumpy feared that both he— and the network had hit gridlock. It was do or die time, and when his boss, Willard Conrad, called for a "breakfast" meeting the following Monday, Bumpy was prepared for the worst.

CHAPTER 5

★ ★ ★

JANUARY 2015

BUMPY COULD SEE CONRAD'S PERFECT coif of silver hair from across the room in the Fifth Avenue restaurant. With his boss's penchant for punctuality, it was no surprise that the old goat had already ordered a latte and was deep into perusing his e-mails on his smartphone, checking the latest rankings that had just broken that morning.

Briskly, Bumpy brushed past several tables on his way to his doom, briefcase and paper sack in tow. Since he had been running late, he did not have time to swing by the office first. When he saw that the meeting was just the two of them, he felt a growing tightness in his chest that he could not shake off, and that had been plaguing him ever since he first awoke that morning.

Conrad rose to his towering height of six-foot-four and extended a tan, manicured hand. His demeanor was predictably calm, but the usual twinkle in his eye and the friendly wink that so often accompanied an opening joke or rib on the golf course, were replaced with a somber pall that unnerved Bumpy even more.

He was a handsome man for sure, and about seven years from a much-deserved departure from a rich career in television management that had won him accolades and a near-perfect performance record that would earn him a cushy retirement in Vail.

He was on his third trophy wife and surely didn't need this unpleasant predicament. He was too old and too seasoned, Bumpy thought. Men like Willard Conrad got into the business to make their fortune and get out.

Conrad's left eyebrow led the inquiry. "Have you seen this morning's numbers?"

"I have." Bumpy shifted in his chair and then reached for the ice water in front of him. He bought a few seconds with a generous swallow. "It's shit. I know. Have known it for months . . .we are not gaining any viewers and are losing on every front in the daytime line up."

"Tell me something I don't know, Captain Crunch," Conrad said as he placed his phone on the table and leaned in.

This was bad all right. Conrad only called someone *Captain Crunch* when they were on his hit list. The pressure in his chest was mounting. He had to do more than let this dinosaur take him down. "I have a plan," Bumpy quickly added. "An idea that will turn all of this around . . ."

"A plan! Well, do tell. What is your solution to the problem that I can't get elsewhere?" Conrad interlinked his fingers like a man praying for a miracle, displaying a garish Citadel class ring and a diamond-studded wedding band. There was the twinkle; only he was not delivering a clever joke, or punch line.

"I—er, my team is working on a proposal that will blow you away. We just need a bit more time to work out the details. I will deliver—I promise. Got some excellent ideas to change this whole thing around. You just have to trust me, Willard. I *got* this."

"Tell me why I shouldn't let you go? Bumpy, you have been at this longer than I have. You are a good man and a great producer, but these are changing times, and the shareholders do not give a flip about what we serve up as long as it makes them rich. I have goddamn pressure on me, so you see... I have to take action. This is not news to you."

"Give me a few weeks. Please, Willard—I'm askin' nice, here." Bumpy was beginning to sweat. His heart was now racing furiously, and he felt nauseated.

The waitress approached. Conrad signed the check and stood up. "You have fourteen days. Call Sondra and get on my calendar for a pitch meeting. That's it, Captain... two weeks. I want to be convinced that you 'got this,' or it's over. *Capiche?*"

Bumpy nodded and fumbled with his belongings. There was not a minute to lose. "Thank you, Willard."

He left the restaurant in agony. His heart was pounding wildly. He felt it in his chest, his throat, and his head. He barely remembered pulling his car into the parking garage at the station and pressing the elevator button for the ninth floor. He stumbled past the empty receptionist desk, retreated to his office and shut the door. Just before he reached his desk, the searing pain gripped him in a vise-like hold like nothing he had ever felt.

He dropped to the floor.

CHAPTER 6

★ ★ ★

GLOBAL STUDIOS. NEW YORK CITY
FALL 2015

THE TWO MEN JOCKEYED DOWN the corridor, mindful of the time. More business suits blurred in all directions, oblivious to the well-oiled machine that Bumpy Friedman's unparalleled know-how had created; years and years of successful television programming. The bulk of which, were shows that aired well before Tom LeMaster and all the rest were out of grade school.

"Wait in here," Bumpy said as they approached his office at the end of the hall. "I gotta use the head."

LeMaster stood at the doorway and peered in. Bumpy's executive suite was another constellation of disarray more tragic than himself. Mountains of paperwork and schedule logs littered the desk and credenza and around his computer. A withered plant drooped lifelessly in the far corner of the room; stacks of files teetered just a tumble from the desktop to the wastebasket below; abandoned demo tapes and unopened résumés were strewn everywhere. The in-box actually contained what appeared to be the remnants of a half-eaten deli sandwich.

"Holy shit, man! What have you got going on in here?" LeMaster blurted, nudging a stack of files piled on the floor with the tip of his Ferragamos. "Don't you have someone to take care of all this?"

Bumpy emerged from the bathroom, zipping his trousers.

"Lorraine was out last week, so I got a little behind," he said, tossing the sodas into a file cabinet, paper bag and all.

LeMaster cringed. Probably wondering if Bumpy had bothered to wash his hands. He would have to let it roll off. No one told Bumpy Friedman how to run the department, his office—or anything else, for that matter.

The clock was ticking, and so was LeMaster. Bumpy could tell by the way he was getting more anxious by the minute, never having been a part of anything as big as this before. He had the jitters, all right, a real rookie casualty. Bumpy could read the signs a mile away. *He'd better not fuck this up,* Bumpy vowed silently. He had too much riding on the dotted line to allow for the kind of stupid mistakes the likes of LeMaster was capable of making.

"Relax, man, everything's on schedule," Bumpy assured him. "Conrad is in there with his people, and as you said, doing the welcome wagon thing, and Mike Cross has the contracts, right? We'll go in together and get it done. No worries."

"Yeah, okay... sure."

"Have a seat," Bumpy directed, patting his bald spot. "I gotta look for something—it'll just take a minute."

LeMaster watched as Bumpy fished through the clutter on his desk. There was only one visible chair, and it was festooned with questionably clean gym clothing. He opted to stand.

Lorraine, Bumpy's assistant, appeared in the doorway. She was waif-like and plain as Melba toast. This was even evident past the outdated wire-rimmed glasses she hid behind.

Limp strands of ashy brown hair sprung loose from two ridiculous braids, and her skirt and blouse were every bit yesterday's news, even by thrift shop standards. She stood teetering on knock-knees, which appeared to be positively taxed under the weight of her sagging self-esteem.

"Good morning, Mr. LeMaster... Mr. Friedman. Sir, your wife phoned. She wants you to get the dry cleaning on your way home. Oh—and she said not to forget, um... something or other. I'm pretty certain I wrote it down with these phone messages. Oh, your e-mail... it is in need of your attention too, sir. I tried to sort through it. Do you want me to—?"

"Just put the messages on the desk, please." Bumpy rolled his eyes, as she stood stuck to the ground. "On the desk, like we discussed before." *Christ but she was stupid!* He had gone over the procedure a hundred times with her, but with loony-moon Lorraine, it never seemed to sink in. She was a mousy little troll that he just never got around to firing. She was totally useless to him—most of the time. It was amazing what an airhead Lorraine could be. She had no redeeming qualities to speak of. Certainly nothing going on upstairs. Why did he even bother? Because he was a softie—that's why. And she needed the job. *This is the thanks I get for hiring the homely*, he decided.

He should have replaced his former secretary of seventeen years with a Harvard grad—if that's what it took these days to get good help. Tons of broads would kill to work in television. And, on top of it all, Lorraine had been hounding him all week to deliver a fan letter to Casey Singer, the young actress and final pick for the show. What was he? A goddamn postman, or a TV producer? *And who writes fan letters anymore? Geez!*

Hastily depositing the messages, Lorraine retreated and then stopped short of the door, timid as a bird—a real dumb one. She seemed to have something on her mind.

Bumpy ignored her and began digging through some of the stray boxes on the floor.

Whack! He hit his head hard beneath the desk. Hence, living up to his namesake.

"Goddammit! Son-of-a-*bitch*!"

Lorraine winced, but with her boss, it could happen twenty-odd times a day... made no sense to warn him anymore.

CHAPTER 7

FEBRUARY 2015

THE EIGHT DAYS FOLLOWING THE surgery were pure hell. Bumpy was restless and sore. But having the triple-bypass procedure was easy. Making Conrad's deadline to produce a career-saving idea would be the harder task. The doctors removed a healthy blood vessel from Bumpy's leg and grafted it to three narrowed, blocked arteries. His rib cage was refitted with wire, and a train track of stitches closed the eight-inch incision. He remained in intensive care for two days, with continuous monitoring of his heart. He was on a breathing tube, stomach tube, and catheter, along with a collection of intravenous lines connected to his veins that pumped nutrition in. A collection of other tubes and lines were employed to drain the chest cavity of fluids and to monitor his blood pressure. Hylda never left his side.

Once discharged, he would have four to six weeks of recovery time, which would include physical therapy and diet counseling. Hylda was on it. She would be there for him and not let him ignore the new rules, or overextend himself. On release day Bumpy wondered how he would convince Hylda to let him take the meeting with Conrad in just six short days. Surely, he could buy a bit more time under the circumstances, she portended.

Somehow, he had convinced her after a two-week respite to allow him access to his laptop. He Skyped in to Conrad's office and conducted the meeting from his sick bed, a notion that he was certain would not bode well for Conrad's confidence in his ability to come back, not only from major surgery, but from the depths of ratings hell, with a winning concept to resuscitate the network. At best, Bumpy managed to buy more time by teasing an idea and promising a full presentation for a show concept format that would blow away the fall book and further rating sweeps to come.

"A new show format? I'm intrigued. What is the concept?" Conrad asked.

"You'll see. I'll have it all laid out for you. We'll present in another four weeks."

Conrad was just getting ready to attend a shareholder's meeting and needed to go in with something more than that. "What am I suppose to tell them?"

"Tell them to be prepared to be blown away," Bumpy said as he clicked to sign off. What did he have to lose by bluffing? He knew with full confidence that he could deliver a ratings bonanza. If the past two weeks lying in bed watching inane daytime television didn't prove to push him forward, then nothing would. He did have an idea brewing somewhere in his brain... he just had to tap into it to get the gold.

Three weeks later, Bumpy was back in the swing of things and dutifully committing to the health club for thirty minutes on the treadmill, followed by a one-hour session with his physical therapist. His meals were artfully created by a private chef Hylda had hired. She wanted to

make sure that he was not straying from the nutrition regimen he'd promised to adhere to. He did, for the most part,
comply, but secretly indulged in drive-thru burgers and
fries when he could get away with it. Old habits die hard.

He was just finishing a punishing walk on the treadmill when he noticed several televisions in the gym were
tuned in to various entertainment programming and real-
ity-based shows, rather than the generic news and talk
show formats that proliferated the daytime lineup. It was
known that ratings had been climbing steadily for more
of the cable programs than network offerings, which, of
course, was the problem.

Just as he stepped off the treadmill, his phone buzzed. It
was Hylda.

"Hi, honey. Can you stop off at the grocery and pick up
a can of chickpeas? The chef wants to include them in the
salads for tonight."

"Chick-*what?* Sure thing, I'll get them. See you in a bit."
He despised Chef Justin with his scraggly man-bun and his
heart-healthy meals, which were fit for a hamster.

"Thanks, love!" she said sweetly and hung up.

How could he ever let her down? She was his muse and
inspiration. She truly deserved better than the likes of him.
He checked the time and headed for the shower.

"Did you see what that Rebecca *did* to her so-called
friend, Skylar... ? It was epic!" The Latina woman first in
line with a cart full of organic produce said to the redhead
behind her.

"I know! I could have *died! Who* says that kind of thing
to anyone? *Right... ?"* Redhead answered, turning to the
woman beside her in the yoga pants. "It was, like, give
that woman another drink and watch her go all postal on
everyone!"

"Right!" Yoga Pants chimed in. "I had to hit pause when
my phone rang, so I wouldn't miss what she would say

next. When Skylar heard what Heather had on her from the previous night's party—it was, like, one way or another, someone is going *down*!"

"Totally! I thought she was going to bust her Spanks!" woman number one said as she swiped at her phone. "Oh, I just got an alert—Taylor Swift just pinned one of my photos to her starlet board!" They all *oohhed* in unison.

"Oh! Hand me that issue of *Star Stuck*," Redhead said to Yoga Pants. "I need my fix. Gotta see what is happening with the latest Bachelor. I hear he's back on the market."

"Are you guys going anywhere for the holiday weekend? I hear that staying in is the new 'going out,'" the Latina woman said.

Bumpy was astonished. *What was this?* He was clearly annoyed by the banter. He eyed the racks of rag and entertainment magazines positioned next to the chewing gum and batteries; each one had a more sensational headline than the next, and he wondered, *What ever happened to real news?*

It took nearly twenty minutes for him to check out with one measly can of chickpeas. Finally, when they had all moved through the line and it was his turn at the register, he swiped his debit card and left.

He pulled the pickup onto the street and began to fiddle with the radio dial to clear his head of the chatter that was still rattling in his mind from the grocery store brigade. He stopped briefly on a talk format on the satellite band that sounded benign enough. It was a woman psychologist taking calls from an audience with personal and professional issues, who called herself *Dr. Mom*. The current caller was a chatty Cathy, just like the three he had just run into at the grocery mart, going on about a relationship issue. "*So I tweeted him and put it out there for everyone to see... .*" The caller was about the same age as Bumpy's daughter Irene. He thought about the way that she viewed her world via a deluge of Tweets, Facebook Posts and Instagram messages—and suddenly, it was remarkably clear.

He hit the brakes, turned the car around, and headed back to the grocery store. He quickly phoned his assistant, Lorraine, and asked her to arrange the troops—the whole production team— for a meeting first thing the following morning. When he pulled back into the parking lot, the same gaggle of women—Produce, Redhead, and Yoga Pants—were still there kibitzing, loading their parcels into the identical SUVs when he approached them. "Excuse me," Bumpy said with a smile. "Can I ask you ladies a few questions?"

CHAPTER 8

★ ★ ★

MARCH 2015

THE NEXT MORNING, BUMPY BURST into the morning production meeting with a pocket full of painkillers, an armload of magazines, and a revived spirit. With less than one week before his fated meeting with Conrad, it was finally time to bring it. His entire production team was assembled and anxious to hear the announcement that many feared would be the end of the line for most of their jobs.

Bumpy dumped the collection of sordid rag magazines and entertainment periodicals onto the table and beamed. "Every headline is a story line. Yesterday's traditional ways are old news. We are going to embrace a new era of daytime talk. We are going to break the mold and produce a fresh, winning product. One that appeals to a range of women and their interests, served up the way they want it." He reached for the pert twenty-something intern's open laptop and commandeered Barry Paige's smartphone and added them both to the pile. "All the latest gossip—scoop—dish—on their televisions, radios, apps—cross-branded and all served up hot with your cup of mid-morning mocha!" He then popped the top on a can of warm soda and began to walk around the room, laying out the concept. "What could be better than *Oprah, Ellen,* and *The View*—on steroids? Daytime snooze-talk goes *Real Housewives, TMZ*-style. We will offer viral topics with headline-worthy guests to meet the current appetite for hot and unscripted gossip served up by the best hosts in the business."

The room was silent at first, and then chatter rose from around the table. *It could work. Why not? Depends on how we position it? Got to have the right advertisers… It's about time!* Clearly, the team was on board.

"We're presenting to Conrad in less than a week," Bumpy said. "I am going to need the best you got. Mike, I'll need you to run the figures on the potential advertisers—the full demographics for women eighteen to fifty-four. Barry, line up the research geeks, writers, and all production support. I'll be choosing the talent. LeMaster, do your thing with some preliminaries for the marketing campaign and launch. Talk is BACK—it's going to be bigger and better than ever!"

"Of course, Conrad is going to want to know whom we have slated for the talent—that's key," Barry said to a chorus of agreeing nods throughout the room.

"Yeah, how many hosts are you considering? Any names?" LeMaster asked.

"Just leave that up to me. Right now, I'm thinking we will go with four women of varying age ranges that will cover our demographic. They have to be leaders in their fields… high-profile and media savvy."

"We have stacks of résumés on file for female hosts, and—" Barry offered.

"No." Bumpy was firm. "As I said, I am going to hand-pick them myself. That's it for now. We will convene here at six a.m. tomorrow to get started. Be ready with ideas."

Everyone began filing out.

"I don't get it," LeMaster said to Bumpy, pulling him aside. "Why are you so set on finding the talent elsewhere? We have tons of prospects."

Bumpy rubbed his throbbing temples. He needed another painkiller.

"It's imperative that we choose the right women to host. The show hinges on it. It's the last piece of the pitch, and we don't have it in place," Barry said.

"We will have to stall Conrad on that issue," Bumpy replied. "Let's first sell him on the particulars. Trust me. I'll find the hosts."

"I don't get it," LeMaster said. "You're going to hire celebrity hosts and social media guests to raise the moral ethics of daytime television?"

"Quite the opposite," Bumpy said, turning on his heel. "I am going to raise the ratings!"

CHAPTER 9

★ ★ ★

GLOBAL STUDIOS, NEW YORK CITY
FALL 2015

LEMASTER HAD SINCE POSITIONED HIMSELF importantly in front of the bank of office windows just behind Bumpy's desk, overlooking Fifth Avenue. Outside, the sky was gray and beginning to spit rain. After he grew bored with the view, he next moved to admiring his reflection in the glass. Then, he dialed up legal on his cell phone to do a quick check on things.

At this time, a commotion had begun to build out in the main office. Some of the staff were congregated around a TV monitor where a breaking news story was unfolding in New Hampshire. Someone turned up the volume.

"Um... excuse me, sir." Lorraine again appeared in the doorway. She had to strain over the noise in the hall. "Is there anything I can do for you before I go on break? Anything else you might need for your meeting?" She already had her purse on her shoulder.

Now she asks! Bumpy dismissed her with a wave of his hand. His head hurt like hell, and it was getting close to show time. He thought about taking an aspirin, but didn't see the sense in it. What he really needed was a smoke, but there wouldn't be time to sneak one, so he popped two squares of nicotine gum from the foil packaging in his pocket.

"I'll do what I can with your fan letter, Lorraine. No promises... just finish the rest of those messages, before I get back, all right? Oh—and call for a car to take Mr. Conrad back to the airport later this afternoon, will you?"

"Aye aye, sir!" she chirped gaily, actually giving a little salute before she vanished.

"Okay, so everything's set, then . . ." LeMaster announced as he swiped at his phone. He touched the knot of his tie for the hundredth time. "Legal is just waiting for one of their lawyers to get back to us. That will make it four for four. I see no reason why we shouldn't proceed. Everyone should be down there by now and—" He stopped short, taking notice of the rising volume in the hall. "What the hell do you suppose is going on out there?"

Bumpy didn't answer. He was oblivious, as usual, and continued to riffle through the clutter on his desk. "Who did you say was holding out?"

"No one's holding out. It's just that one of the lawyers is taking his time around the fine print," LeMaster said. "Trust me, they're locked in. We're locking in the photo shoot for six weeks out. Taping will begin two weeks after that, and—"

"Aha!" Bumpy exclaimed, retracting his arm from a desk drawer. "Hot damn! I found it. I found my lucky pen! Now I'm ready to sign on our new morning show team.

Bring the broads on!" he said, holding the pen up to the light.

From where LeMaster stood, it looked like an ordinary ballpoint. "That's what was so important?" LeMaster shook his head.

"What are you looking at, Hot Shot?" Bumpy challenged, as the two started for the hall. "Don't you believe in luck?"

LeMaster punched the button to call for the elevator and discreetly adjusted himself. "Not really."

"Well, let me tell you something. With that group down there, we're going to need all the luck we can get. One on one, they're dynamic enough for sure, but together? They're goddamned combustible! Yeah, I'm going to hold on to my ass and go with the lucky pen. What have you got?"

LeMaster blinked. "Oh, I don't know. I guess all I got is a quarter million and two months' worth of national buys that says you're a goddamn genius and that every woman in America will be glued to her television Monday through Friday at eleven to see what these four will do to daytime talk."

"You're pretty sure of yourself," Bumpy chided, slapping LeMaster hard on the back. "Too much for your own good. Here's the thing, though," he said, leaning in. "Without this pen and those four signatures, I'd say you really don't have shit, now, do you?"

LeMaster surrendered a bleach-blinding smile. "Well, since you put it that way... sure, what could a little luck hurt?"

"Good man," Bumpy cajoled, quite pleased with his victory. "Like I said, no worries. Right?"

"Right," LeMaster parroted as they stepped onto the waiting elevator. "No worries."

JAMIE C★LLINS

THE Secrets & Stilettos SERIES

BLONDE Up!

DEDICATION
★ ★ ★

To my best friend, and favorite blonde, Monica. Your inner diva is ever fierce and beautiful…!

~ *Mimi*

PROLOGUE

★ ★ ★

GLOBAL STUDIOS
NEW YORK CITY SEPTEMBER 2015

The beautiful girl sat motionless in the parked limo, which had been left running. Her heart was in her throat, as she clutched the door handle with her right hand. She had forced herself to stop thinking about him for so long, but now it was all she could do not to.

Checking her watch, she reeled. The time to decide was now. In just two hours, she could be on the next flight to London. You can do this! she told herself. Just say the words for the driver to take you to the airport instead, and don't look back.

These would be the words that would change everything in an instant. Or not. It was a devil's toss. Gripping the door handle, she gazed out at the studio door, which was looming—beckoning. She bit her glossy lip, as one by one, the precious seconds slipped away....

CHAPTER 1

★ ★ ★

KANSAS CITY, KANSAS
2009

"I DON'T KNOW HOW MUCH LONGER I can take this shit, Roger!" Casey said, in front of God and everybody. Ripping her microphone from its sockets, she sent the transmitter hurling across the set and crashing to the floor.

Her co-anchors sat in stunned silence behind the news desk.

"We're back in two—" a harried voice burst from the sound booth.

"That's real mature, Casey," Bart said from camera three. "Only, why didn't you save that little pissy-fit for the ten o'clock news? More audience!"

The collective laughter only incensed her more.

"Screw you!" She stormed off the set, colliding squarely with red-faced Roger Marshall at the studio door.

He was also fuming. This was the fifth such incident this month, and frankly, it was getting old. Every time Casey had a crisis, he had to clean up the mess; it was always his ass on the line with the general manager. It often meant firing someone to keep Her Royal Highness happy. *Geez!* he thought. *I really ought to stop slammin' the talent!* But how was he to stop? Casey was hot *and* good for ratings.

What could it be this time? Her coffee too cold? Graphics cued too slowly? Too fast? Storm map clash with her outfit? It was always something, and always bigger than life. He was not in the mood for her bullshit. Not today.

Seizing her arm before she could say another word, he ordered, "My office—ten minutes!"

He would make her sit and wait; make her think about what she had done. She had issues all right.

Roger slammed the door, although he was determined to keep his cool and douse her fire with professional valor.

"What in the name of heaven is it now, Casey?"

She unwound her lethally long legs and slowly rose to her full height, towering over his meager five-foot, three-inch frame with her lean, toned body shaking with fury. God, but she was beautiful! He had thought to himself—even more so when she was angry. Unfortunately, it was beginning to turn him on.

"What's the matter?" she hissed. "I'll tell you what! For starters, you cut my segment by forty-five seconds, and you gave it to her!" She drove an accusing fingertip onto the desk to punctuate her point. Her neatly trimmed cuticles had no nails to speak of. She wore clear polish, which was regulation standard for on-air talent. Truth be told, she bit them to the quick.

"Jesus Christ! It's the news! In case you've forgotten, it's what we do here—we report the news. Bethany gets the lead stories as they come in, and that takes precedence over the weather. You know this stuff, Case."

Now she slammed down hard on the desk with both hands, causing a commotion, and drawing gawkers at his door.

"Cows! Cows! Goddamn cows, Roger. You cut me short for a story about some freak fungus growing on a bunch of cows and give my forty-five seconds to that old bat? I don't fucking believe this!"

"That 'freak fungus,' as you call it, is affecting half of the dairy farms in a two hundred-mile radius! Today's local story might be tomorrow's national crisis, and we are obligated to report it. I'm so sorry if that got in the way of your slot."

Casey snorted, folding her arms defiantly across a perfect chest—the saline implants had been a gift to herself for her twenty-first birthday—and to anyone else whom she cared to share them with. "Bite me!"

Roger turned all business. He scooped up his clipboard. "Look—discussion over. I want you to tag this evening's segment with our sponsor's liner, just as we discussed before—no changes."

She huffed, "And what's with this 'Magic Dust Carpet Fairy' crap? Like it wasn't enough that you've got me out there every day with the asinine name 'Casey Sunshine,' which by the way, makes me sound like a goddamn lap dancer, and now you want me to end each weather segment by blowing fairy dust up everyone's ass!"

"Geez, you're a piece of work, Casey." Roger grabbed his throbbing temples. "You are insane, you know that?"

"That's why you hired me, isn't it?" She flicked a strand of honey-blonde hair which had escaped from her tightly wound chignon, which Roger presumed wound more than her hair up too tight.

Casey's killer hair was her trademark, and it matched her killer instincts. Brains *and* beauty at only twenty-two—she had it all. And she knew it.

Unable to resist, he reached for her waist. "C'mon, baby …"

She recoiled.

A twinge of anger tugged at his gut. He was the program director, dammit! He had the power to make her happy. He was the one who hired her, moving her from back-office obscurity to on-air status, from rookie to reporter to weather girl—all in eighteen months. And this was the thanks he got? Ungrateful bitch. She'd been happy to snuggle up to him when she was a nobody, when it served her interests.

"Please, Roger, can't you see I need more than all of this? I'm dying here." She collapsed into a chair and removed her Italian pumps, which hurt like hell, and hurled them one at a time in the direction of the wastebasket. "I'm a journalist, not a goddamn weather-bunny!"

Could have fooled me! he thought to himself. With that one, it was all about sex. It was the only language she spoke.

She'd used her charms to come on to him last summer in a bar after work.

It had been mid-July, the Plaza was bustling with college kids, businessmen, and country locals running amok. The bars were packed to capacity with half-naked coeds lit to the hilt on Heineken, Cuba Libres, and God knows what else, bouncing from barstool to barstool and spilling out into the streets; it was like a Rave /Mardi Gras parade on steroids. The station staffers had arranged to meet at Ransom's that night for a few cold ones. Ratings were anemic, but that was as good a reason as any to rally. Casey had been provocatively dressed in a pair of short cut-offs, a skimpy halter top, and a smile. She flirted all night until she'd gotten Roger's attention. She plied him with tequila and smoke, and then lured him to her apartment. He'd known better than to get involved with a co-worker— especially a young, horny girl who worked close to the executive offices. She had been Bob Draker's intern two summer's earlier, then moved into an administrative role, first in sales, then later in programming; as of fall, she was on the production team. They all wanted to be talent, or close to talent. He remembered wondering which type

Casey would turn out to be.

He got his answer later that night.

Emerging from the bathroom, he'd groped his way through the dark to her, led only by the seductive coo of her voice. He felt for the light switch and then POW! He saw pure, hot, pulsating pleasure sprawled naked on the sheets. Her luscious legs were spread, and resting smack-dab between her velvety thighs was—of all things—a videotape; her demo, strategically placed at the entrance to paradise. He'd stared, dumbfounded at first, then grinned sheepishly and bent down to remove the barricade.

"Uh-uh, not so fast, Cowboy." She stopped his hand to negotiate irrevocable and binding terms of passage. "First, you agree to view my demo for an on-air position, and then I'll agree to try some of my best positions with you."

Roger watched her wriggle with anticipation, stroking the cartridge teasingly. It took him exactly ten seconds to decide.

"Deal!" He nudged the tape off of the cheap sheets, onto the floor.

The demo tape had been awful, a compilation of work from a local college-produced human-interest news show; Casey had been the co-anchor of an entertainment segment called "Hot Beat Chicago." Casey conducted one interview like a flailing rookie, but her quick wit, attitude, and charm delivered, in spite of badgering band members with inane and superfluous questions and comments like: "You speak to the soul of the nation's pre-teen and adolescent population, and your appeal echoes the chant of a repressed generation . . ."

But one thing was certain: Casey looked great in a halter top and skin-tight leather pants. The girl had moxie, but would she be too much for KTBU? That was soon to be determined. She read for station owner Dale Charney, the station manager, and producers wearing a shiny trench coat and patent leather pumps, keeping them wondering what, if anything, she might have been wearing underneath. They decided to try her out on their cable affiliate and see what she could do.

Within ten months, Casey Singer, now Casey Sunshine, was Channel Four's star weekend weather reporter at five and ten p.m. She quickly mastered working in front of a blank green screen, onto which the weather maps and charts were superimposed. It seemed a little unnatural at first—sometimes she accidentally pointed to the Northeast when what she really meant was the Northwest—but viewers were very forgiving with new faces, especially ones as attractive as hers. Within days, calls and letters began pouring into the station, demanding to see more, more, more of Casey Sunshine. Of course, the majority were from male viewers—station ratings and revenue quickly began to rise.

She became a pro at interpreting the forecasts written for her and committing her two-minute segments to memory, complete with graphics cues and just enough time left for playful banter with the handsome co-anchor, Guy Garrison, who led the six o'clock and ten o'clock broadcasts.

Guy's co-anchor was Bethany Peterson-Hall, an aging, angry throwback from New York who had mysteriously landed at KTBU after a nasty falling-out with management at the network affiliate. Casey hated Bethany from the start and detested sharing the same set with her, let alone the same dressing room mirror. Bethany constantly sent Casey seething stares when Casey was on camera in an effort to trip her concentration and make her look foolish, so the feeling was mutual.

"You gave my forty-five seconds to that bitch on wheels, Roger, and you don't understand that I may have just a little bitsy problem with that?" Casey's voice was shrill.

Roger was aware that the tension between the two women was affecting the broadcasts in a highly negative way. One way or another, it would have to be dealt with.

"The cows stole your goddamn precious seconds, Casey. Take it up with them, darling, because frankly,"—he slammed a file drawer shut and stood up—"I'm through with this conversation. If you'll excuse me, there's a newscast to run—and you're up again in exactly twelve minutes. Are you going to do the carpet liner, or not? I can just as easily give it to Bethany."

She seethed and bit her bottom lip.

He took it for a yes, shoved past her, and quickly vanished, leaving her alone as the last of the evening crew headed for the studio.

Casey lumbered through the darkened newsroom over to her desk and eyed her personal belongings: Wizard of Oz coffee mug, miscellaneous photos, an unopened stack of fan mail, peanut M&Ms, hairspray, nail file, a spare pair of panty hose. The large clock looming above the monitors just off the weather department read eight minutes after ten.

Guy and Bethany were perched importantly behind the news desk in Studio A. During a commercial break, and off-camera monitor caught a shot of Bethany flicking her teeth in a hand mirror. *Charming!* Guy was flexing folded biceps, while the giggling intern was tending to a pimple on his forehead. What a beautiful sight they all were!

It wasn't really the cows, or the fact that Bethany Peterson-Hall stole forty-five seconds of her airtime.

Casey glanced around the room for one last look. No, it wasn't those things at all. It was the fact that Bethany Peterson-Hall was the new flavor of the month in Guy's life, and the thought of it was more than she could bear. For three glorious months, they'd had the best-kept secret in the station—in the entire world—a hot and torrid love affair with all the makings of a storybook romance; or so she thought.

Truth of the matter was, Guy was too into himself to ever be real to a woman. He was his *own* biggest fan. The sight of them earlier that night, eyeing each other with sticky lust during the nine o'clock broadcast, was more than she could take. Three long wasted months. She had to get over him. Obviously, there was only one thing left to do.

The floor producer's voice broke her thoughts as he skidded in on his sneakers. You're on in three, Casey—let's go!" He too disappeared in the darkness.

She grabbed the keys to Guy's Porsche from off his desk and shouldered her purse. On a second thought, she snatched up the box of fan mail, and walked out of the newsroom, past Studio A, and out into the night air.

CHAPTER 2

LAKE FOREST, ILLINOIS
2002

NICHOLAS TUGGED AT HIS SISTER'S pillow to rouse her. "Casey... Casey, wake up!"

She rolled over groggily and groaned. "What is it, Nick?" *Had he wet the bed again?*

They both jumped at the sound of a loud crash coming from the downstairs kitchen.

"Mom and Dad at it again?"

The five-year-old boy nodded, rubbing his eyes sleepily. She flung back the covers. "Come on, hop in."

He crawled in close, settling down instantly, but his feet were ice-cold, so he pressed them around hers for warmth. He smelled of urine. Casey winced and pulled her nightgown down around her legs. The shouts were growing louder, and the breakage costlier.

"You *son of a bitch!* That was my grandmother's plate!" Helen Singer screamed.

"And this?" Nat Singer retorted. "Does this upset you, darling?" And then a shattering crash once again, followed by heartless laughter. More cussing, a howling cry, the pounding of feet, then, the slamming of a door. It was over. This time.

The after effects were worse because they reinforced what Casey's three younger brothers were still too young to understand: There was nothing left to say. Fake normalcy. Lies. The kids were pawns in a high-stakes game of broken fidelities and power plays, where choices were being made that hid the truth, but covered nothing. The house was a time bomb.

Casey was wise enough to fear the silence that followed such episodes because it made her mother crazy and mean. Especially since, after each of these episodes, Helen would take out her anger on Casey and the boys, cutting up their clothes if left on the floor outside of the hamper, or tossing their stray toys and belongings into the dumpster, while screaming at them incessantly. Sometimes, Helen would disappear for hours or even days at a time, only to return home, drunk and stinking, and sick. She was never sorry.

The pretense was affluence and privilege, masking every last dream and broken promise behind a facade of the all-American family, complete with a yellow Lab named Rex, private schools, big wheels, soccer games, country clubs, and annual family vacations to Disney World.

On the outside, the Singers appeared to be an ideal family. Justin, Nicholas, and Seth, the baby, had followed Casey, the eldest—all had been under ten years of age when the trouble began. Nathaniel and Helen Singer's union had been a fated omen of misery from the start and had simply gone downhill from there.

The Singers eventually agreed on the final terms of divorce, after six and a half years of bitter battle over the fine print, and the marriage finally came to an end. Casey lived with her mother and brothers until her sixteenth year, when she announced to Helen that she was going to live with her father. By then, Nathaniel Singer had a judgeship and was trying local criminal cases in Illinois circuit court.

He had moved into a high-rent luxury apartment near Chicago's lakefront to be closer to his lady friend, Lana. Arguably, the accommodations were not ideal for rearing a teenage daughter, especially one who was becoming reckless once out of the tyrannical hold of her dysfunctional mother.

Casey would have had to change schools mid-term, from an exclusive private high school on the North Shore to an inner city battleground known for its frequent drug busts, gang riots, and sub-terrain SAT scores. Helen objected, especially to the academic arrangements. So Nathaniel pulled some strings with the mayor's office, then convinced his ex-wife to jointly purchase a fiery red Camaro so Casey could commute from the downtown apartment to her old high school, Lake Forest Academy for Girls, in style.

Both senior Singers were attorneys. Nathaniel had a private practice in Winnetka in addition to his judgeship. Helen taught Business Law part-time at Northwestern University, having ended a lucrative partnership soon after she and Nathaniel got married.

Casey had arrived on their first anniversary, but children did little to rectify the problems that rocked their failing marriage, and they never realized the toll that their ambivalence and lack of love was having on their family until it was too late.

There were no living grandparents, so after Helen returned to work, the Singer children were raised by a series of nannies of varying ages and ethnic backgrounds, due to their parents' demanding careers. The worst was a large European woman who washed her hands with scalding hot water and performed strange repetitive rituals with door locks, cabinets, and desk drawers, which hindered getting anywhere on time.

Although the Singers may have appeared to be a happy family, the truth was that all the material possessions could never repair the damage of their daily existence.

Helen turned into a different woman altogether after the divorce. She began drinking openly, fired the latest nanny, and coddled her sons, insulating them from the rest of the world. Casey would have no part of it, thinking it her mother's pathetic attempt to ensure that they would never leave her. Casey's relationship with her mother was severed the day she chose to move in with her father; Casey felt Helen never forgave her for that.

Nathaniel had no idea how to relate to his teenage daughter, let alone raise her. Casey had been a perfect model child, exceeding in school and extracurricular activities, bright, outgoing, attractive, and articulate. She was an exquisite figure skater, lean, elegant, and disciplined; if she'd applied herself, she could have been champion material. But with puberty, Casey had given up her skates for glossy magazines, MTV, and boys. More than anything, she wanted to be a fashion model some day.

An English literature major, she took her first theater class in her freshman year of high school and loved it. She auditioned for every play, rally skit, and stage production, wrote several articles for the school paper, and joined the yearbook committee. She was insatiable for exposure and basked in the thrill of attention. Eventually, she met kids from inner city schools, who were also involved in performance arts and Community Theater. These kids read very different types of books, listened to strange new music, including Punk and Alternative tracks, and they dressed in dark and rebellious attire. Casey thought herself very "worldly" to be associating with such an in crowd.

Her father decreed that her shiny new sports car was hers to enjoy as long as she kept a B average in her studies and stayed clear of drugs, alcohol, and boys. Casey had excellent grades, drank and smoked pot only on occasion, and always refused offers of cocaine and stronger drugs. But sex was a different story altogether!

Her first experience with passion was on a sweltering summer night of her sixteenth year in a sleeping bag on the rocks at Farwell Pier, with Kirk Cahill. They spent that summer cruising the city in the dilapidated pickup truck he called Tank, usually ending up with a jug of cheap wine down by the lake, where they would drink and talk for hours and make love in the moonlight. It was the acute, monumental, maddening, mind-bending, never-to-be-forgotten first love, the best and the worst a heart could ever know.

Kirk's family was far more dysfunctional than Casey's. His father had deserted his mother before he'd been born. His mother gave him up, unable to raise him on her own, when he was ten months old, so he'd been sent to live with a series of foster families. The Greens were an elderly couple, extremely wealthy but oddly eccentric; Kirk had been with them the longest, fifteen years, and referred to them as his grandparents. Both were well into their seventies and hoarded everything, cooked only by the flame of the stove's pilot light, and reused anything they could, from wrapping paper to coffee grounds.

But by their senior year, Casey was slated for a journalism program at Columbia College, so would remain in Chicago to start classes, while Kirk would attend Notre Dame as a first string starter on a well-earned football scholarship. It was all coming to an end.

"What's going to happen to us?" Casey moaned as she lay with her head resting against Kirk's smooth chest on a blanket spread on the hot rocky ground at Belmont Harbor.

In the distance, Lake Michigan looked like a black, ominous ocean, sprawling beneath a full and brilliant moon, the last full moon of summer. It was ten p.m. and stifling hot. Kirk took a long drag of his Marlboro and flung it into the darkness.

"We'll write... call. We can visit on weekends too, right?"

Casey half-pleaded.

"Right."

A knot in her stomach told her different. She shut her eyes tightly. It was almost over.

The following week, on the day he was to leave, Kirk packed his truck tightly with clothes and books and memorabilia. Casey handed him a care package for the trip—a box of photographs, a carton of cigarettes, and a cassette tape of Journey, because it contained their special song. They had spent their last night together at a cheap hotel with thin walls and leaky faucets out near O'Hare Airport. Casey had told her father that she was at a girlfriend's overnight.

"That's everything, I guess . . ." Kirk lingered, his hands in the pockets of his jeans.

Casey shrugged more casually than she felt. "I'm meeting my dad for brunch, so I better get going then." She felt like dying, but just wanted to get it over with. They both were pretending to be strong.

"Yeah, okay... " Kirk's voice trailed away.

An airplane ripped over their heads, shaking the cement beneath their feet.

"I love you," Casey mouthed, her words drowned by the thunderous engines.

"You too," he returned, squeezing her until she felt that her heart would break.

"I'll call you from school... and don't forget Labor Day weekend!"

Casey nodded. The first tear tumbled, followed by a flood down her cheeks.

Kirk climbed into the truck cab and pulled away, kicking up gravel, waving from the window. "I'll call you, I promise!" his voice trailed on the wind.

Casey stood at the end of the parking lot, watching the truck ease onto the expressway to join the moving traffic, the red taillights fading from view until she could not see him anymore.

CHAPTER 3

★ ★ ★

CHRISTMAS 2005

NATHANIEL HANDED CASEY A GINGERBREAD ornament from the box. "I want you to be happy, honey,"

"I am happy, Daddy," Casey lied as she positioned the ornament on the tree. "Finals are over, there's eight inches of snow on the ground, we're having pasta for our holiday dinner tonight—what more is there?" she added sarcastically. Her father was trying. She did have to give him credit for that, and truth being, Lana was a lousy cook.

"Well, you don't seem to be very happy these days. You stay in your room and just watch TV. School going okay?"

"Yes, I'm fine, really. Everything is fine. I'm a television major, so I watch a lot of television, okay?"

He smiled placidly. "Right. Well, good then. Let's get the table ready. Your brothers will be here any minute."

Holidays were the worst. Casey had to celebrate each one twice, once with her father and brothers, and again with her siblings at her mother's house in Lake Forest. Gone were the warm family photo-album moments when they would all gather together for Christmas dinner. Or had that happened? It was becoming harder to remember.

"Casey!" Helen would intone in her best June Cleaver persona. "Be a dear and help your father put the gingerbread man on the tree."

Nathaniel would beam approvingly from his chair across the room. "C'mon, Daddy will hoist you up there... that's my girl!"

Kirk had not called Casey since Thanksgiving, and she was beginning to think of him less and less. The calls had been frequent at first, with long inane conversations, followed by brief moments of silence or tears and forced goodbyes. Over time, Kirk called less frequently, and it seemed there was less to say. Eventually, he stopped calling altogether. Casey thought the pain of not hearing from him was far more bearable than talking to him on the phone when he had nothing to say. It was truly over.

Several guys at school had asked her out, but she was not interested. Instead, she poured herself into her studies, spending the weekends in town, listening to music in dance clubs with her new friend, Dahlia, when they could squeak by with fake I.D.s, or traveling back to the North Shore to meet with her girlfriends too terrified to venture into the city, preferring the pubs, sports clubs, and coffee bars of suburbia.

"Oh—I forgot to tell you, Daddy, I invited a friend to dinner with us tonight."

"Who's coming, darling?"

The gingerbread man, Daddy! I want to put it on myself, please! Please!"

"A friend from class named Dahlia. She's Jewish, and didn't have any plans, so I thought nobody would mind that I invited her."

"Sure, sweetheart, here's a gingerbread man mommy and daddy for the tree! Can you reach it? Steady now. That's my girl!"

"Not at all, sweetheart," he answered kissing her forehead. "Hope we're not too strange a lot for her! I'll tell Lana. I hope she likes spaghetti."

"It's pasta, Daddy."

Rex ran in, barking and jumping gleefully, followed by Justin, loaded down with colorful bags and boxes. Behind them were Seth and Nicholas, grinning widely.

"Wow." Seth pointed to the heavily weighted boughs. "Are you sure that thing's fireproofed? I've never seen so many lights!"

Nathaniel hugged his sons, while Casey couldn't help but feel a pang of regret that something was missing from the perfect picture. They were fragments of a family. It had only been two years since the divorce, and the scars were still very fresh.

The doorbell rang, but only Casey noticed it over the commotion of laughter and eager voices.

"I'll get it," she said to no one in particular.

Helen came in. Had she forgotten something when she dropped off the boys? Casey hadn't seen her mother in months and was stunned. She looked haggard and fraught with exhaustion—not at all the striking beauty Casey was used to.

"Mother?" Casey said, as if questioning if the woman standing in the doorway were even their mother at all.

Helen just stood there, vacant and rigid, like a person standing outside herself. She looked right past Casey into the room, past the Christmas tree, past the boys frolicking on the carpet with Rex while a cheery Christmas tune was coming from the stereo speakers overhead.

"What the—?" Nathaniel rose from the couch with a jolt. He was the first to see it.

Casey's horrified scream resonated as she saw her mother lift the revolver, lock on her target, and empty three shots squarely into Nathaniel Singer's chest, then turn the gun on herself.

The funeral had been private, a simple service in a small

Presbyterian chapel on the North Shore, with a few close friends and disconnected relatives, clients, and acquaintances. Strangers were in the Lake Forest house, crowding into the large living room and congregating in the kitchen. There were so many apologetic, nameless faces, quiet whispers and stares, pained glances. Pity.

She had phoned Kirk right after it happened, but he never showed. A few days later, she got a trite sympathy card in the mail: *Sorry for your loss. Take care, Babe. Love, Kirk.* It provided no comfort.

Casey just wanted to run from it all. But where in the world would she go? Somehow, she promised herself, she would erase this tragic curse from her life and go as far as her determination could take her.

Her parents had been waked together, but their bodies were buried in separate locations, in accordance with the explicit wishes expressed in their wills—Helen in a mausoleum in Rochester, New York, with her deceased parents; Nathaniel's body cremated and the ashes spread in a field outside his boyhood home in Southern Illinois. All that was left of her parents were memories, ashes, and an unwelcome legacy of relentless public scrutiny in one of the city's most scandalous and high-profile murder-suicide cases to date. The press had a feeding frenzy on the misfortune that had befallen the Singer children, left orphaned and scarred, forever stamped with guilt and confusion over this devastating incident.

Three weeks later, Casey found herself sitting in a church for only the second time in over ten years. She had wandered mindlessly along the frozen sidewalks of the city, up one street and down the next, over and over, until she had ended up at the steps of Holy Name Cathedral.

It was a brutal winter, eighteen degrees below zero and dropping. The icy winds off Lake Michigan ripped through her long wool coat with merciless abandon. Her driving gloves were useless; the frigid temperature still paralyzed her fingers. She wore a knit cap and wrapped her face with a long wooly scarf, which thwarted the winds and provided a welcome shield from the imposing stares of tabloid photographers, reporters, and strangers. Casey was accosted everywhere she went. There seemed no reprieve from the relentless probing into their shattered lives—what was left of it anyway.

For the last few weeks, she had not been able to leave the apartment to go to class, or to the store without the media hounding her for a comment or reaction.

Judge Singer had been a high-profile figure in the law community and had been slated for a possible run at governorship. The press asked, even of his children: Why would his ex-wife murder him in cold blood? Had she discovered an affair that had preceded their divorce? Had she been distraught with grief over an ugly custody battle for the children?

Why had Casey been estranged from her mother? Was there a history of mental illness? Of violence? Of drug abuse? Casey didn't know any of the answers. No one did.

The estates would be handled by the executor for the Singer children. Gabe Lambert had been Nathaniel's lawyer and life-long friend. Not one relative came forward to take the children, except for a great aunt from Rochester, who offered to take the youngest, Seth, but not the other two boys. Gabe declined vehemently. "Nathaniel would never stand to see those boys ripped apart from each other," he rightfully told the aunt, who retracted her offer altogether, citing failing health and a lack of adequate room for three young boys. Casey, though no longer a minor at eighteen, had no means by which to take on the responsibility for her three brothers, nor for herself with out access to the funds, which Gabe was holding.

After much searching, Gabe had located one of Nathaniel's cousins, Elroy Singer, on the east coast, who was more than willing to step up to the charge.

Casey was a basket case. Lana stayed with her for a few weeks, just long enough for adequate arrangements to be made and loose ends squared away.

"You don't have to worry," Gabe assured Casey. "You and your brothers will be well provided for down the road. I've set up your trust funds to mature in advancing increments, according to your father's wishes." He droned on.

To Casey, they were just empty words. What did it matter? It was all a blur. *The gingerbread ornament on the tree, the blood. Oh God, the blood! The screams, the thunderous succession of shots, the explosion of her father's body on the walls, the carpet.* Helen blowing her brain to pulp, leaving her children and this world with the ultimate statement of contempt and desperation.

Was it so bad for you, Mother? Were we so awful that you hated us enough to hurt us in this unspeakable way?

Casey was plagued by questions to which she would never have answers. She prayed alone from the vacant pew to a God she hoped would listen. "Take care of my brothers, please. Make them forget."

A candle flickered near the front altar. The wind stirred and howled, beating against the stained glass windows of the empty church. She prayed for well over an hour, begging God to take care of her brothers and asking Him to save Nathaniel's soul. Her mother, she would never forgive.

When she was finished, she vowed never to look back and to never ask God for another thing. "This is all I want," she told the darkness. "Forget about me; I'll be all right."

Bitterness settled in Casey's soul. It would become her shield, her mask to the world from that point forward. Her way of coping with whatever was far too monumental to bear.

At that very moment, Casey's heart turned to stone.

She moved in with Dahlia in her two-story brownstone on a quiet street in Wrigleyville. Dahlia was happy to lend a hand. She had plenty of room, which she already shared with her seven cats, all named after Greek deities. Dahlia was into astrology and studied mystic religions for kicks. A student of graphic art at Columbia, she was also a quirky and gifted cartoonist.

Casey threw herself into her studies, tripling her workload in an effort to finish college sooner. Two seasons of summer classes would put her one year closer to graduation. She vowed to work extra hard so that she could begin her career climb one step ahead of everyone else. She wanted to be gainfully employed by the time her classmates walked down the commencement aisle.

Time was a precious commodity, and Casey had big dreams of creating a life for herself. Once again, people would take notice, but not for scandal and sensation, but in professional recognition. Her planned career in broadcasting would enable Casey to combine her talents for reportage with performance. She craved attention and validation to fill the void inside her. Sometimes, she would wake in a cold sweat in the middle of the night. Reliving the same dream.

"You're not watching me, Daddy!" she would protest, twirling in circles on imaginary ice skates on the living room rug, where he sat poring over his law journals. "Daddy! Watch me! Watch me!" But he never really saw.

She chose to remember her father as a young man, tall and handsome and strong. He had given her everything imaginable then, except for the one thing she'd needed from him most. She wasn't sure exactly what that one thing was—only that he had left this world with her still wanting it. It was all up to her now, and she would spend the rest of her life trying to find it.

CHAPTER 4

★ ★ ★

KANSAS CITY
2009

SHE HESITATED FOR ONLY A moment before driving onto the pavement. She wondered what everyone would think when they realized that she was gone with Guy's precious Porsche, but she would probably be halfway to Chicago by then. Roger would figure that she was just playing a game, waiting until the final second to jump onto the set. What she wouldn't give to see his face when she missed her cue to intro the last forecast of the evening. She was off to claim her rightful place in posterity, getting as far from Kansas City as she could, and as fast as the Porsche could take her.

Her stealing Guy Garrison's car and storming out into the night would surely trigger interest and speculation. When the story came out about their affair, breakup, and now love triangle scandal, due to Bethany still being technically *married* to her deadbeat philandering husband who owned a string of auto marts, and was dragging out a messy divorce—the media would eat it up.

"That's all you want? To draw attention to yourself?"

he'd asked.

"That's all I want. You tip off the local papers that we were still an item and that you broke it off. Insanely jealous and distraught, I will storm off the set, driving your Carrera Porsche off into the night, never to return—unless you want your affair with butt-ugly Bethany revealed on every social media outlet there is."

"And then?"

"You fly to Chicago two days later to pick up your car, which will be parked at the Fairmont Hotel, on the north end of the lot," she'd explained with a grin. "If anyone asks, you chased me down to retrieve it. But—and this is important—you will *not* press charges. Got that?"

"Are you sure about this, Casey? If it's what you really want... "

"It's going to work out fine for both of us. It's a harmless stunt. You get what you want and every station from here to Chicago will be buzzing about me. It's sure to put the name of Casey Singer front and center, and all people will really remember is a woman asserting herself and controlling her own destiny."

"You did what!"

Shelly was blurred-eyed, hugging a coffee mug with her hands. She had on house slippers and a pretty chenille robe. The light on the stove said 2:35 a.m. Ted was sleeping, oblivious to their late-night visitor.

"I wouldn't be surprised if it's all over the press by daylight," Casey announced proudly. "I'm going to be a household word!"

"Jesus Maria!" Shelly moaned, raking her jet-black hair off her face. "Are you *loca?_Chica*, think about this for a minute, won't you? You walked off a set in the middle of a broadcast! Why in the world would any agent—or station manager, for that matter—ever be willing to hire you again?"

Casey didn't waver; she knew the stunt would work, like she knew her own name. The trick was to get the right people to know it; without a waving flag, she was nobody.

"You once told me that you have to have a gimmick in this business, remember?"

Shelly was incredulous. "I meant something cute, small... harmless. What you are doing—I don't see the hook." She shuffled to the stove, turned a knob, and kicked up a blue flame beneath the kettle. Reaching into the cabinet above the sink, she retrieved a pack of cigarettes from a recipe box. "Don't tell Ted—he doesn't know. Come with me."

Casey followed her to the deck just off the kitchen, where a rush of cold air assaulted her five stories above the city. A light snow had dusted the tarp-covered patio chairs and table. The crisp night air was moist and frosty, the sky still heavy with impending snow at any moment. They each wiped off a seat, sat down, and lit up.

"You got a place to stay?" Shelly asked.

Casey shook her head. "Not yet. I'll manage, though."

The two had been fiends for years. Shelly had been Casey's mentor from the early days at the news station in Chicago, when Casey was young and green. Shelly knew how to anchor the news. She was the best of the best. Shelly was once a fixture on the evening news in the Windy City—and was recently back at five and ten o'clock with a viable competing station.

"I'll prepare the guest room for you."

"Thanks, Shelly. I'll be out of your hair in the morning."

A week later Casey was still there. Guy had since retrieved his car from the hotel parking lot, as planned, and Casey was still working on her own plan. Ted, Shelly's husband, was tolerant and gracious in spite of the untimely intrusion. Late at night, in the darkness, Casey could hear them talking, discussing her, she was certain. Casey remained firm in her conviction, but no one had left messages on her voice mail, wanting to sign Casey Singer to a lucrative television deal. She received a subpoena after the second week; KTBU was suing her for breach of contract. It was all beginning to look frightfully hopeless.

Then, on her way back from the farmers' market one day, she slipped on a patch of ice and tumbled into traffic. Before she could even register what had happened, a car struck her. It all happened so fast. She was walking with the parcels, one in each arm, when suddenly, her boot slipped from under her, and she slammed down onto the ice. She remembered little, except for hearing a *thud* before everything went black. She awoke on the hard ground with a splintering pain in all of her limbs—particularly the one that was broken.

"Can you hear me? Oh, shit, say you can hear me!" a voice pleaded.

"What?" Casey managed through her haze. Her grasp on consciousness was tenuous, but she heard sirens and horns. There were flashing lights, gasoline in her nostrils, and small rocks embedded in her hands and elbows. She was intensely aware of the searing pain in her left leg, and mortified that she had wet her pants. Her two bags of groceries, dinner for Shelly and Ted, were spilled on the icy ground, their contents as exposed as she was.

"Can you hear me?" the voice asked again.

She strained to make out who was speaking. It was a tall man, bending toward her, restless.

"You'll be all right," she could hear him saying, over and over.

And then he was gone, vanishing with everything else into blackness.

She awoke in the hospital, in excruciating pain. Flowers were everywhere she looked. Shelly was stroking long tangled hair away from her bruised and swollen face. She was crying. Tears burned Casey's cheeks too as she let the fear flow.

"Oh my God," Casey cried in fear. "What happened to me?"

"You took a nosedive, honey. But you're going to be fine, praise the Lord." She crossed herself swiftly, then cradled Casey's hand in hers. "Everything's going to be all right."

Casey took her word for it and drifted off to sleep.

The doctors said that it would take six to eight months for Casey's broken leg to heal, but she didn't have that kind of time. She would do it in four. Much to the chagrin of her physical therapist and orthopedic surgeon, she demanded an early release. "I'm not staying here a minute longer than I have to," she announced.

Shelly and Ted insisted that Casey move in with them until she was completely recovered and able to look for work. Shelly thought that with her connections at the new network, there would be something at least in production that Casey could do. Ted was slated to begin filming in Dallas in a few weeks and would be gone weekdays until mid-summer.

Casey had to wear a cast from ankle to thigh. She seethed with hatred toward the stranger who had done this horrible thing to her. The driver of the Lexus, Roe Evans, had apparently cooperated with authorities and was said to have been visibly shaken by the incident. He wasn't speeding at the time of the accident, having just moved out of the intersection from a dead stop when the light turned green; four eyewitnesses concurred. Black ice had caused Casey to slip at just the wrong moment. Nonetheless, having someone to blame for her misery and misfortune seemed to make Casey feel just a little bit better.

Two weeks after the accident, an exquisite arrangement of flowers arrived at Shelly's place, accompanied by a note: *My deepest apologies, Ms. Singer. I do hope that you will permit me to absorb all charges for your medical care. Please let me know if there is anything else I can do.*

The note was hand-written on fine card stock with a familiar logo and was signed, *Best Regards, Roe Evans.* Beneath his name it read: *Executive Vice President, Castle Records.*

Casey figured that Evans must think himself quite important to keep people on hold for nearly twenty minutes. One would think that a conglomerate as big as Castle Records would have better hold music than Michael Bolton.

Just as she decided to hang up, a woman said, "Mr. Evans will take your call now, Ms. Singer."

Casey had music publications strewn in front of her, opened to articles featuring record mogul Roe Evans, the quintessential guru of chart-blowing entertainment management. He turned record labels into franchises, songs into anthems, and performers into megastars almost overnight. The more Casey read about him, the more impressed she was. The man was a genius, a rich, powerful, dynamic, controversial, handsome, alluring, and brilliant music industry heavy. And he had hit her—how lucky could a girl get? If she played her cards right, who knew what she could make of this?

She cleared her throat, suddenly remembering the unflattering condition under which he'd first met her, in a pathetic heap on the pavement in the middle of the street with pee-stained jeans and blood oozing out of a giant gash in her face above her right cheek. Casey felt suddenly and uncharacteristically vulnerable.

"Ms. Singer?"

His voice was low and melodic. Thrilling.

"Is this Mr. Evans?" she asked tentatively.

"Please, call me Roe. Or, if you prefer, The Jerk Who Ran You Over." He had real concern in his voice, but also a refreshing, easy sense of humor. "A thousand apologies for what happened. I never saw you go down. I stopped when I realized, but by then, it was too late. And there you were, just lying there. Christ! I can't get the image out of my mind—scared the crap out of me. I am truly sorry," he nearly whispered, his voice so sweet that it took her aback.

"It's all right—I'm okay, really." Casey found herself consoling him. "I'm fine. You need to know that."

He muffled the receiver to say something unintelligible to someone in the room with him. "Did you get the flowers?" he asked Casey.

"Yes, thank you. You really didn't have to—"

"Do you like music?" he interrupted.

"Well, yes. I like music."

"What kind?" There was more mumbling and much distraction on his end of the line. "Do you like concerts?"

"Yes."

"How about Garth Brooks? Do you like country?"

"Sure, I like Garth. I've seen him at—" Casey started to say that she had once interviewed him at a small bar in Indiana, but stopped short.

"I'll bet you've never seen him up close. I have two media tickets for Friday night's performance at the World Center. How about it? Are you interested?"

"Friday night?" she hedged. It had been only a month since the accident, and she had not yet ventured out in public, except to the corner store for smokes and to the doctor for her follow-up exam. She didn't know if she would have the strength.

But before she could manage a response, he said, "I'll leave the tickets at will call for you and your guest, compliments of the record company."

Casey was deeply disappointed when she realized that he had not asked her out after all.

"Thanks, Roe. You really don't—"

"Forget about it! Take care of yourself. And stay off of

wet curbs," he added with a chuckle. "It was a pleasure meeting you."

"Same here," she replied, caught off guard. "Roe, I really wanted to ask you—"

"Bye now!" He promptly cut her off, and then hung up.

CHAPTER 5

★ ★ ★

Chicago, Illinois
2006

"EXCUSE ME, MISS... ?"

Casey raised her eyes from her text and sized him up in an unfair instant: mid-to-late forties, thinning hair, bad corduroy jacket. *What is that? K-Mart private label? Please!*

She made brief eye contact, although the look registered indifference. She wasn't studying at Pages, the off-campus diner, to entice pick-ups, but because she actually needed background noise to think.

He grinned. "I see that you're reading *Jade and Ashes.* How are you finding it? Or haven't you started it yet?" He had a slight accent, but she couldn't place it.

"Oh, it's not my book; I picked it up for my roommate. She loves this author; he's some sort of an anthropologist-poet who writes a lot of far-out stories about treks to Tibet and dinosaur bones."

"Is that so? Sounds fascinating!" he beamed.

She focused back on her notes. His type of noise was not welcome. Now that he knew that the book was of no

interest to her, maybe he would see that she had work to
do.

He stood there a minute or two, watching her, then
began to leave. "Well, have a nice day, then—hope your
friend enjoys the book."

She waved, not looking up.

Dahlia was probably the best friend Casey ever had;
she was, for certain, the wildest. Her lemon yellow hair
was cut short and spiked out in all directions. She wore
studs and gauges among her earlobes, nose, navel, and lips,
along with a stake through her left eyebrow. She wore
black mini-skirts made of heavy fabrics, opaque stockings
ripped and shredded at the knees, and thick-soled combat
boots from the Salvation Army bin. Casey knew she had
drawers filled with only black T-shirts. The only makeup
she ever wore was a pasty lip stain that was the color of
dried blood. Her skin was porcelain white. A silver choker
with skull and crossbones was her signature accessory, as if
she needed one. Even by artists' standards, Dahlia was in a
league of her own, a tortured soul with few friends, and
who preferred it that way. Being friends with Dahlia was
bold, which pleased Casey, who loved to push the envelope in all things.

The colony of cats that Dahlia sheltered, were believed
to all be reincarnations of her dead relatives.

"Miss Athena, off the table, please!" She swatted the
indifferent feline with a dishtowel. "Thank you!"

Athena was supposedly Dahlia's cousin from six-
teenth-century France, where they had shared a summer
estate while studying music under their great-aunt, Miss
Aphrodite, a gray-and-white tabby with white spotted
paws and a tattered left ear.

The cats all moved as they pleased throughout the apartment, atop counters, in cabinets, in windowsills, bounding
through the narrow hall between the bedrooms and the

kitchen. None of the rooms were neat. Neither roommate was keen on doing housework, and it showed. Textbooks, CDs, paper cups, and fast food bags often appeared in the oddest places, mostly belonging to Dahlia. Due to the limits of student incomes, the cupboards were often bare. Their home was functional at best.

Casey's portion of her insurance inheritance would remain in a trust fund until her thirtieth birthday, when she would receive the first of five installments, per Nathaniel's wishes. What was he thinking? Did he really believe that she could not be trusted with a small fortune in her late teen years or twenties, if the need arose? Apparently, he planned on living at least that long—and banked on Helen doing the same. Huge oversight.

Due to the nature of her mother's death, there was to be no settlement from Helen's insurance policy, and apparently, she was destitute—in fact, mortgaged to the hilt due to her alcohol addiction and reckless spending—there was nothing left in her accounts for Casey or the boys.

Both Casey and Dahlia worked part-time to make ends meet. Dahlia waited tables three nights a week at a coffee house in Wicker Park called Where've You Bean? that served up nightly poetry readings, live folk music, and lots of designer caffeine, primarily to gays and lesbians.

Casey was certain that Dahlia was an authentic, card-carrying, take-back-the-night certified lesbian, even though she'd never admitted to it. This did not bother Casey in the least. She liked Dahlia's offbeat eccentricity, both mysterious and titillating. Although she wondered what on earth two women did with each other once behind closed doors, she didn't have the nerve to ask her roommate for details; she regarded it as a mystery of life best left to the tomboys and sexually adventurous.

"I'm frying soy burgers—want one?" Dahlia asked Casey.

"No, thanks. I'll just have some soup."

Casey lived on Top Ramen soup packets. Sometimes she

strained off the noodles and just drank the broth. One for lunch, another for dinner. She was five foot six and a lean one hundred eight pounds.

"You're going to disappear, Case. Nothing wrong with a little bread and butter sometimes, you know?"

Casey wondered when it was that Dahlia became the food-police, but said nothing.

"Were you able to find that book you were looking for?" Dahlia asked.

Casey dumped her duffle bag, sending its contents spilling out onto the kitchen table. She picked up the book, inadvertently flipping open the cover, and saw Jackson Lovejoy's picture. It was the guy in the coffee shop, wearing the same smile. *Holy shit!* she mused to herself. *It was him!* "Yeah... I did. See?" She held up the glossy cover flap. "The man himself, the great Dr. Lovejoy."

"You just picked it up yesterday. Did you get what you wanted out of it already?

Casey smiled and shoved it back into the bag. "Not yet, but I will!"

Jackson Lovejoy would be Casey's first interview subject, though he didn't know it yet. She had heard that he would be touring the local colleges and universities to promote his newest book, *Rivers in the Steppe,* a collection of short essays on his travels through the Danube and the culture of Central Europe, following in the footsteps of emperors and kings along the imperial waterways. Casey called his publicist and requested an hour interview following his lecture at Columbia. What better choice than Dr. Jackson Lovejoy, writer and world explorer, for her character profile assignment for Professor Donnelley's news reporting class? Lovejoy was not much of a celebrity, but he was an intriguing subject nonetheless, a fascinating author who had published over a dozen travel journals on his exotic treks and excursions.

"I'm sorry, Miss, but Dr. Lovejoy does not do student interviews," the publicist coolly relayed.

Casey's paper was due in three weeks. She would have to get inventive. A little sleuthing and a crisp twenty won her a peek at the guest register at the East Street University Motel to confirm that's where Lovejoy was staying. Casey figured that he would have to eat sometime, so she planted herself in the motel coffee shop's window booth and waited. She knew that he would be in town for the next several days because his lecture series at Columbia would run through the weekend. She also found out that his designated guide, Professor Altergot, would be escorting Lovejoy around campus, dropping in on writing workshops and informal rap sessions with aspiring authors. Casey made a point to be in the student recreation center when Altergot would be touring Lovejoy through campus. That opportunity came later that afternoon. One of the more popular features of the Student Recreational Center was a new karaoke machine donated by former alumni. Casey was not shy about using it. She tied her blouse at the waist, hiked up her skirt, and put enough sizzle into her pouty rendition of "Like A Virgin" to totally distract every male on the premises, including Jackson Lovejoy.

The Grand Hall had been filled to maximum capacity, an impressive accomplishment. Lovejoy sat with his literary agent, Barbara Steele, who had flown in from the West Coast. Lovejoy's lecture was a hit. He had fielded questions for nearly an hour following his presentation.

Afterward, the book signing at Brennan's Bookery lasted nearly two hours. Casey had not missed a moment. She had been in the rear of Grand Hall, taking notes with skillful accuracy and the help of a micro-recorder. Of course, what she was dead-set on getting was Lovejoy's innermost thoughts and revelations, an in-depth interview about the real man behind the public façade.

She was certain that Lovejoy had noticed her little performance at the recreation center—he and Altergot had gaped long enough for him to recognize her from the diner the day before. But she had one final component to her approach. Casey phoned from the back of a bar on Wabash, just across the street from Lovejoy's motel, ordering a carafe of hot cocoa, fresh-baked double Dutch chocolate chip cookies, and a pitcher of ice-cold milk to be delivered to his room at exactly ten thirty p.m., when she figured he would be returning from the book signing. She dictated the accompanying note: *Thought you might be hungry after such an eventful day. Enjoyed your lecture! Sweet dreams, "Madonna." P.S. Your book is terrific—I would love to meet you.* She included her cell phone number.

This interview would enable Casey to not only complete the fall quarter assignment, but would ace her chances for the internship at WLS-TV for the coming semester. She had already impressed the journalism committee and her professors enough to earn their recommendation, but this coup would cinch it.

When she got home at eleven, she slipped her key into the door, just as her cell phone in her purse buzzed twice— she had a message!

He had typed: *Hi – this is Jackson Lovejoy. Thanks for the treats, Ms. Madonna. Care to chat?*

She typed: *Sure!* sending it back with a smiley face.

She bit her lip as she waited. Finally, the phone buzzed again, displaying the incoming call. It was him!

"Hello!" Casey smiled. "It's your stalker— "

"I certainly hope so," Lovejoy retorted. "I dig milk and cookies. How did you know?"

"Just a hunch, I guess."

"Well, you have made an impression. So, you're a student and a karaoke performer?"

"Yes... and a fan. Truly, I just read your book, and it's

brilliant."

"Well, I'm flattered."

"I wanted to make up for being so rude before, at the restaurant."

He paused and Casey waited.

"Would you like to meet, or re-meet?" he finally said. "Perhaps tomorrow for lunch? I know a great diner."

They both laughed.

"Sure, that would be awesome. I'm free for lunch." Casey played it cool. "How about noon?"

"Noon it is. See you then."

Casey arrived at Pages diner on Wabash Street at twelve o'clock sharp. Lovejoy had several hours before his flight back to Toronto. Seeing her through the window, he waved and grinned widely.

"Have you been waiting long?" Casey asked as she sat across from him.

"No, I just arrived. Perfect timing, I'd say." He was staring, making Casey feel self-conscious.

She fumbled through her knapsack.

"I enjoyed your little concert performance yesterday, Miss... *Madonna*? Forgive me—I don't even know your real name."

"Oh, I'm Casey Singer. So pleased to meet you, Mr. Lovejoy."

They shook hands awkwardly across the table.

"I'm a journalism major," she continued. "Third year here at the college. Thanks so much again for agreeing to meet with me."

Lovejoy's smile tightened as he watched her retrieve a mini recorder and steno pad from her bag.

The waitress arrived for their order. When she left, he said, "Please, call me Jack."

"Okay then, Jack. Do you consider yourself to be primarily an author, or a world explorer?"

He was staring back at her blankly. "I don't recall."

"Excuse me?"

"I don't recall agreeing to doing an interview with you, Ms. Singer. If you had contacted my publicist, I'm certain that she would have informed you that I don't do student interviews."

Her face burned. How dare he? She had gone through blazing hoops to get one hour of his time, and now he was going to snub her? She hesitated, and then felt foolish for looking like such an amateur. Of course, she shouldn't have been so obvious—he would have given her all the information she needed if she had just played along properly from the beginning! She had to remain cool and re-think her strategy; she hoped that she hadn't blown her only chance. The last thing she wanted to do was to appear inexperienced.

She smiled coyly. "I was interested in finding out why Jack Lovejoy is hot for Madonna wannabes." She touched his knee underneath the table to be sure that he got the message.

"Well then, I think perhaps we can work something out, Ms. Singer. And a fine singer you are at that! Very alluring."

When the food arrived, Casey snatched the check and deposited a twenty on the table, signaling to the waitress. "We'll be taking lunch to go."

Lovejoy may have been middle-aged, but he performed like a man twenty years younger. Of course, Casey had to compare him to boys her own age. Jack left her breathless and spent, yet still hungry for more. He consumed her with hard, hungry kisses, exploring her mouth with his tongue, making her weak and submissive in his arms. He cupped and stroked her breasts, tugging at her nipples, twisting and sucking them, causing her to teeter on the brink of orgasm several times before he even penetrated her. His sensuous, lingering kisses migrated across her lips, her tongue, her cheek, her breasts, the small of her back; the bristles of his mustache made rough red scratches, but Casey didn't care.

He tasted of cigarettes and scotch; Casey found his scent utterly intoxicating. He was not the most delicate of lovers with his roughhouse touch and hungry mouth every-where on her satin flesh, but it didn't matter. She loved the way he pleasured in her. She reeled with desire, digging her fingernails deep into his broad back, soaring blissfully on waves of passion.

They stayed in contact throughout the following weeks, talking long-distance, sometimes for hours. Casey dili-gently collected insight into his mysterious and fascinating life, an incredible mosaic of journeys far more compelling than she could have guessed. His tales captivated her. He had prayed with Tibetan Monks, ran with the bulls in Pam-plona, hiked volcanoes, zip-lined in the Amazon, floated among the minerals of the Dead Sea, hunted dinosaur eggs in the Gobi Desert, Tiger-spotted in Udaipur, sam-pled fried scorpions in Beijing, and hot air ballooned over the "fairy chimneys" of Cappadocia. There was the story of diarrhea in a crowded market in Dubai, an inadvertent detainment in a Singapore prison for carrying prescription medicine in his backpack, and countless wildlife encoun-ters resulting in lost cameras from Alaska to Tanzania.

"Then there was the time that lust had led me to the very center of destruction. I had met a lovely foreigner at a soccer game in the Leeward Islands in 1989, whom I thought would be the perfect anecdote to my second failed marriage. I followed her to Puerto Rico, where I promptly lost her in translation. I ended up holing up for two weeks in a flea-infested rental on the shore, with rain and winds of 160 miles per hour, as Hurricane Hugo bar-reled through, raking the island's northern half. But that wasn't the remarkable thing... surviving, I mean. I suffered an acute appendicitis attack and had to be operated on under war-zone conditions. I don't even know if the physician was legit. I passed out and didn't wake up until days later, in San Juan."

"What about the girl?" Casey asked.

"Gone. Along with my appendix," he said. "That is this scar right here."

Casey traced the jagged line with her finger and then touched the one she found most intriguing on his neck. "And this one?"

"Vampire. Budapest, 1969."

"What? No way!" Casey slammed him squarely with a pillow.

Eventually, he started trying to coax Casey into having phone sex with him late at night. She played along at first, letting him think that his disgusting dirty talk and sex games were actually turning her on because it kept him coming back for more. Once, she heard the voice of a woman with him. He told Casey she was a dominatrix he had ordered off of the internet, complete with handcuffs and punishing stilettos, ready to get it on with both of them via AT&T teleconferencing.

Casey interviewed Jackson in calculated installments via e-mail and phone calls during his tour. The sex calls, infrequent and brief, seemed separate from their other discussions, as if Jackson Lovejoy were two different men. He only called for sex when he was high on drink or drugs. But the night that he called her at two a.m. with a couple of strung-out junkies he'd picked up in a bar in Detroit was the final straw.

Casey could hear commotion on the other end of the line. "Hey, love... we're havin' a party, and all's missing is you." Broken glass followed by shrieks of laughter rang on the line. Music was blaring in the background.

"Hi'ya, baby," came a woman's voice into the receiver.

"Is this Madonna? Like for real and shit? My girl Patty is gonna be right here."

It sounded like somebody dropped the phone. "Are you there... *babe?*" Jack slurred.

"Jack, I don't think this—"

"It's going to be wild, baby. I just have to get the other one out of the john... Ready to get freaky? Let's do this!"

"Let's not," Casey said as she hung up.

Casey finished the article, changed her phone number, and washed herself clean of his slimy presence in her life, disinfecting her soul with a ritualistic burning of all her notes. Jackson Lovejoy was history.

She got her story back with an *A* and the acclaim of the professor and her classmates, who were most impressed with her treatment of Lovejoy's eccentric nature, a humanistic glimpse into an uncommon aspect of the man.

But Casey had come to claim a bit more of him than she had ever bargained for. Just two weeks before Christmas break, she discovered that she was pregnant.

Casey slipped out after taking her Rhetoric final and walked three short blocks to Dearborn clinic, where Dahlia was waiting with her father's broken down jeep. Dahlia had to have it back to the junk yard he oversaw, where he salvaged hubcaps and what was left of his life after her mother had divorced him nearly six years prior.

"Are you sure?" Casey felt bad about imposing.

"Don't worry, Case. I want to do this for you."

Casey smiled bravely, hugging her friend. "Thanks, Dahlia. You're too cool for doing all this, really."

That evening Casey writhed on the cold tile floor, near the toilet. She clutched her knees to her chest, but it did little to stop the pain. Ripping contractions tore at her innards. A blood-soaked towel was wedged between her legs. She had thrown up again. Her sweatpants were covered with blood and vomit.

"Oh my God!" Dahlia gasped, grabbing a washcloth from the sink.

Casey was shaking uncontrollably, bent in half with crippling contractions.

"It hurts so bad!" she gasped out.

"Shhh, it's going to be all right, honey, you'll see—the worst is over. It's going to be all right."

Casey tried to get up from the floor, but was too weak. She thrashed about, banging her head hard against the tile wall. She despised herself for what she had done. For seducing Lovejoy, for getting pregnant, for ending the pregnancy. She wanted to die.

Images of her mother's murderous rampage flashed in her mind, along with the deafening chants: *Murderer! Killed him in cold blood! The murder-suicide of the decade.*

She was screaming now for Nathaniel. "Daddy! Daddy, please help me. Help me!"

Dahlia held her. "Listen to me, it's over now. Case, it's over, honey. I know it hurts."

Casey shrieked, shoving Dahlia away with astounding strength. "No! Leave me! Make them all shut up!" She doubled over, tears and sweat dripping from her face as the searing pain made her gasp for breath. "How could... you... possibly... know how

I... *feel?*

Dahlia just stroked her hair and said quietly, "There are no mistakes in life—only choices, honey."

Casey was nineteen years old, but she felt like she was ninety.

CHAPTER 6
★ ★ ★

CASEY'S RELATIONSHIP WITH FOOD WAS one of love and hate. She appeared healthy at a slim one hundred eight pounds, but was always obsessing about every pound gained or lost. She kept a scale by her bedside and weighed herself religiously before going to sleep and first thing in the morning. She kept a food diary in her tote bag, although she often lied about her calorie intake, but greatly exaggerated her exercise log. *Why bother?* she thought. She had always had her own system, often fooling her family starting in her teens with clever distraction at dinner, where her meals often made their way into her napkin and then to the trashcan unnoticed. She would sometimes go for days without eating, simply drinking broth from canned soup and tossing the meat or vegetables.

Other times, she would go on a three or four-day binge, like her first year in college, where she would hit every fast-food restaurant near campus on her way home and then hide in her room, consuming entire boxes of cookies and quarter-gallon cartons of ice cream—then, forcing herself to vomit until every last calorie had been expelled. She used this system for years, first discovering how to do it when a friend in junior high showed her how she made herself throw up after gorging on whatever she wanted, to maintain her own weight for gymnastics. Casey became adept at the two-finger method, until she began getting sores on her hands from them scraping against her teeth when she forced herself to puke. That's when she began turning to laxatives to do the job.

Casey knew it was not at all good for her system, but she did it anyway. She figured that she was too young to develop any serious conditions as a result of purging. She was simply too smart and too tough for that. She had figured out how to beat the odds of gaining weight and dodging the gym, and that was all that mattered.

She attributed the compulsion to binge and purge as of late to stress, as she had put a lot of pressure on herself to succeed and make people sit up and take notice. She worked at her lowly production assistant job at the TV station and continued to waitress at banquets at the country club on occasional evenings and weekends for extra money. The television station paid her barely enough for food and rent, and she needed a new wardrobe. Shelly had always said that dressing the part was key to being perceived as talent material, and Casey had her sights on being just that.

Her trust fund was still years out of her reach; she would not receive her full inheritance until a steady lifestyle, family, and career would probably all be well established. The same went for her brothers, who would have much longer to wait.

"All I want is my fair share of what's mine," she told Gabe Lambert in his plush Michigan Avenue executive suite.

"I'd love to say that there was a loophole for you, Case, but I can't release that money to you until your thirtieth birthday. I'm sorry. Do you need some cash? I could write you a personal check."

She accepted the executor's generosity, wondering what it might cost her. He opened an expensive leather check register and scrawled a figure that she could see had four digits. A cool grand to buy her out of his life for a while, maybe until she reached middle age, with its wrinkles, cellulite, and mediocrity.

He gave her the check and stood. "Sorry I couldn't be of any more help to you. I hate to rush you off, but I have an appointment to get to... "

"Sure." She folded the check without looking at it and shoved it into the back pocket of her jeans. "See ya then, I guess."

"Take care of yourself."

She nodded, looking past him at a collection of framed photographs on the bookshelf behind his desk. Gabe and her father on the eighteenth green at Pebble Beach around 1972, she thought. They'd been best friends since college. Next to that photograph was a family portrait of the Singers when her brothers and she had been very young. Helen was holding three-week-old Seth in her arms. Casey realized she hadn't seen her brothers since the funeral.

"I want to see my brothers," Casey told Gabe abruptly.

"I'll call your uncle and arrange it. How soon can you go to Maine?"

"I can't just up and go to Maine. I thought maybe they could come here to Chicago to visit me."

"That's not realistic, Casey. It would mean pulling them out of school when they have settled in so well with Marlene and Elroy—besides, the trauma of coming back to Chicago would just be too much for them. Why don't you wait for Thanksgiving and go there for a visit? It's not that far off."

Casey nodded. "Yeah, sure, maybe then."

Gabe checked his watch. "Well, if you'll excuse me, sweetheart. It was great seeing you."

CHAPTER 7

★ ★ ★

2007

THE INTERNSHIP WAS GRANTED LATER that fall, despite controversy surrounding her alleged affiliation with the alumni author, that had been the talk of the campus for quite some time; an accusation, which Casey vehemently and empathically denied. She was getting frightfully good at burying the truth.

Casey never spoke of Jackson Lovejoy or of the abortion again. It was better left that way. Last she heard, he had headed to Tibet's Mt. Kailas to complete research for his next book. *Good riddance!* As far as Casey was concerned, the farther away, the better. She'd hoped that while he was up there, his Sherpa would push him off the edge!

Casey reported for duty at WRS -TV. Her first week, Casey mastered the fine art of making coffee for an office of twenty, running to the corner office supply store for various members of the programming department, licking envelopes for the executive secretary, and fetching dry cleaning for a time-management-challenged sales manager. She worked after classes and on evenings and weekends— anywhere she was needed. It was a grueling schedule on good days, but she loved every exhausting minute of it.

Over a year passed, and she was just three credits short from qualifying for early graduation. Just as planned, she kept her sights on the brass ring, proving at every turn, that nothing could stop her.

When she was not working, Casey spent her free time hanging around at the TV station, talking and networking with the seasoned veteran reporters and news anchors. She was jokingly known as a sort of "fixture" at all station events and eventually found a way to see to it that she would get on the guest lists for each and every one. Sometimes she would respond to invites that staff journalists or producers had tossed in the wastebasket, or simply show up at station events, acting as if she belonged. Of course, looking fabulous. Ultimately, she so impressed her program manager that she was offered a full-time position after graduation in the newsroom as a news desk assistant where she would aid the staff writers and run copy on the floor.

Casey relished in the realization that her very first "official" media job was at WRS-TV where she was a member of an elite team for one of Chicago's most notable and revered powerhouse stations.

"You are so freakin' lucky!" whooped Dahlia as Casey popped a cork on a bottle of bubbly from the corner Walgreen's. The cork and two cats shot across the room like flying bullets. She had picked it up on the way home from the station to celebrate with her best and only friend right after the program director had delivered the great news.

"Hope you like working long hours, having non-existent lunches and weekends, and don't think much of holidays, he said to me. 'No problem!' I told him. "I'll work twenty-four seven for you if you'd like—just bring it on! Hell, I'll shave my head... turn cartwheels. Whatever!"

They clinked glasses and laughed, gulping down the cheap booze. Casey was in tears. She had done it. She had finally arrived!

Casey arrived for her first day as news desk assistant at her small cubicle at the far end of the corridor, adjacent to a noisy water cooler and a blank wall. A spastic fluorescent light flickered overhead threatening to crap out at any moment. She glanced at her nameplate, the only item on her desk: *Casey Singer, Assistant.* It looked good. It felt right.

Next, she tried out her chair. If she craned her neck to the left, she could see past a bank of tall file cabinets through to the high-rise window pane offering a glimpse of Lake Michigan looming in the distance. From her small desk, she could see across the entire newsroom, filled with staff writers and reporters. The place was a highly charged hub, running hundreds of stories and information into fodder for the afternoon and evening news; turning scandal, controversy, and tragedy into nuggets of gold.

Casey's first official assignment came just after lunch. She would be gathering background information on the birth of triplet marmosets at Brookfield Zoo.

"See what you can find—" the production manager grunted as he thrust some print outs of articles on similar zoo births at her. "Make it fresh."

Casey was on it. Just as she began reading over the first of the clippings, a strange girl with a mile-wide smile peered over her cubicle.

"Hi, neighbor! Look—we're cubicle-buddies!"

Wendy Jozwiakowski was a flighty busybody who Casey remembered from the summer of her internship, always getting into other people's business. She had worked in the accounting department back then. Casey wasn't interested in making a new friend, epically one like Wendy. The girl wore thick spectacles, had a pronounced overbite, and an unfortunate line of dark fuzz above her upper lip. She was at least thirty pounds overweight and constantly feasted on Butterfingers and Diet Coke. She wore painfully tight

spandex skirts over which her stomach pouched in a series
of unsightly rolls. Her hair was another story altogether,
frightfully pulled taunt off her enormous face with a plastic headband.

Unfortunately, Wendy would turn out to be her only
real work-ally in a tight clique of administrative and news
desk snobs who huddled around the water cooler, pointing
and whispering whenever Casey walked by. They scoffed
at her short skirts and accused her of blatant attempts at
schmoozing the department heads. She could hear their
cutting remarks in the lunch room or while waiting for the
elevator as the back-stabbing and snide comments flew—

"Do you think that they're real?"

"No way! She's packing more plastic than a Barbie!"

"I heard that she used her family's publicity from the
murders to get this job... can you believe that? It's like they
just felt sorry for her or something."

Screw them! Casey would declare obstinately to herself.
*Let them think whatever they want about me. Someday, they'll
see. It will be my face up there!* She stared at the studio monitor, intently studying every move the news anchor, Shelly
Escamilla made. As far as Casey was convinced, the way
that Shelly read the evening news was poetry.

Shelly had credibility and sophistication. She commanded the microphone: *"A blessed event at Brookfield
Zoo... the addition of not one, but three young marmosets to the
primate wing. Who couldn't love these adorable little guys? A rare,
but not unheard of occurrence, says resident zoologist, Dr. Trey
Cooley . . ."*

Shelly was a role model, not only to the Spanish community, but also to all aspiring news anchors, especially
women. She was unfailingly positive and approachable.
The public loved her. She *was* Chicago. As familiar as Lake
Michigan, or the Magnificent Mile. Shelly was a mainstay.
Casey knew that all it would take to make it herself in television would be to learn and master the same qualities that

Shelly had; to approach her craft with the same passion. She too could become the perfect broadcast journalist. After all, perfect people got it all.

When Casey asked Shelly Escamilla to lunch one afternoon at the Garden Room of the Drake Hotel, it was worth a half-week's salary and the extra calories.

"It's so great working with you," Casey said, picking at her salad. I really feel that I could learn so much just by watching you."

"Why thank you, Casey. That's sweet of you to say." Shelly was beautiful. She was voluptuous and stunning with her dark smoky eyes and signature crimson lips. She was comfortable in her own skin. Shelly was quick to explain to Casey how no one ever taken the time to talk with her when she was a brand new reporter back in Pittsburgh. "I noticed you when you came on as an intern and I've been watching you grow ever since. You saved my ass one day with a Snickers bar. Remember?"

Casey smiled. "The vending machine was broken and I ran to the Quick Mart to get you your chocolate fix."

"That's right! I said to myself right then and there—now here's a girl who's really going places!"

They laughed. Shelly's eyes were warm and approving.

"Tell me, Shelly. Was television reporting what you always wanted to do?"

"Oh no! God, no—what I really wanted to be when I was a little girl when I grew up was to be a singer. I came from a large family, six brothers and me, would you believe? Me, the only girl. We lived in a small house on the outskirts of Denver with my auntie and little cousin, Estella. Everyone was musical. All of us. I wanted to pursue a career in music, so I took a job out of college working at a small country radio station in Pueblo. She laughed, tossing her head back and flashing that incredible smile. "It made my brothers crazy that I worked there—playing

Conway Twitty and Loretta Lynn records while they were in this struggling punk rock band! They made such fun of me. I wanted to quit! But it was a great experience. Oh, and there was this one guy there—weird Andy. He did the news breaks and he was *so* creepy! He... he... oh my God—it was so unbelievable!" She clasped her hands over her face, fanning her cheeks, which had suddenly flushed the brightest red.

"He *what?* Shelly, tell me... what did he do?"

She shifted in her chair and glanced around for earshot clearance, then leaned forward over her salad as Casey did the same. They were nearly nose-to-nose over the watercress. Shelly arched an impeccably groomed brow and whispered, "He used to masturbate in the studio all the time!"

"Get OUT!" Casey blurted.

"Shhhh!" Shelly giggled, trying to contain it in her napkin, but it was no use. The Chardonnay had worked its magic after a particularly tough week and it had been far too long since Casey had had a good long laugh. Together, they roared. Shelly went on, painting a picture for her captivated lunch guest.

"Casey, I actually caught this guy 'choking the chicken' right there in the news room. He was oogling over some album jacket of Mama Judd!"

"Stop it!" Casey squealed. The tears running from her eyes threatened to turn her mascara into twin black pools. "Stop it already! I get the picture!"

They roared in unison, slamming their hands onto the table, tipping silverware and spilling water on the remains of their lunch. Shelly sighed, dabbing her napkin at her own wet cheeks. "Oh what a place that was! I'll never forget it. But, weird Andy managed to make one critical mistake. He missed so many of his cues that he eventually got himself fired. The station owner, Ted Henner, threw him out on his ass. Then he turned to me and said, 'Hey

Toots, did anyone ever tell you that you have a voice that was made for radio?'" Shelly nodded matter-of-factly. "He offered me Andy's position right then and there on the spot."

Casey was incredulous, "What? Ted Henner? The movie producer?

Shelly smiled coyly. "The very one. Only, he was not famous back then. But I married him anyway."

"So, let me get this straight," Casey recounted. "Your husband is *the* Ted Henner?"

"Yep. The very one. He's my little taco. We've been together for eleven years.

"So, the two of you met in Denver, married, and then worked together in radio?"

"Right. Teddy eventually sold the station and that's when we moved to Pittsburgh. He was just starting an investment venture with an independent film company and I was doing voice over work and TV commercials for a Spanish network. It was Teddy who urged me to get some promotional pictures together and we sent them along with a homemade demo tape around to the local TV stations. We were pretty much broke at that time. He had sunk every penny from the radio station into his film projects. We existed on my pittance as a barmaid. Lot's of beans and rice in those days!"

"Wow!" Casey said. "How did you finally get your break?"

"Perseverance. Prayer. A little luck, I guess. And a lot of balls! I heard of an opportunity there at WNPR and arranged to have a meeting with the program director to discuss a weekend anchoring position. Here I was— me, with no real television experience at all, except for the voice over work I had done. So I just walked right into his office and told him that he should hire me. Teddy and everyone else I knew said I would be great, only the WNPR executives didn't necessarily see it that way. They saw me as an inexperienced Latin girl from the poor side of Pueblo and shoved me out the door. Never giving me a second look."

"And then?"

"And then, I said, *so what?* There had to be another way to convince them to give me a try. It was so tough for women to break in then—especially minorities. But, I just wouldn't let it end that easily. I did my homework... dug a little." She touched Casey's hand to punctuate her point, "Like all good reporters do, and found out all about what

there was to know about the station manager. I asked around. It really wasn't all that hard. I had discovered that he was a huge Knicks fan. So what did I do then? I sent him my one shoe!"

"What?" Casey stared blankly at Shelly who certainly had an amazing way of weaving a tale.

The waiter appeared to clear their plates. Shelly ordered a cappuccino and Casey did as well. It would be her first exotic coffee beverage. Casey felt like doing exotic things when she was with Shelly. She made her feel fearless.

By then several patrons in the restaurant had noticed Shelly Escamilla, recognizing her from the evening news. There were countless stares and whispers erupting throughout the restaurant all around them to which Shelly was not the least bit oblivious. She ate it up.

Casey insisted on competing the story. "You said that you gave him your shoe?"

Shelly nodded. "Yep."

"Why on earth did you—?"

"Because it was my gimmick. You've got to have something to set you apart. I simply boxed up one of my designer pumps along with a demo tape for him to view, of course, all with a note telling him who I was and how I had been trying to get my foot in the door to see him. Tucked in the shoe, just for extra incentive for him to call, were two tickets to the Knicks vs. the Pistons game for that very next night. I, of course, held a third ticket—right next to his!"

"That's fantastic!" Casey squealed. "What a cleaver idea! Did it work?"

"It sure did. He showed up for the game with his program director and even brought the shoe! We had two and a half hours to get to know one another and they agreed to give me a job as—would you believe, of all things, as a production assistant! He said that would get my other foot in the door. So I worked my way up through the ranks. It wasn't until three years later that they put me in front of the camera. And, I haven't looked back since."

"Wow!" Casey said. Her head was spinning from Shelly's remarkable story.

"I've been at six different stations in five and a half years. Now, finally—my first major market position with WRS. It's been an incredible ride."

Casey was happy for Shelly. She was a woman who had it all—a great career, a great family, and a charmed life. She secretly vowed to someday know that kind of success.

"And you?" Shelly asked, resting her chin on her wrist, giving Casey her full attention. "What is it that you want to do?"

Casey peered across the table. No one had ever asked her that question before. She paused only a millisecond. "I want to go out there, pay my dues, and come back to Chicago someday and—"

"Sit in my chair?" Shelly smiled.

"Well, yes ... for starters." Casey demurred.

"And, I suppose, you would like me to give you advice on how exactly to do just that. Right?"

Casey gushed. "Anything at all you could teach me would be great. You're the best in the business, and it would mean the world to me. You see, I don't have anyone behind me. I just have myself."

Shelly paused. "That's okay, *Chica*. "That's all you need."

CHAPTER 8

★ ★ ★

WENDY JOZWIAKOWSKI WAS WAITING FOR Casey outside of her cubicle at ten to seven, finishing off a powdered sugar doughnut and a Mountain Dew.

"Hey, Casey, I've got news."

Casey had had a double espresso to wake up before tackling the big stack of morning newspapers and clippings she was to scan for story leads. She hadn't counted on Wendy first thing in the morning. Her stomach was acting up lately, and the recurring pain had kept her tossing all night. What news could Wendy have that couldn't wait until she had her coat off?

"What is it?" she asked curtly.

Wendy sniffed indignantly. "You don't have to go and be all that way about it—I'm just trying to be your friend! You can just find out like everyone else, see if I care."

"Find out what?"

"Shelly Escamilla is canned!" Wendy delivered her bomb with pleasure on her face.

"What?" Casey was incredulous—Shelly was more than just her mentor. She was her best friend in the business. How could this be?

"It's true. I overheard Warhover's secretary discussing it

with Alan in Programming. She's O-U-T all right. They are giving her the axe this afternoon—hey, where are you going?"

Casey had to get to the ladies' room quickly as the double espresso and the bad news conspired against her empty stomach. She slammed past Wendy and down the hall, but found the restroom filled with busybody assistants and nosy account executives. She barricaded herself in an empty stall until she heard the last person leave. Then, she leaned over the toilet, shoved a finger deep into her throat, and forced herself to vomit.

Six weeks passed, but Casey was still heartbroken over losing her friend and mentor. Shelly had promised to continue to help her with her career goals, but after Shelly had taken a midday anchor position in Minneapolis, she was apparently too busy to return her calls. Casey was once again left to go it alone.

She found solace in binging; eating a whole bag of potato chips, followed by a dozen or more cookies, and then a pint of Rocky Road ice cream. It had started with just a few delectable forbidden delights, but soon, two or three cookies or a single candy bar was not enough. She still felt insatiably empty, and the sweet, rich snacks seemed to soothe both her hunger and her queasiness. She warded off the extra fat grams and mounting calories by making herself throw up after each binging session. It was an uncomfortable procedure, but she could eat whatever she wanted, and as much as she wanted, anytime. A quick trip to the ladies' room erased it all in minutes. And once again, she felt in control.

She knew she could stop if she wanted to. If only her career were on a faster track—that's all she needed. She decided to create her own destiny instead of simply waiting for it to happen to her. What if it never came? She could stay working as an assistant, gathering news articles and transcribing voice mails forever, and no one would notice that she even existed. She didn't belong boxed and hidden in a maze of carpeted cubicles.

She knew she needed a demo tape, a résumé that would feature Casey Singer as a mixture of sex kitten and apple pie; plausible, memorable. She would send it out to mid and large-size markets throughout the Midwest.

"Hugo is the best," Dahlia assured Casey as she deposited a load of dark T-shirts into the washing machine and doused them with blue detergent. She was referring to her girlfriend's brother who taught film production part-time.

"What will it cost?"

"Depends on how fantastic you want him to make you look."

Casey smiled. "Can he make it look like I've done it all?"

The video project took three weeks to complete, using the production studio at Columbia College after hours to tape the mock-interview segment with Eugene Miller, a.k.a. Scartar, another acquaintance of Dahlia's who owed her a mammoth favor. Miller's band was touring the Star Search circuit, so they could use the clip for collateral publicity. Two tech majors, students of Hugo's, assisted them. They shot the interview in several takes until midnight, although they would finish with only sixty seconds of useful material.

It cost Casey $1200 and would eventually win her a response from KTBU in Kansas City.

CHAPTER 9

★ ★ ★

SPRING, 2010

CASEY'S FRACTURE HEALED AS WINTER gave way to signs of spring. The cast was removed in April, just as Shelly announced that she and Ted would be leaving for South America. The film project that Ted had gotten green-lighted on was about to begin shooting. It was an opportunity that he could not pass up. Shelly was granted a four-month sabbatical in order to accompany him. She would be doing correspondent work for the network affiliates in the Midwest. They were to sub-lease their apartment, but the rent was too steep for Casey to afford, so she had just under three weeks to find a place she could manage on her dwindling savings.

"I'm thrilled for both of you." Casey helped Shelly drag a huge packing trunk from beneath the bed. "You always find a way to harness your dreams." Casey tried to sound sincere, instead of sullen and distracted, as she felt. Shelly and Ted had been wonderful, but this was a lousy time for them to be abandoning her.

"Don't worry, *chica*. It's all going to work out for you too, you'll see. Plenty of opportunities are out there, yours for the taking."

Casey smiled, but she feared the worst. Her lawyer was managing damage control with the station's lawyers, ensuring that she would not be sued for breach of contract, but she'd gotten not a glimmer of a job offer from anyone. She had left several messages for Roe Evans, but heard nothing back. She had peddled her résumé and expensive glossy headshots to every TV, cable, and radio station within twenty states, answering ads in *Media Age, R&R,* and *American Broadcaster.* She couldn't even get her former agent to return her call, let alone anyone from the big talent firms.

Casey Singer had become invisible.

Shelly said, "I have a friend in Florida who just got promoted. I spoke to her about you last night. She's directing a show for a cable startup in Fort Lauderdale called The Cable Shopping Network."

Casey had read about shopping channels, real-time interactive broadcasts, where viewers purchased merchandise by phone twenty-four hours a day, seven days a week. The show spokespeople were glorified sales goons—wannabe anchors, not broadcast talent. Casey's stomach pitched. Had it come to this?

"Take it," Shelly soothed as she slid the contact information into Casey's pocket, as if she knew that such a position would be selling out. "She will hire you, no questions asked. It's all set up. You should take it."

Casey nodded.

"Do you need some money? A plane ticket? Anything?" Shelly asked.

Casey shook her head. Her remaining savings would be just enough to get her to Fort Lauderdale; she had no choice but to take the job. She needed work immediately. "Shelly, I don't know what to say... you guys have been so incredible. Thank you."

"Yeah, well, who knows—today, Cable Shopping Queen;

tomorrow, big network talk show host!"

They laughed. Casey knew that Shelly was just being her kind, wonderful self, never believing for a second that such a prediction could come true. Why was it that Casey was the only one capable of ever seeing things the way they could truly be? Where would she be if she'd aspired only to others' desperate-measure dreams for her? Florida was not a life-ring tossed into a sea of doom and uncertainty; it was a wake-up call to greatness! She would take the job and work her way back.

In fact, Casey was certain, she would come back bigger and better than ever before.

The day after she got the cast removed, Roe Evans phoned. It had been eight weeks, and she was thrilled when he seemed to be asking her on a real date.

"Are you free for dinner? I want to see for myself that you are one hundred percent healed. I'm funny that way with all my victims—especially ones as beautiful as you."

Sitting across the table from Roe, Casey felt a magnetic pull between them. Although Roe seemed tired and distracted, she attributed it to his recent return from Tokyo that morning; he still managed to ooze charm and captivated her with his alluring grin. He was more attractive than any of the magazines had shown, sporting a tan in April, with gold-streaked highlights in the thick brown hair that he swiped at whenever it fell across his forehead, a gesture repeated many times throughout the dinner.

They talked about music and the recording industry. Casey didn't bore him with her real life story, but invented a story about growing up in a perfect nuclear family on a small farm in the heartland of Southern Illinois. There was no manic-depressive, workaholic, dysfunctional, homicidal nightmares playing out in this life of Casey Singer.

Casey had no idea how she would explain her seemingly dubious career move to Roe. He was beginning to finally show interest, and she would be taking off. She could feel the disruption in her life as she prepared to leave another home behind. The possibility of asking Roe for help was out of the question. She would do this on her own. Rebuild. Start over. Once she was certain she had accomplished what she set out to do, then luxuries like love would be hers.

Four days later Casey said her goodbyes to Shelly and Ted, then boarded a plane for Fort Lauderdale. Determined to have a fresh start, she deactivated her Facebook page, changed her e-mail account, and left no forwarding address behind.

CHAPTER 10

★ ★ ★

FT. LAUDERDALE, FLORIDA
2010

THE CABLE SHOPPING NETWORK, KNOWN as CSN, was in a warehouse the size of two football fields. It was an ingeniously run enterprise of full-scale mass marketing and also a circus of greed and manipulation. Busy executives and harried producers and production staffers scrambled to find the next hot item to lure viewers into parting with their money.

Casey studied her future cohorts on the TV in her motel room, watching with growing horror as talking heads peddled trinkets, dolls, gadgets, and gimmicks of the day, with tireless wit and ingenuous smiles. The whole routine made her want to throw up.

In fact, she did just that when she reported for duty two days later—all over her Fendi pumps, and inadvertently, on her new boss, who had appeared out of nowhere at exactly the wrong moment. He was in his late thirties, she guessed, and looked more like a veterinarian or computer geek than a business tycoon in his khaki pants, Titleist golf shirt, and sneakers. Actually, she was a bit relieved that he wasn't a corporate suit. He grinned widely, remarkably unperturbed.

"Oh my God! I am so sorry!" Casey said, mortified that nerves and her obviously poor choice of restaurants for breakfast had created such a faux pas for her first impression.

"Not as sorry as I am. Just kidding! Come on, let's get you to the nurse," he said smoothly. The founder of CSN Enterprises extended his hand. "How do you do, Casey? I'm Tim Fraser, and this, is my little empire. I started it with a case of hot sauce and two dozen blenders, then a bunch of floor lamps, and then vacuums—lots and lots of those." He grinned.

Casey wondered how many times Fraser had said those exact words that exact way before.

Attractive show hosts were featured on bright sound stages in the super arena set up to resemble all manner of retail staging, from fake living rooms to kitchens to outdoor gardens. A buxom redhead was practicing her mastery of an easy-to-operate wine opener while standing in front of a fake grotto.

"It should work with one rotation," she said off-mic to the director, who had been calling into his hand radio for more artificial turf. "I can't see you, Jake... are we ready to go?"

Ten technicians ascended onto the set and then were gone in an instant as the studio lights kicked up and a siren sounded for the talent to ready themselves for the segment. A man in a Bermuda shirt joined the woman in the shot, and the two greeted the red blinking light like an old friend. "We are back; and do we have a must-have gadget for you wine aficionados. It's revolutionary!"

Fraser escorted Casey to the first aid station, a small clinic in the middle of a veritable city of lights, sound stages, and backdrops. The show aired around the clock, seven days a week, so everything was self-contained; not only the clinic, but also a commissary, library, swimming pool, and full gymnasium with running track, twelve call centers, and a dry cleaner, day care facility, and a multi-denominational chapel.

"This is Nurse Betty. She'll check you out, and then we'll get you something clean to change into," Fraser told Casey.

Casey nodded, still burning with embarrassment.

"I'm very selective about my hosts," Fraser said. "Your tape was very good."

"Thank you. I'm really happy to be here at CSN," Casey lied, trying to sound as sincere as possible.

"Great to have you." He read a digital message on his phone and frowned. "Oh shit, goddamn freight companies. I'll tell HR to have someone cover for you—go home and get some rest, Casey, and come back when you're feeling well."

"I'm fine, really. It's just a little food poisoning or something. I'm sure I'll be all right." She struggled to pull it together, but the room was really spinning. It had to have been the sausage.

Fraser started down the hall, calling back to her, "Go home—get outta here! You can try again tomorrow—that's an order."

Casey's temperature was one hundred three. So she went back to her motel and to bed.

The digital clock on the bank building across the street read ninety-eight degrees, but the humidity factor was off the charts. Outside, the pedestrians were clad in swimsuits, cut-offs, and halter tops, and littered the crowded beach with lawn chairs, blankets, and ice coolers. Casey watched them through the courtyard of the Bayside Motel, where the second floor end unit caught every ray of the afternoon sun, which converted the three-room efficiency into an Easy Bake Oven. The air conditioner was turned on all the way, but still, she alternately shivered and burned beneath her sheets. She had tried to eat some soup, but the thought of it, let alone the taste, repulsed her. The smell of the ocean air was powerfully foul and seemed to permeate everything.

Like it or not, Florida was going to be her new home.

Within a week, she had found an apartment near the studio that was more convenient than safe or attractive. It didn't matter. She hated Florida, almost as much as she hated CSN and its formulated circus format, which coerced its viewers into parting with their money, feeding their weaknesses with ploys to manipulate their induced compulsion to shop. The whole thing disgusted her, but she had a compulsion of her own—to survive, so she sucked it up and smiled and sold her way through each shift.

That she was one of the inane talking heads made Casey feel that she had indeed stooped to a new low. The pay was less than half of what she had earned in Kansas, and the hours were insufferable. She'd been assigned the daybreak shift, which was from five a.m. until nine a.m., then would spend the balance of her day—seven more hours—preparing for the next day's show, familiarizing herself with all the details and merits of electromagnetic feather dusters, weed whackers, glue guns, and fake gems.

Casey glanced at her cell phone: One message waiting. It was already sundown. She must have fallen asleep and missed the call. She checked the voice mail. *"Hi, Gorgeous!"* It was Roe.

Casey was delighted to hear his voice; she hadn't spoken to him since she left Chicago nearly a month ago.

"Just wondering how you are doing, you lazy bum. Getting any good leads? Call me."

She had to decide what to do. Should she call him back

and fill him in on her relocation and position as a host of the Shopping Network? For all he knew, she was wait-ressing back in Chicago, just biding her time until the right offer came her way. She did not have the money to fly back to have drinks and dinner with him. The choice, in her mind, was basically made. She would not call him back. *No sense in starting what cannot be finished*, she thought. Besides, Roe was unpredictable, and the last thing Casey needed was another disappointment.

CHAPTER 11

★ ★ ★

CASEY WAS IN NEED OF an agent who could really kick-start her stalled career. She had remembered hearing of an agent who had once helped a co-worker land a gig with an economist show that later went syndicate. The girl had sworn by the agent's moxie and killer instincts. Casey remembered that the agent was on the East Coast and hoped that he was still in business. She'd kept the tiny slip of paper scribbled with his cell number on it in her wallet all these years. What did she have to lose?

It took several weeks and leaving a deluge of persistent phone messages to get a call back from Jordan Turner & Associates. In the process, Casey became acquainted with Jordan Turner's assistant, Cheyenne, whose life partner, Doreen, sold life insurance. Together, the couple raised two adopted siblings from Uganda. Cheyenne was a very big-hearted woman with a weakness for shopping.

Once Casey's promotional packet arrived on Cheyenne's desk, the rest was cake. Casey soon learned through her new ally that Jordan Turner went by the name Jordy, was a former pro-tennis player, a huge Streisand fan, and a *Star Trek* enthusiast. He also happened to be gay, with a lover of twelve years named Marcel. Cheyenne was a babbling brook of information.

"Oh my God! I love your show!" the woman gushed.

Casey winced on the other end of the line at the words, "*Your* show."

"Thank you," Casey said. It was recognition, at least.

Cheyenne continued, "I have to admit—I am so hooked on that channel. Last week, I watched a handbag go from ninety-five dollars to twenty-nine ninety-nine. I couldn't help myself—it was so cute, I bought two!"

"That one was from the Marilyn Moriarty collection, right? I do remember that handbag. As a matter of fact, it was a designer original... with side pockets and the detachable sunglasses case, was it not?" Casey said.

"That's the one!" Cheyenne said.

"Gorgeous bag, all right. Tell me, Cheyenne... is Jordy available at all?"

"Sure. Hold on, Casey. I'll get him on the line."

One week later, Casey met with the elusive Jordy Turner at a Taco Hut on Davie Boulevard. It was not exactly lunch at the Ritz. Just as a safety measure, she had arranged for a shipment of two new Marilyn Moriarty handbags and a collector's edition of Streisand shiny CDs to be sent to his office—to help matters along.

Jordy was beefy and jovial. He had curly silver hair that sprang out all over his head and sported a tasteful diamond stud in his left ear. He wore a Prada watch and matching belt. He had a quality about him that reminded her of Kris Kringle.

Casey got the idea that with Jordy, the clock was always ticking. That was fine because hers was clicking too.

"Let's see, you've got skills reporting weather in a small market, good camera presence, a journalism degree, news desk experience with a major network; cute hair—and a hot bod! Well, I don't see why we can't get you into something a little more deserving of your talents, honey."

They spoke between bites of dripping tacos. Casey was glued to her chair. "Anything—I don't think I could stand to remain another day peddling push-up bras and exercise bikes. I'm better than this, Jordy. I know I am."

"Of course you are! But what about the walk-off at KTBU? We're going to have to spin that little faux pas to your advantage." He eyed the hot sauce, his baby blues twinkling. "It might be a tough sell. This business is very unforgiving, you know. Now, if you were Lady Gaga that would be another thing altogether. God! I love her style."

"Can you help me or not?" Casey said, half-pleading.

"I honestly don't know, but... what the hell! Let's try and see what happens. It might take some time," he said with deadpan gravity. "Meanwhile, you don't have to send me gifts, okay? I charge plenty for my time... and besides, who listens to CDs anymore? Welcome to 2010 and iTunes!"

"How much are we talking about?" Casey asked, referring to his cut.

"What you pay is not so much in dollars, sweetheart, as it is in dedication and drive. I am going to take a chance on you. Got it?"

She nodded.

"I can get you in, but you will have to take it from there—and not go Miley Cyrus on me. Do you know what I mean?"

He was referring to her little stint in Kansas City. "I won't be embarrassed by a client who can't manage her responsibilities. I won't tolerate it. One fuck-up with me, Princess, and you're OUT."

"I was just trying to—"

"Shush!" He thrust up a plump finger. "Don't want to hear it. I saw your tape, and you're good. Good enough to make it in any market. Only, I don't think that weather is your gig, sweetheart. You're too dynamic and attractive for that dog and pony show. Perhaps we should spotlight your versatility and personality more, explore the playing field.

Have you done any commercial acting?"

She shook her head.

"How recent are your headshots?"

"Did them four years ago—at least."

"*Oy!* I'm setting up a session with a stylist for Saturday. We'll go blonder!"

"Okay," Casey beamed.

He checked his watch. "I've got a one thirty. Put my number into your phone. Pick up when I call," he said, scooping up the check.

"Do I owe you anything?" Casey asked.

He winked. "Let's just say that if you make money, I make money. In the meantime, though, don't quit your day job—okay?"

"Thank you. I won't let you down." Casey was relieved. If anyone could turn her career around, it would be Jordy. She knew that she could do anything she put her mind to. She just needed someone else to believe in her.

Over the next four months, Jordy turned down twelve offers from small to medium markets—everything from pawnshop ads to a walk-on role as a deaf-mute for a cable pilot, citing that none were the "right fit" for Casey Singer. It was Jordy's intention to get her out front and noticed; to create a buzz about this five-foot-six dynamo whose face, style, and finesse could sell products, impress the critics, and win viewers.

Finally, Jordy agreed to let her do a public service ad for a pharmaceutical company that would appear on billboards from Miami to Chicago. The lead came from a modeling agency in Detroit. It was slightly controversial, featuring a nearly nude woman in bed with an attractive man beneath rumpled sheets. The copy read: VENEREAL DISEASE IS NOT SEXY—PREVENTION *IS*. SILVER SHEIK CONDOMS.

The campaign was a success. The manufacturer committed to seventeen more cities and a slew of print ads in twenty-two magazines nationwide. Seemingly overnight, Casey became known as "The Condom Girl."

Thanks to Jordy's business plan, she was on her way

CHAPTER 12

★ ★ ★

THE NEXT TIME ROE CALLED, it caught Casey entirely off guard.

"Hello, beautiful. I was beginning to think that you have been avoiding me."

"I've been busy with work... sorry. I've meant to call," she said, walking into her apartment with a stack of mail under one arm and a grocery bag in the other. The sound of his voice distracted her, nearly causing her to drop her keys, along with the overdue bills. She kicked off her shoes and then took a seat on the coffee table.

"I've missed talking to you, Case." His voice was soothing, familiar. She liked the way he had come up with a nickname for her—already. "How are things going with the job hunt?"

"Pretty good. I'm in Florida now, working for CSN—just to keep my skills sharp in between modeling gigs." *Yeah—and food on the table*, she thought. She had cut her hours at the cable network job and it had been weeks since the last check came in from the condom ads. Work was not exactly pouring in.

"That's great! I didn't know that you had moved. Look at you—are you hosting those swanky infomercials? I'll bet that you are killing it," Roe said encouragingly, causing her to feel less self-conscious about the whole thing. It was work, and she was just biding her time until her real break came through.

"I'd really like to see you again—that is, if you would like to."

"I would like that very much," Casey said, trying to remember to breathe in between words. She sounded calm and nonchalant, but inside, it was high school and butterflies all over again. She wondered what was happening to her. Truth being, the harder she tried to stay away from Roe, the more she missed him and wanted him to pursue her.

"Turns out, I have a conference in West Palm Beach coming up next month. Would you be up for a visit?"

"Yes!" Casey said, and then added, "Of course, I'll have to check the date to be sure that I will be available. I stay pretty busy between the show and picking up bookings with my agency."

"Impressive!" Roe said. "No rest for the beautiful, I guess."

Now Casey actually blushed, a skill she did not even know she had.

"It's a two-day conference—I have to fly back to LA for a meeting the day after it ends. I'll text you the particulars, okay?"

"Sounds like a plan," Casey said, pumping her fist at her reflection in the hall mirror. She coolly signed off, promising to get back to him, closed her flip phone, and then dropped down onto the couch with a delirious smile on her face. Things were looking up indeed.

Four long weeks dragged painfully on before the weekend of the conference finally arrived. Casey drove to the hotel in Palm Beach and was a full thirty minutes early for their agreed upon time to meet. She couldn't wait to see him. Roe had called her earlier that day to say that his plane had touched down and he was on his way to the conference. They made plans to rendezvous that evening in the lobby for dinner.

She used the restroom to kill time, fussing with her makeup and hair with compulsive tenacity. It would all be for Roe. She scrutinized her image in the mirror with disdain. Casey was her own worst critic. She berated herself silently for not going with the yellow sundress she had considered. White always made her look too washed out. Her hair was cut neat to her chin, honey-blonde with soft golden highlights, setting off her blue-green eyes. She was sporting an All American Girl look these days, with a flawless complexion, high cheekbones, and those unusual eyes whose color were all her own. Casey had perfect vision to match her perfect look. Her eyes were her trademark, along with a bright smile that could sell anything from toothpaste to tornado insurance.

Just for good measure, she threw up in the stall. Old habits die hard. *Just this once*, she thought. It actually helped settle her nerves.

She was certain that Roe would be able to read the things in her she would rather hide. Talking to him on the phone from time to time was perfect. It was safe. Distant. Being in his presence was another thing altogether. The prospect both unnerved and excited her. She had so much to be proud of—a decent job, a major modeling contract with a successful ad campaign, and a kick-ass agent who was always schmoozing with some executive bigwigs, trying to figure how to get her hired to sell their products. But what if Jordy couldn't really help her? What if spokesmodeling for the shopping channel was the best she could do? What if the condom ad was a one-hit wonder? Such were the thoughts that kept her stomach in knots. Jordy was in her corner, she decided—that would make all the difference. She trusted him.

As for Roe... he was in her heart.

No man had ever affected her the way he did. When she was in Roe Evans's presence, all rationality ceased, and she became the best version of herself she could be. The thought of him assured her that everything was going to be all right. Finally, she was beginning to think that she might be ready to believe in love.

He had been waiting in the lounge, and waved when he saw her. Stepping out of a throng of tourists and business suits, in a haze of booze and bar smoke, there he stood, looking handsome and cool in his Levis and button-down polo shirt. Their eyes locked. She practically ran toward him. "Roe!" Her breath was shallow, and her legs unsteady as he reached down from his towering six-foot-four frame and enfolded her in a warm embrace. It was the first physical contact between the two, and she hoped he didn't mind her lingering. She drew in a breath, settling into his neck. His scent was sweet and fresh, like traces of citrus aftershave and Downy.

"I can't believe you're here," he whispered in her ear. She never wanted to let go.

Together, they sat at the bar, catching up on the past months and reminiscing about the unusual way they had come to know each other.

Dinner came and went. Neither ate a bite. They feasted instead on conversation and stolen glances; a brush of a hand in passing the salt... pressed knees beneath the table.

"How are you enjoying the conference?" Casey asked as she sipped her Chardonnay.

"It's perfect—now!" he said.

"It ends tomorrow?" Casey asked.

"Yes. Then I am going to try to play eighteen holes with a new distributor before going back to LA, and then on to London." He explained how he had been spending more and more time in London as of late. His record company,

Castle, was acquiring additional outlets and opening new offices at the speed of light. He was heavily involved in the chain of things. "I caught your show on channel six. Very impressive work there with the silver polish, Ms. Singer. I nearly bought a case, but then I remembered that I don't have any silver." He chuckled. "And the ads ... Casey, they're magnificent. I've seen them all over the place—in Philly, Nashville, Vegas... and LA. Super sexy! There is definitely a side of you that is under-played. Tell that agent of yours I said so."

Her face reddened. "The shopping channel is a temporary gig, you know, just until my agent, Jordy, lands the 'big one.' He says we're very close. Every week, someone else asks for my comp."

"Well, I don't doubt it." He smiled, taking her hand and not letting go. This caused a surge of fire to radiate up her arm.

"So you like my ads?"

"IN–CRED–I–BLE!" He bit his clenched fist in restraint. This made her laugh, and now it was his turn to blush. He was charming and boyish, and yet, when he spoke about the record business and industry trends, it made her feel like she was in the presence of greatness. She even noticed several people staring at them as they passed by their table. *Who is this guy?* she wondered.

Roe's Blackberry buzzed, and he excused himself to take a call.

Casey loved every minute of being with him; the stares and commotion meant that he definitely was someone special. Much to her surprise, while she was waiting for him to return, a rocker type approached the table.

"Excuse me, but are you the girl in the Sheik Condom ads? You are! Can you sign this?"

Casey was stunned.

"Your ads are wicked great," he said. "And you are *way* hotter in person. Hey, is that Roe Evans with you—is he your boyfriend?"

She smiled, carefully inking her signature onto a cocktail napkin he had provided along with a hotel pen.

"Yeah, I thought so... lucky guy! Thanks so much."

"You're welcome," Casey said.

He paused and stared an awkward moment longer and then disappeared back to his table holding up the napkin. The table of assorted rocker types erupted in a round of high fives.

Roe returned, frowning.

"What is it?"

"Oh, I have to put out a little fire, that's all. I've just been summoned to a committee meeting in our president's suite. Looks like it's going to be an all-nighter."

Casey looked at her watch. It was nine forty. She had an early morning herself; she had to be up at three thirty a.m. to prep for her five a.m. call.

"It's late for me anyway, I'm afraid. I'd better be getting back myself." Who was she kidding? She would have stayed with Roe straight through the night, talking and just being together, if only he asked her.

"I hate to cut our evening short," Roe said.

"Me too, but I understand."

He reached for his gold bankcard. "Can I see you again before I go?"

"Definitely," Casey said.

Roe paid the bill and escorted her outside. The valet fetched her car. It was a cherry-red Jeep purchased soon after she started at CSN. He watched as she slid behind the wheel.

"It suits you," he teased, leaning with his elbows propped on the curve of the hood, peering into the open window on the passenger side. He looked positively edible standing there in the luminous moonlight. "Tomorrow night, then?"

"Sure," she replied coolly. "How about a late dinner? I'm

a great cook."

"I don't doubt it." He smiled. "Text me your address."

"Say, nine thirty?"

"Nine thirty it is."

"Come hungry!" She flashed that priceless smile and blew him a kiss. Then she dropped into gear and sped away.

Casey needed a plan, and she needed it fast. Why in the world did she offer to cook Roe a meal? She wasn't even mildly effective behind the stove.

A new emotion permeated her hazy utopia—*panic*. In twelve short hours, Roe Evans would be there, in her home, ready to be wowed with salad and sauces and sautéed things. What would she do?

She went to the health club and hit the treadmill. At the peak of her target heart rate, she master-planned an exquisite menu. Lucky for her, she knew the head chef at Pier Blue, located on the outskirts of the strip.

She would start with shrimp cocktail and a beet, blood orange, and quinoa salad before serving the main attraction—monkfish with a light dill sauce and polenta with sautéed kale. After giving Stefan full use of her tiny kitchen and explicit instructions for a gourmet extravaganza, she was delighted to see that she still had plenty of time to take a luxurious bubble bath.

She coiled her hair around jumbo-size rollers, tweezed her brows, waxed her underarms and bikini line; and polished her fingers and toes. She checked the condition of her diaphragm, retrieving it from a plastic container shoved under the sink. Just for safe measure, she had picked up some condoms from the grocery quick-mart on her way back from the gym—Silver Sheik, of course.

She slipped into a relaxed pair of blue jeans and a gauzy designer T-shirt, in an effort not to look too over done.

By nine o'clock, Stefan had finished preparing the meal,

had cleaned up, and was ready to leave. Casey got right to work, returning a few pots and pans to the stove for effect. With time to spare, she set the table, lit scented candles, and settled on a playlist from her new iPod on the stereo, remembering that Roe liked classic blues covers.

The tiny apartment looked radiant and inviting. The chilled wine and catered dinner glistened on the table around a cluster of peonies, arranged in a crystal vase scored from Goodwill for a song. She could not believe that all this was actually happening; that this night had finally come.

At exactly nine thirty-seven she got the text. He was detained at a meeting and would not be able to make it after all.

CHAPTER 13

★ ★ ★

JANUARY 2011

THE NETWORK WAS A FRENZY of activity. Rumors of a buyout had been proliferating since Casey came on board, six months ago. In some ways, it seemed like a hundred years ago that she was back home in Chicago; back at WRS-TV dreaming of making it big someday, being someone everyone loved and admired. Kansas had been a detour on the journey that went awry, partly because she faltered—got sloppy and broke her own number one rule: *Don't become emotionally involved.* Some lesson. It had cost her Guy Garrison and nearly her career.

The re-building of her life was not going nearly fast enough for her. If there was one thing Casey lacked, it was patience. All she had ever wanted was fame—to reach the top and to denounce her miserable childhood and reclaim a place that was *hers*. She knew that she did not have the means to get there on her own, which was precisely why she hired Jordy Turner. It was his job to resurrect Casey Singer. She had put her fate in his hands. She needed a hero. Only, she had hoped that it would be Roe Evans who would do the saving. *Better to keep things strictly busi-*

ness, she reminded herself yet again. Even though she was disappointed about Roe's change of plans, she decided to let the matter rest. He would call her, if and when he was ready. She could not let it rattle her.

She sat at her desk, a circular cubicle she shared with four other anchors. Stacks of scripts and program sheets crowded her desk. Morale was low at CSN, as everyone was working under the looming weight of a ticking time bomb. *The Wall Street Journal* was predicting the franchise's demise, citing the impending presence of a Norwegian conglomerate as the vulture waiting to pounce.

Tim Fraser had been implicated in a possible import/export ring operating under one of his subsidiary companies out of Peru. The news did not bode well, with the investors threatening to pull their shares at any moment. As it turned out, Fraser's tidy tale of starting his little business in his basement with a toothbrush and a toaster was all bunk. Six independent manufacturers who were about to be exposed in the scandal and who had been generously financing him, were ready to talk. Word was that CSN would be gone in less than five months.

Modeling opportunities could not have come at a better time. The outdoor ads were great, but Casey needed more. People were already starting to forget her, and she would need a lot more than one good run to reach her goals.

She slumped at her desk, head in her hands. She could feel the walls closing in. It was if she were suffocating. She had bills to pay, was barely making rent, and was quickly falling behind on her car payments. She had been sinking what little money she had made into photographers and wardrobe for go-sees and sample shoots. It didn't help that she had a shoe-buying habit that had grown to around five hundred dollars a month, and she was quickly maxing out her credit cards. She would rather wear Prada than eat. Life was crashing down hard, and once again, she was beginning to spin out of control. Desperate thoughts berated her to distraction. Was it Helen, her mother's genetics that predisposed her to depression and self-abusive behavior? She did not know.

Instead of binge eating, she began finding solace in rum, vodka, or gin. Every night was a party at The Cove, and Casey became the beautiful blonde who had a perpetual claim on stool number five.

It was Jordy who found her, facedown in a bowl of peanuts. "Goddammit, girl! What are you doing?" He yanked her arm, while everyone around stared.

She giggled and pointed at Jordy's red corpuscles, which were threatening to blow. "Hiya!" Her hand flopped down hard, sending the assorted bar snacks everywhere.

"Let's go, Sunshine," he commanded, scooping her in a heap over his shoulder.

"Don't call me that!" she slurred, kicking and flailing.

The bartender nodded. "All's I know is that she's in here most every night, running up her credit cards. Thought maybe we could get a car for her or something, but we don't know where she lives, and the TV station won't give out the information. Finally, she gave us your number—she just kept sayin' 'Call Jordy,'" he explained.

"I'll take it from here. Sorry for the mess," Jordy said as he stumbled out the door with Casey dangling awkwardly over his shoulder like a lifeless puppet.

Back home, he placed her in the bathtub, not bothering to remove her sandals or her skirt. He was not being delicate with her.

"Listen, Princess, I am not paid to be anyone's mother. You may be my responsibility professionally, but you'd better get your act together, or you are going to really fuck things up. I've invested too much in you to see you piss it all down the drain." He looked hard into her eyes. "Did you take anything? Casey, answer me! Goddammit—what did you take?" He turned on the faucet jets and yanked the shower lever. A blast of cold water shocked her to full consciousness. She stood unsteadily, groping for the knobs.

"I hate you, Jordy! I hate CSN! Why did I ever come to this God-forsaken place?"

"Tell me! What did you take, Casey?" He was prodding her with a loofah brush as she squirmed to escape the assaulting pokes. He was relentless.

"Nothing! Listen to me—I didn't take anything, you stupid fuck! Stop jabbing me! What are you trying to do? Drown me?"

"Tempting, yes; practical, no." He shut off the jets and then sat down on the commode lid, lit a cigarette, and stared at her. "There's a pot of coffee in the kitchen, and you and I are going to have a little talk—*Capeesh, bitch?*" He handed her a towel and smiled. "You've got five minutes."

She grabbed it from him and yanked the shower curtain shut and began peeling off her wet clothes as the pink-tinged water from her red blouse swirled down the drain.

"Way to go, shithead. This was dry-clean only!"

"Nice mouth." He chuckled. "Very attractive of you, passing out in a bowl of Planters. Very classy."

"Fuck you!" she huffed. "You're my agent, not my warden."

She climbed out of the tub, naked, dripping wet from head to toe. She stepped onto the linoleum a bit more sober, no less fuming. She padded across the tile floor and snatched her bathrobe from the hook. She glared at him as he sat all smug and self-righteous, perched on top of the porcelain throne, legs crossed all prim and prissy, smoking one of her Virginia Slims like the queen that he was. "Do you mind?" she said, shooing him out. "You said that I had five minutes."

Casey emerged exactly five minutes later, bare-footed in the kitchen of the tiny efficiency in which there was little room for much else except for a small glass patio table and two café-style chairs.

Jordy poured two strong cups of sludge and ordered, "Sit down. For God's sake, you look like shit."

Casey winced and refrained from telling him to kiss her ass. Her head hurt too much to fight. The caffeine sounded good. So she slid into the chair and waited for the lecture.

At first, Jordy just sat there smoking. It was two thirty-two a.m. and for the first time, Casey realized that he was wearing pajama bottoms with a ragged Miami Vice tank top and flip-flops.

"*What*?" he said defensively. "Did you expect *très chic* at two in the morning? I was in dreamland when Bartender Bob called—let me tell you, Marcel is none too happy about this late-night vigilante brigade. You owe me for this one, sweetheart!"

Casey softened at the thought, picturing Jordy rolling out of bed, fumbling for his clothes in the dark, having to explain to his Latin bedmate that he had to go rescue a crazy client from a drunken stupor. It was, if nothing else—*funny*. They both began to laugh. Casey laughed so hard that it caused her to break down in a mess of fitful sobbing. Once again, Jordy was at the ready with a box of tissues.

Casey dabbed her eyes and shook her head. "I just got sad. That's all... it happens to everyone."

"What's his name?" Jordy leaned back in the chair, making himself comfortable.

Casey knew that it was useless to resist. Jordy had super powers, so she spilled.

"His name is Roe. He hit me."

"He hit you?" Jordy flicked an ash onto a gravy boat he found in the back of the cupboard.

"Yeah, the bumper of his Lexus met my entire body on an icy street in Chicago last winter, and well, it was a cute meet for the record books. We stayed in touch after the accident... met up for dinner once or twice. He's really busy. I mean, he runs a division of a record company and—"

"Hold on, Sally! You are not talking about Roe Evans—the Castle Records guru? Wow. He is definitely a catch—I mean, if you like Ivy League, executive type, music industry straight men."

"Yeah, well, he just might be like all the others. Too soon to tell, but—"

"But he's already made you cry, and that is not a good thing. Listen, don't you worry an iota about this guy. He isn't going to be looking out for your best interests. He has his own uber-career to pilot. Besides, you are destined for great things, and you have to keep a level head to get there. I just don't want to see you blow your chance at really doing some great things with your life. Sorry to say that you're just going to have make some sacrifices. You can't have it all—not in this arena."

Casey knew that Jordy was right. What was she thinking?

"I'll tell ya—we all do stupid stuff when we're scared. It's okay."

Good ole Jordy. He was the closest thing to a guardian angel she had ever had. She didn't deserve him.

"You are your own worst enemy," he said, pouring another round of brew. "We'll get your car later this morning and get back to work."

Casey nodded. No one had ever done anything even remotely as kind as this for her before. "Thanks, Jordy. You really saved my ass."

"Drink your sludge," he ordered, then lit another smoke.

It would soon be dawn. She was exhausted. Jordy's words were still burning in her ears, and yet, Casey wondered what Roe was doing at that exact moment. The thought of calling him later flittered through her mind and was just as quickly dismissed. All that coffee had hit her stomach hard, stirring things up that didn't need stirring. She would have to call in sick. There was no way she was going to do a show in this condition. All the makeup and studio lighting in the world could not make a presentable spokes-model out of her—not today.

Casey spent the rest of the day in bed and the follow-ing one and the one following that one. She slept right through the entire weekend—and two full shifts at the station. Still, in all the hours that she logged alone and depressed beneath her one good set of bed sheets, Roe never called.

She met with Jordy for their usual lunch meeting at the Taco Hut. She was off on Mondays from the network and relished getting back into her routine.

"Hey," Jordy said, cleaning the last drop of sauce from his plate, "do you know what you need?"

Casey shrugged.

"A vacation. You ought to come with Marcel and me. We're sailing on Friday over to Key West for a little get-away. It'll be fun. Just us three—what'd ya say? Take some vacation days and burn 'em, baby, before that place goes under. You've earned it. It's probably just what you need in light of your little nervous breakdown and all." He grinned. "C'mon, Casey... just say yes. You'll love the Keys, I promise. It's a great way to kick off the new year."

Casey hesitated. A hundred thoughts ran through her mind of things she had to do: clean her apartment, run some errands, update her comp, obsess over Roe... the list was long and endless.

"We'll have you back in a week," Jordy pressed. "The station can spare you for that long."

I really could use the rest, she thought.

"All right!" she blurted, surprising even herself.

"You'll go, then?"

"I'll go." Tim Fraser could manage without her for a few days.

"Fabulous—I'll let Marcel know we've got a stow-away! We're going to have the best time, and you'll end up thanking me, you'll see." He snatched up his fanny pack from the back of his chair and fastened it around his paunch waist. "Be down at the marina on Friday morning at eight, sharp. Pack light. We'll be sleeping on the boat. Don't worry about food, we've got all that handled. Oh—and bring your best bikinis, we'll get some candid photos out about the island. Have you ever been to Hemingway's house? It's amazing. Bring good walking shoes... and lots of sunscreen!"

She laughed. He was chattering like a mother hen, the way he always did when he was really jazzed about something.

"I can't wait!" she said, wondering what she had just done.

He kissed her squarely on both cheeks and sighed. "You are taking charge of your life and are about to have an adventure." His tone was serious and scolding. "You really gave me a scare there the other night."

His blue eyes looked like they had weathered a hundred storms in life, and she regretted having added one more. He looked younger at a glance, but Jordy was pushing fifty and knew a thing or two about just about everything. So she took his advice for what it was worth—plenty. He was one of the best men she had ever known, and she trusted him implicitly.

CHAPTER 14
★ ★ ★

JAMES OF VIS-À-VIS AGENCY NEVER made phone calls. Her "people" contacted models—if they deemed fortunate enough to be invited to the esteemed agency for an audience with the grand dame herself. So how did *she* get so lucky, Casey wondered as she attempted to decipher the CSN receptionist's hieroglyphics, scrawled on a tiny pink slip of paper that read: *Emarie James. Vis-à-vis Agency… call her back.* "What on earth?" Casey was dumfounded. *Could this be real?* She searched the note for a phone number, but there was none. "Interns!" Three days away from the office and everything went to hell in a bucket.

She did a Google search for the number; her heart was pounding out of her chest as she carefully punched the numbers on her phone. Why would Emarie James be calling her? Emarie was the one of the most coveted agents in Hollywood—she alone represented the very top talent on the coast: vocalists, rappers, actors, models, comics, and sports gods. Her track record was legendary. Funny, she didn't remember ever sending a composite to Emarie or to any of the West Coast agencies.

She held her breath as she checked her watch. It was three p.m. in LA. Casey silently berated herself for nearly missing the message. She really needed to better organize her desk, even if she was riding on a sinking ship. If she hadn't glanced at her sagging plastic inbox before heading home herself, she would have missed it. It was Thursday evening, and half of the office had already bolted for happy hour. She needed to head home herself soon to pack for her excursion to the Keys with Jordy and Marcel.

"Good afternoon. Vis-à-Vis Agency... how may I assist you?" The voice was smooth by design, with just a hint of an exotic accent. Everything connected with Vis-à-Vis made one feel that they were crossing into an enchanted dimension.

"Yes, this is Casey Singer. I'm returning a call from Ms. James. I believe she tried reaching me earlier."

"One moment, please."

The hold music was discothèque chic—Studio 54 pulsating over the cell line. Casey's heart pounded with every synchronized breath. Suddenly, a voice broke in. "Hello? This is Emarie James."

Casey was alone in her cubicle, but felt a compulsion to stand a little taller in Emarie James's presence, even if it was only a phone call. The two-pack-a-day smoking habit of the woman on the other end of the line made her sound like a cross between Marlene Dietrich and Joe Cocker.

"Uh... yes. Hello, this is Casey Singer... returning your call, Ms. James."

A pause. Casey's heart tripped.

"Marvelous! Who are you? Oh—the condom girl from out east. Yes, I remember now. How long have you been modeling, dear?"

"For about half a year. I'm also currently hosting a shopping show on channel six here locally, weekday mornings."

"Question, Casey—are you happy in Lauderdale? I mean, would you be willing to trade up? Relocate if need be? No promises, but Vis-à-Vis would like to take a closer look at you."

Emarie wasted no time. She could be heard inhaling a deep, indulgent drag before asking, "How soon can you be here? We'd like to take a look at you and go over some of your past work. Bring whatever you have. How does tomorrow sound at, say… around one o'clock?"

Casey blanched.

"I'd like to send you on an open audition on Monday."

"Yes, ma'am. I suppose I can make that happen." Casey was dumbfounded but not stupid. She already had an agent, and agreeing to meet a potential rival was not something she was altogether comfortable with. Then again, one does not say no to Emarie James! "I'll be there," Casey said, deciding she couldn't afford to miss this opportunity.

"Wonderful. I'll switch you over to my assistant, Charles. He'll give you all the details."

Then, the line went silent.

Casey could feel her head spinning. A young man came on the line and asked her for her e-mail address.

"I'll send you an itinerary and some agency notes. Okie dokie, then, if there are no questions—"

"Just one, if I may ask," Casey broke in. "Who referred me to your agency?"

"It says here… a Jordan Turner."

"What have you done!" Casey was beside herself, laying into Jordy on her cell phone as she hurried to her car.

"Nothing that a good agent wouldn't do for his best client," Jordy said. "I gave it much thought, and I know that I can do nothing more to really help you. Not here. It is time, Casey, time for you to go further."

She paused before turning on the ignition. "But what about Key West?"

"There is no Key West, darling—at least not for you. Listen, I got you to get the week off, so there is no reason why you cannot take advantage of this opportunity and just go see Emarie—she and I go way back."

"So this is a *favor* she is doing for you?"

"A favor that I am doing for you—now stop asking questions and get your pretty little ass home to pack. Bring all of the good outfits and shoes. I have booked you on the red-eye this evening. Check your e-mail for the hotel and car information that Cheyenne will be sending you. I am so proud of you, girl! You are going to wow that old bitch!"

Casey was incredulous. She could barely think, let alone speak.

"Oh my God!" she said, her heart pounding.

"*Ciao, bella!* Call me from the airport when you arrive at LAX—and good luck!"

The next move came to her in an instant. She would not bother to speak to Tim Fraser personally, or to just limit her absence to one short week. Rather, she called into the answering desk in Human Resources at CSN and told them that she had quit.

Ready or not, she was now Hollywood-bound and one way or another, she knew that she would make it. She pulled onto the interstate with her hopes high, setting her sights on moving forward and not looking back.

CHAPTER 15

★ ★ ★

CASEY ARRIVED AT LAX AHEAD of schedule. She had dozed off a bit just after takeoff. The flight attendant jolted her awake from the most wonderful dream with the drink cart hitting her squarely in her elbow. She had dreamt that she was walking on a sandy beach in the Keys with Roe beside her. He was carrying her sandals and kicking up sand, laughing. The warm Pacific air stirred his hair, and his boyish grin flashed in the sun; her spirits soared like the cranes coasting on the breeze.

She was happy and carefree. It was just the two of them, until—"Excuse me, watch your elbows."

Too late! Ouch! It was glorious while it lasted.

Once she landed, finding an available electrical outlet was impossible. Business executives and tourists were everywhere, jamming their fingers into their ears, shouting into their devices. She only had a quarter of a bar left on her phone, and was unable to pick up a signal. She decided to grab a cab and call Jordy as soon as she got to the hotel.

"I'm here!" She could barely hear him over all the static. "Jordy?" The reception is terrible!" He was on his cell, speaking to her from the boat.

"You are going to do great, Casey. Emarie is going to love you! Have fun, and be sure to avoid the mid-day UVs, all actor-types, and bad sushi."

She laughed. He was such a crack up. Forget about the fact that she was nervous, she had Jordy on her side, and he believed in her.

"Go get 'em, Princess! When you... remember to . . ." He was breaking up badly. He said a crackling goodbye and then was gone.

"Hey—wait!" She wanted to thank him before he hung up. She shrugged and smiled instead. *Oh, well that was weird. Remember to do what?* she wondered.

Little did she know, that would be the last time she would ever speak to him.

It was twenty to one when Casey's cab pulled up to the glass and granite high-rise office plaza in Century City. It was massive; far bigger than the stumps they called high-rises in Lauderdale. Los Angeles was more fabulous then she had imagined. She was a native Chicagoan, and most cities had much to prove if they were going to hope to compete with the Windy City. Of course, nothing ever did, but LA truly was in a league of its own.

Casey took the elevator to the twenty-fifth floor and entered the reception area with confidence. Gripping her portfolio tightly, she approached the beautiful waif perched behind the colossal reception desk with bolstered confidence. Brunettes never intimidated her, no matter how beautiful they were. This one resembled a young Audrey Hepburn with a pricey haircut and cat eyelashes.

"Take a seat. Ms. James will be right with you," she said.

Emarie made Casey wait an excruciating twenty minutes before emerging from her office.

"Casey! Welcome... I trust that you had a good flight?" She greeted her with a blast of stale cigarette breath mingled with Channel No. 5. Casey smiled and nodded, taking in the plush modern surroundings, where a gallery of framed photos—comedians, actors, and other celebrities, framed the walls.

Emarie led her to a large room with a wall full of television monitors, several leather couches, a huge conference table, matching console, and two teal-and-black swivel chairs positioned near a smaller desk.

"This was once our screening room," she explained. "I chose it for my office because of the view." The walls were encased in glass from floor to ceiling, revealing a spectacular view of Burbank, the Hollywood Hills, and the ocean.

"Have you just come in off the plane, dear? You look a bit knackered." She settled into a chair nearest the ashtray, motioning for Casey to sit as well. Methodically, she lit up, flipping open a Cartier lighter as thin as a lipstick and masterfully returning it to its sheath all in one graceful movement. "You must remember to keep hydrated, especially out here."

Emarie was a piece of work; a real relic. She was pretty well-preserved, though, for seventy-*something*, Casey guessed. "May I ask how it is that you know Jordy?"

Emarie took in a long drag and paused. Her red lipstick, which had migrated into the cracks around her mouth, revealed a graveyard of nicotine-stained teeth when she smiled at the memory.

"Jordy and I were old friends from The Laughing Stock, a small comedy club out in Miami, about a hundred years ago. Jordy was one of the very first comics I ever signed. And he was a pretty bad one too. Then he decided to take up tennis and become an even bigger bomb! After his tennis days were over, he begged me to teach him the business and eventually opened his own talent agency. By the time he was up and running, I had relocated out west and survived seven husbands, until I could afford to hang my shingle right here. We go way back Jordy and me. I would do anything for that old fag."

Casey gave a nervous smile.

"Anyway, he called the other day and said that I should take a look at you—he thought you might be willing to move out here permanently. I said that I would be happy to."

So that was it. Jordy told Emarie that Casey was thinking about making the move for her career. Typical Jordy, always working the angles.

"I arrived early this morning. This is my first time here," Casey said. "I'm going to take things as they come."

"Well, that's certainly brave of you. Jordy said that you are a tough one. May I?" She reached for Casey's portfolio before she could answer. Casey sat motionless as Emarie donned her spectacles, which dangled from a chain around her neck, and slowly surveyed each page.

"Oh, this is a sweet shot... I like the back lighting here. Great smile."

"Thank you," Casey said, slowly gaining confidence.

Emarie paused and then shot a succession of rapid-fire questions at Casey: "How long have you been with Jordy?"

"Nearly a year."

"Born?"

"Chicago."

"Modeling experience?"

"Yes. "

Emarie's eyes peered over the rims of her glasses, and her pencil-thin eyebrows tightened. "Could you expound on that, dear?"

"Well, there's been print work in the various catalogs you see there. Of course, the outdoor ad for Silver Sheik most recently. I have done some runway and spokesmodel stints in several malls ... and many trade shows. I also did some voice-over work in Chicago, as an intern. I anchored weather in Kansas for KTBU-TV, then moved to Florida, where I was working for the cable network there as a product host for the shopping channel."

"School?"

"A BA in journalism from Columbia College in Chicago… and a minor in theater."

Emarie closed the portfolio. "What is it you're hoping I can do for you?"

Casey stiffened. She was unprepared for the question. "Well, I… thought I might try my hand at acting. It's sort of a passion of mine—next to broadcasting, of course."

Emarie removed the ebony eye frames and bore a hole right through her. "I see. Well, Casey, we are in the business of representing talent, not creating it, you understand."

"Yes, ma'am. I think you'll find that I am not like most other—"

"Hopefulls? I'm afraid you are. Let me make myself clear: I'm seeing you today because you are a client of a dear friend of mine, but Jordy and I play in far different leagues."

Casey blanched.

"He says that you have *chutzpah*. I like that far more than fancy rèsumé or demo tapes. I'm a believer in gut feelings. I'm just that kind of broad. Do you know what I mean?"

Casey was certain that she did not, but nodded and eagerly smiled, sitting a little taller in her seat.

"I know what sells. I don't really give a rat's ass about anything else. That's how you make money. You would have to already have—or be able to create—one hell of a name for yourself."

"Exactly! And I—"

"Stop right there, honey." Her gruff voice startled Casey. She watched as Emarie clenched the tiny eyeglasses, turning them over and over in her grotesquely venous hand. She took another long, slow drag on the cigarette. "I am aware of the scandal in Kansas that you… for lack of a better term, left behind."

Casey swallowed hard.

"What you did was irresponsible, and it takes people a while to forgive and forget. What you didn't do is use it to your advantage. In my opinion, it was a lost opportunity. You will need to turn things around if you ever hope to make your mark. You will need to use your faults to your advantage."

"How?" Casey asked.

"For starters, you'll have to drop at least eight pounds—maybe more. I don't care how you choose to do it. I doubt anyone will be able to place you until you do. And if I were you, I'd chop up that prissy bob and take up the blonde a few million watts—go as freaking bombshell as you can. I would also look into a top-notch acting school. Reporting the weather is a far cry from a dramatic role. Frankly, we couldn't even take you on at this time on spec. Go get the experience—and then we'll talk again."

"I see." Casey fumbled with her things as she got up to leave.

"Sit down. I'm not done," Emarie said. "There's an audition tomorrow morning at seven a.m. at Chase Models—the one I mentioned on the phone. It's a cattle call for some Australian denim company. They're doing a search for a spokesmodel. The suitable candidate has to not only be attractive, but she has got to be able to string two sentences together, and have poise and a strong camera presence. I think you should go out for this. I could get you on the call list."

Casey brightened. "I would truly appreciate it!"

Emarie stubbed her cigarette into the ashtray and checked her enormous watch. "Wait right here." She exited the room and returned with a folder containing the particulars.

"Chase Modeling Agency is about forty minutes from downtown. Go there first to get registered. The audition is at Aussie's main plant in the Fashion District. Here's a phone number. Ask for Baltimore—he's a fabulous agent."

"I don't know how to thank you, Ms. James. I really appreciate the opportunity," Casey said as she reached for the folder.

"It's up to you, dear," Emarie croaked. "Luck has nothing to do with it." Then she turned on her heel and was gone.

CHAPTER 16

★ ★ ★

THOUGHTS OF THE NEXT TWENTY-FOUR hours dominated Casey's mind as she rode down the marble and brass elevator to the lobby, where the air was fresher. Where would she spend the night, for starters? She had a little cash and a few credit cards, but they were maxed-out to oblivion. The round-trip ticket in her purse back to Florida was her safety net. If things went bad, she could always return to Fort Lauderdale and beg for her inane job back at CSN. *Fat chance!* She had five days to claim a miracle; to turn her flailing career around.

She hailed a taxi to check out the location of Chase Agency first. It was not too far toward the city. She then asked the driver to suggest an affordable place to stay. The Royal Orchard Motel was just eight blocks from the modeling agency and would seem as good a choice as any. Until she learned that there was nothing "royal" about it.

The dump advertised a thirty-nine-dollar room rate on the marquee, along with hourly specials; free television, telephone, and adult movies. It even offered discount vouchers for the strip club just up the street. It would have to do under the circumstances.

Casey asked the cabbie to wait as she checked in, then

she requested that he take her to the nearest shopping mall. The next item on her agenda was to locate a department store to prepare for the audition.

There was a Macy's downtown, at which she purchased a pair of Aussie boot-cut jeans in a deep indigo blue, along with a crisp white blouse and a reptile-print belt. The outfit cost her three hundred dollars, but she was more than pleased with the investment. Back at the hotel, she had to stand on her suitcase in front of the dresser mirror to see her full image.

Not bad. The jeans fit her perfectly in all the right places. Casey liked her curves. And she knew how to use them. She released her hair from a plastic clip and let it fall down around her chin. The Pacific Coast sunshine had lightened her mousy blonde mane to a golden hue, but could she sport peroxide blonde? In spite of what Emarie said, Casey felt that she had never looked better. Tan, vibrant, sexy. "This job is mine!" she repeated to the image in the mirror smiling back at her. "Hello, Aussie Girl! Goodbye, bad streak!"

She took a quick shower and then walked up the street to a Chinese restaurant. She ordered a virtual feast: pot stickers, egg rolls, hot and sour soup, Moo Shoo pork, vegetable fried rice, and her favorite—crispy noodles. It was comfort food, and she hadn't eaten since the day before. She carried the cartons back to the room, taking special precaution to make sure that no one was following her. Being on her own in a strange city unnerved her.

The front desk clerk was a stern-faced older man who looked like a former Marine, and that suited her just fine. A lanky German Shepherd lay curled at his feet. He quickened and stood when she entered the lobby through the glass door. The dog's snout probed the air as the aroma of Chinese food drifted from the grease-stained bags wafting in the heat. His tail happily thumped against the old man's leg, alerting him to the arriving visitor. The dog lowered his head with a low whine as she passed them on the way to the courtyard to her room.

She ate with the television on and checked her phone at least a hundred times. No messages. She resisted the urge to leave Roe a voice mail. She would wait to hear from him when he was ready. If she was on his mind as much as he was on hers... well, she would just have to wait.

Jordy and Marcel were somewhere on the ocean, on their way to the Keys. She knew that Jordy would be pulling for her tomorrow. She just had to do her best. She just *had* to get this job. From what she could already tell, Los Angeles was the place to be. After the audition, she would rent a car for the day and explore the area. Maybe drive to Venice Beach to see what all the hype was about.

Each minute that she spent contemplating the possibilities, she became more convinced. She would need to be in LA if she was ever going to make a real career for herself. Even from the no-frills, remote confines of the tiny motel room, she could feel the power of the city humming all around her, and she couldn't wait to get out there.

There was only one direction for Casey Lynn Singer now. And that was full speed ahead.

She arrived at Chase Modeling Agency twenty minutes early. This cab driver, it seemed, was determined to break the sound barrier—nearly causing her to spill her latte all over her lap. Caffeine gave her the shakes, but she drank it anyway. She entered the waiting room and joined a sea of blue jean-clad models of all shapes and sizes, touting their portfolios, audition faces, and large plastic bottles of designer water. They seemed not to notice her in the least.

She approached the reception desk. "I'm here to see Mr. Ramirez and to audition for the Aussie call," she said to the stone-faced transvestite with tattooed eyebrows and glitter eye shadow. She was directed to sign her name on the call sheet and wait. A moment later, an attractive man rounded the corner.

"Hello, Casey," he said, thrusting out his hand. "I'm Baltimore, director of Chase Models." He was handsome; Hispanic, with a broad, white smile and sleek black hair.

"Let's get you over to Maureen, who will help you with the paperwork—it will just take a minute. We'll talk later. Welcome to the agency... I'll see you inside."

Casey's heart raced as she sat on a chrome chair and signed the endless forms, while the woman named Maureen attached agency labels to the backs of her stack of headshots. "We need at least two good numbers to be able to reach you... an emergency contact, and a local address."

"Oh... " Casey paused. "I don't have a permanent address just yet."

The woman seemed unfazed. "Leave it blank—an e-mail address will do.

Returning to the waiting area, Casey stepped over two doe-eyed girls who were sitting on the carpet with stick-thin legs stretched out in front of them, chattering incessantly; their cascading manes were coiffed to perfection.

Casey slid into a vacant seat next to a blonde who, like herself, wore a reptile belt. The girl's nails were obviously fake; square edges with pristine white tips. *Way too glam!* Casey thought. She was certain this was not the look the client was after.

Casey had Googled the Aussie Corporation on her smartphone and studied their ads well into the night. It was clear that the company had an image to uphold and that their brand did not rely on the overt use of manufactured beauty to sell their jeans. The Aussie Girl was "Every Girl USA." She would wear the jeans like she wore her own skin; she'd be wholesome and organic. Casey had purposely downplayed her look to become that image.

She hoped that she had made the right call, suddenly feeling overly plain in the company of pageant queens and would-be starlets.

She thought about leaving several times. One hour turned into two... two slipped into three. Finally, at eleven fifteen, her name was called.

She was escorted to a large room, where a photographer had set up shop. There was a backlit screen, umbrella trees, and a camera positioned on a tripod in the far corner. A boom box blaring Usher pulsated from somewhere near the makeup station. Baltimore and some people from Aussie were standing there, talking.

"Casey... come in," Baltimore piped up. "This is Mr. Liam King, Executive Marketing Director for Aussie Corporation, along with his Vice President of Merchandising, Ava Walker."

The woman was a ball-busting thirty-something, with a designer suit, killer shoes, and an Australian accent.

"Great. Let's give it a go, then," the young woman said, checking her watch. It was obvious that she loved her job, the way that she moved about with her notepad and two-way radio, ordering everyone around. "Won't you take your seats?"

The troupe sat on folding chairs, and everyone stared at Casey.

"Could you slate for the camera, please?" A tech assistant's voice filtered in through the glare.

Casey nodded. "I'm Casey Singer... with Chase Models."

"Just look at the camera if you will, Casey. We are going to ask you a few questions about yourself, okay?"

The audition took less than five minutes. A brief biography about herself, previous modeling and on-camera experience, and finally, two profile poses.

Ava, who was giving Casey's portfolio a quick flip, took note of one of the photos, and paused. "'Ang on," she said, leaning into the executive director's ear and then nodding.

"We would like to take some Polaroids of you, Casey. Give us a good go, won't you?"

The photographer snapped away as the executives debated and pointed at the proofs. In less than half an hour, a representative from the agency asked her to return to the holding room and wait. Incredibly, she had made it through the first round.

Baltimore greeted the six finalists. "Really great job, everyone. You have an hour and a half for lunch. Be back here at two thirty—sharp!" Then he leaned toward Casey. "Hey, Midwest, I could tell that they were impressed with you," he said, scanning his iPhone texts. "Well done!"

Casey was elated. She could smell victory, but still had a second hurdle to clear. There would be more cuts. If nothing else, scoring a big-time agency like Chase and an agent like Baltimore was huge. A few jobs with them would no doubt lead to bigger things; the kind of attention that would make the likes of Emarie James sit up and take notice. There were five contenders left, including Casey. Two were blondes—herself and little Miss French Manicure. Two were brunettes, and the fifth was a tall girl with very pale skin and a fiery red mane. It was anybody's game.

Casey noticed the tall redhead with the freckles from earlier that morning, now standing by the elevator. She had a fantastic smile, eyes the color of Hollywood swimming pools, and a knockout figure—a triple threat. She had a Julia Roberts way about her that simply lit up her entire face when she smiled.

"What a morning," the girl said, as the two stepped onto the elevator.

"I know. The waiting is the worst part," Casey said, pressing the button for the lobby.

The friendly rival nodded, sliding her tote bag further onto her shoulder. "Guess if we made it this far, the rest can't be all that bad. I'm Glenn, by the way," she added.

"I'm Casey. Nice to meet you."

"Would you like to get some lunch? We've got an hour and a half to kill before we have to be back." Glenn looked at Casey as the doors popped open. It was an awkward moment best remedied by a kindness.

"Sure, I'm famished," Casey said. "Do you know where to find a decent salad around here?"

"I can definitely help there," Glenn said. "My dad owns a restaurant up the street. Best grub in LA."

Harvest had the best of both worlds—everything from bean sprouts to bacon burgers. The lunch-hour crowd was in full swing. It was the Fashion District's busiest new deli and promised to be a goldmine for investors who saw gourmet sandwich fare as the new next big thing. The two found a vacant table along the back wall and plopped down. Glenn ordered a vegan salad and an iced tea. Casey broke protocol and opted for a plain burger with diet soda. More dangerous caffeine, but the summer heat was sweltering, and denim was not the coolest thing to be wearing on a ninety-eight-degree day.

"So where are you from?" Glenn asked as she dug into the bib lettuce.

"Chicago, originally," Casey said. "But most recently I've been working in Fort Lauderdale. How about you?"

"Been here for three years now. I was born and raised in Iowa. I'm one of those who got out," she added with a glint in her eye. "Better late than never, as they say." She removed the hard roll from her plate. "No carbs for me."

Casey suddenly felt guilty about her bun. "What made you leave? Did you come here to be a model?"

"Not at first. I was doing some modeling in Sioux City, but not really going anywhere with it. I really wanted to be an actress. I guess, in a way, I was doing just that—I 'acted' like I wanted to get married and settle down. I said yes when my boyfriend, Eddie, asked me. Only, I changed my mind one Sunday right in the middle of Walmart. I was working there at the checkout one minute and the next, I was running out of there like a crazy person. I just kept running—all the way here, I guess."

Casey stopped chewing.

Glenn's voice softened. "I didn't tell my mama or pa, or my brothers and sisters goodbye. I just hopped a bus here to LA, with less than two hundred dollars in my pocket. I lived on the streets for a while before I finally found work at an after-hours club. Then, one day, I walked right into Chase Modeling Agency—with no comp, no experience, and just said, 'I'm here!'"

Casey was transfixed. "You really did that? It was that easy?"

Glenn threw back her head and roared. Her fiery curls sprang in all directions. "No! I'm just messing with you. That's just something I made up to test out my acting skills. You bought it, didn't you?"

"Shut up!" Casey had to give it to her. This girl was definitely different. She was impressed by Glenn's quirky personality. Casey admired anyone who could pull one over on her.

"You had me there!" Casey said. "Well played."

"I'm sorry." Glenn giggled into her napkin. "I just love doing that. Last week I was an Irish exchange student working as a governess for a producer in Encino!"

"Maybe you should think about becoming a writer instead," Casey said.

"Actually, I am a native—*really*." Glenn sat up straight in her chair. "Born and raised in the Valley... just me and my step-sister, and my mom. My parents divorced when I was ten. My mom remarried in 2004 and had Aggie a year later. But, he was a flake and she divorced him a year after that. In spite of all that dysfunction, my life story is far from exciting."

Casey could relate to a broken family. That was for sure.

Glenn continued, "Been modeling since I was four... I've done commercials, runway, trade shows, print work—tons of it. I think I've only eaten a total of five doughnuts in all my life. I was forced to take dance lessons, ballet, piano, speech, and I attended charm school since I could speak. My mom is a former model; my dad a working actor, until 2004, when he broke his collarbone doing a stunt. He left my mom for some no-talent actress with one name. They live in the Hills. He buys and sells restaurants now. But hey, when I'm here, I eat for free—just sign my name on the receipt and it's all on daddy!" She sniffled. "I know what you're thinking, why don't I ask my dad for help with my own career? He knows anybody who's anybody in Hollywood."

Casey stopped eating and leaned forward.

"No," Glenn said. "I'm going to do this on my own, or not at all. I'm studying under Fiona Dewitt at her studio in West Hollywood and trying to make a real career for myself. It's bad enough he pays for it." She brightened. "At present, I have done exactly one television commercial for an insurance company, which only ran locally, and," she concluded, chasing an unexpected tear from her eye, "I would *kill* to become the next Aussie Jeans Girl."

Casey was surprisingly uncomfortable. Glenn and she were not all that different. "Is that it?"

"That's everything," Glenn said, dabbing her eyes. "Sorry for the blubbering. I must be premenstrual."

"Or mental!" Casey said.

They both laughed.

Casey picked at her half-eaten bun. She was glad that there wouldn't be enough time for her to recount her life story.

"Well, I'm really glad to have met you, Casey." Glenn's Julia Roberts smile was sincere.

"You too," Casey said, happy to note that in a city of strangers, she had just made a new friend. "We've got each other's backs, right?"

"Right," Glenn said, shouldering her tote bag. "Oh—look at the time! We have to hustle."

Casey reached for her portfolio and smiled. "But you know, I'm still going to beat you out for this job."

At two-thirty sharp, the second round of the audition was underway. It consisted of a twenty-minute photo shoot in which each candidate was asked to reveal her best Aussie Girl personality for the lens.

Casey dominated the session with panache, working her honey-blonde mane and uninhibited abandon as the shutter clicked. She was sexy, confident, and captivating. Particularly convincing was a candid shot taken once they had finished. As Casey stood with legs astride, her hands on her hips, she struck a most captivating pose. She had since unbuttoned her blouse and tied it about her waist to cool off, revealing just the slightest curve of her back and bare midriff. Her sandals were off and casually flung over her shoulder, dangling by the straps from her fingers. She ran her free hand through her hair, and—*pow!* The photographer captured the perfect shot!

He ran it into the war room and tacked it up on the work board. The Aussie team rallied. This was what they were after; the quintessential free-spirited, renaissance woman. They had found her—the new Aussie Girl 2011—and her name was Casey Singer.

CHAPTER 17

★ ★ ★

DRIPPING WET, CASEY WAS STANDING in Glenn's mother's kitchen with the phone pressed to her ear. Glenn and her younger sister, Aggie, were taking turns jumping from the water slide into the pool. The stereo speakers on the deck were cranked full blast, and Adele's "Rolling In The Deep" was bouncing off the concrete patio and into the summer heat. Casey could barely hear Baltimore on the other end of the line. It was a miracle that she had even heard her phone signal the message at all. Luckily, she had been reaching in her tote bag for her sunscreen when it went off.

Was this it? Did she get the job? Her heart raced as she dialed the number to Baltimore's office. *What if someone else got the job? What if it was Glenn?* He could have been trying to reach her to tell her thanks, but—no, thanks.

Casey had already decided that she was going to stay in LA no matter what. She had a friend in Glenn as it turned out, and the two were a great team. One picked up where the other left off. It was a true friendship; like a cosmic bond between soul sisters. It felt wonderful to have a true friend again—someone she could trust. Plus, Casey simply adored Glenn's mother, Donna. She was a beautiful older version of Glenn, with long red hair twisted into a horse-tail braid down her back. She had creamy, freckled skin, high cheekbones, and stunning blue eyes. She was a young forty-year-old who interacted with her daughters more like a sister than their mother. Donna O'Keefe could sell moisturizer or breakfast cereal commercially if she wanted to. She was still stunning. Casey liked the fact that all of the O'Keefe women were self-sufficient, smart, and care-free. Even little Aggie, at six, ran around topless most of the time, shunning proper clothing and sandals, choosing instead to exist on Pop-Tarts and Tang.

"She's a bizarre child," Glenn would say about her step-sister, but Casey found her simply adorable. She often found herself noticing things like children and their little games and funny ways of doing things. She adored Aggie, who was the third of the O'Keefe contingency, lanky and lean like her sister with a face full of freckles and a cap of unruly raven curls. Her eyes, though, were a muted brown, and her features a bit more angular, evidence of her biolog-ical father's paternal claim on at least one of the O'Keefe offspring. Despite Glenn's outward apathy toward her own father, he did provided for her mother and step-sister nicely, making it so that none of the O'Keefe girls would ever want for anything.

Baltimore picked up the line. "Congratulations, Casey! You got it—you are the new Aussie Jeans Girl!"

"Oh my gosh!" She had to steady herself against the sink, a hundred thoughts racing through her head.

"They loved you, girl. Said that you were a natural. They want to start shooting next week."

Her mind was a whirlwind of questions. Through the kitchen window, she could see Glenn. She had just emerged from the deep end of the pool and was adjust-ing the straps on her bathing suit. She waved for Casey to hurry up. *What will this mean to our friendship?* She would have to tell her. If she had not gotten it, she would have wished it to be Glenn. But it was her.

"I'll be in touch with the particulars," Baltimore said and then hung up.

Casey ended the call and said a silent prayer. It was the first time she had spoken to God since she was eighteen. *Thank you,* she whispered.

The next thought that came to mind was—now what? That, and an irrepressible desire to call Roe. He would be so proud of her. How she wanted to celebrate this with him... wherever he was. And, of course, there was Jordy. She tried his number, but only got his voice mail. She decided not to leave this type of news in a message. She would wait and tell him when she could reach him.

Aggie was calling now at the top of her lungs from the diving board. "*Cas-eeee!* C'mon!"

She slid open the patio door and stepped out into the sunshine.

The call came as a jolt in the darkness. She had been staying at The Royal Palms Motel for nearly a week and still was not accustomed to her surroundings. She fumbled with the cell phone in the dark, nearly disconnecting the call in the process. "Hello?"

It was a man's voice, and he was crying. "Casey—Oh my God... it's Jordy... he's dead!"

The news made her snap to her senses in a sobering second.

"What!"

He had suffered a massive heart attack and died instantly on the steps of the beachfront condo. Marcel horrifically relayed the moments leading up to his finding Jordy there, when he had returned from the market. There would be no funeral, but a lavish memorial would be held back east. Jordy Turner had a large family. Parents, siblings, friends, past clients, former lovers, they would all be there to say goodbye.

Marcel choked on his words as he gave her the details. She scribbled them down through her tears in the darkness. "There's a flight out of LA in the morning," she informed him, feeling as if she were dreaming the worst nightmare. "I'll be on it."

CHAPTER 18

★ ★ ★

THE MEMORIAL WAS QUAINT BUT powerful. A steady flow of mourners descended on the tiny chapel in North Miami to pay their respects. Jordy Turner was said to be truly a one-of-a-kind soul, loved by many. Casey, heartbroken, believed that he was one of the few people in her life who ever really understood her.

Standing before a large portrait of Jordy, Casey said her goodbye. She was no stranger to death. This loss would leave a permanent scar, which she would simply add to the others on her heart.

When Casey returned to LA, she had reduced all her worldly possessions to just five suitcases. A few remaining boxed items she would have shipped to the O'Keefes'. Donna had insisted that when she returned from settling her affairs in Florida, she come to live with them. "You're not going back to that dump motel if I have anything to say about it!" she said. "We're not the Ritz, but you're more than welcome to stay here with us until you get on your feet."

"I appreciate it so much," Casey said. No one had ever shown her such a kindness.

The O'Keefes' sprawling Malibu home was palatial, with

its terra cotta and stucco Mediterranean design, towering palm trees, and stone pavement leading to a guesthouse above the garage. The O'Keefes owned a Volvo, a mini van, and a sporty blue convertible that Glenn's father had purchased for her when she turned sixteen. It reminded Casey of the one she once had as a teenager, which she'd had to sell her second term in college to pay for living expenses. Those days, she'd hoped, would be well behind her soon. She parked the Jeep on the driveway. Presently, she was three months behind on the lease payments. The threatening notices from the bank had already started coming in. The timing for landing the Aussie gig could not have been better.

While she was grateful for Donna's offer to live with them, Glenn was less than enthused.

"What do you think you're doing?"

Casey was caught off guard by Glenn's condescending tone. "What do you mean?"

She reached over the kitchen counter and knocked the glass Casey was holding out of here hand, sending it crashing to the floor. "You stand here in my mother's kitchen, in our house, drinking our tea and sleeping in our bed, and you ask 'what do I mean'?" Her eyes flared, and her flesh grew nearly as scarlet as her hair. "What do you want from us? It's obvious that you have nobody, or you wouldn't spend every waking minute here, pretending that my family belongs to you!"

"Excuse me?" Casey said. "You're just jealous because I won the account. Admit it—you're dying of jealousy. You want to be me."

"At least I don't have a psycho family who goes off the deep end and blows each other's heads off!"

"You did not just go there—you bitch! How DARE YOU!" Casey lunged and, grabbing a handful of Glenn's hair, pinned her down against the granite counter.

Donna walked into the commotion. "Stop it! Both of

you!" She pulled Casey off of her daughter, who was still screaming.

"She's evil! She's trying to take everything!" Glenn slid down into a heap on the tile floor, sobbing.

"What? No, Glenn... please don't cry, baby," Donna said, trying to console Glenn, who pushed her away and bolted from the room wailing.

"I can—" Casey stopped herself.

"Jesus, Casey. Don't you get it? I think you just need to go." Now Donna was crying too. "This clearly isn't going to work."

Casey felt horrible. It had never been her intention to hurt Donna or her daughter. Glenn was right. They were not her family.

"I'll find something as soon as possible, so that you can have your lives back," Casey said, leaving Donna standing in the shards of broken glass.

Casey knew that it wasn't going to be easy, but regardless, she was determined to keep her word. It was the least she could do, having made such a mess. She packed her things, loaded the jeep, and left in the night.

She found an efficiency apartment in West Hollywood, which offered furnishings, and free Wi-Fi. The building was adjacent to a Chinese restaurant and a thrift store, and sat near a busy intersection. It would have to do. She offered her modeling contract with Chase as proof of employment. It was good enough for the Korean landlord, who quickly looked it over and then gladly took the security deposit and first month's rent up front in cash, which all but cleaned out her checking account. She would be running on fumes until she got her first paycheck from the agency. She would have to charge a few essentials on credit at Walmart, like clean sheets, towels, and sundries for the place. *It is just temporary*, she kept telling herself. *I'll be out of here in no time.*

Later that night, after settling in, she curled up on a worn-out couch, and halfway into a cheap bottle of grocery store chardonnay, phoned Roe's business line, knowing he wouldn't be there, and left a message on his voice mail. "Hi—it's me... just called to check in and see how you are doing. I know you're swamped. So am I... surprise! I'm working in LA now." Her nervous laughter trailed off into silence. "Well, call if you get the chance... bye."

Then she re-dialed just to hear his recorded voice greeting again.

The shooting was going fabulously. The first of several print ads were beginning to appear in national magazines and on billboards, bus ads, and plans for the filming of the commercial spots were well underway. Casey had been working steadily for the Aussie account for going on four months and squirreling away her paychecks. She had several print ads currently running, billboards in cities everywhere, and an avant-garde thirty-second television spot on national television. She was booked solid into the next year with personal appearances from coast to coast. She was well on her way, to say the least.

Suddenly, people started recognizing her from the outdoor ads. The large billboards featured Casey wearing nothing but a pair of Aussie low-riders and holding two pythons coiled artfully around her middle, covering all the questionable angles. The copy read: TAMING THE OUTBACK—GET A PAIR—AUSSIE JEANS.

The contentious ads were provocative to say the least. They offended some, mesmerized others, and effectively branded the Aussie Jeans trademark—a silhouette kangaroo logo—on America's minds and on the backsides of teenage girls and young women everywhere from Miami to New York as a kind of throwback to the jean craze of the seventies.

The provocative campaign prompted manufactures to commit to seventeen more months of buys, twelve more cities, and several additional print ads in over twenty-seven magazines nationally. Seemingly overnight, Casey became a sensation. It appeared that America couldn't get enough of her!

CHAPTER 19

★ ★ ★

CASEY SCOURED THE PAPERS FOR a new place to live. She had promised herself that as soon as she could afford it, she would move to more suitable real estate. The noise and commotion from the Korean grocery, where there was a ruckus nearly every night, was more than she could stand. Hoodlums and gangbangers ran the neighborhoods and the nights, threatening her safety. Especially now that she was becoming increasingly more recognizable. The thought of remaining stuck in her current apartment indefinitely was not an option she could entertain for much longer. What she needed was a prime location, close to the agency, with privacy.

The very next week, Baltimore sent her a link for a listing that had just become available on the Internet. The owner was a friend of Baltimore's, and from what Casey could tell, the ad looked promising. *Lovely, quiet coach house on gated estate available for suitable boarder. Newly furnished and renovated. Includes all upgraded amenities. References required.* She phoned the realtor, and he agreed to meet with her that afternoon.

Casey sped along the Interstate in her new Miata Roadster fresh from the showroom. It was stormy blue metallic with tan leather seats, and it smelled like one hundred Louis Vuitton handbags. It suited her. She liked the way the car felt, taking the curves and whipping along Highway 5 like a bullet. Michael Jackson's "Thriller" thumped from the Bose speakers as she sped with the top down and the air conditioner running full blast. Things were definitely looking up for Casey Singer.

She pulled up to the estate, which was concealed behind a wrought iron gate at the foot of the driveway. The numbers on the mailbox matched those that Baltimore had given her over the phone. Ian Redwine was a renowned Hollywood director who was first an acquaintance of Baltimore's father, Benjamin Ramirez, who was the "R" of Ramirez, Ahern, and Mason Studio, affectionately called RAM for short, and who was, at the time, currently in production of one of Redwine's scorching blockbusters. On occasion, the three—Benji, Baltimore, and Ian—would play racquetball at The H. Club, an exclusive Beverly Hills fitness emporium where membership came by elite selection.

All over town, Benji Ramirez's name was golden, and the Ramirez namesake was all one needed to gain access to a bounty of riches. Casey was learning this lesson well as doors seemed to fling open at every turn now that she had Baltimore Ramirez's exclusive representation.

Baltimore had remembered Ian mentioning that he had been looking for a tenant to replace the recluse scriptwriter who previously occupied the residence. "I never much liked the guy," Ian told the Ramirez men wryly as the three towel-clad comrades had lazed in the healing Eucalyptus steam room at the club.

"He was a queer—for sure. That was number one. Number two, he was just fucking weird. So I upped the rent and he bolted. Made a real mess of the place too. Had to have the whole goddamn thing re-done. Now he's hounding me to do his movie. Yeah—like I give a shit about what that freak shits onto a page!"

Ian was not a man to mince words. He hadn't managed to achieve stratosphere status—nine Oscars, to be exact—by being a light touch.

Casey liked the idea of living in a coach house. There was something regal about the sound of it. Plus, it would afford privacy. From the looks of the palatial Redwine manor from the curb, she was very excited about the prospect.

She pulled in, and the gates automatically parted. She steered the Miata carefully, snaking along the winding pavement to the side entrance. Obviously, somebody had let her in, but no one came out to greet her. Pensively, she emerged from the car and stepped onto the hot stone pavement, still wearing a pair of jeans from a shoot that morning, along with a Versace tank top and punishing high-heeled mules. The denim was barely tolerable in the blaring heat. She wished that she had changed into a sundress.

The sound of a springboard and the splash of pool water beckoned, just steps away, from behind a wall of towering shrubs. She peered over and saw the most extraordinary swimming pool she had ever seen.

"Holy shit!" she said, removing her Gucci shades. She marveled a moment longer, first at the pool and then at the young teenager who was evidently perfecting his diving technique. She watched as he climbed up the chrome ladder and paused, adjusting his crotch, and then plunged headfirst into the chlorine ocean below.

The set up was fantastic—like some magnificent stone emporium built on the side of a mountain with brilliant white balustrades, chaste blue water, and exotic naked sculptures glistening like Grecian gods. *Wow—Redwine really went all out*, Casey thought. The fair-haired boy in the baggy swim trunks looked out of place, as if he had left his buddies back at the mall or at some other hang-out that teenagers frequent. He must have activated the gate before deciding to take a dip. At first, it appeared that he hadn't noticed her.

"Hello?" Casey's voice floated across the patio.

The teen emerged from the water and wound a plush towel around his waist. He eyed her head to toe and brightened. "You must be Casey—the Aussie chick!"

"I am that." She smiled, shielding the sun with her iPad. "I'm here to meet—I'm guessing, your father, Ian?"

"Nope. I'm supposed to show you around. He had a thing come up. Said he'll call in around noon."

She waited as he slipped into some beach shoes and mopped at his chlorine-tinged blond hair; clipped close to the crown, preppy style, not at all the typical surfer type.

"I'm Rush Redwine." He thrust a wet hand toward her, continuing to drip on the pavement. Close up, she could see that his fair skin was peppered with freckles and was pink in some places from the sun. His voice was pubescent, unsteady and oddly deep for his size. His arms and legs were gangly and still had much growing to do. She figured him to be no more than sixteen years old.

"Nice to meet you, Rush, " she said, smiling.

"Come this way. I'll show you around. The place you'd be renting is on the other side of the property."

The coach house was not more than fifty feet from the main residence. It had one entrance and an exterior spiral fire escape that extended from the second-floor loft. Rush fumbled with the key retrieved from a nearby flowerpot and unlocked the door. The cool air prickled their skin when they walked in. Casey was immediately struck by the smell of fresh paint and new construction. A huge plus.

"Very nice," Casey said.

The kitchen was large and opened into the living room, which had bay windows against the back wall, a tiny brick fireplace with mantel, and a winding wooden staircase leading to the loft. There were ceiling fans in the kitchen, living room, and bedroom upstairs and skylights built into the vaulted ceiling above where the bed would go.

A small powder room was just off the entrance hall, and a second, larger bathroom with shower and sunken tub was connected to the master loft bedroom.

Casey was, as far as she was concerned, home. "I'll take it!" she said, already decorating it in her mind.

He smirked. "Don't you even want to know how much the rent is?"

"Oh, yes—what is your father asking?"

"Twenty-two hundred, includes utilities."

"Fine."

Rush thought for a second, and shrugged. "Oh, and there's one month's deposit."

"Done," Casey said and smiled.

They shook hands to close the deal.

"Is that your Miata out there?" he asked, shifting the conversation.

"Yep." Then she asked him, running her palm across the gleaming marble countertop, "Do you like cars, Rush?"

"Hell, yeah. Who doesn't?" He readjusted the beach towel around his waist, looking as if he liked the way she said his name.

"Want to go for a spin?"

"What? You'd let me drive your car?"

"Sure. You got a permit, right?"

"Just got it last month... sometimes I take my dad's Mercedes around the cul-de-sac. When he lets me. As long as I have an adult along, I can drive on the streets."

"Great. Put on some dry clothes, and we'll go for a ride. You can show me around the neighborhood."

He grinned and then bolted toward the main house. "Give me five minutes!"

Three days later, after her application checked out and her deposit cleared, Casey was ready to move in. Baltimore arranged for a moving crew as his housewarming gift to her. This turned out to be quite a joke, as it only took five men one trip and all of an hour and forty minutes to fully move her in.

The coach house had some furnishings, and everything was new. Still, she would have to start from scratch to acquire everything else, a concept that suited her just fine.

After a few days, when he was certain that she was completely settled, Ian Redwine appeared at Casey's door with a bottle of Dom Pérignon. He was wearing expensive jeans torn at the knees and a Hugo Boss polo shirt. He smelled like the men's fragrance counter at Barney's.

"Miss Singer! Welcome! Rush tells me that we have a princess-goddess living in our coach house. I had to see for myself if this was true." Eyeing her lustily, he stood in the doorway and grinned. He was tan, overconfident, and handsome. He lost his grip on the bottle and sent it crashing to the pavement. "Whoops—let's consider this a christening, like for a new ship. Congratulations, and bon voyage and all that." His eyes glistened. He was apparently plastered.

"How do you do, Mr. Redwine? I—"

"Call me Ian, please." He shook her hand. His palm was small, but firm, surprisingly smooth. She noticed things like hands on a man. It told a lot. He had probably been blond-headed in his youth, like his son, only now he sported a white-capped brush back style like the old-time movie stars. "I know I'm old enough to be your... uncle, but spare me the harsh reality. You are quite gorgeous."

"It's nice to finally meet you, Ian. I was beginning to believe that Rush was the real owner of the place."

"Shhhh... " he said, placing an index finger to his silver mustache. "Don't tell him he isn't. He lets me live here for free!"

They both chuckled at the innocent attempt at humor.

It was an awkward moment. Ian could not take his eyes off of her breasts.

She stared at the bottle of bubbly that had exploded on the pavement and gave a nervous smile.

"Oh, hell!" he declared, throwing up his hands. "Here's to your new home. I hope that you will be happy here, my dear."

"Thank you," she said, thinking about inviting him in, but then deciding against it. It would be best not to become too friendly with the landlord. Inside locks could easily be changed.

She knew by Baltimore's previous rundown that the Redwines were solo males in a mansion of many rooms. Ian's former, and second, wife had vacated the premises last June, along with their infant daughter and their prize white Alaskan Huskies. The last Baltimore had heard, they were stowed away in Encino, not too far from there. It must have been pure hell for Ian, knowing they were so close, Casey figured.

Rush was Ian's son by wife number one, Phoebe Johnson, who was serving time in San Quentin for embezzlement, done to fund a nasty narcotics and shopping habit she had picked up before Redwine had made his millions in film. He had no trophy wife to grace his mantle currently, but from the looks of things, Ian was not hurting in the companion department. It was just his preference to be single, and, in his words, his "goddamn right to be left the hell alone" and thus avoid the inevitable minefields of romance, or so Baltimore had confided in Casey about him. It was common knowledge that Redwine avoided relationships like the plague. "Work was his bride," Baltimore had said. "Everyone else was either servants or whores to the man."

"Well, I just wanted to say welcome. My housemaid, Juanita, lives on the premises. I'll have her clean up this mess," he said, looking at his jeweled watch.

"Well, thanks, Ian—for everything. I think I'm really

going to like it here."

He turned and strolled back to the main house to a bottle of waiting brandy, like a man without a care in the world.

CHAPTER 20

★ ★ ★

BALTIMORE HAD GREAT DESIGNS FOR Casey, the Midwestern girl with the wild persona and limitless energy. Especially with Casey, though, the very thing that made her stand apart made her a nightmare to work with. She would go berserk at a shoot if something wasn't going her way, pulling down light trees and stomping off the set. She had something to say about every shot.

"Excuse me—I just think that this shot would come off better if we could do it over, with me moving around instead of anchored to this one spot."

A victim of her own creative vision, she would cause shoots to go overtime and over budget—much to the client's annoyance.

"She can't keep doing this, Baltimore." Ava's rant was full of Australian expletives as she unloaded into the phone. "I know she's got the goods and all, but I really don't care if she bangs like a dunny door—bloody hell, she's got to be reeled in!"

Baltimore knew this all too well. On a good day, Casey was brilliant, animated, and engaging. She was a real pro. On a bad day, she was an unraveling child, spewing orders and throwing raging tantrums that often shut down shooting for days until she cooled off sufficiently, or until a new photographer could be found; when she would return to finish the project, profusely apologetic and raring to go. She was, in a word, problematic.

Such behavior was not foreign to Baltimore Ramirez, it was just exhausting and expensive to have to monitor. Casey's moods were unpredictable. He was constantly checking in with her to make sure that her appointments were met and her obligations fulfilled. In desperation, he arranged for a personal assistant to tend to Casey's schedule and to keep an eye on her.

Her name was Kendra Hoffman, and she was a first-year intern from Berkeley. Her major was in fashion design, and never in her wildest dreams did she ever imagine that she would have to babysit a twenty-something-year-old supermodel. She was just nineteen herself and hardly a lightweight at one hundred forty-five pounds. Baltimore thought that the two could connect, and in some ways, help each other.

Casey dragged Kendra everywhere, like a purse puppy, working the poor girl to death with her absurd litany of demands that ranged from requests for large shipments of bottles of Evian to asking Kendra to stand in for her at photo sessions so that she wouldn't have to endure endless hours sitting under hot lights prior to shooting.

Kendra ran all of Casey's personal errands, cleaned her home, and organized her snail mail, e-mail, and social accounts. This left Casey with more free time to pursue offers from other clients clamoring for The Aussie Girl. National recognition gleaned two and three-year exclusive contracts with cosmetic and clothing companies, although she had a non-compete clause with Aussie on denim apparel for the next five years running.

Casey's was a calculated one hundred eight pounds. Any fluctuation, one way or the other, could render her contract with Aussie null and void. This was part of the commitment. It kept her in the gym four days a week and reduced her from binge eating to counting carbs and drinking blended juice drinks on the go.

In spite of her average frame, she did occasional runway modeling and product sessions with top New York photographer Günter Van Adel for public service spots about bullying, along with other industry super-beauties such as Isabella Eton, Adrienne Jones, and Rachael Reuben.

Casey was the token blonde made to look sultry and subdued when she was featured with the others in a group shot. Critics loved to single her out, though, as Casey was by far the most newsworthy member of the bevy of beauties. Always cutting up, and in a sort of unapologetic way, she seemed to snub her nose at the whole superficiality of the modeling industry. The industry that had delivered her back to the world.

"I'm here to have fun... " she once told *Flash!* Magazine during an interview. "I'm not a serious-severe anorexic type with a goddess complex. I'm just me!"

This did not bode well with her peers and started a rivalry in modeling circles. The media ate it up and couldn't get enough of her.

"Screw them, Baltimore! I'm better than all that. What I really want to be is an actress."

He cringed. She was standing in his office wearing cut-offs, Uggs, and a "Save the Whales" tank top over an exposed hot-pink bra. She was eyeing an expensive vase on his credenza.

"Oh, really?" he stalled, moving the precious artifact from her reach. No breakables—priceless or otherwise—were safe around Casey Singer. Baltimore had already lost two ashtrays and a crystal decanter to her "antics." She was as clumsy as she was temperamental.

"So you are saying that you don't want to model anymore?"

She studied his face. He had sincere brown eyes and a

smile that turned his whole face into a fiesta when he grinned. He constantly sported a five o'clock shadow, although the rest of him was manscaped to perfection. He was, by far, one of the most handsome men she had ever met, except, of course, for Roe. The gold wedding band on Baltimore's left ring finger put a halt to any thought of pursuit. *Too bad, Ladies,* she often thought. Baltimore Ramirez was one sizzling Hottie!

"I'm not saying that exactly. I'm bored, Baltimore—it's as simple as that."

"I see."

"Please don't get me wrong, I appreciate everything you've done for me. God knows I do. It's just that, as soon as I have honored my current obligations, I would like to, you know, branch out. Challenge myself even more."

He smiled.

"What is it you're asking for? You know we're committed to clients the rest of this year."

"I realize that. In the meantime, I just want to work on my craft; keep improving. I'll take some classes. You know... begin putting out feelers." Baltimore Ramirez was a bottom-line kind of agent. Leveling with him was the only way to go. He appreciated frankness more than bullshit. "No more new accounts. I'll finish my obligations with Aussie and then, that will be it."

"Have you found someone to represent your new... career aspirations?" He stroked his chin, as was his habit when he was agitated. It was clear that she had hit a nerve. However, if he was bitter, he was not showing it. Baltimore was always the consummate gentleman. Casey knew that she was one of his most lucrative models. The news couldn't have been as easy to take as he was playing it off to be.

"Not yet," she said. "I'm thinking of approaching Lucas Morgan. I admire his taste in protégés. Maybe he'll see his way to represent me too. Who knows?"

Baltimore simply nodded. She could see that he was thinking intently, but he kept his cards close to the vest. The uncomfortable silence lingered a beat or two longer, so she went on. "I just started taking lessons at Astor Lane Studio, along with private acting sessions with Fiona Dewitt—she's fabulous."

"I see," Baltimore said, not raising his voice, which confused her even more. "Then I wish you the best, Casey. You know that." He rose from his chair and patted her shoulder; the gesture translating, at best, as patronizing.

She felt a tinge of embarrassment. Was this the way to repay someone who had done so much for her? *This was business,* she had to keep reminding herself. *Just business.*

He walked her out into the hall. An elevator was waiting as if on cue.

"I tell you what—I'm not going to process you out just yet. No more new bookings, but we will keep your file here active, okay?"

"That would be awesome. Thanks, Baltimore. I wouldn't be anywhere if it weren't for you," Casey said.

"Good luck with Lucas—I hear that it's easier to get into a White House dinner than to get a meeting with that guy," Baltimore said. "Hey—come to think of it, isn't he supposed to be at the big screening coming up in a couple of weeks?" He casually dropped the bait, escorting her onto the elevator.

"What screening? Where?"

"It's a little shin-dig at the Mansion two weeks from tonight," he said.

Casey held the DOOR OPEN button. The only "mansion" referred to as such in LA was the infamous Playboy estate. She had attended one or two publicity events there in the past months, and was aware that from time to time, Hugh Hefner threw screening parties to showcase new film releases.

"We received an invitation, but my wife and I can't go.

Say, why don't I phone over there and get your name on the guest list?"

Casey was speechless. She was certain that Baltimore might just be the coolest guy who ever drew breath.

"Really? You'd do that for me? I don't know what to say."

He reached over and pressed the lobby button. "Just tell old Lucas that I said hello and that the son of a bitch owes this mad Latino lunch at The Palm!"

Casey laughed. "I will!" she promised, and then disappeared behind the shiny chrome doors.

Baltimore returned to his office and closed the door. He would be making the call to Aussie to inform them that Casey would not be signing for a second year. Moving forward, she would be someone else's storm to weather

CHAPTER 21

★ ★ ★

SHELLY TELEPHONED CASEY JUST AS soon as she
and Ted returned to the States.

"Brazil was a fright!" Shelly lamented. "Nothing but
pesky roaches and slimy reptiles—and *that* was just my
camera crew."

Casey collapsed into the overstuffed couch in the center
of her new living room. It was on loan from the designer
she had hired to re-decorate the coach house. Currently,
she was living with pencil sketches and fabric swatches
everywhere, but reveled in the process. She kicked back
with a fruity pinot and let Shelly entertain her with tales
of her and Ted's adventures in the exciting world of correspondent reporting abroad.

"It wasn't easy finding fresh topics to cover. I hired a local
to keep his ear to the street—his name was Juan Julio—
and I thought that Ted was going to divorce me 'cause that
guy could not keep his *piroca* in his pants. He was such a
man-whore! However, he did speak Portuguese and was
very connected with the Brazilian heavies and younger set
on social media—that's how I scored stories way before
any other foreign outlets."

Casey laughed. "Oh, so you didn't just crank out fluff

pieces about samba and soccer for the past eighteen months while Ted directed sexy Brazilian starlets? Why am I not surprised?" Most fascinating to Casey was how, in spite of it all, time and distance did not tarnish their friendship one bit. Shelly was exactly the same person she was when Casey had first met her anchoring the nightly news in Chicago.

"Speaking of sexy, I heard that somebody has gotten herself a national modeling contract with a big-name agency."

Casey wondered how long it would take for Shelly to finally get around to *her* good news. "I'm exclusive—or at least I *was*, with an agency out here in LA. I've recently decided to pursue acting. I've got a few more months on my contract with Aussie Jeans, and then—"

"The kangaroo people?"

"Yeah, I guess you really have been living on another planet. Geez, Shelly, the ads have been running everywhere."

"*Chica*, that's great! You really have made it, girl. I mean, really, that is huge."

Casey reveled in her friend's praise. "Well, I did bust my ass for this gig."

Shelly was juggling the receiver and trying to switch lanes on Lake Shore Drive. "We bought a new house in Evanston. Oh my God, Casey—it's so beautiful! You'll have to come back home and see it sometime."

The way that Shelly said the word *home* made Casey pause. She thought about Chicago and the things she remembered: hot dogs and deep dish pizza, Italian beef with sweet peppers, the stunning lakefront in the summertime...Wrigley Field. It all seemed like a million miles away. Her tiny sun-filled coach house was like a cocoon, insulating her from the world. She was safely tucked away at Redwine Manor, far away from her past; from memories she'd sooner forget.

"Listen, Casey—we have some other news . . ."The cellular connection came in and out, reducing Shelly's message to fragments. "The babies come, and... "

"What?" Casey sprang to her feet. "Did you say, *babies?*"

"Yep! We're expecting twins! I'm due in February. I'd love it if you'd come for a while, at least when they're born. Then you can—" A loud drone was followed by dead silence. They lost the connection.

"Damn cell phones!" Casey said, tossing hers onto the empty counter. How lucky Shelly was to have it all, a husband, new home, and now, a family. The realization of it flooded her first with happiness, and then was quickly followed by a dose of old-fashioned self-pity. Something about Shelly's news saddened her as well. She shook it off and dismissed the emotion. It was getting late. She padded to the fridge. For the first time in almost two years, she craved a binge. She suppressed the urge and had a single bowl of cereal instead. Every day was a struggle. It always would be.

She had much to do if she was going to be attending the screening at the Playboy Mansion in less than two weeks. Number one was to actually sign up for classes with Fiona Dewitt. The second was to find a killer outfit. "Look out, World," Casey shouted at the top of her lungs, standing in the bay window in her bathrobe and slippers. "This diva is about to break out!"

And why do we *act?*" The question was lobbed as tactfully as a hand grenade in the window of a nursery school. Everyone held their breath as Fiona surveyed each of her pupils with cutting scrutiny; a frozen stare emitting from her one good eye.

The troupe, comprised of actors, writers, and Hollywood *wannabes* were a sorry lot. They knew this because she had told them so. "Only two or three of you—at best—will be chosen to study under my direction. I'm looking for something special, and not everyone possesses it." She pointed her walking cane toward a timid brunette, who first cowered and then was reduced to giggles out of sheer nervousness. It was either that or wet her pants, which Fiona Dewitt was not above inducing in less worthy novices.

Fiona's body was frail, but she had risen from ashes on more than one occasion. From the ghettos of Warsaw to the glitter of Gershwin, stricken with every disease and ailment known to man, nothing had felled her yet. It had been the cancer, though, that most took its toll. On top of it all, urban legend had it that she was as crazy as a loon, but no one knew for certain if it was that, or just plain creative genius.

"I'll thank you not to have outbursts of any kind in this classroom—unless I command you to have them. Understood?"

The girl nodded and sank farther into her seat.

"And YOU!" Casey jolted. She was not yet finished extricating the weak ones first, as was her practice. The crease-faced woman was standing over her like a school matron, prodding an arthritic finger in her face. "Stand up, please."

Casey untangled her arms and legs. Halfway up, she was halted by Fiona's shrill directive.

"STOP!" The cane crashed down onto the wooden floor, shaking the foundation beneath all of their folding chairs. "Wrong! Wrong! Wrong! First, listen to my direction—all of my direction. Then act."

"Yes, ma'am."

"Now. Stand up, please... and... become for us, if you will... an oak tree."

A collective gasp erupted from the room, but Casey obeyed. Falling to her knees, she huddled herself into the smallest place, stoic and silent, and simply remained still. Snickers reverberated here and there in the silence.

"What kind of tree is *that* supposed to be?" the old lady shrieked, already mentally noting that the skinny blonde was O-U-T.

"I'm the acorn," Casey explained. "You didn't specify at what stage of growth. Her face was still fixed on the floor, arms and legs pulled tightly about her, refusing to break the scene.

Suddenly, Fiona lost her frown. "Get up, girl! Go back to your seat." Her earrings jostled as she broke into a hacking laugh. She was old; a real dinosaur in the theater world. She might have thought that she had seen it all. The feeble woman with the black eyes of a sage grinned widely. "Next!"

Casey sat back down, fully knowing that she had just aced the toughest audition of her career.

CHAPTER 22

★ ★ ★

CASEY ARRIVED EARLY AND HAD to circle around to kill some time. The last thing she wanted to do was appear eager. A line of Jaguars, Porches, and Mercedes had begun to file into the winding stone driveway, so she followed suit, parking the Miata behind a Bentley.

She thought about Glenn, and how much she had always wanted to visit Hef's place at 10236 Charing Cross Road. She and Glenn hadn't spoken since the incident so many months ago. Casey missed her friend and Donna's motherly ways. Tonight, she was truly on her own. Casey was not shy when it came to hobnobbing with the rich and famous. These were not your standard garden-variety rich—Hollywood royalty, they were Tinsel Town's freaks and Nouveau riche. Hefner's soirées were the best. No one passed on an opportunity to "do the Mansion" in style.

A spattering of kamikaze paparazzi, as she liked to call them, littered the treetops and ivy-lined fences on either side of the driveway, where they risked life and limb to catch a glimpse of some of the famous guests pausing before moving through the security check point, which was an intercom built cleverly into a rock, where all visitors had to announce themselves.

Rich, young, and sexy were the rights of passage; that, and one: your name had to be on the guest list; and two: you had to be free of guns or weapons.

Two well-endowed Playmates in tank tops and shorts were directing cars at the valet stand. A number of similarly hot-pantsed beauties—all teeth and hair—parked the cars like seasoned pros. It was, in a way, quite a show in itself.

Past the threshold of the infamous mansion, things got even better. Casey fell in step behind a gay male couple busily chattering about some foreign production that the other had just seen. "It's going to be at Cannes, and I already predict that it will far outshine any of his earlier work—that queen is due his props by now."

She squeezed past them, smiling coquettishly. She would smile at everyone. That was her plan; to look cool, confident, and like she belonged there. She followed the couple through the entrance, at which point yet another Playmate directed them through the foyer, past the living room, and out onto the patio.

Several people were milling around the main rooms of the house, admiring the furnishings and artwork, soaking in the aura that was the Playboy Empire.

Outside, barbeque grills were fired up. A lavish spread of seafood, imported cheeses, exotic fruits, and crudités loaded four banquet tables. Seafood and pricey steaks were being served on china plates. Champagne flowed from Grecian fountains. It was said that Hef liked to feed his guests before anything else.

Signature bowls of M&Ms were placed everywhere, another trademark of the gracious host; reminiscent of the child in every adult—a metaphor not lost on Casey. Oh, to be so rich and famous as to have every luxury at your disposal! To indulge yourself and your guests' every whim!

The summer air was sweltering. Acres of rolling grass and trees afforded a wistful illusion of being someplace else, like a stately respite on the Riviera. With the exception of the blasting heat, it was nothing short of paradise. The eccentric pajama-clad host even had a zoo built right on the premises, filled with exotic creatures that hammed it up for onlookers. Casey marveled at the collection of strange and exotic birds that moved freely about the expansive backyard.

An in-ground pool with adjacent Jacuzzi provided pre-show entertainment as scantily clad men and women frolicked about the lagoon grotto, while others, dressed to the nines, postured at the open bars, closing deals and sealing fates with a handshake, a smile, a friendly stab in the back.

Already, cliques were forming, indicating who belonged with whom. Casey kept moving to assess the possibilities; to hopefully spot Lucas Morgan and figure out a way to meet him. He was Hollywood's "king of agents"—the master; a Guru of sorts among players. She figured that he wouldn't be too difficult to find. He would be the one with fifty or so aspiring actors surrounding him, with their lips flagrantly attached to his ass.

It was surreal, and Casey felt that she deserved every wonderful minute of it. She reached for a second glass of champagne from a waiter who looked oddly familiar. He caught her staring.

"Thirst-aide."

"Excuse me?" Casey said.

"I did the Thirst-aide spot with you back a couple of months ago. It ran during the Grammys. You remember, right?" He mimicked downing an imaginary bottle of the sports drink.

"Oh, yes! That's right... we did that together, didn't we?" she said, having no idea what he was talking about.

"Yeah, I never forget a face... especially a gorgeous one like yours!"

What gives with this loser? "Great seeing you," she said, quickly taking a sip of the bubbly. Making conversation with a commercial actor side-lining as a waiter was not her idea of high-profile company.

"Name is Darren," he said. "Have you been at it long? In the business, I mean?"

"Yes, quite a while. I'm surprised that I haven't run in to you here before."

"Well, I'm new. I've never worked the Mansion before. Been out here ten months now."

"Are you supposed to be fraternizing with the guests, Darren?" she asked wryly. "No offense, it's just that I don't want to get you in trouble."

"No, it's all right. We're not paid enough to not take a little advantage of the room, if you know what I mean."

She did.

"So," he said, "where else might I have seen your work?"

"Some small projects... overseas mostly," Casey lied. *Why am I even wasting my time with this geek?* she wondered. She loathed waiters, with their overly friendly personas and quick lines. *No wonder most of them were aspiring actors!*

She was devising her quick escape when he asked, "What's your latest film?"

She thought fast. "*White Orchid.* I'm not the lead or anything, but I have an integral part in the story."

"Cool!" He looked all of twenty-one, with a Gold's Gym physique, a beach-bought tan, and enough time on his hands to maintain it. "I've done—"

"Have you seen Lucas Morgan here tonight?" she cut him off, ready to cash in on his usefulness, if any. She couldn't afford to waste any more time being seen talking to a waiter when there was serious networking to be done.

"Lucas? Yeah, he's around here somewhere. That's his Maserati out front. Won't let the staff valet it, so he parks it himself wherever he damn well pleases. He's got a thing about it—that and for making millions." He laughed, and it was then that she noticed the huge gap in his front teeth. "The guy is awesome, really. He shits hundred dollar bills.

Always has the hottest tail. I've seen him blow twenty-five Gs one night right here at a poker game... crap tipper, though. Figures!"

He adjusted the tray of empty champagne glasses and surveyed the lawn. "There he is. He's by the fishpond. And, if you're wondering, lot's of luck—word is that he's not taking on any more clients. It's pretty much useless to try."

"Really?" Casey said.

"Well, unless you're willing to put out. That guy is all about the V-card. Good luck."

He hoisted the tray and slipped off into the crowd toward the bar.

"Is that so?" Casey said to no one. *It has nothing at all to do with luck.*

She walked casually toward the pond, taking her time. Finally, there he was right in front of her. Lucas Morgan—tall, wiry and thin, with untamed blond hair, all pocked-faced and coked up on blow, no doubt. He probably had never been considered good-looking. In fact, he resembled a spindly jester. His skin was anemic, and he was wearing expensive athletic shoes, boutique running shorts, and a black designer T-shirt—evidence of his irreverence for fashion and conformity. He was, as advertised, an avid runner. He was a freakish six foot nine, with a cocked grin and a nervousness about him, compliments of too many years pushing the hard drugs and booze.

His Hollywood credentials were impressive, if not downright astonishing. Rumor had it that he swindled a middle-aged wealthy foreign heiress into marrying him. Others say he made a fortune the old-fashioned way, embezzling from foreign investors. A professed bachelor, Lucas Morgan made Hugh Hefner look like a monk. Supermodels, divas, coeds, and other people's wives... he had them all, and he had a reputation that defied logic.

Casey waited patiently near the edge of the patio, sitting

alone, eyeing him alluringly from her chair until she was certain that he was catching her signals. It didn't take long.

The swarm of hangers-on crowded around him, flipping their sun-kissed hair and flashing bleached white smiles, chattering about their latest endeavors. Scriptwriters circled him like starving wolves, even though the last thing Lucas Morgan used a manuscript for was prospecting... bathroom reading was more likely. Sure, he knew directors—box office heavies—producers constantly clamored for his client list, but as with his drugs and his money, Lucas was a stingy bastard. With his roster of top talent, he could wait out countless projects until only the best deals begged for his expertise. And pay off they did. With hot commodities like Nicolette Davis and Christian Steele at the top of his talent roster, Lucas could retire on the dust that fell from their golden Oscars alone. The rest of his clientele were mostly snot-nosed rookies; Hollywood's next generation of J. Los, Denzels, and DiCaprios... ripe for grooming.

It was one of his newcomers being featured in the premiere that evening, Shay Sorrentino. She was appearing opposite Keanu Reeves in a modern-day thriller. The release would be two weeks early. Hef always had first-run showings before they ran in theaters. None was more awaited than *Mindbenders,* a high-action ride into a computer-generated nirvana controlled by alien mutants who pirate their way into the Pentagon's national security systems.

Lucas was not even aware that he was repulsive to be near; he drew hangers-on like few others in the business, and for that, he rarely got a moment's peace when he stepped out in public, but that never stopped him. He was a social narcissist. Tonight's screening was a favor for his buddy, who was the film's promoter. It was rumored that Shay was expected to make a quick appearance that evening in the flesh, but that might have only been talk. Word had it that she was in Canada filming with Spielberg, so it was anyone's guess.

Casey made it a point to purposely flirt with Lucas long enough for him to notice when she had left her chair. She watched from across the grounds as he strained his neck in several directions, looking for her. She treated him to a lingering eyeful as they all filed into the miniature theater inside the house, promptly at eight.

She found herself seated two rows directly behind him, purely by fate. He was definitely alone. Seated to his left was the film's promoter, and the open chair on his right was reserved for Shay—should she make the event.

The house lights went black, and the screen jumped into action with pulsating Dolby sound. That was the end of the dance for the next two hours.

Men like Lucas Morgan were the gatekeepers and simply for the sexual thrill of conquest, would gladly give the keys to any babe who would oblige them. In a playing field of such high stakes, unfortunately, one often started on one's knees. This is what she was thinking as she pleasured his paltry cock, for but a chance at gaining entry through what, for most others, was impassable. The thrill of the challenge alone made it nearly bearable. In times like these, Casey kept her eye on the prize.

The last time Casey could remember being in such a position with a steering wheel in her back was when she was sixteen and giving Kirk Cahill the thrill of his life. She hated like hell to resort to this, in the front seat of Lucas's Maserati, but one look at him and she knew she would have to speak his language to get what she wanted. This was clearly a man to whom tawdry compliments and clever gimmicks meant nothing.

Thoughts of the last five years—since she drove out of Kansas in a Guy's Porsche—

had only led up to this pivotal point.

"I saw you staring back at the party... just before the

movie started. Did you like watching me?"

Casey continued smacking her lips hotly and telling
him that she did, until he exploded in her mouth, bearing
down on her head with a visceral grip, releasing a grotesque noise that signaled that it was over. Unfortunately
for her, that was the easiest part. Sleeping with him would
be close to impossible.

"What did you say your name was?" He was struggling
to zip his pants while eyeing his reflection in the rearview
mirror, satisfied in more ways than one. No one caught
them, parked in the quiet, dark driveway of a neighboring
mansion. She figured that Lucas would love adding danger
to the mix. The threat of getting caught would only make
it hotter.

"Casey Singer," she said, scrambling into the passenger
seat, rearranging the straps of her dress.

"So, are you a singer, then, you say?" he asked fuzzily.

"No. I'm an *actress*. Singer is my last name."

"Oh," he grunted.

He riffled through his pockets for the keys.

"Are you looking for these?" She dangled the key ring in
front of him. He puzzled, obviously forgetting how eager
he had been to let her drive, what with the Herculean
hard-on he had been sporting, it was a piece of cake for
her to score the keys, once she got him alone. It was simple. She had slipped him a note a few minutes into the
movie, relaying that some idiot in a metallic blue Ford had
just grazed his bumper and that he should move his car
pronto if he didn't want to further tempt fate.

"I was passing by your car when I was leaving, and I saw
the whole thing happen."

The blue paint streak on the fender of his precious white
Gran Turismo told the story. If not for her intervention, he
could be looking at a lot worse, she had told him. A couple
of drinks later and after much flirtation, her incessant pleas
for taking a spin were granted.

"You say you got a good look at the asshole that scraped my baby?" he said.

"And the plates too. My uncle's a cop. I'll have him run them for you. I'll bet it was one of those waiters."

"Yeah, thanks... uh, Casey. I really appreciate this. It's goddamn late. I've got an early morning. C'mon, I'll drive you back to your car."

"What about the offer?" she quickly parlayed.

He scratched the bristle on his pocked neck.

"What offer?"

He was still so drunk and high that she could have fabricated the whole night. It would have been a lot less risky than dragging her own car across the paint of his precious Maserati. "You offered me a chance to read for *Jersey Nights*... remember? See—you gave me your card," she lied. It had been easy enough to swipe from his wallet.

She held it in front of his bloodshot eyes. "Sure, doll, whatever you say. Hey—I think I'm gonna hurl—!" He lurched over the side of the car and threw up onto the driveway.

Casey was thoroughly repulsed and waited as he collected himself. Wiping his slimy mouth, he slurred, "Are you ready? Let's fuck. "

She thought fast. "We already did it, baby—don't you remember?"

"Oh, then, I gotta split. You got a ride?"

Casey's car was still parked back at the party two and a half blocks away, safely out of sight. She decided that the walk back would be safer. "Yeah—I'm good. I'll contact your office in the morning," she said. Then she slipped out of the car and started down the street, leaving Lucas Morgan, his Maserati, and his deflated hard-on alone in the darkness.

"Well, is Mr. Evans expected back anytime soon?"

"I'm sorry, Miss, he's out of the country. I don't have any further information. Would you like his voice mail?"

"No, thank you." Casey hung up, defeated. This was her eighth attempt to reach Roe in several days. It was as if Roe Evans had disappeared off the face of the earth.

How much business could there be? He was always jetting away to a conference, meeting, or to the home office in London. What was going on? Why wasn't he returning her voice mails or messages? She had scoured the music trades for clues. There were no mergers, no takeovers, and no emerging deals that would consume him to such an extent, at least none that she could find.

The silence was deafening. She missed hearing from him; his checking in like he used to, just to say hello. Today, she could have really used Roe's special brand of encouragement. He made her feel like she was invincible; like she could do anything. She wanted to prove that she could. And she wanted him to be watching.

Soon after Casey had drifted to sleep, the phone on her nightstand lit up. She squinted to see who was calling. It was midnight.

"Hello?"

"Hello, Sunshine."

"Roe!"

"How are you? Lovely as ever, I presume!"

She sat up in the darkness, as if doing so could make him hear her better.

"I'm great. Are you back in the States?"

"Yes, but I'm afraid I am going to be stuck out east for a while."

"You've really been busy. I can't seem to keep up with you," Casey said.

"And I can see that you haven't slowed down yourself— the ads are fabulous! I've been seeing them all over."

"I'm reading for a part tomorrow," she said, sounding

carefree. "It's only a bit part. I'm called GIRL IN HOTEL LOBBY BAR, or HOOKER IN GARBAGE CAN... at least, that's where I end up. Can you believe it?"

He chuckled. "Oh, no!"

"Oh, yes! It's tragic, really. Of course, I do have a line or two before I get drugged and dragged into a dark alley."

"Well, you'll knock 'em dead. I know it. "

The cobwebs had cleared, and she was now fully awake. "Yeah, well, I'd give my eyeteeth to get the part. Nicholas Cage is the lead, and it's filming right here in LA."

"You're a natural. I'm sure you'll land it, Sunshine."

She loved it when he called her that. Hell, she just loved it when he called, period. There was a pause, and she rested on the blanket of silence that stretched between them. If only she could crawl through the phone. She wanted to curl up in his arms and just disappear for one glorious moment.

"How long will you be out east?" she asked, in spite of her determination not to pry. *Why do this? What was to gain?*

"I have some work to do here before I have to go back. I'll be here into the end of next week... and then on to London."

"I see," Casey said. *London—again!*

"Hey, did I ever tell you that you look like Barbie? No—a Casey doll. Maybe you should talk to that agent of yours about this. You could be the new modern Casey Doll."

She was certain that they would not be changing the mold for her, but she liked the compliment just the same.

"Thanks, Roe." She blushed, but it was a wasted gesture in the darkness. Then she blurted, "I miss you."

"I miss you too." His words made her heart quicken.

"Well, I gotta run. It was so good hearing your voice." She could hear the airport announcement for the flight in the background.

"You too."

"Bye, Sunshine!"

"Goodbye," she whispered, and then, upon hearing the click on the other end of the line, she let a single tear trickle down her cheek in the darkness, as once again, he slipped away.

CHAPTER 23

★ ★ ★

CASEY'S CALLS TO LUCAS MORGAN only resulted in deafening silence. She was certain that he neither remembered nor cared who Casey Singer was. She had to act quickly if she was going to score a chance at reading for the part in *Jersey Nights*. She would show up and give the performance of her life.

First, she had to get on the call list for the audition. Several calls to Lucas's staff resulted in dead-ends. No one was giving out information about the film auditions. She had nothing but a crumpled calling card and Lucas's good-for-nothing word that he would get her seen for a private reading. That promise, she was certain, had faded with the memories of the night before. Then she had an idea.

"Emarie here." Her gravelly voice made no indication of recognition.

"Hi, Ms. James, it's Casey Singer. We met about a year and a half ago. I was working with Jordy Turner at the time."

"Oh, yes—what a tragedy that was with Jordy. I still can't believe that he's gone. Tell me, was it a beautiful ceremony? I sent an arrangement."

"Yes, they received them. Quite the shock for all of us

who loved him."

"It's just impossible to imagine a world without him. He used to say that 'cupcakes are just gay doughnuts'. Oh, how he'll be missed. Was there something I can help you with?"

"As a matter of fact, there is. I was given an opportunity to read for the director of *Jersey Nights*, the new Nicholas Cage film being cast today, and unfortunately, I lost the address to the studio, and I was wondering if you could tell me where exactly I am to go."

"Who is sending you for the reading?"

"Lucas Morgan—it was a last-minute thing and—"

"Really? You have signed with Lucas? Kudos to you!"

"Well, thanks... but I've done a stupid thing. I lost my cell phone, and I'm too embarrassed to let his agency know that I cannot retrieve the information about the audition; it would not bode well. It's my first audition with his agency, and I am driving around downtown, but I can't remember the building."

"Heavens, child—that is cardinal rule number one. You don't show up late—the casting director won't even consider seeing you if you miss your call time. Hold on."

She jumped off the line, and Casey waited the longest minute of her life, her heart pounding out of her chest.

"We have that they are seeing people up until two p.m. at Stagg Studios, fourth floor—and make sure you look like a street walker."

"Got it. Thanks so much, Ms. James. I really appreciate this."

"Anything for a protégée of Jordy's. So, *the* Lucas Morgan, you say? How in the world did you manage that? I hate that bastard, but that is impressive that you have won him over, young lady. Good luck—you must have had something he was after."

The phone went silent. Casey cringed and exhaled at the same time. *You don't know the half of it*, she thought, as she sped in the opposite direction for Burbank.

Casey arrived at the fourth floor of Stagg Studios, breath-less and sweating. It was ten minutes to two, much to the annoyance of the young Latino woman behind the desk, who was clearly on a personal phone call.

"I'm here to read for the casting director," Casey said, producing Lucas Morgan's business card. "I'm with the Lucas Morgan Agency."

"Name?" the girl cracked her gum, never taking the phone away from her ear.

"Casey Singer—I'm reading for the part of the hooker."

The girl scanned the sign-in sheet and shrugged. "I don't see your name here on the list... sorry. Plus, we are wrap-ping up for the day."

Casey grabbed the girl's phone and yanked it away from her ear. "Not on the list? I suggest that you take another look at this card," she said, shoving it into the girl's face. "See where today's date is written in? That's Mr. Mor-gan's writing, and this puts me on your fucking list—or should we call him directly and maybe involve your boss in this misunderstanding?" She spoke into the girl's iPhone directly. "She'll have to call you back." Then she discon-nected the call and handed the device back to the girl. "Go ahead... call Mr. Morgan yourself. Tell *him* I'm not on the list."

The girl's mouth dropped. Silently, she peeled a label with the number forty-eight on it, wrote Casey's name at the top, and attached it to two pages of script with a few lines of dialogue printed in faded ink. "Right through that door," she said, waving a collection of acrylic nails.

"Thank you," Casey huffed and walked across the empty waiting room. She would be the last, all right, but they always saved the best for last.

Lucas called Casey immediately when he had gotten

word that she had been chosen for the part of Lorna, in the film *Jersey Nights.*

"Refresh my memory, but I don't recall signing you to my agency," he said. "Who the hell are you?"

Casey hesitated and then, lowering her voice, she said, "We met at an industry party a while ago. You gave me your card."

"Oh, hell! Yes, I remember." She was certain that he did not.

"Well, Candy—"

"It's Casey."

"Whatever. You just can't go around using my name to crash into auditions. Do you actually have an agent?"

"Yes, Baltimore Ramirez at Chase Models. You told me you would get me the read. I am sorry. It won't happen again," Casey said, her words lost in the silence. He was probably deeply immersed in checking his phone texts.

"Damn right it won't. We'll put through the forms for this one booking."

"Thank you, Lucas. I won't let you down," Casey said.

"You bet you won't. Like I have time for this shit," he said and then hung up.

It was done. She was in.

CHAPTER 24

★ ★ ★

SIX WEEKS LATER CASEY RECEIVED the sweet-est of surprises. Roe had sent an elaborately wrapped gift delivered to her dressing trailer on the set of *Jersey Nights*. They had been communicating regularly for the past month and a half with e-mails and texts laden with swirling heart emoticons and smiley faces like a couple of schoolkids. Casey became accustomed to checking her phone incessantly. His latest text read:

I hope you like your surprise.

It was the last day of filming, and a package arrived right on cue after a grueling ten-hour session.

"What do you think it is?" Casey asked her assistant who signed for it and placed it on the dressing table in front of Casey. The two stared at the large rectangular box with a white ribbon encircling it. Kendra, who had been currently helping Casey run her lines and keep her on schedule with makeup and wardrobe calls, was well aware of Casey's secret crush. The return address was Castle Records.

"One way to find out," Kendra said, sliding the package in front of Casey. "Open it! The suspense is killing me."

Casey's face was a fright. It was caked with blood and

bruises from running the murder scene earlier. All she longed for was a container of cold cream and a hot bath—until this moment.

Casey ripped open the package. "It's a doll," Kendra said. "A Barbie... and she's all dressed up to go to a party!"

"Why in the world . . .?" Casey asked, confused.

"Wait, there's a note. It reads: *My lovely Casey, get dolled up and meet me at eight. The party awaits, and so do I....*

"What? Give me that!" she swiped the card from Kendra's hand and read the note for herself. Also inside the box was an airline itinerary for two days from then, and an invitation that she had to blink twice to be sure was the real thing. *The President and Mrs. Obama of the United States of America request the honor of your presence at a benefit dinner for Harvest Bounty and the fight against child hunger. Black tie required.*

Casey could not contain her excitement. "Oh my God, Kendra! I'm going to the White House!"

Kendra took a closer look at the invitation. She held it up like it was the World Cup. "Well, not the White House exactly, but, yes, you are going, girl. It's at the Ritz Carlton!"

The two embraced, screeching and jumping up and down. Kendra's headset flew clear off her head, and Casey's makeup ran in a stream down her face. They collapsed in a heap onto the floor, laughing.

After a sobering second, Casey gasped, "What in the world will I wear?"

The release of *Jersey Nights* was a moderate success. The film did well at the box office, beaten out by two other films. The Ian Redwine thriller, *Rail Box Nine*, was still drawing millions in first place, and in second was a mindless teen comedy called *Lucky Vegas* with cameos by legions of comics from Will Ferrell to Russell Brand. Having Nicholas Cage at top billing in *Jersey Nights* didn't hurt matters in the least. *Jersey* would be a well-received contender.

A dozen roses arrived on the set of her twenty-fifth and final shoot for Aussie Jeans. The contract had come to an end at precisely the right time. The company was now skewing toward a younger demographic. The image revamp would best be conveyed by a younger, more uni-sex-appearing model. Casey was happy with the decision. It was time to move on.

The enclosed card was from Fiona Dewitt, Casey's eccentric acting coach and mentor. *Way to go, Blondie! You make a fine screen whore... where I come from, that's a compliment!*

Casey smiled. Receiving Fiona's praise was no small feat. When her SAG card finally came in the mail, she danced on the bare wooden floor of her bedroom like a fool, shouting at the top of her lungs. She had arrived. She had earned legitimate screen time, and that meant a lot. What she would do next was anybody's guess.

Lucas Morgan did not acknowledge her existence. Frequent calls to his agency only resulted in an occasional reading for a bit part in some obscure documentary or offshore production. Gone were the prize parts that could launch a no-name into fast-lane status. Lucas never returned her calls. It was going on three months since she had finished *Jersey Nights*, and Casey was growing impatient. She needed to get noticed by him if she was going to be taken seriously and score the best auditions.

She thought about talking to Ian about some projects at RAM, but decided it was better to avoid mixing her worlds. Ian Redwine was her landlord, and the last thing she wanted to do was to send up flares that she was desperate for work. Thankfully, there was always modeling to see her through, although Baltimore Ramirez's representation was not going to get her noticed with the big-time studios.

There was just enough work locally to keep her afloat. Baltimore saw to that. He kept pushing her into new print work and increased her runway bookings. Hot Looks Cosmetics had approached with a two-year contract for their hair care line. Baltimore had strongly urged her to take it. Even though it meant cropping off more than half her beautiful mane and settling for a sassy ultra-short coif dialed up several shades brighter in shocking platinum.

"I'll get you out of it if something opens up for you elsewhere," Baltimore promised.

She agreed. When Hector, the stylist at Hot Looks, revealed her new look, she was more than pleased. Her coif was short and could be styled spiked high, or smoothed to sleek perfection. It was a brand new Casey Singer—only more youthful and edgy. She darkened her eyeliner and pitched vibrant colors for a pale, natural lip. In spite of it all, she was determined to get noticed.

Remarkably, Casey's new transformation did get the attention of more than a few cosmetic giants, fashion houses, and agents—namely, Lucas Morgan.

Flipping through her portfolio, he tore into pastrami on rye and explained to Casey, who had been ecstatic to get the call to meet with him, "There I was, sitting in the freakin' waiting room at the dentist's office the other day and nabbed a magazine from a stack on the table. I open it and see your face on an ad, grinning behind a bottle of shampoo. I recognized you from the *Jersey Nights* audition you hijacked, right? Which, by the way, you were good in. Anyway, I popped on the cell right away and called my assistant. 'Hey, Trish,' I said. 'Find a current copy of *High Style* magazine and get me the girl on the inside cover. I think I just found our Nikki!'"

"Really?" Casey could not believe her luck. Did he actually say that she was good?

"The girl we previously cast in the role is freaking out

of control from a cocaine habit. She is a real train wreck on the set. The role of Nikki West needs to be delivered by a hot, smart girl with a mix of edge and charm like a young Scarlett Johansson type; shit—someone, like you, Casey. You got the balls all right."

Lucas was in rare form, talking through bites of the sandwich. He was wearing torn jeans, a tight silk T-shirt, and Italian loafers without any socks. When he had invited Casey to meet with him over lunch, this was not what she had in mind—deli sandwiches from across the street of his Beverly Hills office suite. *Geez!* Didn't she even rate a table at Wilshire's?

He never mentioned the night at the Playboy Mansion... the front seat of the Maserati, the gratuitous quickie, or her leaving him there drunk and in the dark. She doubted that he made the connection. He just thought that she was but one of hundreds of faces that, hopefully, would translate to dollars. It was fine with her that he did not remember who she was. It was probably better this way.

The script was wretched, but she didn't care. It was prime-time television, and already, the show was beating out two of the major networks in the nine p.m. time slot. The only competition was the cable reality shows. The pilot featured seven coeds who spend a summer internship working at a Club Med-type resort on the island of Maui. Shooting would begin in a month, which coincided nicely with the end of spring break, when most vacationers and students would retreat back to their usual worlds and the islands would be blissfully vacant.

Before dismissing her, he belched. "We'll send copies to your previous agent, along with a right of exclusivity waiver. Trish here will take care of any additional paperwork. Any questions?"

"Just one," Casey said, her heart racing in her chest. "Where do I sign?"

The agreement that Lucas had his assistant process would

have Casey sign on as exclusive with Morgan Enterprises. The agreement would prohibit her continued representation with any other agency, which meant that Baltimore was out—for good. No one, not even Emarie James herself, could steal her away under this ironclad agreement. Casey would be allowed to ride out the terms of any and all previous commitments, including the Hot Looks Shampoo spots that had her locked in until the following year.

"The director will want to see you right away," Trish had said as she plied Casey with the last of the paperwork. "Can you drive to Malibu on Wednesday to read for him?"

"Yes, of course," Casey had said. It would be just two days before she was planning on flying to Washington, DC, to meet up with Roe. At the rate her life was going, she was clearly going to need someone to pinch her, for her own reality check.

She returned home with a bag full of groceries and even stopped off at the florist for a fresh bundle of peonies. She loved the way they smelled like roses, but lasted longer. She decided that she would keep the coach house while she was on location. It would be an off again, on again schedule, and she wanted to have at least one place in the world where she could feel rooted. She would work six weeks in a row shooting the series in Maui, then have two weeks off back in LA, until the season was finished. If the show continued to do well, there was talk of extending taping into the holiday months and beyond.

Casey figured that she'd pay Rush to look after things for her while she was gone, if, of course, Ian wouldn't mind. She would have no need for her car on the set location, so the Miata would have to stay behind. She was certain that Rush would love looking after it as well. It would soon be time for him to start pre-college classes at UCLA, and he would need a set of wheels at his disposal. She would speak to Ian about it. She was thrilled with the way that everything seemed to be coming together.

It was nearly dusk, and the California sun had baked her skin a tawny bronze. She decided that she would take a quick dip to cool off before scraping up dinner. She would pack later that night for the upcoming trip to Washington.

Thoughts of Roe Evans danced in her head as she grabbed a towel and headed out to the swimming pool. She fantasized just how wonderful it would be when, after the festivities, the two of them would finally have a chance to be alone. She wondered if she would have the courage to tell him how she felt, once and for all; to open up to him completely. There was still so much about him she did not know. He was an enigma.

She approached the pool with anticipation, happy to have the place to herself. The Redwine men were gone for the week in Tahoe, and the area was well sheltered by the ivy-lined gates and spiral towering shrubbery.

Stripping down to nothing, she reveled in naked bliss, letting the warm winds caress her skin before tossing her thong onto a beach chair. She padded up to the diving board, launched herself airborne, and dove into the jewel-toned water below—just a fraction of a second before the shutter of a camera lens caught it all, frame by frame.

CHAPTER 25

★ ★ ★

CASEY BRACED HERSELF AS THE wheels of the jetliner met with the pavement at Regan National Airport. She could hardly wait. It would still be hours before she and Roe would be together, but just being in DC gave her a feeling of excitement.

Imagine, she thought giddily, *Roe and I are in the same place.* She couldn't believe that the day had finally arrived.

Casey checked in to the JW Marriott located on Pennsylvania Avenue. She was thinking of staying on through the weekend, renting a car, and driving up the coast to Connecticut. Maybe she could talk Roe into staying on longer and spending the entire weekend with her. *Depending on how tonight goes,* she cautioned herself. She had to curb her expectations. Most likely, Roe would have to fly off to some client meeting or merger. She would just have to wait and see. Either way, she would be happy with the time they would have. No matter how brief.

Washington, DC, was electric. Casey had always been fascinated with its history; its monuments and artifacts. She especially loved the mystique of the Kennedys and the incredible aura that was Camelot. Being on the "other" coast conjured up images of warm, noisy bars, exquisite restaurants, world-famous chowder, seaside landmarks, and sailing. She'd remembered how much Jordy loved to sail. She was grateful that he and Marcel had been able to take the boat out one last time together before he died. Jordy often talked of one day wanting to complete the English National Challenger Championship. If anyone could have done that sort of thing, it would have been Jordy.

She wondered if Roe liked to sail. She smiled, imagining him in a captain's hat, herself seated beside him on a schooner, watching him work the ropes and pulleys, flexing his muscles in the sun, adjusting the sails masterfully. It felt exciting and wonderful to daydream. It was a pleasure that she seldom allowed herself to indulge in. Nonetheless, as great as it felt, it frightened her at the same time. This evening, she would finally have Roe's attention all to herself; a chance at telling him, perhaps, how she felt. For once, she didn't want to think, or plan, or scheme. She just wanted to get ready for her date and to let the evening go where it was meant to go.

She spent the afternoon browsing in the little shops downtown. She found a beauty salon, where she had her hair and makeup styled to perfection. When she passed a couple strolling hand in hand, she smiled. Her guard had been up for so long, she wondered if she could ever appear as serene and blissful in another's company.

She stopped cold when she saw three young boys huddling on the sidewalk near the park over a brown-and-white puppy. Their fits of giggles and charming Northeastern accents made Casey laugh out loud.

"C'mon, Sparky! Let's go home *naw*. We're going for a ride!"

"Let's go, boy! Let's get in the *car!*"

"Move over ... I wanna see um!"

"No! I'm holdin' um. Let me!"

She instantly thought of her brothers, Justin, Nicholas, and Seth. They would be nearly grown by now, but she remembered them as little boys. Sadly, she had lost touch with them sometime after the death of their Uncle Elroy. Casey often thought of them and hoped that someday they would try to contact her.

It was three years ago that she learned through Gabe Lambert about her younger brothers' whereabouts. "Seth and Nick are with a foster family in Milwaukee. Nick is enrolled at a college on the east coast and will be starting in the fall. They're doing great," he had said. That's all that mattered.

On the east coast. She figured that Nick would be a junior by now. She wondered if he could possibly be close by. Wouldn't that be something if they just ran into each other? It was a ridiculous fantasy. Still, she couldn't help but study every fair-haired teenager's face that she met in passing. After seeing the young boys with the dog, the thought of her own family consumed her. *Someday, when things slow down, I'll find them.* It was a promise that she had made to herself and vowed to keep.

She returned to the hotel at four o'clock and opted for a luxurious bubble bath before getting ready to meet Roe. She laid out her dress, a Vera Wang gown, and studied it. Would it be all right? Would she? She sat on the edge of the bed, staring at the wallpaper, trying to breathe.

She had spent the past eighteen months thinking of Roe. She could not get him off her mind, or out of her dreams. Tonight, she vowed, she would tell him how she felt. She simply had to. She had to know if he felt the same. Here she was, about to embark on the first six-week round of shooting in Maui, having landed an incredible role as Nikki West on *Paradise Cove*, and she was shaking like a schoolgirl on prom night. She remembered her high school days, and images of it made her shudder. Being alone like this with nothing but her thoughts and memories to consume her was not her idea of a relaxing weekend. It would be good to be getting back to work again. She thrived on it like breathing.

At promptly seven thirty, her cab pulled up to the Ritz Carlton. She and Roe had planned to meet in the lobby. Instantly, she felt reassured about the black beaded gown when she saw the plethora of similar ensembles stepping from black town cars, Mercedes Sedans, and limousines, accompanied by tuxedo-clad escorts ranging from millionaire moguls to actors, recording artists, and senators. She had spotted an NBA star and his entourage pull up in a gold Rolls. The media was on hand, covering the gala with an eye on the heavy players, who came out to see and be seen at fifteen hundred dollars a plate.

Local police held back the throngs of onlookers who dotted the streets and entryways to the hotel. Surveillance was everywhere; on the rooftops and sidewalks stationed outside and on every floor of the hotel—in the service elevators, the kitchens, lobby, and ballroom. Helicopters flew overhead, and each and every guest was patted down and passed through a metal detector before entering the foyer. A red carpet was unfurled under the massive iron canopy. An American flag heralded from stanchions high above the hotel moniker.

Scheduled to perform that evening was Adele, but rumors had been buzzing for over a week that she was ill and wouldn't show. There was a stand-in scheduled to appear from a rival label—Castle Records. She was a new recording artist from Canada named Devon Laurent. She was a singer with a unique, ethereal tone and booming vocal presence that had pegged her as the next big break-out star.

"Tonight is pivotal," Roe later explained. "It's a chance to showcase the record label's newest star." What were the chances? When he had heard that it looked like a stand-in would be needed, he offered Devon. It was Roe's job to see to it that Ms. Laurent was ready to wow the fastidious

Washington elite—and the world. Once she performed her opening set, Roe would be free to enjoy the rest of the evening with Casey.

Casey entered the grand hall of the ballroom and scanned the crowd. For a frantic moment, she feared that he wasn't going to be there; that he would just leave her there, waiting. She felt strangely vulnerable and small in the middle of a stage she knew little about navigating. The world of politics had never appealed to her, and the pretense and power-positioning made her feel more uncomfortable than dealing with the plastic posers and phonies back in Hollywood. Here, she was, much to her regret, a fish out of water.

In a glorious instant, though, her fears subsided as she found herself staring at the most trustful, beautiful brown eyes in the world.

"Roe!"

"Hey, gorgeous!" He scooped her up into an embrace that lasted a full minute, charging her body with electricity. "You look incredible," he breathed, nervous and trembling just enough to convince Casey that he was indeed just as happy as she was. It was like a dream, sweetened by months of delirious anticipation. She could have given herself to him right there on the spot.

"You look pretty great yourself." She smiled.

He touched her face sweetly and stared languidly. The last time they had been together was in Palm Springs, which felt like a hundred years ago to Casey.

She caught herself blushing. Roe was perfection; tall and handsome, with a quiet dignity about his towering frame that just pulled people toward him. Women could not help but look. He was as crisp as a groom on top of a cake in his sleek designer tux. A security badge hung from a gold cord around his neck, and he carried a two-way radio to communicate with his production crew. It was countdown to showtime.

The radio squawked, and he pressed it to his ear. "They're just finishing the sound-check in the ballroom. I'll need to break away. Darling, will you be all right for a little while?"

She nodded. "Go! Do your thing."

"Great—have a drink. I'll find you when I get back. Stay in this area."

Twenty minutes later she found herself backed into a Grecian urn with a glass of some overpriced Washington reserve in her hand. A brash Harvard-type was inching his way dangerously toward her, giving her an occasional oily smile and a sly sideways glance. He was drinking fast and talking loudly, trying desperately to get her attention. A reporter with all-access press credentials was tearing at the crudités while his covered lens missed four dignitaries, a state senator, and Maria Shriver walking by.

"Oh, my God!" Casey gasped, nearly dropping her glass. Could it be? Could her eyes be deceiving her? *So many people look like other people, right?* But Casey's radar was never wrong. She carefully glided over to the main staircase to get a better angle. It was definitely her—in the flesh, whooping it up with a cadre of pickle-faced crones—none other than Bethany Peterson-Hall.

Nearly six years had passed since Casey had left the Kansas City newsroom, where she could have only hoped that Bethany would have rotted into oblivion after that day. Instead, there she was, looking "reconstructed." A nose job was easy to spot at any distance, and her eyes were so tucked into her forehead that she looked painfully and perpetually surprised. She had gained the customary ten pounds that television always strapped you with, and sagged disgracefully in a low-cut Valentino gown that should never had found its way off the mannequin and onto her lumpy frame. Her hair was dyed a cheap blonde, and cut in a bob with severe little bangs that made her appear like a bloated Cleopatra. She flashed her wrinkled cleavage and her pasted-on smile, flirting shamelessly with every male in the room. Casey presumed that by the manner by which she conducted herself that either she was on her third martini, or was working to piss off her husband to no end by playing to the clueless admirers milling around her.

Casey watched as a man sidled in next to Bethany and reached down quite matter-of-factly and patted her ass. It had to be her husband, Casey figured, by the way she did not so much as flinch at the intrusion. When he cocked his head in Bethany's direction to catch her leathery cheek, Casey got a look at his face and gasped, this time dropping her drink onto the marble floor. It was Guy Garrison.

He looked in the direction of the commotion that sent two plain-clothed security guards to the scene. Casey blanched and tried to look unaffected, but it was much too late for that. They had already seen her.

"Casey!" Bethany bellowed in her phoniest falsetto. The two ambushed her.

"Look who's here, darling, it's Casey Singer. The little weather girl from forever ago! How are you, honey? Still pointing at storm clouds?"

Casey cringed. Bethany was her tight-ass, bitchy self. She wanted blood.

"So, Bethany, what have you been up to all these years?" Casey asked through clenched teeth.

"Oh, we've been married for going on five years now— Guy and me."

Casey smiled and nodded. *First mistake of many*, she thought to herself.

"What about you? Where did you land?" Bethany said, drawing Guy in with a death-hold grip of acrylic nails around his arm.

"Actually, I'm in LA now. You know, modeling and acting and such. Perhaps you've seen my print ads for Aussie Jeans? I suppose you don't wear the brand, though, as it is geared for the younger set."

Bethany's zip-lock eyes narrowed at the blow.

Casey continued, "I'm in between pictures right now. Just finished a film with Nick Cage. Oh—and I will be taping a new pilot, *Paradise Cove,* this summer in Maui, and—"

"Let me fill you in on us, " Bethany jumped in. "Guy is still anchoring on weekends." It was clear that in her presence, Guy did absolutely none of the talking. He just stood there, dumb and obedient. The past several years had been kind to Casey, and she knew it. She let him take it in. She knew that they would talk about her behind her back the minute she walked away. Bethany never would admit that Casey had what it took to make it. In her opinion, she was just another messed-up rich kid with a curse on her pathetic life; a little tramp from Illinois who would ever amount to anything. As for Guy, he was too obtuse to even form an original thought. He was Bethany's bitch now, for sure.

"And what about you, Bethany? Are you still doing the news?"

"Heavens no, that was ages ago. I'm freelancing now for *Entertainment Digest.* I have a blog. You should click on sometime, dear."

Translation: not really working.

"We're tremendously happy," Bethany added, through a forced smile, suddenly panicking at the notice that her martini glass was empty. "Guy, darling—would you mind?"

"Not at all, sweetheart." He nodded toward Casey and smiled, she figured in case it was goodbye for another six or sixteen years. "Good seeing you, kid... best of luck out there in Hollywood."

She feigned a sincere smile, although what she really wanted to do was to kick him in the teeth—all thirty-two capped beauties. Wouldn't sweet Bethany like to know how much of a creep and dirty dog he really was, pestering her for months on end after the Porsche incident, begging her to meet him for a hot little sexual reunion. "One last fling, for old time's sake," he had pleaded. The phone calls and texts ensued for several months afterward. Of course, all that stopped after the rumors died down about their torrid on-set affair and the dust swirling around their staged breakup settled.

"So, who is representing you out there?" Bethany's interrogation was well underway.

"Lucas Morgan," Casey said, retrieving a fresh glass of champagne from a passing tray. She let the information sink into Bethany's peroxide-infused brain.

"Oh, really, you say? Lucas Morgan? It just so happens that I did an exposé on him just last year. What an asshole that one was!"

Casey smiled. *It certainly takes one to know one*, she thought. As far as she was concerned, Bethany could give lessons. She wished that Bethany would just slither off and drown herself in the punch. Scanning the crowd, Casey searched for Roe, willing him to return and rescue her.

"Are you here alone?" Bethany said over the jazz trio that had just struck up a tune in the corner. After all, she had no escort, and the doors would be opening for dinner any minute.

"I'm here with a good friend, Roe Evans of Castle Records."

Bethany's eyes widened from slits to dimes, and her eyebrows arched. "Is that so?"

"Yes, I'm just waiting for him. They're getting ready for Devon Laurent's performance tonight—in place of poor Adele. Tonsillitis, we're told." Casey liked sounding in the know. It made her feel superior to Bethany, which was not in the least a stretch.

"I know your Roe Evans. As a matter of fact, didn't *Rolling Stone* do a piece on the Castle spin-off label not too long ago? Their Nashville division is really producing the megastars. Devon, for one, is fantastic."

Casey nodded and played with the chain on her purse.

Wait for it…

"Well, he's quite the trooper, that Roe. I mean, in spite of everything that he's been through. It's no doubt, though, that his heart's in London."

"Yes, of course," Casey said, certain that she did not know in the least what Bethany was talking about.

"Please do tell Roe that I said hello. He might remember me from an interview back in April. Now, I really should find out where Guy has gone off to get that drink. *Ciao, Bella.* Enjoy the party."

She vanished, or rather, everything in the room vanished as Casey stood on unsteady legs, taking in the blow that Bethany had squarely delivered to her gut. Few people in the industry even knew about Roe's personal life. What did she know that Casey didn't? Maybe there was some sort of mistake. Maybe Bethany was confusing Roe with someone else. He never mentioned anything that she could remember specific about London, just business.

The room felt smaller by the minute. It was all she could do to move her trembling feet in the direction of the lobby to the ladies' room. She ended up in a stall. She was shaking uncontrollably, as if she was going to be violently ill. Bethany was a liar; a two-faced liar who was insanely jealous of her, and that was the God's honest truth. Why should she buy into it? It was bait! Bethany was just trying to mess with her mind. Casey took a few deep breaths to compose herself and refreshed her makeup, all the while willing Bethany's ridiculous words to evaporate from her mind.

There was one sure way to settle her fears, and that was to confront Roe directly. It couldn't have been at a more inopportune time, but she would have to do it. She mechanically reapplied her lipstick and snapped her handbag shut. She would ask him at dinner.

Dinner came and went. It was a blur of banquet dishes,

coffee refills, and flowing wine between strategically timed speeches and formalities. Roe and Casey were seated at the media table, which, unfortunately, was only two rows away from the Garrisons, or was it the Halls? Who knew what they went by? Midway through the main course, Bethany shot Roe an animated smile and flagged her napkin at him, causing a commotion that made the whole table look to see what the big deal was at table twenty-eight.

"That's Bethany Peterson-Hall from *Entertainment Digest*."

"Yes, I've had the pleasure of working with her back in Kansas."

"Was she always such a pain in the ass?" Roe asked.

Casey stroked his arm and smiled. It was just what she needed to hear. "So, you know her well, then?"

"We've never formally met. You'll have to fill me in on what I've been missing."

Casey sighed and felt instantly relieved. What was there to worry about? Obviously, Bethany was playing games. False alarm.

Roe checked his watch. The show in the Amphitheater was scheduled to begin promptly at nine thirty, just minutes after President and Mrs. Obama arrived and were seated.

Minutes after the final encore, Roe leaned over to Casey and whispered, "Let's get out of here."

They had a second dessert—two swirls of Rocky Road yogurt purchased from an all-night Frosty Freeze a few blocks from the hotel. They ate unabashedly as they walked along the grass of a quiet park in the middle of the city, barefoot in their formal clothes, stealing, for the first time, alone time. In the distance, they could see the festivities as camera crews and a few lookers-on still milled around the entrance to the pristine hotel.

Beneath a cloudless night sky, what stood before them was

so much better, a vast cityscape and a magnetizing moon. Still, the words Bethany had spoken earlier hummed in Casey's head, refusing to be quieted. *He's quite the trooper... considering everything. No doubt, his heart is in London.*

She held her breath and went for broke; there on a park bench he had cleared for them, laying his tux jacket down for her to sit on. "How long do we have? I mean, when do you have to go back?" Casey asked.

Roe was silent for a long while, as if he didn't hear the question at first. He just sighed, looking up at the starless sky. "I have to leave tomorrow for St. Louis. I have—"

"A meeting?" Casey finished his sentence.

"I hate like hell to go, Casey. But I can't stay. Believe me, I'd love to, but I just can't get out of this. I have to meet some people. I'm so sorry. "

The wind stirred up among the trees and then retreated, taking with them Roe's words and Casey's hopes for an unforgettable weekend. They sat in the silence.

For once in as long as she could remember, Casey did not know what to do. Then, as if in perfect answer to her confusion, he took her hand in his, leaned forward, and kissed her mouth with a power so real that it made her want to sob.

They made love that night like Casey had never experienced before in her life. They stayed awake all night, talking, and then, again and again, making love until dawn, with their clothes strewn about the hotel room and memories of the night before, the fundraiser, the concert, the park, still dancing in their heads.

Casey awoke to the sound of running water in the bathroom and felt the cold, vacant space next to her where Roe had lain hours earlier. She braced herself. There was always the dawn to expose the damage. She had not been strong. She did not press Roe for answers.

Her pounding head and sore bottom were keen reminders of the night before. Too much champagne and too much—

He bounded into the bedroom, fully dressed and smelling like heaven. "I've got an early flight." He shouldered his garment bag, which was expertly packed. He was ever at the ready to go, to leave her.

Kissing her forehead sweetly, he groaned. "Bye, beautiful... I'll call you when I can, okay?" He blew her another kiss from the door, and then he was gone.

She recoiled beneath the covers like a helpless child, moving into the empty spot his body had made, seeking comfort. She slept deeply.

It wasn't until many hours later that she awoke and regarded the time on the clock radio with disbelief, as some sort of mistake. It was half past four, and afternoon had already begun to fill the hotel room with heavy shadows. Uneasy with the unfamiliarity of her surroundings, and prompted by the memories of the evening prior, she was more than eager to go home and deal with her feelings on familiar ground. She wanted to get out of Washington as soon as possible.

She padded to the bathroom and took a quick shower. Traces of Roe lingered all around, yet his presence seemed to wash away, sadly, with the drain water, until she was simply left with a sanitized version of herself. Being clean was starting to bring her back to life. It gave her a sense of control again.

She scrubbed her face with the tiny bar of glycerin soap in the bathroom and swished some of the neon blue rinse in her mouth. She hated to slip back into the party dress. It smelled of smoke and was covered with grass and was so badly wrinkled that she wondered if she shouldn't just pitch it and opt for something from the gift shop to wear back to her hotel, which was about ten blocks away. Luckily, she had some spare cosmetics in her evening bag. She dabbed on some powder and blush to create a presentable face. A touch of lip gloss and she was ready to bolt. If she hurried, she could make the seven o'clock flight back to LA. She would get her things, check out, and head back to the airport.

Stepping over a strewn bath towel that Roe had left on the floor, she spotted a terry cloth hotel bathrobe left on the chair. He had worn it. She lifted it to her face and inhaled. The scent of Roe's neck was infused in the soft fabric, sending her, once again, heaven bound.

Her eyes scanned the room for one last look at the bed in which they made love all night into the dawn. Just before turning to leave, she spotted a small leather case sitting squarely on the nightstand. It was Roe's planner—in a world of technological gadgets, he had an actual old-school planner! It was small and thin, with a section for business cards and photos, along with a month at a glance calendar. The gold embossed monogram on the front verified that it was his. She held the planner in her hands and caressed it, wondering if he would be greatly inconvenienced without it. Hopefully, his assistant had a backup of his appointments and contacts at the Minneapolis office. She decided that she would try to contact his office as soon as she got home.

"See, Roe Evans," she said, curtailing her irrational fears and placing the planner in her clutch, "what would you do without me? You need me."

Walking to the elevator, she regarded the incident with a smile. *Who uses anything as antiquated as a physical planner anymore?* she wondered. The bell for the elevator chimed, and the doors sprang open. She stepped into the car along with a short, disheveled man with a camera around his neck. He eyed her curiously all the way down to the lobby floor. She figured that he recognized her and dismissed the intrusion. He didn't say a word. It was only moments later when she noticed him frantically snapping photos of her as she was hailing a cab, causing a commotion around the entrance to the hotel. Mortified, she bounded into the taxi and covered her head with her hands. Some onlookers, who had recognized her from the night before, began calling her name.

"Casey! Hey, Casey Singer! Why are you still in the same dress from last night? Who were you with?"

"Go, go!" she ordered the cabbie. "Get me out of here!"

CHAPTER 26

★ ★ ★

CASEY GLANCED THROUGH ROE'S PLANNER on the flight back to LAX, noting its contents: a few business cards, receipts, and a slim address book. She resisted the urge to search it thoroughly. She had noticed that he kept his bills and identification in his front pants pocket folded in a gold money clip that the president of Sony Records had given him when he left their employ back in the nineties. She loved the fact that she knew at least some things about him—yet so little. She'd hoped that the planner would be the key to her getting even closer to him somehow.

She arrived home spent and grateful for the peace and quiet of her little haven. It had become increasingly difficult to be inconspicuous, and it was about to get even more difficult with the new TV series, which would put her face in front of millions weekly. She unpacked quickly, and once again came across the planner in her purse. She decided to stow it safely in a wire basket on the kitchen table for safekeeping. It was usually filled with fruit, but was currently empty. She hadn't been to the store, hating to leave the house at all. She did not want to give the lurking paparazzi any opportunity to follow her. Hopefully, the ambush at the hotel that morning would not be mentioned in the entertainment rags. She still managed to fly under the radar where they were concerned, and that was fine with her.

She had put a call in to Roe's voice mail from the airport terminal and had hoped to have heard from him by now. She had simply asked him to call her back, but that was hours ago, and still, no word. She knew that he was in St. Louis. She felt comfort in knowing his whereabouts. She especially liked having his planner on her kitchen table in her peach bowl.

It was Sunday morning, and Casey was still in her bathrobe at nine a.m. She would lumber around the house all day if she had to, determined not to miss Roe's call. She poured herself a cup of coffee and parted the mini blinds over the sink. She could see Rush traipsing from the main house to the garage. He was newly seventeen and Ian let him take one of the cars on occasion. He had his golf clubs with him and was shoving them into the back of the SUV.

Sassy, a Bichon Frise, barked at his heels, jumping high into the air with glee. She had recently been to the groomer and was sporting a perky pink ribbon on the top of her head. She was a handful, Ian had secretly complained to Casey. However, Rush completely adored her, and so the dust mop became a permanent member of the family— one of which Ian was loath to indulge. Rush scooted her back into the house through the patio door, calling for Juanita, their maid, to fetch her.

Casey smiled. She eyed the leather planner, which she had since moved to the counter. It loomed, looking important, prompting her to try to reach him once again. She had already left several messages, but maybe for some reason, he was not able to retrieve them. *This is ridiculous,* she thought. *Call me, Roe... call me!*

She tried to forget about the whole thing and busy herself by preparing for her upcoming trip to Maui. Suitcases were propped on the bed, and clothes for the next six weeks were pulled from closets and drawers, strewn everywhere. She laundered and ironed essentials and made a list of drug store items that she would need to pick up. All of her travel and shooting itineraries were stowed away in a file folder in her carry-on, along with her credit cards, passport, and other identification. Instructions were written for the cleaning woman about the azaleas on the back deck. She pulled the spare key to the Miata so that Rush could drive it in her absence. He had said that he would be happy to look after things for her.

She never did get around to asking Ian if he was all right with that. He had been gone himself, in Peru, filming a spy sequel with Bradley Cooper for the past eight weeks. It was not uncommon for Rush to be left alone so often. It was a plus for Ian that Rush was as responsible as he was. Above all else, the kid was trustworthy. Rush was a pensive, artsy-type like his father and was content to pursue his passions and studies, listen to music, play golf, and swim. Plus, he knew unequivocally that if he were ever caught with something like drugs or worse, Ian would kill him. It was as simple as that. Juanita looked after him like a mother, keeping him fed and in clean clothes. She was even teaching him a bit of Spanish. What more could a kid want? Plus, he had Sassy to keep him company in the forty-acre fortress. That would be any teenager's dream.

At five o'clock, Casey ordered out for Chinese and dined alone at the coffee table. Then, she settled into the window seat of her bedroom nook in her fuzzy slippers and designer sweats, and with a glass of merlot in hand, she cracked open the script to *Paradise Cove*. She placed it on her lap, and began to read.

As of seven thirty, Roe still had not called.

She had rehearsed her lines, over and over, but somehow, still seemed unsatisfied. She had to be better than good—

she would have to blow everyone away at Star Casting, and play the part of Nikki West to perfection. Who was Nikki? Casey wondered. Did she really have what it would take to play a pre-med coed on summer sabbatical from her studies and demanding, soul-crushing, rich parents and philandering playboy boyfriend who was one letter grade short of being dropped from law school, who was working her ass off at a scandalous island resort as the young, hot yoga instructor? The premise seemed tired, at best, but there were plenty of stunning outdoor shots and hard bodies in yoga outfits, skimpy bathing suits, and surf gear to appeal to the masses. Nikki was a virgin at nineteen, which Casey loved the most about her. That, and the fact that she was extremely hot for Damien, the beefcake Latino hunk, island native, and resident diving instructor. Nikki was pegged to be the foil to megastar Mandy Mitchell, who was playing Kimber, the daunting spoiled heiress to the Moncrieff fortune, and whose family owned Paradise Island, as well as most of the neighboring resorts on the island. It would be easy for Casey to identify with the character of Nikki. She would just have to tap into her fearless, take-no-prisoners self. As far as she was concerned, she wrote the book on prima donna bitch behavior; it was up to her to unleash it.

Casey was immersed in a scene on the sands of Blue Surf, where she finds Damien checking the tank gauges on the diving barge, bobbing at the lip of the pier on a postcard-perfect morning ...

NIKKI: Are you going out today?

DAMIEN: Yep—got a corporate group from San Francisco. The head guy wants to take his sales team to Skull Reef.

NIKKI: You're not going out there with them, are you? It's way too dangerous for amateurs. Besides... what about the curse?

DAMIEN: What curse? You are way too paranoid. They want the best, and I am the best. Ain't no one else got the proper equipment, let alone the know-how to take them down like me.

NIKKI: Well, you will be careful, won't you? I mean ... we want everyone back in one piece.

He smiles. The two exchange a knowing glance. Enter KIMBER and her flowing amber hair, tan, rock-hard body, and launch-ready missile projectile breasts, enjoying a slice of mango. Her jealousy radar cocked full tilt; she eyes NIKKI with disdain.

KIMBER: See you tonight, Damien? [She calls from the pier, posing provocatively in the morning sun].

DAMIEN: Tonight. I'll be there. [He answers over the crash of the waves and smiles. KIMBER waves him off and trots back toward the resort. NIKKI peers through her Ray Bans with seething disdain, delivering steel daggers into KIMBER'S back. DAMIEN ties off a slipknot on a nylon fastening, and his biceps bulge and glisten in the sunlight].

NIKKI: We'll see about that, won't we . . .? [NIKKI mumbles under her breath, waving them off].

The phone rang, and Casey shot off the seat cushion like a cork, letting the script fall to the floor. She grabbed the cordless on the nightstand.

"Hello?" The anticipation in her voice made Shelly laugh on the other end of the line.

"Hey, girlfriend. Who were you expecting? The President of the United States?"

Casey sighed. "No, I saw him last night."

"What?"

"Never mind—hello! How is the little mother-to-be?"

"Huge!" Shelly said. "I swear, I am the size of a house.

Teddy won't stop teasing me about it."

"Is everybody healthy?"

"Yes, we all are."

"Then, so what? You lucky bitch—stop complaining! I hate you, and I'm jealous."

"Of what? Morning sickness, bloating twenty-four seven, and I swear to God, Casey, I haven't seen my feet in months. Don't be crazy."

"I'm sorry, Shelly. I'm just a little razzed. I've been going over the script for *Paradise Cove,* and I've got to ace this scene. It's all happening so fast. It's times like this, I really miss Jordy. He was great for studying lines. He always told me when I sucked."

"Well, I'll tell you that you suck!"

"Thanks, Shelly. You're a true friend."

Casey paused.

"What is it, *Chica?*"

Casey threw herself backward onto the bed and stared blankly at the ceiling fan. It was turned off, but somehow still looked like it was moving. "I'm going nuts waiting for Roe Evans to call me back."

"The record guy?"

"Yes, the guy who hit me with his car, remember? We've been in touch ever since; had a sort of 'thing' going. Shelly, I think I'm in love. I mean, I'm not one hundred percent sure, but what does it feel like? I mean, real love?"

"It's about time!" Shelly shrieked. "*Jesus Maria!* When did this happen? Is it serious? Tell me everything, girl— and don't leave anything out."

"There's nothing to tell. I'm just saying that I think that maybe ... I'm not sure. I don't know what I'm sure of any-more!"

She flipped over on the bed and kicked her feet up like a teenager. "Do you really want to know?"

"I really want to know."

"He's gotten to me, Shelly. It's to the point now that I

can't think of anything else."

"Did you guys kiss?"

"Yes, we've kissed." The memory of it made Casey smile

"Have you . . .? You know!"

"What?" she teased, knowing full well what Shelly meant. "Have we, what?"

"Dammit, Casey! Have you done it? You know, DONE IT?"

The sweet silence said it all.

"*Ariba!*" Shelly howled. "Oh my God. You did! Now spill it all, honey... and don't leave out a single detail."

They talked for an hour. Casey watched the clock migrate from ten to eleven o'clock. She had call waiting, and still, the entire time, there was no click on the line from Roe's long-awaited call, or on her cell phone. Finally, Casey confided about Washington, the night at the park, at the hotel, and the next morning, with Roe's abrupt leaving. She relayed her fears concerning something possibly being very wrong. She was in the kitchen now, throwing together a tuna sandwich. Obsessing made her hungry.

"It's strange—you know, that he has not responded, especially in light of leaving his organizer behind. It's really strange. I thought that maybe he did it on purpose, you know, unconsciously. Either way, surely he must be looking for it."

"So he might not know that you have it?" Shelly asked.

Casey sighed. "No. I didn't want that to be the only reason he called me back. I suppose I should say something about it on my message to him. I just said to please call. Maybe I should try to contact his assistant or something."

"Oh, honey. It's only been a day, give him a chance to figure it out."

"He knows that I'm leaving for Maui in the morning. I told him last night. He implied that he would call. It's just so odd, that's all. The guy is such an enigma. It's driving me crazy!"

"Hang in there. He will show you what he's about soon enough. I promise."

"You'll never guess who I ran into at the party last night," Casey said, changing the subject.

"Who?"

"Bethany Peterson-Hall and Guy Garrison—can you believe it?"

"You're shittin' me!"

"Nope. Big as day, there they were. The happy couple."

"Wow—did Bethany talk to you?"

"Oh, she talked all right, and..."

"And what?"

"She said something odd. Something I haven't been able to get out of my head since yesterday. I'm sure it was nothing."

"Nothing my ass! What did that old bat tell you? Spill!"

Casey moaned, annoyed with her own foolish paranoia. She noticed through the blinds that Rush had returned, and he was with a girl. They were pulling up noisily in the driveway. The engine woke Sassy inside the house, and she started yapping from her pillow near the door.

"She said that she felt 'Sorry for Roe, considering what he was going through.' What do you suppose that means?"

"That's obviously code. She's thoroughly jacked that his life is in some sort of turmoil. Could be anything ... bankruptcy, criminal charges... ooh, maybe a mysterious illness."

"Shelly!" Casey was incredulous. How could she suggest such things?

"Truth is—it could be anything, or nothing. Look, the woman is a gossip hound, right? I wouldn't worry about it. Scandal, baby. Ole Bethany either knows something, or ..."

"Wants me to think that she does?"

"Exactly."

Casey peered through the small kitchen window and watched Rush and the girl. "She also said that he'd be better off in London. Isn't that strange?"

Through the window, Casey watched them stumble into the house, laughing and pushing each other playfully. It was obvious that they had been drinking. Rush fumbled with the keys and unlocked the door, juggling two brown bags, acting gallant and goofy to impress the girl, who was wearing a gauzy halter top and cut-offs. He bowed deeply, ushering her in the large dark house with put-on bravado. The girl giggled. Moments later, the light in his bedroom window illuminated, and the sounds of Smash Mouth blasted from the upper floor across the courtyard.

Shelly took this in and quickly delivered a cutting conclusion. "Check the organizer."

"What for?"

"Just check the planner. See if there are any clues. I know I would. Honestly, Casey, I don't know how you could have been in possession of that little goldmine of information for almost twenty-four hours and not seen your way to look at it. Have you lost your edge? The old you would have immediately torn through it for any scrap of information you could find."

"Shelly, I did—sort of. It's just that it's his, and it's personal."

"Yeah, so is your sanity. Besides, whatever Bethany knows was gleaned through that magazine of hers she writes for, and we both know how those people get their facts."

Casey winced. She eyed the leather planner, sitting safely in the wire bowl as if it were forbidden fruit. In a way, it was. It held the truth. And Casey was not ready for it.

"Go on, Case—you know you want to. The answer is probably staring you in the peaches."

Shelly laughed, but Casey was unmoved. What was she asking? For her to betray Roe's trust? Would it be that easy to find what she was looking for?

"Don't worry, *Chica*. You'll decide what to do." Shelly yawned. It was time to sign off. "I have an early morning, my friend. You call me if you need anything. I mean it; go kill it in Maui. I can't wait to see your first episode."

Casey air-kissed the receiver. "Okay, Shelly. You take care too."

"These little monkeys will be born by the time you come back—they're boys, God help me!"

"I knew it!" Casey said. "Take care of yourself and my nephews."

"Love you!" Shelly gushed.

"You too," Casey echoed, and then hung up.

She bounded into the kitchen and snatched the planner from the peach bowl. What would it hurt to take a little peek? She started to open the leather case and then stopped short. *No!* She wouldn't do it. Roe's private life was his. Besides, she needed to go see Rush. Five a.m. would come early, and she had to square things away with him before she left.

Sassy jumped into action, yapping wildly after being awoken from sleep atop her plush puppy pillow just next to the door. She was waiting for Ian to come home, and thirty days past did not dampen her determination to keep the vigil. Casey could see Rush's bedroom light from the front of the house, but no one except Sassy was stirring.

She bent over the potted mums and felt around for the spare key.

"Ah-ha!" Right where Ian had told her he left it. That and the four-digit code would get her in and past the security system in any emergency. Well, she reasoned, it was an emergency of sorts. She had to see Rush in person before she left. It was now or never.

She stood on her bare feet in the moonlight, working the key into the lock, and then punched the code numbers on the keypad. She was good with remembering things. She had the entire first script to *Paradise Cove* memorized just that evening; not only her part, but of every character.

She was remarkable that way.

She pushed the heavy door open and peered inside. The cool air hit her immediately like an Artic blast. Ian kept it like an icebox.

"Hello?" Her voice echoed in the stillness.

Sassy swirled at her feet, nearly causing her to trip as she moved in the darkness across the hardwood floor. The house smelled of leather couches and expensive teak wood; of scented candles and cedar wood beams. Even in the shadows, she could see that the Redwine mansion was a glorious showplace of opulence and wealth. A grand piano glistened in the great room to the right; quiet oil prints loomed priceless and haughty in the half-light.

She tiptoed over an exquisite Persian rug into the kitchen, where she laid the keys on the marble countertop. On second thought, she decided that instead of disturbing Rush, she would just leave a note, when suddenly; she felt something move behind her.

She spun around and gasped. There, standing in the doorway, wearing nothing but his boxer shorts, socks, and a petrified stare, was Rush—pointing a gun at her.

"Rush! It's me, goddammit. Put that thing down!" she shrieked, so loudly that Sassy growled at the sudden jolt of excitement.

Rush immediately retreated and bent in two, panting and wagging his head, his shaggy blond hair falling across his eyes. A trickle of urine spread rapidly around the fly of his boxers.

Casey bit her bottom lip to keep from smiling and calmly pointed out the obvious. "You sprung a leak there, Bud. *Jesus!* What were you thinking, dude?"

"No shit, Singer—you scared the piss outta me! What the hell are you doin' sneaking in here like that?"

He looked like Ian with his crimson face and veins bulging in his neck. She felt mortified and relieved all at the same time. Rush could take care of himself, all right. There was no doubt about that.

Before she could answer, a nervous wisp of a girl scurried up behind him, covered only in a sheet, which she had obviously dragged from the bed.

"Hi!" Casey said, growing more amused by the moment. "What do we have here?"

The girl said something unintelligible and buried her reddened face in Rush's back.

"We were just . . ."

"Watching TV?" Casey smirked, helping herself to a cigarette from one of Old Man Redwine's discarded packs of Marlboros on the counter. She slowly lit the tip and drew in several calming drags, holding the two teens with her stare. It isn't every day that one busts two teen-agers doing the nasty. It was different than what all unchaperoned horny kids would do when given an empty mansion, a sack full of Red Bull, and free rein. And what was that sweet spice she first detected when she walked in? Must not have been cedar beams after all!

Rush shifted uncomfortably. The girl clutched her pink acrylic nails onto him for dear life.

"Are... you gonna tell my dad?"

Casey boss-eyed him as if she were surprised that he could even think such a thing.

"Of course not. We're buddies, right? You're a responsible guy, right?"

He nodded.

"Relax then. I'm here to give you the keys to my car and the coach house." She held up a sterling key ring. "This is my entire life, Rush. Got that? I mean it. Be careful, and don't fuck up."

"I won't," he gushed. "You know I'll take care of things."

"Good. Then we're all clear here. Are you sure that Ian will be okay with this?"

"Yeah, he's chill. Oh, this here is Amber. Amber, Ms. Casey Singer. She's going to Maui to become a big megastar."

He smiled patronizingly, as if "megastar" was an impressive accomplishment to a boy who grew up on countless movie sets. Amber's father was an orthodontist, so the novelty of it all was not lost on her.

"Cool." The girl smiled vaguely, averting her eyes.

Casey needed to put an end to the awkward moment. She finished her cigarette and extinguished it in the sink. "I'll be back in six weeks; home for a few days, and then I'm off again for four more. Here's the number where you can reach me if you need to. Put the digits in your phone—and on the fridge."

She smiled. "I'll show myself out. Rush, remember—if anything happens to that car, I will personally hunt you down, got that?"

He nodded. "Bye. And good luck, Casey; sorry about the gun thing."

"No problem, Bud." She planted a quick sisterly kiss on Rush's cheek and headed back across the courtyard, calling in her wake, "Aloha, dudes!"

CHAPTER 27

★ ★ ★

THE NEXT MORNING, CASEY WAS up at dawn. She had a bowl of corn flakes and watered her azaleas. She placed the garbage bags out on the driveway and had just rolled her luggage into the living room when she noticed the time. It was eight o'clock in Minneapolis. She decided she would try Roe's office once more before she left, and this time, she would leave a message with someone about the organizer.

"I know that Mr. Evans is traveling today from St. Louis … I just wanted to notify him that he has misplaced his leather planner, and—"

"I'm sorry," the assistant informed her. "Mr. Evans is out of the country. He arrived in London yesterday. May I ask who's calling, please?"

Casey was taken aback. She could have sworn that he had said that he would be back in the Minneapolis office on Monday.

"I can connect you to his voice mail, Miss, if you like. You say that you have his organizer?"

"Yes. Can you tell me when Mr. Evans is expected to return?" Casey tried to sound casual, although her heart was pounding.

"Who did you say this is?" the woman asked curtly.

"A friend," Casey said. "A good friend."

"Oh, then excuse me for saying, Miss, but perhaps he has not informed you. Mr. Evans does not have a return flight scheduled."

"I see. Thank you." Casey ended the call and slammed the phone onto the counter. What was going on? Why did Roe tell her the other day that he was going to St. Louis for a client meeting when he really went to London? And was not returning?

She berated herself for being so gullible. Bethany's words returned with a vengeance to taunt her, drumming in her head. *No wonder his heart's in London.*

Was there another reason that Roe was not returning her calls? And moreover, was that reason in London?

She snatched up the planner and riffled through it. A quick perusal confirmed her greatest fear as she counted the days aloud. Much to her shock and disbelief, it seemed that Roe had traveled to London twenty-four times in the last four months.

He had lied to her!

And, more disturbing, she was stunned to find that on the entry for that very day, April twelfth, in Roe's hand-writing, marked in caps and starred with asterisks across the top of the page, was the dagger that pierced her heart: SIX O'CLOCK – DINNER WITH JANE.

"Oh my God!" Casey gasped, dropping the planner to the floor. *He has a woman in London.* And from the looks of things, he had been seeing her on a regular basis. Rage quickly overtook disbelief and shot right to the core of her being.

"Son of a bitch!" Casey screamed. Roe Evans was nothing more than a sleaze and a sneak—just like all the rest.

Was it yesterday's news that Roe Evans was a cheat? Did everyone in the universe know? Apparently, the joke was on her! She berated herself for ever believing that maybe,

just maybe, he was different. She was through with it—
through with him. She would not waste another moment
of her life on the likes of a dog like Roe Evans. As far as
she was concerned, it was now a closed chapter.

She gathered her suitcases, shoved the fated planner into
her carry-on, and slammed and locked the front door. She
waited silently on the stoop with her bags for the limo to
arrive to take her to the airport.

It was a quiet, still morning. The haze would soon give
way to the glaring sun. The forecast called for cloudless,
sunny skies, and the paper said that it was already nine-
ty-two degrees in Maui. *Perfect!*

It was good to be leaving; to go as far away as she could
fly. She felt dizzy and sick inside. What would she do now?
There was only one thing she could do—nothing. Roe
Evans would never hear from her again. With her silence,
she would send the bastard a message loud and clear that
she was not into playing games, and that she was not going
to be made a fool of. He could have his little tart in London for all she cared.

But care she did. It was going to take more than simply denouncing him to exorcise Roe Evans from Casey
Singer. He was in her bones.

CHAPTER 28

★ ★ ★

CASEY ARRIVED ON THE SET that afternoon just in time to meet the producer and the director for a late lunch. They dined in the resort's full-service restaurant amidst an arriving crew of staff, productions assistants, and camera operators. Much of the staff had been on the island for weeks, preparing for the first taping. Already, several script revisions had been made, and one major character was cut from the pilot due to creative re-writes dictated from the network.

Everyone was scurrying from the implications of a major character change. The new actress, Lee Ann Daniels, would be too young to play the part of Abigail Moncrieff, the proprietor's wife of the resort, so they would be casting her as the sister-in-law instead, alluding to a non-existent missing brother that would make for some interesting storyline possibilities. This did not affect Nikki's character in the least, and for that, Casey was grateful.

"You'll be rooming with Lee Ann. She's playing Mia Moncrieff, the sexy sister-in-law," the production manager explained. "Trailer number eight is for the women—it's on the west side of the lot. All sleeping rooms are at the Outrigger. A bus will shuttle you to and from the set each day. Be ready at four a.m. sharp for call. All meals, except for lunch, are at your hotel in the Kahului Suite. Lunch is what you can catch in between takes. There will be deli and salads on the set. Got all that?"

The production manager, Dottie, was a forty-something lesbian with a short buzz cut and a ring in her left eyebrow. She had non-existent breasts, a survivor of a double mastectomy. She wore a tank top, khaki shorts, and hiking sandals, always. In a comforting sort of way, she reminded Casey of her college roommate, Dahlia.

Dottie was canonized the saint of "Making All Things Happen," and happen they did, when she was at the helm. After all introductions, Dottie handed Casey over to the production assistant for a tour of the set. Her name was Amelia, and she looked and sounded like she has just walked off the set of *Downton Abbey*. She was plain, mousy, and all of about twenty-two.

"You won't mind 'et mooch working 'ere, sweet pea— the vistas are breathtakin' and the blokes ain't bad to look et neither!"

Casey learned from Amelia that Dottie was married to a French-Canadian biotech engineer, who was conducting research somewhere in Greenland. It was a strange arrangement that was better left unexplained. Dottie had been contracted with Beacon Productions for the past seven years, and the task of den mother to the stars suited her just fine.

"We would all be piss wit'out her," Amelia said. "Dottie makes it all happen."

That night, in her hotel room, Casey laid awake listening to the lulling sounds of the ocean rushing up on the beach. It had been an exhausting day. She must have met over fifty new people; unfamiliar faces and names, pouring forth energy and enthusiasm.

Paradise Cove's launch episode would have to be nothing

short of phenomenal, right out of the gate. With television, there was little time to build a following during a run. The show had to be hyped well before it even aired. Promotional photos would be taken in the morning, and then shooting was scheduled for two p.m. Casey was on the call sheet for scene four of the first episode. Makeup was at seven a.m. and again at noon.

She turned over on the stiff mattress in the darkness and regarded her roommate, Lee Ann's, back in the shadows, breathing shallowly in the bed next to hers. Casey could hardly believe her fate. She was really here. Her heart skipped in her chest as she contemplated how far she had come.

You can do this, she assured herself. She knew that she could do anything she set my mind to. She willed herself to ignore thoughts of Roe that kept tugging at her, threatening to distract and throw her off course. She ran through her lines for the next day in her head until she couldn't hear his voice anymore.

Casey worked harder than she ever had in her life. Set calls were at all hours. It was nothing to report for makeup at five p.m. and shoot well past midnight. The waiting in between scenes was the worst. She studied her lines constantly, oftentimes teaming with Lee Ann or one of the other cast members on the beach or holing up in the trailer with the inept air conditioning that made her actually long for her hotel room that was miles from the set.

The second Saturday there, they took a schooner up and down the southwest coast near Molokini Crater, and for the first time ever, Casey tried her hand at snorkeling. It was adventurous and new, and she loved every minute of it. More exhausted than she could ever remember being, she fell into bed each night, satisfied with her work and eagerly looking forward to the following day, when she would get up and do it all over again.

When she wasn't working, Casey scoured the Internet for information about her cast mates and the show heavies to learn more about her new "family." She found the director, Selma Bateman, a dream to work with. She respected Selma's directing style and took to the rigorous hard-driven shooting schedules and difficult scenes with professional valor. For once, Casey didn't mind being worked to her full potential. In fact, she loved it. And she relished in the concept of *Paradise Cove* being directed—as well as produced—by women. Selma did not take crap from anyone. She had stamina born of her European roots and homegrown values. A child of immigrant hopefuls, she embraced unpleasantness all her life to make good movies and to win approval. When she failed to produce another Oscar after many attempts, she was dismissed in the industry as a has-been. What the industry didn't know was that great directors never die—they move to television.

Dragged out of early retirement, Selma had to be practically begged to read the pilot for *Paradise Cove*. A lover of the younger generation, she was content to stay home and raise her teenage children in peaceful chaos. It was her youngest, Hyden, who convinced her to take the job.

"You're hip enough, Mom. Everyone loves you. We've all seen *Melrose Place* re-runs. How hard could it be?"

Armed with a baseball cap and a perpetual thermos of hot coffee, two assistants, a tech crew of fifty, twelve camera operators, fourteen actors, and a stick of gum, Selma could whip more asses into shape than Spielberg and Scorsese combined. That won Casey's deepest admiration and respect.

Surprisingly, *Paradise Cove* had must-view TV-potential, at least with the twenty-something set. The chemistry and smart script writing promised a new, edgy television drama that would captivate viewers, causing them to not even think of dialing into another inane reality bore-fest. Casey was convinced in its merit now that she was fully vested. It would be nothing but sandy beaches and sexy bitches on Monday nights at seven.

Casey kept her cool and conducted herself like a seasoned pro. She pulled no punches with Selma. Selma was fascinating to watch at work. She let it all consume her, helping Casey to feel the same. She actually helped Casey to became Nikki West—confident, fresh, and cunning; her trademark blonde hair, her crowning glory, highlighted in the tropical sun, with the help of chemicals, to sleek perfection in a short bob that perfectly framed her sun-kissed face, giving Nikki a hint of distinction from the other female characters, whose appearances favored any variety of the Barbie doll brigade.

Casey still possessed a curvaceous, yet athletic frame; a look that served her well in a bikini, with long, lean legs and a full, firm bust line. She was easy on the eyes, and the camera lens loved her. Portraying nineteen-year-old Nikki West was natural for Casey, who would turn twenty-eight by the final day of taping.

Shooting was slated for the entire summer, with a four-week break in the fall. Then, they would resume again until just before the holidays, through the New Year. If the show got picked up a second season, another twenty episodes would be taped for the following sweeps period. Everyone did the best they could to stay focused on creating the best show they could. The rest, it was believed, would take care of itself.

As the show began to catch on, fans started frequenting the set and began to make it increasingly difficult to shoot in the middle of the day. Beach scenes were then shot as early as possible, affording, in the process, better natural light, as well as assured privacy.

There were several nightclubs where the cast and crew members liked to go to dance and socialize, or to sample the island's best Mai Tais or Mango Margaritas. Most of the time, Casey declined, taking to her room to study her lines for the next day and to catch up on some much-needed rest.

She resisted the urge one hundred times a day to phone Roe. He was on her mind constantly. Still, she made no attempt to contact him. It was better this way. Even if he did want to talk to her, he had no idea that she had pushed him and all hopes of ever seeing him away. She busied herself, instead, in checking her Facebook page for the onslaught of posts and pleas for her reply. Her fan base was growing by the thousands, and the thrill of it all was beyond anything she could have ever imagined.

Lucas Morgan's office e-mailed weekly progress reports and industry updates. Whenever she noticed that the voice mail light was on in her hotel room, Casey could bet that it was Trish from Lucas's office, wanting to check in with her. It was easier to talk on the hotel phone to the mainland. Lucas preferred to Skype and bothered her constantly for updates. His little "pep talks" as he called them. At least the contact made her feel somehow connected to someone back in LA, even if it was slimy Lucas.

She stumbled in from a particularly enjoyable wrap party at the Tiki Torch Cantina, feeling unusually giddy and light-headed from the rum. Lee Ann had challenged her to a game of darts in which the loser had to buy a round for everyone. By midnight, Casey was feeling no pain and stayed on with the others, drinking and celebrating the success of another great season behind them. The chemistry of the cast members, both on the set and off, was remarkable. She had grown very fond of each and every one of them.

Selma and Dottie were holed away at a corner booth, smoking Cubans like chimneys. Her co-star, Enrique, who played Damien, was table dancing for a cadre of tourist groupies, and the techies were flirting with the mega hunks' discards on the dance floor. Few of the women cast members dared to go out to such public venues as Tiki's, but Lee Ann and Casey didn't care. The burly camera guys, along with the security goons, for the most part, kept the psycho-fans at bay.

Therefore, it was not surprising that the two actresses had no inclination that a reporter from *Star Beat* had followed and captured every moment of their drunken revelry with his digital camera. Not least of all, the moment of debauchery as Casey and Lee Ann danced hip-locked, bumping and grinding their way across the bar top in a hot tango of tongues and wet T-shirts... putting on a show for everyone to see.

The hotel room was blissfully cool when they stumbled in at four a.m., happy to be reunited with their beds. Casey was exhausted, secretly thankful that the next day was Sunday and that there would be a three-day reprieve before taping would begin again.

"Your phone dinged. You have a message," Lee Ann said, facedown on the bed. She didn't even bother to remove her clothes or to crawl beneath the bedspread.

Casey appeared from the bathroom, reaching for her cell phone on the nightstand. "So, who could this be? Oh— maybe I have been nominated for that Emmy." Casey smiled at her own prediction through the dripping toothpaste.

Lee Ann was already snoring. Casey slapped her hard on the ass, but she didn't move. *This night would be one for the record books*, Casey thought of the innocent horseplay between the two of them.

Casey spit in the sink and then quickly crawled into bed.

The lure of the incessant missed call light got the better of her curiosity. She swiped the screen to see who had called. It was Lucas.

The connection was full of static, but the recording clearly revealed a frantic Lucas Morgan. "Casey! I've been trying to reach you all night ... *shit!* Where are you? Call me right when you get this. I have some horrible news. Oh, God... just fucking CALL ME!"

CHAPTER 29

★ ★ ★

THE LINE CUT OFF, BUT his words rang eerily in her head. She looked at the clock radio. It was four thirty-five a.m. She quickly ended the call and selected call back feature. It was three hours ahead in LA. She waited, exhaling deeply, her mind racing in a frenzied attempt to decipher his cryptic message. Could she be fired? They hated Nikki? Or, no—

maybe they hated her. Maybe they had found another actress to play Nikki—the same type, only better.

An anxious Lucas Morgan answered on the second ring. "Casey?"

"Lucas, what's up? Talk to me . . ."

An eternal silence stretched across the Pacific, causing her to blurt out, "Goddammit, Lucas! Why did you call me? Is everything all right?"

"Thank God you're there. Listen, there's been an accident, Case. A horrible accident on the Santa Monica freeway. Your car…it was involved. At first, I thought you might have come back over the break, but that's impossible—you were still on set."

"Of course I'm here. I lent it to—" Her heart stopped cold. "Oh my God! Rush... I lent my car to Rush Redwine!"

Silence.

"Lucas, was Rush driving?" she demanded.

"Yes."

"Alone?"

"No. There was a blonde—Jesus, Casey, she fit your description so perfectly ... I freaked out. And then it came out that she was a teenager also."

Amber! "Are they ... " She couldn't bring herself to form the word.

"Both killed instantly. Case, I'm so sorry."

She drew in air, but there was no oxygen. Her head was spinning. She was going to be sick.

"They jumped a median," Lucas explained. "There was no chance."

"No, no, no . . ." she whispered, struggling to assimilate the news.

"There's more, Case. I don't know to tell you this, other than to just come out with it."

She was sitting on the edge of the bed, so she stood as if changing position would better prepare her for what as next.

"Ian Redwine—the boy's father . . ."

Her stomach lurched. The Mai Tai's were burning a hole in her gut and singing her throat with lethal bile. "Does he know?"

"They contacted him last night. It happened around eight p.m. He should have arrived on a flight from Peru an hour ago."

"So I should go back right away too. He'll need me to— "

"No, Case. He doesn't want to see you. In fact, we think you're in danger if you come home. You might be in danger now. Is someone with you?"

"What are you talking about? I'm at the hotel with the other cast members."

"He blames you, Case. For giving Rush your car."

She collapsed onto the bed, unsteady on her legs.

"They were forced off the road. Redwine believes that the hit was intended for you. Don't you see? He blames you, and now he wants retribution. He is grief-stricken, and, well, Case, I don't need to tell you that he's a very powerful man."

Casey agonized with every unbelievable blow. "Me? How can that be?"

"Your place, the coach house. It was torched this morning. Everything is gone."

"WHAT?" Casey could not believe what she was hearing.

Lee Ann roused in the darkness, the sound of Casey's horrifying gasps too much for even her drink-addled mind to block out.

"To make matters worse, Redwine's missing. He touched down at LAX, but never showed up after that. We're going to get extra security for you. Just until they locate him. I always heard that he was a crazy son of a bitch, but this is over the top."

Casey hushed Lee Ann, who was frantically tugging at her arm.

"I've already contacted the island police. I suggest you take this seriously, Case. I won't have you, or any of my people, terrorized."

Tears stung her eyes. She doubled over as she tried to comprehend the nightmare that was unfolding.

"Casey!" Lee Ann screamed, then ran for the door to get help.

"They are going to ask you questions, okay? Detectives will be there shortly—as well as the media. I want you to prepare yourself for the frenzy. We'll tell you what to say. How to handle this. Do you understand? Kirsten Frey, with our public relations firm, will be there later this morning. You are not to talk to anyone about this, not a word to anyone. Got that?"

Casey nodded as tears streamed down her face. She was in a bad dream.

"Wait until Kirsten gets there, okay?"

Casey wiped her nose with the back of her hand. She was trembling. "Okay." Her voice was weak and unsteady. Who on earth would want to run her off the road? Surely, there had to be some mistake. How could the hit have been aimed at her? She could not believe or make sense of any of it. *And Rush…poor Rush and Amber!* Maybe they did target Rush. He was Ian's son, and the man did have enemies. He was a multimillionaire. The whole thing was unfathomable. It was like a bad movie; a horrible, demented joke. The thought of it made her want to vomit.

"Hang tight, Case. We'll get you through this, I promise. I'm thinking we can even spin it to our advantage, if we play our cards right. My phone has not stopped ringing."

Spoken like a true businessman, protecting his investment. She wanted to stab him one hundred times. At that exact moment, she hated him more than she had ever despised anyone. The heartless bastard was showing himself for the slime that he truly was. Two teens were dead, and all he could think about was how to make the six o'clock entertainment news. *Fuck you, Lucas Morgan…fuck you!*

"I'll be in touch," he said. "Try to keep it together, all right? You'll hear from me again soon."

Casey shuddered, freezing in the blasting air-conditioned room, shivering with her knees pulled up to her chest. She would sit there and wait, alone in the stillness.

She would sit and wait for the sun.

"Good morning, Casey. I'm Kirsten Frey, with The Morgan Agency." The woman offered Casey her hand. It felt lifeless and damp, like a limp glove in the ninety-degree heat. She was clearly out of her element, up to her Prada pumps in sand and sweltering in a silk sleeveless turtleneck beneath her gabardine suit jacket. "Whew! Sure is hot. Is there someplace we can talk, privately?"

Casey led her to her trailer, where two undercover cops were standing guard. Her name, along with Lee Ann's, had been removed from the outside of the flimsy door. Inside, a burly gentleman greeted her with a grizzly handshake. He was a Pacific Islander.

"Miss Singer, I'm Sergeant Roach," he said, extending his giant hand.

He was bald, and his head glistened with sweat. Kirsten invited them all to sit down in the tiny quarters. Roach had on a short-sleeved shirt with serious perspiration stains snaking beneath the armpits. A squawking two-way radio was fastened around his enormous belt.

The three sat down at a folding card table.

"Ian Redwine, the old man, is also dead," the cop announced from behind his gray-flecked mustache.

Casey gasped.

"He was discovered this morning by the maid. Shot through the head and tossed, naked, in his own swimming pool."

Casey winced at the sickening image.

The detective folded his hairy mitts around a crumpled report. It was then that she noticed that he was missing a finger. He was wearing his wedding ring on his middle digit.

"It was a hit. We're certain. Redwine, let's just say, was not a model citizen. He dealt in some very heavy stuff—designer drugs, to be exact. Let's just say he got greedy in his dealings and leave it at that. These goons play hard."

Casey nodded, her thoughts a blur of unanswered questions.

He went on. "We think they might have torched the coach house; to make it look like he did it to punish you."

"For loaning Rush the car?" Casey asked.

"Who knows, ma'am. That's one theory. Ian Redwine had a boatload of enemies. He was not the warmest, if you know what I mean. There's no telling who could have had it out for him. We found photographs in his possession, at his office—particularly of interest are these candid shots of you." He reached into a vinyl duffel bag and handed her a small brown envelope. "See for yourself."

"Oh my God!" Casey gasped. There were several shots of her back in LA, coming and going in the shiny blue Miata to the mall or to yoga class. There were others too—Casey shown swimming naked in the pool... and the latest shots taken at the Ritz, in Washington, the day after the fundraiser and her night with Roe. "This is so creepy," Casey said. "But why? Why would Ian have these photos?"

"I am sure you were not aware of them having been taken. He may have had someone photograph you for his protection."

"Protection? I don't understand."

"Blackmail. The man was a paranoid freak. We don't know all the reasons behind the actions that were taken." He went on, "The crash was made to look like an accident. The teens' blood work came back clean. We can only assume that whoever did this, thought it was you in that car. It all still has to be sorted out. There will be a thorough investigation, though. You can bet on that."

"I don't understand why—" Casey tried to get a word in, but Kirsten ran interference. Damage control was more like it.

"I'll handle this, Casey. We'll make good and sure that none of those photographs get into the wrong hands. You don't have to hear any more of this. No more questions, Sergeant Roach. Ms. Singer is tired and obviously shaken. I have five reporters waiting for a statement and a five o'clock plane to catch, so, if we're through here... "

Sergeant Roach lifted his hefty frame, which shook the trailer when he stood. Here's my card, Ms. Singer. If you should want to talk—about anything—just give me a call."

"Are these the only copies of the photos?" Casey asked, almost as an afterthought.

"No telling, ma'am," he said.

She nodded and watched him duck beneath the low doorway and lumber down the metal steps. A pack of nosy crew members and some hungry photographers were milling around near the trailer. They could smell blood.

"Move back!" Kirsten shouted. "You must be careful to stay out of view for now as much as possible," she cautioned Casey, shutting the tinny door and drawing the trailer's curtains. Then she swiped at her phone and sighed heavily. "The first thing we're going to do is to get you a good lawyer." She said this as if she were dialing up a pedicure.

In moments, she was buzzing into the phone, no doubt consulting with Lucas on what to do next.

What followed was mostly a blur. Casey was awash with images of Rush and Amber, tangled in a ton of steel wreckage, with blood and glass everywhere; the images grotesque and agonizing. She secretly blamed herself for giving Rush the keys to her car. If only she had known, but then again, how could she? She was just as much a victim here.

Kirsten droned on, but Casey heard nothing; nothing but the sound of tires squealing and the crash of steel and metal on concrete, imagining the horror-stricken teens just moments before they were crushed painfully to their deaths. And Ian's tormented heart that, no doubt, broke into a million pieces when he had learned of Rush's demise. She wondered if he really had blamed her for giving Rush the car. It wouldn't have mattered, though. They were followed. Followed and hunted down, just like Ian. Perhaps they had meant to kill all of them and it was just fate or dumb luck that she was not in the car as they thought. Ian's killers wanted to make sure he died in agony, knowing about the fate of his son; seeing his place burn before his eyes, watching his entire world come to an end.

She waited until Kirsten was distracted, heavy into conspiring with Lucas on how to spin the tragedy in favor of almighty publicity for the series and the agency. "She's a total innocent, here. Yes, really, Lucas, that's what I'm saying. Get TMZ or CNN down here right away, and we'll have her do a spot right here on the set with goddamn palm trees in the background and tears in her baby blue eyes. I'm seeing it, man, for real... it's freakin' gold."

In less than fifteen seconds, Casey grabbed her tote bag and was gone. She raced past the crowd of gawkers, who had pitched their lawn chairs just feet from the trailer. She ran through the set grounds until she couldn't breathe, to the open road, where she flagged a cab. She had exactly sixteen dollars in the pocket of her denim shorts. "Take me to the farthest beach this will get me to." She tossed the crumpled money over the seat and stared out the window. The driver stole a few glances at her in the rearview and then floored the gas pedal, heading along the lush pineapple fields toward the sunrise.

Casey walked in the wet sand for hours, deep in thought, calmer than she had felt in years. *They'll want me to play this off as a good thing.* Bad for Ian and Rush Redwine, but good publicity for Casey Singer. What a tragic turn of events for the director and his son! Headlines would read: TV ACTRESS CASEY SINGER OF PARADISE COVE FAME – RAVAGED OF HOME AND ALL WORLDLY POSSESSIONS. WHAT CONNECTION DID SHE HAVE WITH THE REDWINES? DID SHE ESCAPE THE SAME TRAGIC FATE? Once again, she would need to rebuild her life. After all, she still had her precious career intact. Or was it? She could see Bethany Peterson-Hall having a field day with the story. *Nobody cared about her. Nobody gave a shit about Ian and Rush, just like her dear father and mother all those years ago... no one!*

From the top of the cliff, she could see the entire island. She kicked off her sandals and felt the jagged rocks cut into the soles of her feet. She reached into the tote bag and extracted Roe's planner. She still had it. All this time, she kept it close, and kept him waiting, for *her*. The surface of the cliff felt sharp and slippery at the same time. The morning sun was burning high in the sky.

She thought about Helen. All those years ago, wondering how she might have felt just before she pulled the trigger. *Did you feel like this, Mother . . .?*

The waves churned and crashed beneath her, taunting. Moments flashed in her mind: *Her father's strong embrace... Justin's dirty frog... Kirk in his football uniform... Lovejoy's scotch, warm breath on her mouth... the Kansas City newsroom... Guy's silver Porsche... Jordy's quirky laugh... a heavy leg cast. Roe's boyish grin and his placid brown eyes watching her... the senseless nightmares of her alone, all alone, in a sea of nameless faces... the explosion of the photographer's flash.* She held the planner out in front of her. Then, opening her hand, slowly, she let go of it. The small leather planner plummeted in a spiraling free fall into the ocean.

Then, leaning forward without so much as a second thought, she flung herself over the ravine behind it.

"Casey... Casey!" It was Roe's sweet voice, mingled with the soft hum of the respirator and other mechanical things that beeped and pumped and whisked life and morphine into her veins. The pain was distant and fuzzy. Her senses were floating on clouds not connected, but hovering somewhere near her body. She could hear him, but his distant voice could not reach her. Not in this place.

Seconds after she had hit the water came the eeriest feeling of calm. And in an instant, she saw before her, emerging from the light... Nathaniel, her father. He was frowning and telling her to stay. "It's not your time, Princess, not yet."

*"But I want to go with you, Daddy—really. Why else would I
have jumped? Please, take me with you... Daddy!*

He only frowned and shook his head, retreating.

His image started to fade as the water got colder, drawing
her deeper in its rhythm until it lifted her up, depositing
her as if with human hands, onto a smooth rock. Divers on
their way to the Crater spotted her within minutes. They
rescued her and took her the mainland. An emergency
team met their boat and transferred her immediately to
the trauma center.

It was four days before she regained consciousness. The
island officials had turned the waterlogged planner over
for identification. It had washed ashore not fifty yards from
where Casey had jumped. Several business cards tucked in
the corner flap led them to Roe Evans, the owner.

He arrived the next day.

"Everything is going to be all right, Case... I promise. I
am so sorry, baby," she could hear him say, his words filter-
ing in the distance.

He kept vigil at her bedside for three days, feeding his
words over and over into her dreams, telling her that everything was going to be all right.

That's how she knew that it would be okay. Roe had said
so. And she believed him.

When he couldn't stay a moment longer, he kissed her
pale cheek, apologizing over and over. "I have to go now,
Sunshine... I'm sorry." He choked on the words, letting
them fall on her seemingly lifeless body along with his
tears.

She heard every word from somewhere deep and distant inside, where it counted for everything, and it had the
power, once again, to rescue her.

CHAPTER 30

★ ★ ★

"WHY DON'T YOU CONSIDER TAKING some time off?" Lucas looked insipid in his Lululemon shorts and sleeveless tank. His nose was peeling, and his lobster-red shoulders were well on their way. His pale skin rarely saw the sun. Now that he was away from his LA office and there in Maui, to monitor Casey's recovery, he was really racking up the UVs. They ate outside on the verandah of the Grand Wailea Resort, where Lucas had been staying on during the shooting of the remaining episodes of season two. He was determined not to leave without taking her with him.

"I'm fine, Lucas, really. I want to keep working."

"I understand, babe, but it's only been two months since—"

"Since I tried to kill myself? Jesus, just say it, Lucas. That's what happened. I know what I did was foolish; I realize that now. Don't you think I do? Shit!" Her eyes were bloodshot, and she looked ragged. All those weeks in confinement at the clinic made her appear thin and gaunt. She had lost her curvy figure and looked downright skeletal.

He stared at her and her untouched salad. His lunch sat uneaten as well, save for the numerous Bloody Marys he was tossing back like iced teas. "Yeah, of course you do. I know you're getting better, but the producers, they don't see it that way, you know?"

He had said it—the awful truth she had feared all along. She knew something bad was up when Lucas appeared on the set unannounced, all those weeks ago. Up until that morning, she had thought that Lucas was heading back to LA for good, where he belonged. He wouldn't continue to be on her ass twenty-four seven, babysitting her as if she were a helpless child.

The waiter approached, and Lucas ordered another Bloody Mary for himself and one for Casey. He was clueless about twelve-step programs and recovery. Her therapist had her on a strict regimen that definitely did not include alcohol. "Just give it to me straight," she demanded, fidgeting with a paper napkin that she had twisted into a knot.

"They want to cut Nikki. She's off the show."

He said it as if "Nikki" were someone else, and not connected to her in any real way.

"What?" Casey could feel the old panic returning to her gut.

"She's being shipped back to Vermont, or wherever the fuck she came from. They just don't want to continue with the character—with you. I'm real sorry, kid. What can I say? I tried every way to Sunday to convince them otherwise. You can't beat the machine."

She was speechless, but couldn't say that she was surprised. Finally, she asked, "When?"

"In a week. Script's already been written. These guys don't waste any time. Nikki will get an emergency call back home. You'll tape through next Friday, and that will be it." He belched matter-of-factly. "You'll be paid through the terms of the contract, of course, no changes there."

She nodded. Her head was whirring.

"Casey, I am—" he began to soften, a real stretch for Lucas.

"No, don't. Really, I'm fine. It's been wonderful. Every-one's been wonderful. I understand, really I do." She was struggling for control, fighting back tears.

The check arrived, and he quickly signed for it. "Sorry, kid."

She looked away. *So was she...*

"I'm not going to drop you," he said, as if he read her mind. "You're still signed with us—that is, if you want to be. I can always get you modeling bookings. You can take things as they come."

She noticed a family settle into a table near theirs; a mother and father with three boys, on vacation in their Hawaiian shirts and sandals. The scene seemed so surreal, all of it did.

"Sure. Yeah... I'd very much like to stay on with the agency."

"You'll need a place to stay when you get back to LA."

Her mind was adrift, flooded with so many thoughts, but frankly, this was not one of them.

He produced a toothpick from his pocket and checked the time. "I'll tell you what—you can stay with me. I have plenty of room, and I'm never around. Perfect roommate. We'll work out the details back in LA. Just until you get on your feet again, okay?"

Why was he doing this? Why was he being so human? she wondered. He never did anything without a motive. She was one of his clients, and supposedly, he had an obligation to her, but this was way over the call of duty. Then again, what choice did she have? "I'll think about it, okay?"

Lucas grinned, his Gucci aviators flashing in the sun-light. "Here's the address." He jotted some numbers down on a paper napkin in the shape of a pineapple. "It's in Turner Towers near Century City. The doorman's name is Victor—he'll set you up. I'll leave a key with him, if you should decide to take me up on the offer. It'll be waiting for you. Okay? You take your time deciding, but you have to be out of here at the end of next week."

"Thanks, Lucas." Casey felt like her world was completely spinning.

"Sure, babe. No problem. What are agents for?" He cracked his gum and smiled, slipping another glance at his watch. "I gotta sprint—got a thing." He gestured to a woman across the patio. She waved back, sun-kissed and stunning in a mesh mini sundress, carrying several shopping bags from the spa; her face hidden by a floppy hat and dark Chanel shades. She was the *thing* he had to do; some millionaire's bored wife, no doubt. Lucas was nothing if not predictable.

"See you back in LA, then?" he said.

Casey nodded. "I'll take you up on the offer—it will just be temporary, though, until I can find my own place."

"Great—see you back home then."

He was being nice, but she definitely didn't trust him. He was way too happy for her liking. She hated like hell to be indebted to him for anything.

"Oh, and keep a low profile, okay? Say nothing to the press or anyone about any of this. If somebody wants to talk to you, they are going to have to go through me or Kirsten first. Got that?"

"Sure. Got it," she said as she watched him slink away, feeling defeated and broken, and deeply fearing she had made a mistake, like she had just made a deal with the devil.

The return flight to LA was brutal. Raging turbulence tossed the plane in all directions, making her feel even sicker than she already was. Saying goodbye to everyone would have been unbearable. So, she just slipped out earlier that evening, before anyone would have noticed that she had even gone. Lee Ann, along with several of the cast members, were planning a farewell party for her at the sports bar at the Marriott. They would all be disappointed when they learned that she had taken an earlier flight off the island. *It was just easier this way*, she wrote Lee Ann in a note taped to the bathroom mirror. *Keep working hard, and think of me when you meet Spielberg someday.* She drew a rough sketch of an Oscar and signed her name with swirls and flourishes. Goodbyes sucked, and Casey was the worst at them. This would just have to do.

She knew that Roe cared enough to fly four thousand miles to see her in the hospital. But the gesture was tainted. He had left a note, which she did not receive until the day of her release, along with all of her other belongings. He had texted her right before he left to explain:

Princess, I stayed as long as I could. They told me that you would be all right. I've missed you.

She reached into her purse. She still had his organizer. It was given back to her with her belongings when she was discharged from the hospital. *Why didn't Roe take it with him?* she wondered. There were so many questions; things she wanted to ask him. She closed her eyes and felt the weight of the massive jet finally make contact with the runway. She turned on her phone and swiped the screen for her messages. There was another one from Roe:

I am moving to London to open a new office for the company. You are a star about to launch into spectacular horizons. I only wish the best for you, Casey. You deserve it. Shine brightly. Be well, my sweet. Roe.

The words felt so final. Pain arched through her heart like a volt of current. How could she lose something she never had? Once again, and quite likely for good, he was gone. Now, day after day, with each passing hour, she would work to try to get Roe Evans out of her mind. She had to. If ever she were to succeed at her dreams, and rebuild her life, she would have to let him go. Something in London had lured him and commanded him to stay—*or someone*— so powerful that even his feelings for her were no match to convince him otherwise.

Casey walked purposefully through the jetway. No one bid her welcome at the gate. She was well aware of just how alone she was. She would have to face another uncertain future.

She claimed her bags and then hailed a cab. Giving the driver Lucas's address, she settled in for the ride.

The doorman, Victor, had been off duty since four and was not on again until the morning. His replacement was a genteel silver-haired man who let Casey in with his master key. She had to leave a copy of her driver's license for security and sign a waiver.

"Just until Victor comes on in the mornin'," the old man explained, "and can verify that you are to receive a key," he said, reminding her of an elf with his charming accent and grandfatherly ways. He made Casey feel better in spite of everything.

"You're sure pretty enough, Miss," he said, escorting her into the ornate brass-and-marble elevator that would take them to the thirty-fifth floor. "Have I seen you on TV, or in a movie, yet?" he asked, his blue eyes twinkling. She figured that he took all of Lucas's guests to be clients.

He wasn't exactly the demographic for *Paradise Cove*, so she decided to skip mentioning it. "I don't think so." She smiled, focusing intently on the lighted number panel ticking off the floors as the car climbed directly to the penthouse. The elevator stopped, and the door lurched open. "Here we are, Miss. Mr. Morgan's suite—top o' the tower!"

He led the way, pausing at the entrance. An impressive urn adorned the threshold, and at least a half-week's newspapers were stacked, untouched, directly in front of the door. "Mr. Morgan will be back on Sunday, Miss," the old man explained, stooping to pick up the bundles.

"No bother," Casey said. "I'll take care of that."

She waited as he unlocked the door, stepping back gingerly to let her pass. "Well, goodnight then," he said, disappearing into the waiting elevator. In a moment, he was gone.

Casey pushed open the door and deposited her bags into the small marble foyer. It was an eerie homecoming, walking into Lucas Morgan's apartment without him there. She felt strangely like an intruder.

Maybe this was a mistake, she thought, questioning the decision once more as she slowly surveyed the surroundings. It was a large, modern suite. It had large picture windows overlooking the city from every angle. The spacious living room was expertly decorated with luxurious black leather couches, chrome lampstands, and expensive modern-print rugs. There were men's fitness magazines and copies of *GQ*, *Variety*, and *Hollywood Weekly* strewn on the coffee table; exquisite abstract sculptures, exotic plants, and provocative prints of naked women ensconced in light boxes. It appeared to not be lived in. It was cold and lifeless. She had expected nothing less.

She made her way through the rest of the apartment, surveying the dining room with its Scandinavian designs and sheer imported floor-to-ceiling drapes. The unit had three bedrooms, each smartly decorated in masculine tones of black and taupe, with contemporary accents and minimalist designs. The master bedroom was dark and smelled of Lucas's cologne from the doorway. She did not explore it any further than that. Only one of the other bedrooms had an adjoining bathroom of its own, so that's the one she claimed.

The kitchen was massive, with dark granite counters, gourmet pot racks, a center working island with expensive industrial quality range, built-in grill, state-of-the-art appliances, and artfully appointed faucets and gleaming ceramic tile flooring. The condo was the product of a high-paid designer, and the upkeep the handiwork of a twice-a-week housemaid.

In the scheme of things, she could have done a lot worse. It was bachelor-chic, all right, but it would definitely do. Warming to the idea, Casey decided to make the best of the situation and settle in. It was late and she was exhausted.

Casey slept for some twelve hours and awoke to the sounds of commotion in the next room. Someone had turned on a stereo, and the sounds of Rascal Flatts was pulsating through the apartment. She slid from beneath the covers and fumbled for her jeans from one of her many suitcases on the floor. Tentatively, she emerged from the bedroom, braless beneath a thin cotton camisole, barefoot and groggy. The aroma of fresh-made coffee and the sound of bacon crackling and popping in a skillet lured her to the kitchen.

To her surprise, a beautiful girl with gorgeous eyes and cupie-doll lips, swathed in a terrycloth bathrobe, was standing at the stove. Her golden blonde hair was cinched in a scrunchie on top of her head, and she wasn't wearing a fleck of makeup. Regardless, she looked as fresh and dewy as the eggs she was frying.

"Hi! You must be Casey. How do you like your eggs, darlin'?" Her accent was straight from the bless-your-heart backwoods of someplace like Arkansas or Missouri, and immediately, Casey gleaned that this one must have just fallen off the turnip wagon from some God-awful place.

"I'm sorry," Casey said. "You seem to know me, but who are you?"

"Oh—I'm Taylor. It's a pleasure to meet you. Lucas filled me in. He said that you'll be staying here a while with us. It'll be fun... just like a big ole pajama party."

Casey slid onto one of the tall stools near the counter and rubbed her temples. "You are his... *girlfriend*?" She couched the word carefully.

"Well, sort of. *We have an arrangement.* I just got into town last week. I signed with Lucas a month ago, but it took a little longer than I expected to get out here. He's puttin' me up just until I can find my own digs."

"Where are you from?" Casey asked.

"Cole Camp, Missouri. It's about ninety miles from Kansas City." She poured them each a cup of the strong brew and then looked intently at Casey. "Lucas told me that you were once the weather girl for KTBU back in Kansas, weren't you?"

"A long time ago," Casey said. "Tell me, Taylor from Cole Camp, Missouri... did you win a pageant or something?" Casey yawned after pitching the question.

"Yes. As a matter of fact, I did. I was Little Miss Corn Husk two years running, and most recently, second runner-up for the State Pageant. That's amazing that you picked up on that—how'd you ever guess?"

Casey smiled. She knew the route—first the child pageants, then local talent contests, various modeling agencies in the surrounding towns, a state crown or near-miss, and then finally, a headshot sent to an LA agent who takes a liking to your look, inviting you out on your own dime. "So, you're here to... do what exactly, may I ask?"

Taylor might have felt interrogated. It was obvious what Casey was implying, and she didn't appear to appreciate it.

Casey didn't care. The girl was no more than nineteen or twenty, and she was certainly a long way from home. She had not paid any dues, she hadn't made Lucas's agency any money. She was young and clueless, and to top it all off, they would be sharing living quarters like a couple of strays. If Taylor from Missouri knew what was good for her, she would hightail it right on back to Green Acres.

"I'm modeling right now. Very soon, Lucas says he is going to get me some acting work," Taylor said, with conviction. "My print work is good. As good as anything a city girl could turn out."

Touché! Casey liked the girl's spunk. She knew all too well how feisty farm girls could be. She wasn't exactly up for a hen fight. She would just have to make the best of it. It beat being alone with Lucas and the dangers that that situation could invite. Better that he had a new playmate to entertain him.

"I'm sorry," Casey said. "I didn't mean to insult you, really. I've just come off taping a television series, and I'm exhausted. Not really up for socializing."

"Sure. No problem," Taylor said, eyeing her apprehensively.

"Do you mind if I ask how old you are?" Casey asked with sudden renewed interest.

The girl scooped the eggs neatly onto a plate. "Eighteen this August. Lucas said, 'You know Casey Singer—Nikki from that *Paradise Cove* show? I can make you bigger than her someday.' He said to trust him. So here I am. I want to be an actress like you, Casey, on one of them TV sit-coms."

So that was it! Lucas intended on using her to groom his next protégé? The set up was so obvious; so convenient. What did she look like? A nanny? A babysitter?

"Is that right?" Casey said, smiling. "Do you have enough eggs there for two?"

Inside, she was seething. She would deal with Lucas as soon as he surfaced, and set him straight.

CHAPTER 31

★ ★ ★

LUCAS ARRIVED ON SUNDAY, BEARING gifts from his recent trip to Milan, spouting on about what a wonderful season it was for Cabernet. He showered and then slipped on his bathrobe and strutted around the place like King Dick.

Later that night there were over twenty people crammed in the apartment to welcome him back, all industry types, laughing and drinking and getting high on Lucas's drugs. Poor Lucas, he was far too stupid and too strung out to see that he was being used for his money and his coke. But Casey figured he used people too, so it was all fair in the end. She tried to act the part, chatting with thin, wasted women who came with their freaky boyfriends and lovers. All hangers-on. All Hollywood wannabes. She stayed up until two a.m., at which time things were still in no way winding down.

Casey had to chase a lip-locked couple out of her bed. They did not care, and just took their act to the couch, where they proceeded to copulate in full view of the other guests. Most everyone was too hedonistic or too wasted to care. She locked the bedroom door and buried her head beneath the pillow. What was happening? It was all so surreal.

Earlier that night, Lucas, in an inebriated state, had tried to kiss her. He cornered her in the kitchen, and, grabbing her ass, put his grimy mouth all over her, groping her breasts and pressing his cock into her leg. She shoved him off.

"Are you kidding me?" She pushed him hard against the sink.

"Aw, c'mon, baby... is this the thanks I get for taking you in?" Taylor appeared and ran interference, grabbing his hand and leading him to his bedroom.

"C'mon, baby, I'll show you gratitude," she said, eyeing Casey with baby blue daggers.

First chance I get, I'm out of here! Casey promised herself. It couldn't be soon enough. She was going to be a star. And this she knew with certainty—one way or another, Lucas was going to help her.

The next morning, Casey showed up at the agency. She approached the receptionist's desk and smiled. The girl, who had just unpacked a tall latte and muffin, was settling in to enjoy it before tearing into the giant stack of mail on her desk. A hundred résumés and composites a day crossed the door into The Morgan Agency. Everyone in Hollywood wanted to be the next Jennifer Lawrence or Channing Tatum.

"Hi. Is he here yet, *Rhonda*?" Casey asked, reading the nameplate next to the phone. She knew that Lucas would not be up for another half-hour, and then would go on to the gym, followed by a shower, trip to the juice bar, and then to the quick mart for the latest *Magnum* magazine and the *Wall Street Journal*.

"Health club," the girl offered dryly. "Then he's got a breakfast with Bob Haley, the executive director of Fox, a ten o'clock, an eleven o'clock, a massage at noon, lunch with a new scriptwriter at one—and who are you?"

"Casey Singer. I'm not a client, honey. I'm talent." It was obvious that Lucas went through receptionists like printer ink.

"It's like this from now until Christmas. If you want to get on his calendar, it will be about three months."

"No, I'm—" Casey stopped. What she really wanted was access to his office, not to see him. She thought quickly, and then asked, "Is his assistant, Trish, in?"

The annoyed receptionist shook her mane of extensions. "On vacation. She'll be back on Tuesday."

Casey's heart quickened. *This could work*, she thought to herself. "Mind if I pop back there a minute, Rhonda? Lucas had asked me to pick up something from his office my next trip by. I don't think I need Trish to help me find it." She reached into her Prada wallet and extracted a twenty. Placing it on the desk, she smiled. "Do you mind if I just go have a look?"

Rhonda was easy to peg. She was a temp with bills to pay and no idea where her next job was going to land. She gazed at the Jackson and raised a waxed eyebrow. Casey kicked in another twenty, and the girl buzzed her in.

Casey found Trish's desk just outside of Lucas's office at the end of the hall. His was a plush corner suite with expensive artifacts and large windows with a spectacular view that he kept concealed behind a veil of the tiniest micro-blinds she had ever seen. She had remembered having lunch with him back when she was just breaking out and wondering then why he kept his office so dark. *He thrives in the shadows,* she reasoned, *like a maggot.* She did not trust him in the least.

There was one thing only that she was interested in: his calendar of bookings and potential work on the horizon. She had already tried to see if she could ever find his smartphone lying around the condo unattended, but the control freak even took it into the bathroom with him when he showered. There was no separating Lucas from his precious portal of data, which was further password protected, along with all of his porn. She figured that Trish most likely backed up everything from Lucas's device on a regular basis onto her computer. She had hoped to do the same, only to transfer the information out of Trish's system into her own smartphone.

She took a seat at Trish's desk and flipped on the computer, making certain that no one was watching. It was far too early for the typing pool crowd, and most of the other agents didn't arrive until well after nine. She clicked on a few key icons, and within seconds, the screen displayed Lucas's entire schedule from then until 2020. She produced a white cord from her purse, attached it into her phone, and then plugged the other end into the back of the computer. She clicked onto iTunes, and the Mac whirred into action as the data was in full sync. A few short minutes and a few clicks later, the transfer was complete.

Cameron Hatch's film career was shaky, at best. He had made two domestic shorts, and although they each received recognition at the American Independent Film Festival, they never found mainstream acceptance, faring only slightly better at the box offices overseas. He was a visionary with a passion for the avant-garde, a style far more suited for audiences who embraced Indie films rather than that of the Hollywood set. When he had decided to produce *The Dress Maker*, a little Irish film about an immigrant seamstress who was born mute, he appealed to Lucas for a face; a perfect starlet to portray the fiery Bernadette. He had, as of yet, waited for Lucas to send him the perfect candidate, but without a finished script, Lucas was loath to comply.

Casey learned of the project while snooping through Lucas's notes he had left open on the mahogany dining table one morning, when he and Taylor were doing the

deed. His electronic calendar confirmed it. She had information on the projected filming site and start date of the
production: October twelfth the following fall—London,
England.

CHAPTER 32

★ ★ ★

MEANWHILE, PLANS WERE IN PLACE for up-and-coming actress Shay Sorrentino's return from Paris. She was one of Lucas's most lucrative commodities. Coming off *Mindbenders* with Keanu Reeves, two years prior, she had just recently completed a romantic comedy in a film with Clooney that was slated for release some time in the summer. Shay was an overnight success that took ten years in the making. Her remarkable debut three years prior in Paramount's epic blockbuster, *Maximillion,* won the then-twenty-two-year-old actress a Golden Globe nomination, and she had not slowed down since. Now with the phenomenal success of *Jilted*, she was poised to turn any role she took on to gold.

Shay was a director's dream. She had natural talent and keen business sense. She was making Lucas a very rich man, and by the looks of the way in which she regarded him, it was clear to see who was in control. She could dump him at any time for representation with any number of mega-agents vying for her attention.

Shay's homecoming back to LA was not to be overshadowed by the fact that it would be her twenty-fifth birthday. It was Lucas's self-proclaimed purpose in life to treat her to the birthday party of the millennium. He had rented out Tank, one of LA's most trendy nightclubs, and a hired event planner extraordinaire, Gaylord Ross, to oversee arrangements. Tank was a trendy new haunt that only those in the know would gain admittance to, as it was strictly by invitation only. Lucas had gone all out. He ordered a ten thousand-piece balloon drop, search lights and red rope stanchions at the entrance, and hired an up-and-coming alternative band out of Norway to play all night. He plastered large glossy promotional photographs of Shay all over the walls of the nightclub, custom-ordered an eight-foot birthday cake, and handpicked the beefcake male dancers to mingle with and pump up the crowd. A buffet of barbiturates and hallucinogens were ordered and were on hand, out of view, but easily accessible to anyone for the asking.

The party was to be exclusive, but everyone who was anyone in Hollywood knew that such restrictions could never be kept. Two rag magazine editors were on the guest list, and the others had staff members posing as guests at the ready to crash the party. There were photographers crawling for blocks, hoping to get a shot of the privileged few who were granted entry into Shay's big soiree.

Lucas was a basketcase the days leading up to the bash. He was boorish and more cynical than usual at work and an impossible bastard at home. Casey and Taylor aptly stayed out of his warpath. Mostly, Casey stayed in her room, reading scripts and even attempting to write one. She was working on a one-act scene that would serve as her signature audition monolog.

Later, Casey learned that the bottled blonde in the large hat who Casey remembered seeing waving at Lucas in Maui, was moving in. Her name was Holly, and incidentally, she had become the newest member of the cast of *Paradise Cove* upon Nikki's departure as her long-lost ball-busting cousin, Victoria West. Casey wanted to retch when she found out. She acted unaffected when Lucas mentioned in passing conversation that Holly had gotten the part. "You remember Holly, don't you? She was with me in

Maui... "

Screw you, Lucas! Casey was incensed. Luckily, the show's ratings didn't reflect a booming reception in any demographic, and last Casey heard, the show was being dropped. This gave her far more pleasure than any news she had heard in a very long time.

On occasion, Holly would pop in and stay for several days, causing Taylor to have to move from Lucas's bedroom back to her own—most likely causing her to regret not originally claiming the guest room with the adjoining bathroom, which Casey had laid claim to and would never relinquish. It was a degrading and cruel game he was playing with their lives, giving each girl just enough booze, drugs, and sex to keep them hungry and coming back for more. From her bedroom, Casey could often hear Taylor's sobs as she cried herself to sleep at night.

Lucas Morgan was the truest bastard to every draw breath. With Casey, though, he was different. It took him several tries and a stiletto to the balls for him to get the message that she was not putting out for a roof over her head. He left her alone after that, and that suited her just fine.

Casey crossed paths with Taylor in the ladies' room at the party. It was a circus of primping and chatter, hair spray and gossip. Everyone was going on about Shay and about how thin and raw-boned she looked, secretly despising her for it. They were all angling for how they would get Lucas's attention for themselves. Those who didn't already have a deal were posturing for limelight out on the floor, working their fifteen minutes of fame for all it was worth.

Taylor emerged from the stall, pale and peaked. It was no

mystery to Casey why. She had suspected for several weeks. Only two things could have been the cause, and Casey was all too familiar with both. She was pretty certain that Taylor was not too keen on making herself vomit for vanity's sake, so it had to be the second possibility.

Casey rinsed a hand towel under cold water and handed it to her.

"How far along are you?"

"Two months, maybe three. I'm not sure." She breathed into the towel.

"Is it his?"

She nodded.

"Are you positive?"

"What? That I'm pregnant, or that it's his?"

Casey felt sorry for Taylor.

"Oh, I'm sure, all right. Sure on both counts." She dabbed her mascara-streaked cheeks with a tissue and faced herself in the mirror. "Shit."

Casey touched her shoulder and then pulled her in for a hug, holding her as she cried.

For the next couple of months, Casey did her best to avoid Lucas as much as possible. She mostly dealt with his office directly for photo shoots and auditions. The winter market was dragging, and the offers were slow in coming. She managed to snag a catalog shoot that had four days worth of work in Burlington, North Carolina. When she returned, Taylor was gone. No explanation. All her things were missing, and not a trace remained.

"It didn't work out for her here," was all Lucas said. "She up and left."

Two days later, a petite Asian girl named Nya moved in.

CHAPTER 33

★ ★ ★

CASEY STUFFED THE BILLS INTO an envelope and then affixed an overnight label to the outside pouch. It was chump change to Lucas—five hundred thirty dollars. It was everything she could find on his bureau and after checking all of his pants' pockets. He would suspect the new girl, Nya, or one of her freak-strung-out-friends. They were all shifty and bizarre, every last one of them.

Casey had discovered that Nya was not even listed with the agency. She was just one of Lucas's little whores he had picked up at one of the clubs, or online, no doubt. She had a ready and willing array of female lovers who literally came and went in and out of the condo at all hours that she was happy to invite into she and Lucas' bed.

Lucas never knew how much money he had at any given time anyway so she doubted he would even miss it. She addressed the envelope to Dorothy Hunt, 21 Rural Lane, Cole Camp, Missouri, then added the zip code and several stamps. She would drop it off at the post office when she checked her post box. She had been waiting all month for a special package of her own. Pushing through the revolving door, she stepped into the bustling street. It was nearly nine a.m., and she had work to do.

After the post office, her next stop was Cups Café. She ordered wheat toast, two poached eggs, and coffee. Armed with a stack of industry magazines, she combed through them with a red marker. Nearly fifty subscriptions arrived at the condo each month. Lucas was a glutton for information, though he barely read more than a few pages of any of them. The only one of any interest to Casey was *Variety*. She had lifted the current copy from the coffee table before leaving that morning and then purchased four others from a drug store on the way. *Rolling Stone, Stage & Screen,* and *Entertainment Review*—the usual fare. She also had the LA classifieds open and was scanning them for all open auditions. She also perused the entertainment sections for any news about Roe and Castle Records. She was able to find some information on the whereabouts of the current London office. There was, however, no mention about a new office opening, or any artist releases in the spotlight.

She retrieved her smartphone from her purse and paused. Sadly, her contact list was short and only contained one entry that mattered to her—Roe Evans. She punched in the address for the London office and smiled. *Roe... sweet, wonderful Roe. I wonder what you're doing right now; right this very minute.* She berated herself for dreaming. Why did she torture herself?

Next, she scanned the ads in the magazines for leads. The quicker she was able to find a viable project, she figured, the quicker she could extricate herself from Lucas. The work was not coming in as promised, and she knew that his "generosity" had its limits. What worked for her in the past was no longer necessary. She didn't need to bed Lucas to keep his attention. She had already proven herself. What she needed was work.

The waitress appeared. She refilled Casey's cup and gave her a knowing glance. "Anything promising out there?" she asked, referring to the newspaper.

"No—big surprise, right? What is it with this town?"

"That's why I wait tables," the woman said. "If I left it all up to my agent, I'd starve to death. They don't call it *waiting* tables for nothin'."

Casey smiled nervously, touching the bulky package she had burning in her purse. "Who is your agent?"

"I am!"

They both laughed. The woman was attractive, middle-aged, and had a great way about her. Casey thought that she would be great for any number of commercial projects. Instead, she was stuck there at the diner, serving bacon grease and day-old apple pie.

Casey grabbed the check and the *Variety*, leaving several dollars and the other magazines on the table. On a second thought, she fumbled through her wallet for one of Baltimore's business cards and tucked it beneath the plate. Then she headed up the boulevard to Lucas's office.

Casey stormed right in. He was in the middle of dictating a letter. Both he and Trish startled at the intrusion.

"What did you do, Lucas?"

"What?" He was clueless, as usual.

Trish was notably not amused. "Hello, Casey," she said, rolling her eyes and moving closer to the desk phone.

Never mind that Trish was an old maid at thirty-seven. Her biggest problem was that she dedicated her miserable life to serving a boss like Lucas. She protected him like a mother hen.

"Why don't you get us all some lattes, Trish, okay?" Lucas said, cutting her loose.

"And for you, Casey? Would you care for anything, or are you not staying?" Trish asked, in an annoying falsetto.

"No, thanks. I'll just be a minute."

Trish huffed, hightailing it out of there. The errand would be good for ten minutes of Lucas's undivided attention. It would take far less than that for Casey to say what was on her mind.

Lucas leaned back in his chair and cracked his knuckles, drawing a cocky grin. "I assume you are referring to Miss Taylor Hunt?"

"I am," she said, her heart pounding. *C'mon asshole, lie like the bastard you are.*

"She just wasn't cut out for the business. Didn't have the chops, I suppose." He grabbed a rubber ball off the junk on his desk and began to squeeze it. "Although she did have talent, I'll give you that—too bad, really." He bounced the ball off of the far wall, and she caught it midair.

"Bullshit! Like you don't know why she *had* to leave?"

"I don't know what you're talking about. Now, what is so important that you had to barge in here? I'm working here, in case you hadn't noticed. Can I have my ball back, please?"

She dropped a copy of *Variety* onto his desk, causing a small avalanche of memos and reports to tumble onto the floor.

He eyed the glossy cover. It was a bad photograph of Gwyneth Paltrow, trying to be a brunette.

"So?"

"Page sixteen. I marked it for you. It's a piece on Cameron Hatch. I want to be considered for the lead in his current project, *The Dress Maker*. I know that it's filming in London."

"And you want me to arrange it? Set up a reading for you?"

"Yes. That's exactly what I want," she said, giving the rubber ball a firm squeeze.

"Well, I can't do it. I'm sorry."

"Why not?"

"Because."

"Because, why?" she asked, her face reddening.

"Well, for one, Casey, I haven't seen the script. How would we even know if it was the right part for you?"

She reached into her shoulder bag and produced a thick brass clip-bound manuscript and smiled. "You mean, this? Is this the script you mean?"

He leaned forward in his chair and narrowed his eyes. "Where? How did you get that?"

She added it to the pile on his disheveled desk and placed the rubber ball on top. "Don't ever underestimate me, Lucas—I'll always surprise you." The ball cracked in half like a magician's trick.

His eyes darted between the screenplay and the ball with disbelief.

"I'll wait until you finish it," she offered. "I'm planning on reading scene four—the one in the smokehouse, when she meets her father for the first time and he doesn't recognize her. Let me know what you think."

She turned to leave, treating him to a glimpse of her backside. "And if you think that Trish is taking good care of you, well, I'd think twice. You wouldn't want to leave yourself *exposed*."

He laughed nervously, left with the destroyed ball on top of the manuscript, looming on his desk. She was certain that he was damned if he knew anything at all.

Casey had exited Lucas's office, but not the building, stopping off on the second floor to use the restroom. When she was certain that no one was watching, she slipped into an empty conference room and punched an outside line. She dialed a number taken from Lucas's digital planner—it was an overseas extension. It took the crackling connection several seconds to connect, and then a faint, quick series of rings sounded on the other end of the line.

"Cameron Hatch here."

"Hello, Cameron, this is Trish Landry from Lucas Morgan's office in Los Angeles. We wanted to thank you for sending the script. Mr. Morgan has it now and is reading it. He saw the piece in *Variety* and was thrilled. He's so glad to see that the project is underway."

"Well, that's wonderful... you don't know how encouraging this is."

"Yes, indeed."

"I'm so glad that Lucas changed his mind. I am sure that with the right casting, it will be smashing."

"We have someone in mind already. We're just checking her availability. We'll be in touch," Casey said, quite pleased with herself. It would have been easy enough to Google Cameron's office posing as Trish to try and bypass his assistant, but why bother when she had his direct line right there at her fingertips?

"Thank you so much," Cameron said. "Looking forward to a meeting. Cheerio!"

CHAPTER 34

★ ★ ★

CASEY DESPISED NYA. EVEN PRINCESS, the cat who belonged to Nya, avoided her for unknown reasons that Casey could only imagine. The discerning feline was content to stay on Casey's pillow instead, or slumber on the windowsill. Luckily, Lucas was allergic to cats, so he had even more motivation to keep a respectable distance from Casey's bedroom. Her bathroom, however, was another story. Nya habitually helped herself to Casey's personal things, and it drove her crazy. She constantly used her makeup, perfume, and even took several prescription vials. When she went for Casey's shoes, it was war.

"That's it!" Casey raged. She was at her wit's end with the unruly roommate. She had no recourse but to retaliate. She replaced the contents of a bottle of expensive shampoo with hair remover. It was childish and ruthless, but Casey did not care. She would be happy to teach the little nymph a lesson. Three days later, she heard a scream come from the hallway bathroom. Casey smiled, satisfied that the showdown would end in her favor. *That'll teach you to mess with my things,* Casey raged to herself. The very next day, Nya came home with a short-cropped hairstyle that bordered on bald. With her distinctive Asian features, she looked like a teen boy. Casey was vindicated.

Lucas and the girls' escapades continued. They slept in all weekend and partied all night. It was nothing to stumble over bodies lying on the living room floor after a wild debacle, or to find strangers leaving the condo at all hours of the morning. Once, Casey awoke to the sound of running water and found a stoned-out anorexic girl she had never seen before standing in her shower—fully clothed, tripping on acid. An ambulance had to be called. The evening that she returned home from a movie to find Lucas and Nya on the couch engaging in sex with a young black girl was the end for Casey. Lucas would definitely be made to pay for what he did to women. He made them need him, and then he took what he wanted and discarded them. Casey knew that he was not interested in her career. He was only interested in what he could gain for himself. He exceeded professional boundaries, and he ruined people's lives. All she could think about was poor Taylor. For that reason alone, she decided to take him down. The only remaining question was how?

She would get Lucas where it counted. He wouldn't even know what hit him. It was the only way to settle the score with him and to get what she really wanted all along. She already had all of Lucas's appointments synced on her digital phone, but she could get more—all of his pin numbers, passwords, and accounts. She could download all of his client information, talent files, invoices, financials—contact numbers. It would be easy enough to do.

Casey packed her things and moved out the next morning, into a four-star hotel downtown. She donned a long dark wig and checked in under the name Liz Frechette, posing as a Canadian consultant. No one knew a thing about her. She was a mystery. An enigma. It felt wonderful. Living life under a shroud of anonymity gave her a rush.

"I'm here on business for the Lucas Morgan Agency,"

she told the front desk manager. "I'll be conducting staff evaluations, sometimes here at the hotel. Privacy is paramount during the length of my stay, as well as complete discretion. I will require a fully appointed suite for at least two weeks; all charges will go to Mr. Lucas's account." She knew that Lucas had set up clients in the hotel in the past, so no further questions were asked.

"No problem, Ms. Frechette. How does the Westwood Suite sound?"

It sounded perfect and was even more spectacular than she had imagined. The luxury suite featured two bedrooms, each with sizable master baths and fireplaces; a parlor, a dining room, full kitchen, fully equipped office, state-of-the-art entertainment room, and a small gym. "I'm home!" Casey shouted after the bellman retreated and the door to the garishly opulent suite was closed.

Her task was clear: she would infiltrate Lucas's computer files this time and get it all—his coveted contact list; all the names, addresses, and phone numbers of every actor, agent, writer, director, producer, and promoter in Hollywood and beyond. She would have his lifeblood, all right. And the color was gold. She would make a backup of everything. Then, once she had his attention, he would be desperate to retrieve his precious data—at any cost. She wasn't interested in stealing from him, really. She was just planning on withholding a little intellectual collateral; enough to make him very agreeable to her terms. It would be simple enough, but first things first—she would ditch the wig, strike up the fireplace, draw a Jacuzzi bath, and pop open the bubbly chilling in the fridge. After all, she would hate to put all the wonderful amenities to waste.

The next morning, she was up early and ready to get to work. She phoned a local florist, ordering up an exotic arrangement of flowers to be delivered to his office with explicit instructions to have his assistant, Trish, sign for them personally. This was key. Casey knew that The Falling Leaf only delivered as far as the building lobby, so Trish would have to get up from her desk and go to the main security desk, sixteen floors down; a venture that would take approximately fifteen to twenty minutes. It was plenty of time for Casey to do the deed. The important thing being that she make it all appear to be an accident. According to Lucas's calendar, he was in Georgia, golfing in a tournament for the Guild, and wouldn't be due back for another three days, and Trish had free rein of the office—that's when she would get sloppy.

Casey waited in the lobby until she saw Trish emerge from the first elevator bank. She had decided to wear the wig as part of her disguise. Dark sunglasses and a Hermes scarf further concealed her identity. A thousand times or more, she had walked through that lobby in the past. No one recognized her. She felt like a spy, or one of those paperback novel-type private eye's who solved crimes in Pradas and packed heat along with their lethal double Ds. She had to giggle at the irony of it all—she was an actress by trade, so playing the part was a piece of cake.

Quickly, she slipped, unnoticed, into the very same elevator car that Trish had exited and headed up. She stepped off on floor sixteen and headed down the back hall leading to the kitchenette, bypassing the receptionist. Once inside, she hurried past half-empty offices and deserted conference rooms. It was Friday at five to five. Most everyone was long gone for the weekend.

She approached Trish's desk and re-synced her smartphone once again with Lucas's current files. She shoved the phone back into her purse and looked over at Lucas's office. Her good fortune was almost too much to believe—the nitwit had left Lucas's door open. Trish was a heavy smoker and had obviously been sneaking cigarettes in the clandestine sanctuary of her boss's office. Only with Lucas safely out of town would she be bold enough to actually light up at his desk. He smoked in there all the time, having no regard for the rules, but he would never allow his staff to follow suit. Only Lucas Morgan was permitted to break the rules. The privacy of the large mahogany door and concealing panels of micro-blinds were inviting to a secretary too fat and lazy to relegate her puff sessions to the designated smoking room on the twentieth floor.

Casey could not believe her luck. She had planned on spilling coffee on both their keyboards after she had downloaded what she came for, but this? This was a gift!

Quickly, she grabbed a sheet of letterhead and ignited the end of it with a lighter she found in the top drawer of Lucas's desk. She waved the makeshift torch directly under the sprinkler jets. Within seconds, the system went off. She extinguished the flame and wadded up the evidence, shoving it into her purse. Water spewed everywhere, and alarms sounded loudly, sending dazed office workers into the hallways and stairwells. Within seconds, Lucas's desk was drenched with torrents of water. Everything was soaked.

Casey worked fast in the commotion, back at Trish's desk to perform a few commands, calling up Lucas's address directory and appointment files and deleting them

with several adept clicks of the mouse; an operation worth every excruciating minute she had spent on a date with the geek from The Computer Shack the week prior to learn how to do it. Information came easy when one was blonde and nearly famous, especially in Beverly Hills. Instantly, all of Lucas's electronic files were deleted, and any hard copies he might have had were surely destroyed in the torrential downpour pounding his desk and file cabinets. A burning ember from a cigarette left unattended would be found to be the culprit, and Trish would be long gone before anyone could utter the words, *you're fired.*

Lucas rightfully blew a gasket when he was called back to the office from his trip, right around the time that the first invoice from the Four Seasons arrived in his mailbox for Casey's stay at the luxury hotel. Casey was lounging comfortably in a bathrobe and slippers, eating the large chocolate-dipped berries she had ordered from room service. She had originally planned on leaving a simple but direct message for Lucas on his voice mail, but he picked up instead, growling into the phone. "CASEY! What in the fuck is going on?"

"Hello, Lucas. Having some unexpected troubles? Perhaps we should talk."

CHAPTER 35

★ ★ ★

CASEY HAD LUCAS MEET HER that afternoon at Harpy's, a bar of her choosing, located just east of Hollywood and Vine. It was a neighborhood-type haunt. Nothing special, just a couple of dartboards, a few pool tables, and one of those antiquated bowling machines with the heavy silver puck that looked like a paperweight and skidded on rosin toward the flat bank of pins. It reminded her of a bar she once went to with her father when she was around nine years old, back in Chicago. She would sit on a high stool at the bar and watch him play pool. It was there that she had her first taste of ginger ale. She remembered how the place smelled like beer and Old Spice and how it made her feel so grown up to be there, just her and her dad. Harpy's was exactly the kind of place that Lucas would never be caught dead in, so it was perfect.

She waited for him in a back booth. She was wearing a baseball cap, a designer T-shirt, and tattered jeans. She had just come from the gym and was finishing off a turkey burger and a basket of potato skins. Lucas, on the other hand, was on his way to an important client meeting and was uncomfortably stuffed into a Hugo Boss double-breasted gabardine suit sans the tie. His chin was marred with nicks, and he was in need of a haircut. In haste, he had slicked down the sides of his thinning strands, making him look like a clown. He was clearly off his game. It was obvious that he had little time to spare. And from the looks of him, his blood pressure had suffered as well.

The waitress arrived with a glass of ice water for him, and he waved her off.

"I need to be across town in less than an hour, and the 405 is shit. You care to explain what the fuck this is?" Large veins were protruding from his neck, as he shoved the hotel invoice in her face.

She remained calm. "It's an invoice for my hotel accommodations, I presume. I have to stay somewhere. Your little playmates have made it impossible for me to live at the apartment."

His face reddened. "You suck, Casey, you know that? I'm not paying for this. It's bullshit! You were living at my place for free. You just think that you can get away with whatever you want, don't you? You're fucking crazy!"

"I'll take that as a compliment," she said, staring him down in the dim light. "Do you have any idea why I asked you to come here, Lucas?"

"No clue, but I'm sure you will enlighten me."

"Now, I'm just as anxious to get out of your life as you are to get rid of me. But, unfortunately, I have a three-year contract that says I work for you. That means you have to place me. If you don't utilize me, you don't make money. Right?"

"What are you getting at, Casey?" His forehead was beading with sweat, but he did not remove his suit jacket. He wiped his face with a napkin.

"How do you expect to make any money if you don't have your precious contacts and client files?"

"What?"

"Your files. You know—pity how they all perished in the 'accident.'"

"How do you—? You *bitch!*"

Casey beamed. Not her finest, but it was a proud moment indeed. "Relax. I have all your precious data safely stowed away. All of it."

He blinked wildly with mounting fury. "How do I know that's true?"

She held up her phone and gave it a swipe, giving him a quick gratuitous look at the contents on the screen. It was all there, his entire client list and personal contacts for starters. "You want to think twice before you underestimate me, Hoss."

"I don't fucking believe this!" Lucas stood up, causing a scene that made the two tourists at the bar look over.

"Oh, but there's more. Sit down, dickhead," Casey said, adding a bluff to the deal to sweeten the stakes. "I also have drafted an e-mail that I am prepared to forward to each and every one of your contacts, announcing the folding of the Lucas Morgan Agency, as it seems that you have decided to sell your little empire to start up a flash-frozen ice cream franchise in Santa Monica that was always your life's dream. Would you care to see a copy?" She pulled up the draft and whisked it off to him with a flourish. His phone dinged as the fated e-mail arrived in his queue.

From the look on his face, it was evident that he would kill her if he did not need her to release his contacts and lifeblood.

She continued, "They're all ready to go. Not to mention the blasts on Twitter and Facebook as well, announcing the shut down of your agency. I'd say the news could have you leveled in a matter of weeks, or even days, once everyone starts bailing and the lawsuits from the default on talent contracts start pouring in. Yeah, I'd say it's all going to start *pouring down*, like some freak sprinkler going amok in a corner office."

She had definitely hit a nerve. "Jesus Christ, Casey! What do you want from me? Money—is that it? How much?

How much will it take to get you off of my balls and out of my fucking life?"

She frowned, looking innocent and a tad disheartened by the blow. "You don't have to be a total asshole about it, Lucas. This is business, right? Besides, it's not your money I want."

He smirked. "Yeah, right! And I'm the son of Elvis— fuck you, you witch!"

She scooped up her keys, dropped a twenty on the table, and shouldered her gym bag. "This conversation is over. I have to go back to my hotel room and send some e-mails. *Ciao!*"

He reached across the table and grabbed her arm. The look in his eyes was manic. He squeezed hard until she sat back down. He could have snapped it off in an LA second; or paid someone to do it.

"What do you want?" he said between clenched teeth.

"I want three things." She looked at him dead-on. "One, I want out of my contract with the agency."

"Done," he said. "*And...?*"

"And... I want the lead part in Cameron's movie; the one shooting in the fall in London, as a free agent."

"That's it? What's number three?"

"You will contact Taylor and do the right thing by that child. You will own your responsibilities—for the duration."

He barely hid his relief. Now it was his turn to push back. "That's all you want in exchange for returning all of my data and not sabotaging my company?" His laugh was cocky and infuriating.

"Yes, that's all I want—and for you to stop being such a prick to women."

He threw back his head and roared. "You are some piece of work, Singer. So, if I do all that... you'll call off the dogs?"

She nodded.

"No masse-mails—no social media homicide—no bloodshed?"

"No. And you'll get everything back—well, digitally, anyway."

"Well, I think I just might be able to do that. Yeah—deal."

"Good," Casey said. "Everything has been saved to a flash drive. It's in a safe place. Deliver me the deal, and I'll deliver you the data. It's as simple as that."

CHAPTER 36

★ ★ ★

BALTIMORE HAD FIRST HEARD ABOUT the casting call in March, when he flew to New York for an agency seminar. He had dinner with his college buddy, Garrett Thompson, and his wife, Merrill. Garrett was a set designer, and Merrill spent her time co-producing a news show for Global Network, number three in the major market race for ratings.

It was the first time that Baltimore had ever met Merrill, and she was every bit as charming and witty as Garrett painted her to be. The two had met in graduate school and didn't marry until ten years, and two failed marriages between them, later. With dual television careers, and no children, they had nothing holding them back. Truth being, they were like a couple of teenagers, still crazy in love after a decade already behind them of wedded bliss.

"Sorry that Connie couldn't make it. I was really looking forward to seeing her."

"Didn't want to take any chances with the pregnancy. Doctor says it's best for her not to fly," Baltimore explained, regarding addition number three to the Ramirez clan. "We're all going to Puerto Rico when it is all over to see her family. She can't wait."

"For the baby, or for the trip?" Garrett asked good-humoredly.

"Both!" Baltimore said, grinning.

The couple smiled. It was great when old friends could get together and laugh and reminisce. They talked about the usual fare: old times, the best places to eat around town, overdue vacations, work life, and life in general. Merrill let it slip somewhere around dessert that her network had big plans for a weekday woman's talk show scheduled to air in the spring. "It's slated to compete with the tired old model of dinosaurs hashing out yesterday's headlines. It is expected to draw a newer, younger demographic. It will have wide appeal with women, but with a real *edge*. It will do for the industry what HBO did for cable, and Kimmel did for late night."

"Really?" Baltimore was intrigued.

"Oh yeah, " Merrill said. "It's going to be unlike anything out there. Supposed to blow the doors off the snooze-fest talking heads currently sinking in the afternoon ratings war. It will be the greatest thing since late night—only daytime banter and even better."

"Exactly how do they intend to do that?"

"With the anchors. Each will be a well-known personality, diversified in age range and backgrounds, but these gal-pals will be bigger than life, sort of like Real Housewives meet real topics and real people. Still searching for the perfect divas to fill the couch. The aim is to create a show that offers viewers a slice of life bigger and better than their own. *It's not your mother's talk show*—that's the tag line."

"Merrill came up with that. Clever, huh?" Garrett said, spearing the olive in his dirty martini like a pro. "People like celebrities, and celebrities are never boring. You know, like when crazy girlfriends get together and blow it up. From what I understand, they're still casting."

"Who's making the decisions?" Baltimore asked, tipping

his hand. His interest now peaked to new heights.

"Bumpy Friedman—the executive producer," Merrill added. "He's here in New York, but ultimately, he'll be making the decision, along with the parent company."

"The guy's at the top out in Holly*weird*," Garrett offered, proving that, apparently, Baltimore was the only one at the table—possibly in the entire industry—who was out of the loop on this.

"*Anchors,* you say? So they are looking for more than one? Well, Merrill! You've got to get us in there. We have great talent at Chase, and—"

She cut him off, fearing that she had said too much already. "You'll have to wait like everyone else, Balt. You know I can't divulge trade secrets." She slurred her words a bit, slightly tipsy from the wine. She nuzzled against Garrett's arm like a schoolgirl.

"She's not kidding, man. It's top secret. I sleep with her, and still—I can't get the scoop on the people they're thinking about hiring."

"Geez—this is HUGE! I haven't heard or read a thing. Nothing's buzzing on the coast. C'mon, Merrill, how many hosts will there be? Just tell me that."

"Four." She gifted him with the first critical confidence. "It's hush-hush, Balt. I'm serious. They'll have my uterus for this—really." She sighed. "They're media-types, you know—not exactly hard-core journalists, but not all fluff either. Casting's primarily out of New York—that's probably why you haven't heard."

Baltimore posed a question: "If they're starting up in spring, they've got to be close to final casting, right?"

Merrill smiled dreamily at the crème brûlée that the waiter had just deposited in the center of the table. She was loath to talk about work on weekends.

But Baltimore was persistent. "C'mon, who am I going to tell? How many have they already signed?"

She held up several limp fingers and cracked up.

"Two? Three? One? What is it? How many, Merrill—c'mon!"

Finally, she formed a "three," which took two of her hands to accomplish.

Garrett shifted uncomfortably. "She doesn't get out much... I swear."

Merrill fake-punched her husband's arm. "*Pooky!*"

Baltimore didn't care; he was just happy that this was the night she chose to let loose. He figured he'd go for broke.

"Who's left? What type do they still need?"

Merrill frowned when Garrett pulled her half-full glass of Chardonnay from in front of her. "Hmmm... Miss Generation X!" She drew an "X" in the air. "Tell you, if I were twenty-five years younger, I'd go out for it myself! It would be such a sweet deal... "

"Yeah," Garrett offered. "I hear that Friedman received over a thousand resumes from inside tips alone."

Baltimore grinned. He had a kind, bashful way about him when he got a flash of brilliance.

Merrill was fading fast and yawning uncontrollably. "Well, they're still on the hunt for host number four. If you think you might know a brash, hot twenty-something with half a brain and a mouth for the censors, you'd better get in there. I guess, so far, no one's been right."

"As a matter of fact," Baltimore said as he brightened, "I think I just might."

Baltimore could not dial fast enough. He had just returned from New York and mapped out the best proposal of his career entirely on the plane ride home. Chase Modeling Agency meant little to the Wall Street-types, but they did pay attention to Hollywood. With big box office clout the likes of which Lucas Morgan was capable of delivering, he, if anyone, could get Casey's name in the hopper for consideration with Global Network.

He hadn't spoken to her since she got back from Maui. He didn't say a word about her "accident" or the tragedy at the Redwines. He had been at Ian's memorial, and did not have to wonder why she wasn't. He never mentioned Lucas either, or the buzz about her being fired from the television show. None of it was news to those in "the know."

The line rang for an eternity before being snatched up by a sleepy Nya, who had been napping on the huge leather couch. *Jerry Springer* was on the tube in the background. She sounded like she had a whopper of a hangover. The noise of a housekeeper vacuuming in the distance didn't help matters. He could hardly hear her Minnie Mouse voice.

"Hello? Morgan residence," she said as she yawned.

"Yes, is Lucas there, please? It's imperative that I speak with him."

"Hey, man, have you tried his office? I think he's working or whatever. " Feigning interest was not her strong suit.

"No—I just tried. No one is answering there. Doesn't he have an admin?"

"Beats me." She couldn't have been more correct.

Baltimore's tone intensified. "Well, if you see him, could you tell him that I'm looking for him? It's Baltimore... Baltimore Ramirez from Chase Modeling Agency. This is very important—it's about Casey Singer. Are you getting all this, young lady?"

"Uh-huh . . ." He could tell that she was pretending to be writing it all down. Then, much to his surprise, she offered. "Did you try the hotel?"

"Excuse me?"

"DID YOU TRY THE HOTEL?" she shouted into the phone stupidly, as if Baltimore was suddenly hard of hearing. "She might still be there... maybe; or maybe not. I heard that she was leaving for London to do some film."

"Which hotel? Do you happen to know?"

"The Four Seasons... I think. Yeah. Good luck, mister."

The line went dead. She was done being helpful. It must have taken far too much energy. He was heading out of his office with keys in hand to the parking garage. The call went through as he slid into his car. The front desk immediately connected him to the hotel operator. "Casey Singer's room, please," he said, pulling out of the stall, and then stopped with a jolt.

"I'm sorry, sir. No one by that name is registered here."

Four days later, Casey had a ticket to London, an audition with Cameron Hatch and his production team, and Roe's address burning in her pocket. *Maybe,* she thought. Maybe there was something to salvage. How else would she ever know? She did still have Roe's leather planner. She would take the opportunity to return to him what was rightfully his, and possibly to claim for herself what was rightfully hers—the truth.

CHAPTER 37

★ ★ ★

LONDON, ENGLAND

THE SIGHT OF PICCADILLY STREET was something straight from a Dickens novel. Casey wasn't a bit tired from the journey, and the jet lag had not hit her yet. She decided to explore the area. Every doorway, every storefront, every passing face was a discovery. She felt an underlying reassurance in knowing that she was now closer to Roe and that they were no longer an ocean apart. Just knowing this made her feel invincible.

She stepped into a pub off of the main thoroughfare. It was dark and warm inside, with a trilling buzz of chatter and laughter. Televisions were glowing in the bar light just like back home. People crowded the bar, ate, drank, and flirted with one another just like in any other bar in any American city. Not much seemed different, except for the accents.

"Hi, I'm Emma," came a voice above the din. "Pleased to meet you. First time 'ere?"

Her lively cockney accent made Casey smile. "Hi." She offered a firm handshake to the pale, thin woman sitting cross-legged on a stool. Two packs of Chesterfields were anchoring her place at the bar. "I'm Casey."

"Ah! American, are ya? Are you one 'ove them tourists then, Sweet? Are you gonna ask us all kinds 'ove questions 'bout the queen?"

Her companions seated with her all laughed and nodded knowingly, having a little fun at her expense.

"No, actually, I'm here to work. I'm an actress from California. I'm working with Cameron Hatch on a film." It sounded good to affirm herself as an American artist traveling through Europe, even if it was only in a bar to a group of drunken locals. It felt good to be associated with Cameron and his movie. He was supposedly highly regarded in London.

This hit home with Emma, or appeared to. She lit up like a Christmas tree. "Ow! I luv the theater! Don'cha luv it too, Shawny?"

Her jovial companion chimed in. He was very rotund and wearing a wedding ring—only it didn't appear that it was Emma who was his wife. "Oh yes, indeed we do, Mummy!"

She was his mother? Casey puzzled. What did it matter? This was a new world.

It was all the same to the likes of Shawn and Emma. They were dear spirits, she could tell. Her first real encounter with the London set; so very far from the pretentiousness of LA, but then again, not really all that different.

Casey drank her warm beer and savored the strange flavor of both it, and the local color of the bar. The faces around her were kind and non-judgmental. She felt strangely content.

Later that night, she returned to her motel room feeling strangely invigorated for the first time in months. The Mayflower Motel was a far cry from The Four Seasons, but was nice enough. The agency would continue to support her for the duration of the filming. After that, she was on her own—for good. That was the agreement she had made with Lucas. She had answered an ad online for a room rental in the affluent area of Chelsea, once home to the likes of the Beatles and Rolling Stones. She was excited to be meeting the landlord the next day, a widow and retired cook named Mrs. Perryman, who sounded like quite an eccentric character. The bright, spacious bedroom in the detached brick walk-up built in the early 1800s sounded perfect. It was said to have a separate bath and sitting garden on a tree-lined street in the heart of Central London. Hopefully, it would be as magical as it sounded.

She drew a bath in the antique claw-foot tub and settled into the bubbles with delight. The black-and-white penny tiles on the floor reminded her of a restaurant in Chicago that she had gone to with her family what seemed like a lifetime ago. She closed her eyes and let her thoughts drift and mingle with the vapors of the scented bath oil. Casey figured that the project would last four to six weeks. Long enough, she hoped, to get what she had *really* come for.

Cameron warmed to Casey immediately. While he decided she wasn't the right age to play the lead of Bernadette, she was perfect for a supporting role in the film, and she accepted the role with aplomb. It wasn't Lucas's fault that the casting director didn't see things her way. She brought fire and life to the main character's young cousin, Meagan, who served as Bernadette's ears and voice. The poignant drama was said to play out in the autumn meadows of Dublin, but would be filmed right there in the English countryside.

Casey was introduced to Cameron on a Tuesday, and her first costume fitting was then scheduled for the following Friday, the same day that she moved into Mrs. Perryman's flat. She was delighted that everything was falling into place, and equally excited to be involved in such a spectacular and important project. Cameron's films were epic, and she had to pinch herself to make sure that she was not dreaming every minute of it.

Lucas was notorious for not returning phone calls, but when Baltimore left his fifteenth phone message in a row, it was clear that he was being ignored. Baltimore, in all his wisdom and modesty, knew that there was more than one way to catch a degenerate like Lucas Morgan—lure him. One well-placed phone call to *Vibe Magazine* would be the spark that would ignite the Lucas Morgan Agency's notable CEO into action. It would be bait that a fox like Lucas could not pass up.

The very next morning, back in LA, in his silk robe and boxers, Lucas nearly choked on a Pop-Tart when a document screamed off of his home-office fax. The headline on the lead page of the entertainment wire's *Inside Report* read: GLOBAL NETWORK TO COURT CASEY SINGER AS FOURTH AND FINAL CO-HOST FOR NEW DAYTIME TALKFEST—*THE GAB*. The article went on: *The dynamo model/actress of television's* Paradise Cove *fame is said to be a strong candidate for the show. Sources close to Singer's agent, Lucas Morgan, say it is just a matter of negotiations at this point. "If the network has the dollars, I'm sure that Morgan will release her from any current project to take on this exciting venture. She is the missing gem in the crown they have been searching for," the unnamed source speculated.*

Lucas was incredulous, knocking over his coffee onto the print out with a litany of expletives. "What the—?" Son of bitch! That conniving little whore!"

A call to his contact in New York would verify the prophecy. He would find out who had tipped off the press... and more importantly, how in the hell it was that he was the last to know. It was probably a hoax, he concluded at first; only moments later to concede, with a splitting headache that had him digging through his stash of pharmaceuticals for the Vicodin, and wondering, *but what if it was true?*

He decided to phone the magazine and speak with the reporter directly. He had a litany of the pariah bastards on his speed dial.

"How did you get this information?" Lucas demanded. "Who is this source?"

"It's in all the trades," the frat-boy staffer said. "Word leaked, I guess. It's everywhere, man. We're just reporting what everyone else knows. Casey Singer is the front-runner. You *are* her agent, right?"

Not anymore. The perfect opportunity was about to fall in his lap, and he no longer had claim to Casey's future. *How did this happen?* He raked his hands through his thinning hair, pacing like a wild animal around the coffee table. He concluded that there was no way it could have been Casey. His little trump card was a million miles across the ocean. She was pursuing the Cameron Hatch deal. It didn't add up. He had no means by which to get her back now, and no idea who was using his name to pitch Casey to the network. He was being played.

The house phone rang, and Lucas snatched it up in a flash. "What!"

Another reporter with the same magazine introduced himself and pressed, "Mr. Morgan, are you denying or confirming that Casey Singer is in contention for the Global Network deal?"

"No comment!" He hung up, and a moment later, when it rang again, he yanked the cord from the wall and threw the phone across the room. Suddenly, his cell phone lit up with a deluge of messages and texts. *Relentless bastards!*

Lucas threw on some clothes and headed out the door to the parking garage, racking his brain. If it wasn't her doing, then who could be behind this? A thought stopped him in his tracks. The irritating mope who had been pestering the piss out of him for the past two weeks—Ramirez!

He jumped in the Maserati and, releasing the clutch, he opened full throttle, squealing along the Santa Monica

Freeway toward the city.

CHAPTER 38

★ ★ ★

CASEY SLIPPED OUT OF THE doorway of Mrs. Perryman's flat and breathed in the London air. Her eccentric landlord had several cats, which didn't bother Casey in the least.

"Leave it to 'em strays to find me!" she would say, explaining how she went from one orange Tabby to a brood of five felines. "'Taint a problem for this ole gal," she said, referring to the Tabby. "She luvs to make new friends, and so do I." Her blue eyes sparkled when she spoke, matching the rhinestones on her vintage housedress. Casey imagined that if Mary Poppins were a grandma, she would be Mrs. Perryman with her sweet nurturing ways and rosy red cheeks, although she doubted that Julie Andrews's character hit the schnapps as much as Ophelia Perryman.

Casey was excited to have a couple of days before filming to explore the area and immerse herself into the culture. London was such a marvelous place. It was unlike anywhere she had ever been. Where punks and hippies once populated the bars and bohemian cafés, things were now giving way to business-types in suits, who were snatching up townhomes and ordering up Uber and dinner reservations on their smartphones along the streets and thoroughfares. *No wonder Roe wants to be here,* she thought, noting the progressive and electric vibe.

Casey reached into her Louis Vuitton satchel for a Starbucks receipt on which she had written the address for Castle Records. She had been contemplating tracking Roe down for days, since she first arrived, but chickened out each time she got even remotely close to actually doing so. The words of his last letter were still seared in her brain: *I have moved to London permanently to open a new office for our company. I will miss your light . . . .*

What am I doing? she asked herself as she flagged a cab. *This is crazy, right?* The drive took forty-five long minutes, starting along King's Road, on to The Mall, and then on to St. Martin's Lane. It was a three-story building with clean lines and an extended frame, and glass-pierced brickwork. It looked like an old schoolhouse with its chimney stack and brown and tan-hued stone that had been renovated into a contemporary work of art. It was beautiful and far from corporate-looking, by American standards. A gold decal above the glass entrance doors touted the distinctive Castle Records logo, confirming that this was the right place.

What would Roe do when he saw her? *Maybe I should have called first,* she thought. She felt silly standing there on the curb, her heart pounding. What if Roe could see her right at that exact moment from the window at his desk? He could be straining to look, wondering who the strange girl in the leather coat and leopard-print scarf with dark shades and sleek spiked boots was, standing at the entrance.

The stoic receptionist looked up from a *Harper's* when Casey entered the waiting lounge.

"How do you do?" Casey tried to conceal the fact that she had never uttered those exact words out loud and seriously meant it.

The receptionist blinked. She was plain. Un-pretty.

"I would like to inquire as to if Mr. Roe Evans is in,

please." She could barely breathe for the pounding in her chest that squeezed the words into tiny, wet, raspy syllables.

"And you are . . .?"

"Casey Singer, from the States. I don't have an appointment exactly. I'm a friend."

"I see. Wait here, please."

Casey wondered if the woman could tell that she was trembling.

The woman disappeared behind a corner and left her in the small waiting room with cranberry-colored walls and bold abstract print art, potted plants, and glossy magazines. A vintage jukebox in the far corner was the only music-related vestige. It looked out of place.

A moment later, Roe appeared. "Casey! What an incredible surprise!"

She could see that he was slightly heavier, but was still as tall and handsome as she had remembered. He offered an awkward, near-miss kiss to her right cheek and then squeezed her tightly. "You look smashing!" he said.

She could only manage a silly laugh. "You do too!" The frosty receptionist was looking on, and it made Casey feel uncomfortable. Roe seemed to know this.

"Wait right here." He ducked behind the corner and emerged seconds later with his jacket—a vintage black leather motorcycle bomber from the Springsteen tour. He had keys in his hand. "I won't be back today, Justine. Color me gone."

Together, they walked across the street, where he was parked. Her chariot was a '68 vintage Harley in mint condition. A far cry from the typical luxury boats she was accustomed to seeing him drive.

"Since when do you ride a hog?" she asked.

He grinned and helped her onto the back. "A guy's gotta have a vice, right? Mine's collecting things with wheels."

Another thing Casey did not know about him. She wrapped her arms around his waist and savored the feeling of flying as the cycle burst through the narrow streets out onto the M4 Highway.

They drove a short distance to a café not far away, along the river. It was nearly noon, and the bustling bistro was filled with lunchtime diners. The maître d' greeted Roe with an exuberant smile, waving his arms as if he were landing a plane.

"Ah! Señor Evans! Welcome, my friend. Will there be two of you this afternoon?"

"Yes, Carmon. Meet my beautiful American friend, Miss Casey Singer. She's an actress from Hollywood."

Carmon feigned a painful stroke or heart attack of sorts, gripped her hand, and kissed it gallantly. "Ah, so beautiful is right! Welcome, mademoiselle, to old Italia!"

The two followed him to a tiny square table, where they would sit for the next several hours, drinking fine wine and watching a picture-perfect view of the sun cast brilliant shadows on the plaza.

Roe was smooth. He selected a full-bodied Merlot, along with a generous fruit plate with crackers and Brie. Neither could eat a bite. The impromptu date felt as if it had been planned. It was as if Roe had been waiting for her to arrive.

Finally, she said, "Are you wondering how it is that I found you?"

"You have my planner," he teased.

Casey smiled.

They both laughed.

"I wouldn't expect anything less from you. I had hoped that you would come. I just had no idea when."

"What do you mean?"

"I guess it was just wishful thinking, but when I left you there in Maui, I left the planner on purpose. I wanted you to think of me; to miss me. I hope that's not silly."

Casey touched his hand. There were so many questions she wanted to ask. Things she had wanted to say, for so long. She hesitated, tracing her glass with the back of her hand. "Then, why did you write me that note?"

Roe looked at her painfully, as if his heart forbid him to hurt her. "Tell me," he asked, changing the subject abruptly, "will you be in London long?"

"That depends." She let the words catch and then hang in the air, floating on the sweet aroma of the pizzaiola sauce.

"A day? A month?"

"I'm filming," she finally said, giving validity to her unexplained visit.

Somehow, the answer seemed to sadden him a notch. "Oh."

"I'm cast in *The Dress Maker* at Stagg Studios on lot B. It's a Cameron Hatch film, and Roe, it's really a wonderful project."

"Top-billing?"

"I'm a supporting character, but she's fabulous. I'm playing Meagan. At first, I found her dull and uninspired, but then... I don't know, we came to terms, she and I. And now, it's like we are one and the same."

"What do you mean?"

"I don't know. She just does things right. She sees the world... others, herself, for what they are, and although she doesn't have much of anything, it's all right with her. She's got something more. She's got enough."

He smiled, his eyes shining in the soft light. "I'm so glad for you, Case... and I'm so glad that you're here. I want to show you something; do you mind?"

"Not at all," she said, trusting him completely.

"Tomorrow," he declared, lifting his glass and touching it gently to hers. "I'll show you tomorrow, then. Will you be free in the afternoon?"

The next day was Saturday. She was free. She reached into her purse and carefully lifted out the weathered planner. She placed it on the table and smiled.

"I believe this belongs to you."

Casey lay awake in the half-light. The moon cast a soft glow on the bedpost. One of the tan-and-black cats was curled up beside her, purring rhythmically, not really seeming to mind the lumpy old mattress. Mrs. Perryman's afforded no luxuries, but the price was right, and her wheat cake biscuits and tea each morning was something of a wonder to wake up to.

But who could sleep this night? She had found Roe and was beginning to close the gap that was between them. She trusted him, in spite of the separate manner in which their lives played out, as if by her just being there, fate had given them permission to explore whatever it was that existed between them. Once and for all.

He had dropped her off that night after cappuccinos and biscotti. She was exhausted, still not acclimated to Great Britain time.

"I'll come for you around nine o'clock tomorrow. We'll take a drive to the country."

How positively quaint! Casey had thought. It would be like something out of a Jane Austen novel. Roe was truly the most romantic man Casey had ever known. It seemed that everything he did was poetry.

You're falling, Singer! She could hear Jordy's immortal words echoing in her head. And then, Shelly's wise mantra: *But what is success for, anyway? I mean, if you don't have someone to share it all with?* Shelly was certainly someone who had it all—why couldn't she? What would happen, Casey wondered, if her worst fears about Roe were confirmed? Either they would end up together, or their relationship would have to end. There were no two ways about it. She would have to confront him once and for all.

CHAPTER 39
★ ★ ★

THE RECEPTIONIST STARTLED AT THE sudden intrusion. "Can I help you, sir?"

"I need to see Baltimore Ramirez right away. It's urgent," Lucas demanded.

"Yes, sir. Did you have an appointment?" The stoic matronly woman was somebody's kind mother, seated behind the paneled reception desk.

"No, but he'll see me. Tell him Lucas Morgan is here."

The woman picked up the phone. "If you'll have a seat, sir, I'll see if he is available."

He sniffed nervously and stepped over to the magazine rack and placated himself with the current issue of *High Style*, where, ironically, a spread featuring Casey on page two touted an ad for Hot Looks cosmetics. They were still using her print work copiously. She was still the face of their Lash-out mascara line.

The receptionist delivered the blow. "Mr. Morgan, regretfully, Baltimore's assistant informs me that he had to take an early flight this morning. He's not here."

Lucas cocked his head and smirked. "Is that so? Did she say where he went?"

The woman, now irritated by the interrogation, said, "I

don't exactly know, sir. Gladys says that he is expected back on—"

"Thank you for your help," he said, cutting her off. Then he lurched for the door and headed toward the lobby, taking the stairs two at a time.

Once outside, he drew a deep breath and fumbled for his cell phone. It was nearly eleven thirty. He checked his voice mail on the drive back to his office. There were twenty-seven new callers. Most were reporters from not only the less-than-reputable rags, but from the large entertainment magazines. Some were from colleagues, some from competitors—all inquiring about the big deal with Global Network. The kid from *Vibe Magazine* was still relentlessly trying to reach him, but there was not one call from the network.

He blew into the office like a thundercloud, asking loudly in his wake, "Who has my messages?" Trish was long gone, and no one had yet replaced her. No one wanted the job. Not any assistant worth her weight. Most were college-age acting students or aspiring talent; the type didn't always come with the best of administrative skills, and after Trish's mishap with the cigarette, no one wanted to work for the crazy tyrant. Jacqueline, the Jamaican beauty from across the hall, was the exception. She was desperate for a modeling break, and therefore, was happy to come to Lucas's rescue.

"I have your messages, sir, along with your mail and all of your appointments for this afternoon," she said, placing the stack on his desk, mindful at the same time to offer him an eyeful of her incredible stack as well.

"Cancel my appointments."

"What?" She blinked.

"Did anyone call this morning from New York?"

"No, but about an hour ago, a gentleman... " She checked her notepad. "I think his name was, yes, Baltimore Ramirez. He phoned about an hour ago. He said it was about Casey Singer."

"What? What did he say?" Lucas practically lunged at her. His head was beginning to split; his pulse pounding against his skull in painful blows. She rounded his desk and bent over, letting her Cleopatra-length hair brush against his arm.

"He wanted to know about her availability or something. I don't exactly remember."

He ignored the pass and fished a cigarette out of a pack in his pocket and lit it. "It's important that you remember, Jacqueline. I'm asking you to think. What *exactly* did he say?"

"He asked if she was still with the agency. I said that she was no longer with us. Of course, I first checked her file to be certain and confirmed that the contract had been terminated."

Lucas banged his fist hard onto the desk, sending everything flying.

"Well, she has, hasn't she? Gerilyn in Human Resources has already processed her out."

Fuck! He couldn't believe his ears, or his shit-luck. Casey was a free agent now, and Baltimore knew it. He was probably well on his way to New York at that very moment to pitch her to Global.

He stared out his office window at the brown LA sky. It was a shit storm, all right. *Wait a minute!* he suddenly thought—only Baltimore knew that Casey's contract with the Morgan Agency had been terminated. He was, in actuality, still presumed to be her agent in the real world. *Maybe... just maybe,* he thrilled, *there was still time to get her back!* Casey was well across the ocean, and he was the only one who knew exactly where she was. If only he could get to her in time—he could win her back. There was no way that little selfish brat was going to screw him out of a deal with a network like Global—*no way!*

"Get me a flight to London," he ordered. "I want to

leave as soon as possible. And not another word to anyone about what you told Baltimore—got that?"

"Sure, Lucas. Consider it done."

He rubbed his face. The two-day stubble felt like sandpaper. He had failed to shower and was wearing yesterday's gym clothes. Who were they going to believe at Global? A two-bit modeling agent, or him? He was a bonafide talent mogul with a superstar roster for Christ's sake. He would place the call. He had a contact on the inside that would provide him with the proper connections to the heavies at Global. But first, he would need to call the kid at *Vibe Magazine* and set the record straight. He would tell him that yes, Lucas Morgan was indeed about to seal the defining deal of Casey Singer's career. Then, he would track her down and get her to come back. She *had* to. He would offer her the world... anything she wanted. He knew that they were two of a kind. She had beaten him once before at his own game, but she had him to thank for everything that had fallen into her lap—including this. No one made a fool of Lucas Morgan a second time—especially not America's newest blonde phenom. He was sure of it.

Lucas arrived at Heathrow at noon London time. He was tired but far more famished. He took a cab to his hotel, the Radisson, near Soho on Mercer Street, and checked in. He walked to a pulsating club just two blocks away that was alive with a lunchtime crowd of media types, and fashion forward trendsetters feasting on bar food and beer. A liberally tattooed waitress in jeans and a tank top offered him a menu. She wore several nose studs, eyebrow piercings, and had a Mohawk.

"No breakfast items until eight a.m.," she said when Lucas tried to order eggs.

He studied his options. "Can I get a BLT, then?"

She didn't look amused. "Does it 'ave bacon on 'et?"

"Yes," he said.

"Then 'et's breakfast food. Sorry, bloke!" She cracked her gum. Her front teeth were a war zone.

He stared disbelievingly, and then noticed her relent. "It's jes'ta joke, mate! Don't lose yer rag over 'et!"

She took back the menu and had herself a good laugh. "Keep your pecker up. I'll be right back."

He scowled. He wasn't in the mood for wise-ass waitresses, especially not at four in the morning, or whatever the hell time it was.

He hated London.

CHAPTER 40

★ ★ ★

LONDON, ENGLAND

"HE'S 'ERE!" MRS. PERRYMAN PEERED through her ancient curtains out onto the street. Five locks—three deadbolts, a chain, and a knob-latch had to be unhinged in order to let the guest in. A colony of cats paraded across the linoleum and on the countertops to greet the visitor. Mrs. Perryman patted her auburn wig and threw open the door right before Roe could knock. The bell had been broken for years. Since before Jesus wore sandals, Mrs. Perryman was fond of saying.

"Good mornin', Mr. Evans," she greeted grandly.

He gave her his sweetest smile and a slight little bow, as if she were the Duchess of York. It was a sight to watch. Casey ate it up. She never had a real grandmother, and she imagined that if she did, one like Mrs. Perryman would be just the kind she would have wanted.

Mrs. Perryman was thrilled with all the attention and the opportunity to show off her teacakes. "I baked 'ew two a few treats for the road. 'Ew don't want to get out there and come up hungry, now! There's plenty an' more where 'at come from right 'ere."

Ophelia Perryman was not well-off, but she could put on airs like royalty. She had been left a small stipend from her dear dead husband, Ollie, a former gentleman's butler to a distant relative of the Castle, gone now twenty years. She got a fair draw from the occasional boarders who came to stay on from time to time. "No worries 'ere," she would say with a toothy grin. "Not as long as I has half my noggin' and me cats!"

Casey adored her. And from the looks of it, Roe did too. He kissed her vein-riddled hand and presented her with a small bouquet of pansies that were originally intended for Casey. No matter. It was the perfect thing.

Mrs. Perryman actually grew pink-cheeked and exclaimed, "Ain't he just the mutt's nuts?" Then, she hurried off to the pantry for a vase.

Roe and Casey said their goodbyes and accepted Mrs. Perryman's delights, which were lovingly wrapped in folded dishtowels over tin pot lids. "You bring those lids on back 'ere t'night, missy, or I'll 'ave your security deposit!"

They all laughed and waved. Mrs. Perryman stood watching as Roe helped Casey into the passenger seat of the vintage '78 Mustang and the two sped away for the afternoon.

They drove for an hour, which felt like minutes. Casey watched the scenery change from bustling highways to rolling meadows. The trees and countryside changed colors right before her eyes. They stopped in Runnymede and parked alongside the riverbank beside the Thames. It was the perfect picnic spot.

"Hungry?" Casey tempted Roe with a whiff of Mrs. Perryman's finest crumb cake. It was thoughtfully cut into two perfect servings, with a plastic fork for each of them. The other tin had tea biscuits with ham, but those could keep for hours. A day like this called for having one's dessert first. Casey had to pinch herself. She couldn't believe that fate had brought her to this perfect place in time. Parking beneath a shade tree, she and Roe were finally alone. It was bliss. With Roe, she didn't have to prove a thing. She couldn't think of any place she would rather be. And she could not remember ever feeling as glad to be alive.

Just then, Roe reached over and touched her chin. It was a signal that he was about to kiss her, the way that she had fantasized so many times. She gave him her cheek, and then her lips. She wanted to give herself to him right there in the front seat of the red vintage Mustang, with the radio playing hits from the eighties and the fall breeze stirring the leaves all around.

"I've missed you," she whispered, pulling him into her.

He held her close, and stroked her hair. She felt strangely like crying.

"I feel foolish, Roe. I don't know what's wrong with me." Tears were not her style, but she was losing the battle to control them. In fact, she had not felt anything so powerful since the day after her parents' funeral, in the church back home in Chicago. She had done everything she could to forget all about it. To put behind what was too overwhelming to bear. Yet, this was different. Usually, she just shut down, like at Jordy's memorial, or when her sorrow and despair had brought her to the edge of that jagged cliff on a beach and she found herself empty of even the most basic of emotions. But now, the floodgates were open, and the tears began to pour out.

"Shhhh," he soothed, holding her gently.

Still, she longed to ask him things about himself. Things she might not want to know, but the moment was too perfect to destroy.

"Do you like cricket?" he asked.

"What?"

"You know, the game. It's like bowling, sort of."

"I don't know," Casey said, wondering what he was up to.

"Let's find out. My friend has a field not far from here."

She didn't care where they went. She would accompany him quite happily to the moon; as long as they could be together.

That night, she stayed with him in his small but tidy flat not four kilometers from his office. It was a studio efficiency with an open living room with a Murphy bed, a miniature kitchen, and tiny bathroom. Roe lit a candle on the windowsill and selected a CD, which he popped into the stereo. Soon, the smooth, rhythmic sounds of Usher were bumping through the speakers. She was pleased to see the manner in which he lived. No evidence of another female in sight. The place was under-decorated. It was sparse and plain, and in some ways, like a page out of time.

"My real home is in the south of France," he announced, retrieving two wineglasses from the cupboard. "That's where I perfected my cricket game." They had stopped earlier for supper at a roadside inn, where Roe had not stopped gloating over his merciless victory on the playing field.

"After all, you cheated. I didn't know the rules," Casey said. "Unfair advantage."

"You didn't do too bad for a Yankee," he chided.

She jokingly tossed a punch at his arm, reminding him that he hailed from the oh-so-noble state of Oregon, where cricket meant something very different.

"So you want to play rough!" he said, tackling her to the ground. They wound up on the couch, kissing and groping madly until their clothes were in a tangle on the floor.

The CD gave way to a low humming drone on the stereo.

Finally, Casey had the courage to ask. "Why are you here, Roe? Why did you decide to leave the States?" she said, as they lay in each other's embrace.

"I had to."

"Was it your job? I mean, this office is so much smaller

than Minneapolis, or St. Louis. You oversaw a staff of fifty or more back home. I don't get it."

"Well, I... " He looked at her intently. He seemed like he wanted to say something, but couldn't find the words.

The phone rang. It was a peculiar sort of chirping from an antiquated heavy black unit mounted on the wall. It was vintage kitsch.

She'd hoped that he would ignore it.

"Excuse me." He slid from the couch, carrying a small throw pillow modestly over his privates. His bare backside was a vision Casey savored from her vantage point, now comfortably nestled, naked, in the crevices of the couch cushions. She began to feel a creeping dread as it became soberingly clear that it was a woman on the other end of the line; one with whom he was closely acquainted.

He spoke low and calmly into the receiver. She could barely make out any words, but she could not avoid the realization that she was witnessing the undeniable, excruciating communication between an estranged couple.

She held her breath as Roe negotiated a meeting time, while painfully trying to be inconspicuous. Casey's heart sank. A sickening feeling welled up in her stomach.

He hung up the phone and returned to her, crouching down at the side of the couch. Casey sat up and faced him dead-on, stunned and confused.

"Who is Jane?" she asked.

Her eyes begged for clarity. The truth. His seemed filled with dread.

Casey could see his desperateness. "You just said her name, goddammit, I heard you! That woman... on the line just now. Was that Jane?"

His voice was soft. "No, Case, that was not Jane. That was Jane's mother, Angelique." He then went on, "My ex-wife."

Casey had remembered seeing the entries in his planner marked *Jane*. It was the name that broke her trust in him all in one single instant. She was confused.

"Come with me, Case. I want to show you something. Please, trust me. I'll explain everything."

They got dressed and walked out into the night air. It was cool, and the clouds hung low, covering the stars. She had never seen such a black sky.

Together, they drove in silence to a small street on the edge of town. Roe pulled up to a grassy embankment and shut off the engine. Before them was a beautiful old house. Casey could make out the white shutters and tiny lawn ornaments and chimes spiraling in the wind. It was a picture-perfect Victorian, which resembled a storybook cottage. Lace and ribbon curtains skirted the windows, of which one was aglow with soft lamplight.

"It's pink...Jane's favorite color. I had it done right before we brought her home from Parkside—that's an institution. Jane, my daughter, is severely retarded. She was born with Cerebral Palsy. It's a brain disorder that affects her motor function. She might have had meningitis as a newborn, but the doctors were not sure."

Casey touched his hand.

"That's her room up there," Roe said. "Her nurse is with her now, reading her a story, I suppose." His voice trailed off.

Casey was numb. If she felt or thought anything at all, it was impossible for her to speak. She was taking it all in.

"I don't love Angelique anymore. Things have not been good between us for the past three years now. The divorce was final in June. It was happening when we first met. I swear, I wanted to tell you that it was all just a mistake—Angelique and I getting married in the first place. Two single people who met in an airport terminal. We just hit it off. She was from here. I was glued to my job in the States. We got married after knowing each other only twenty-four days. Isn't that ridiculous?"

Casey wanted to tell him that no, she didn't think it was, but she couldn't form the words. Her eyes pleaded for him to go on.

"Anyway, she got pregnant right after the honeymoon. That next summer, Jane was born—with complications, three months early. She nearly died. Both of them nearly died. The prognosis was bleak. Angelique was devastated." He paused and swallowed hard. "She fled back to England with Jane, to be with her family, I suppose, mainly. I stayed in Minneapolis. Needless to say, the marriage crumbled soon after that. I waited and hoped that they would return. One year turned into two... two into three... I started commuting to London. Used the company as an excuse; a reason to work between both continents. To see Jane."

His mouth tightened, and tears crept from an ocean within, rolling first from one, then the other eye. Casey squeezed his hand gently.

"We agreed on a divorce. No contest. No hassles. But when it came to custody and Jane's care, we differed greatly. Angelique wanted to keep her in the hospital at Parkside. She said that they knew best how to help her and take care of her. Angelique had her music, her work with the symphony; she had her life, and I felt that she was not rightfully putting our daughter first. So, I got the best lawyer I could afford, and I fought Angelique. I fought the system. I fought with myself. Blame... shame... fear. You name it. It was all there. Always with me." He wiped his face with the back of his hand, his nose dripping. "And I won the right to keep my daughter here, in her home."

Casey cringed when he said the words, "my daughter." It was like a bad dream, but she listened as Roe poured out his story.

"They awarded me joint custody—in theory only. Jane is not mobile and cannot be transferred easily from place to place. I knew that there was no other choice but for me to move here permanently. I tried commuting for well over a year. That was what you saw in my planner. Bi-weekly visits... in the park ... at the hospital. Sometimes just with

Angelique at a restaurant or at my lawyer's. There were papers to be signed. Discussions to be had... arrangements to be made. I lived a divided life for longer than I can remember. It took everything I had to manage two lives. I was most concerned about keeping Jane and Angelique out of the public eye. The press, for the most part, did cooperate. I was played to the masses as being single— available even, to dissuade any controversy. I didn't want to make a circus of my family."

"I understand." Casey's eyes shone wet in the half-light. It was all she could manage to say, although she felt more. She felt completely swallowed by the magnitude of Roe's story.

He took hold of her hand in both of his. He was shaking. "If I did anything to hurt or mislead you, God, Casey, I am so sorry. I only wanted to protect you from... this." He looked at the quiet house through a fresh stream of tears, and choked on his words. "I wanted to tell you, but I didn't want to lose you."

She pulled him close as he sobbed in her arms.

The drive back to Mrs. Perryman's was silent. Roe kissed Casey sweetly on the forehead just outside the door. "Take your time with this. You don't owe me anything. I don't want to get in your way. I won't do that. I told you once that you are going places, Case. And you are. See... it's already happening." He touched her hair that shone nearly white in the moonlight.

She was exhausted. She would need time to think; to figure things out. It was all a shock, learning of Roe's double life and watching him break down in front of her like he had. He still was, in her opinion, the most honest and forthright person she had ever met. Roe's love for his daughter was noble. Of course he would choose to be with her.

Was she jealous? Angry? Confused? All of the above. She knew that when she arrived in England, all she wanted was a life that included Roe. Every day, she wanted him, like she had never wanted anything before. But now... everything was changed in an instant, never to be the same again.

She pulled away from his embrace. "Goodnight."

"Goodnight, Princess," he whispered, blowing her a kiss in the breeze. She turned and went inside, slipping into the darkness of the house, closing the heavy door, leaving Roe and her dreams on the other side.

CHAPTER 41

★ ★ ★

LONDON, ENGLAND

LUCAS WAS ON THE PHONE with Stone Kendall, a network consultant for the daytime talk show *The Gab*. Stone had returned Lucas's call from his beach house in Nantucket. It had been nearly fourteen years since they had worked together at Gallant Productions—an independent film house that shot industrial videos, just outside of Berkeley. Lucas provided warm bodies for their then-fledgling director/writer, Stone Kendall, fresh out of UCLA. Lucas was busy himself, humping for deals at the time, and major studio projects were still a far-off dream.

Stone went on to produce documentaries for public television, and some cable affiliates. Eventually, he landed at Global Studios, where he produced a daily news program, and a series of game shows, and a daytime soap drama, which was where he met executive producer Aloysius T. Friedman—affectionately known in the biz as Bumpy Friedman.

Stone had heard through the grapevine that Lucas was representing Casey Singer and was positioning her for the new talk show—his and Bumpy Friedman's brainchild right down to, and including, the casting.

"Yeah, we've been following the trades and Casey Singer's career with some degree of fascination. She's a bit of a risk, though, wouldn't you say?" Stone said. "I mean, her work is spotty at best, and there was the whole suicide thing."

"*Accident*," Lucas quickly corrected. "It was an unfortunate slip-up that's all. Casey's got it all together now. She's presently filming as we speak. She's fielding offers, man. I can vouch for her stability, if that's what's got you worried. She's booked until 2020, for Christ's sake!" Lucas paced with phone in hand, across the all-business carpeting in his London hotel. An obstructed view from the permanently sealed high-rise windows showed a dismal sky. Fall had come to London with a vengeance, bringing cold rain to spit onto the quiet gray city. He sucked the life out of a Marlboro as he paced. This was what he needed to get in to see Bumpy—Stone's blessing. The two were tight as a gnat's ass.

Stone went silent for an agonizing ten seconds and then said, "So if she's so much in demand, how is she going to tape ten shows a week? Not to mention promos, live appearances, photo sessions . . .?"

"Ah! Anything's possible, man. You know that the young ones run on piss and adrenaline—especially that one. She can do it. I promise. Casey Singer will not disappoint."

Stone went silent once again.

"Hey, you're not still sore about all that water under the bridge bullshit, are you, Hoss? You gotta watch those actress types," Lucas said, referring to a falling out that remained a touchy subject between the two. Lucas worried that Stone was still harboring ill feelings over the fact that he had bedded Stone's then-fiancée just three months before their wedding. Since she later turned out to be quite the whore—according to Lucas, making the rounds in Hollywood, so to speak, Lucas figured that Stone just chalked it up to experience and had forgotten about it by now. Fourteen years of mutual dislike would not dissipate with a polite ten-minute transatlantic conversation with the offer of a lifetime pending. Lucas knew this and had to try to play it down. "She would have just bled you, man. You can't trust broads—what was her name? She won an Emmy, or some shit, didn't she?"

"No. A Tony, in 2010," Stone corrected. He was always so good with remembering things, especially the trivial.

"That's right. I wonder what ever happened to her. What was her name . . .?"

"So you say that Casey is exclusive with you?" Stone asked, all business.

"Yep."

"And she's fielding offers right now?"

"Affirmative." Lucas stopped and pumped his fist in the air, catching his reflection in the mirror. He really needed to get back to the gym. The late nights were killing him.

"Is that so?" Stone said. The connection crackled a bit, and his voice was thinning.

"So tell me then, *Hoss*... how is it that I sat in a meeting with Bumpy, his program director, marketing goons, and the network general manager just this morning—along with a Mr. Baltimore Ramirez, who claims that your Casey Singer is no longer under your representation?"

Lucas froze. Stunned down to his stocking feet.

"According to Ramirez, my friend, Casey's a free agent."

Lucas choked. "But, Stoner—"

"Right as we speak, in fact, we are working with Ramirez's people to draw up a deal that we feel will be mutually acceptable for everyone, pending Casey wants to sign on, that is. We still do not have her commitment yet."

Silence.

"Sorry, man," Stone said. "It looks like you were just a little too late on this one. Too bad."

Lucas stammered. "Stoner—what are you talking about

here? Ramirez is a nobody.

He's a fucking thief, that's what he is! Listen to me—!"

"Yeah, well, excuse me for saying, Lucas, but do you even know where your so-called client is?"

"Of course I do. She's right here in London." *Shit!* He'd hunt her down and drag her back himself if he had to. "I'll get a hold of her. We'll come in, sit down, and talk things over with you and Bumpy. What do you say?"

"Give it up, Lucas. She's on her way to New York. She and Ramirez have a meeting with the team on Monday afternoon. Hey—always nice talking to you, though. Oh, and regarding your question about what ever happened to old what's her name? Devin and I have been married for thirteen years now, and we have three beautiful children and a Pit Bull named Fred, so fuck you, man."

With that, the line went dead.

CHAPTER 42

★ ★ ★

THE INTRUSION CAME AT THE peak of dawn. The threadbare curtains were quite ineffective against the stream of sunlight that splashed onto the floor of her room. The sound of Mrs. Perryman's voice calling was grating. "Casey! Casey, darlin', come on down, luv. There's a gentleman vis'tor to see you!"

The clock on the nightstand said seven a.m. She was groggy, just having fallen asleep not three hours earlier. The smell of pancakes, however, wafting from the kitchen burners, further compelled her to pull herself together.

A gentleman? It had to be Roe, she thought. He was back. How much more could her heart take? She wasn't sure that she was ready for more surprises.

"Casey! Did you 'ear me, gal?"

"Coming!" Casey quickly slipped into her robe and splashed cold water on her face to summon color to her cheeks. Her eyes were swollen from crying most of the night. She feared that she looked a fright with her hair clamped into a messy twist, but little could test her natural beauty. Tightening the robe around her, she headed for the kitchen, her bare feet stinging against the cold wooden stairs.

"Oh, 'ere she coms now!" She heard Mrs. Perryman talking to a figure who was standing in the shadows with his back against the window.

Upon seeing him, Casey immediately knew that he was much too thin to be Roe. Then, her breath caught in her throat when she saw who it was. "Lucas!"

He mocked her surprise. "Hello, Casey, you look... well, you look like shit."

He smiled with a grin that looked like it belonged on a serpent. He was holding court in Mrs. Perryman's kitchen with her cadre of cats, who were wreaking havoc on his sinuses. He was swollen and blotchy; his nose raw from blowing.

"You don't look so great yourself. What the hell are you doing here? Are you stalking me?"

"I tracked you down. You're not mad, are you? Mrs. P. here has been entertaining me since dawn... I'm full of tea and crumpets."

"Sit down, luv," the old woman piped. "I'm 'bout to serve me Swedish pancakes!"

A calico licked its paw from on the windowsill defiantly and then leapt toward Lucas's leg. He convulsed and sneezed rapid-fire for one full minute.

"Blimey!" Mrs. Perryman hollered. "You're not going to be able to tolerate Little Lou mooch longer. I'll jost wrap the pancakes up an' you can take 'em with you."

Lucas caught his breath and drew a Marlboro from the pack with his teeth. "I need to talk to you, Casey. It's about business."

"Well, I'm busy right now." She was unconvincing. "And besides, I have nothing to say to you. Our deal is over, remember? God, why did you come here? I have nothing to say to you." She turned and started back upstairs.

His eyes were on fire and tearing badly. The cat dander was prickling every inch of his skin. He swiftly followed her up to her room, much to her fury.

"I said, get out! You can't be here, Lucas," Casey said, gesturing angrily toward the door.

He ignored her and walked in anyway, his heavy footsteps pacing out the length of the small room. He stopped at the open window and lit his cigarette. "Ahhh, to breathe."

"What do you want, Lucas? And make it fast—I mean it. I swear to God, I'll call the police. Say what you came to say. I'm really not in the mood for this. You picked a really bad time."

"Oh, really? Isn't the film going well?"

"Actually, I haven't started shooting yet. We begin in two days."

He paused, thinking. "What would you say if I told you that Global Network back home was interested in signing you to a two-year deal as an anchor of their new daytime talk show? It's called *The Gab*, and you would be one of four co-hosts—little Miss Millennial for the Gen Y demographic."

"I'd say you're full of shit, Lucas. Why would I believe anything you say? Now, will you please get out of my room, before I scream bloody murder and Mrs. Perryman is up here in a flash with a frying pan!"

Lucas smiled. "Are you insane? Oop! Bad choice of words—scratch that. I mean, are you *high*? There is this deal of a lifetime with your name on it—you, Casey Singer. Your name is on the desk at this very minute of the biggest goddamn network executive in New York, and I need you to make a decision. I didn't fly all this way to punk you. Look, I brought the papers; your flight itinerary. You have to trust me." He waved the crumpled proof in front of her.

"You will be back in the States by tomorrow afternoon. You have a two p.m. meeting with the network on Monday. I can go ahead and deliver the deal. All you have to do is sign this. I'll see you at Global on Monday, and we can cinch this thing—"

"What's the rush?" She yawned. She was still thinking about the pancakes, her stomach rumbling. She couldn't trust anything Lucas said. *Wasn't there already a glut of day-time talk shows with pretty talking heads sitting around a table, whining about PMS or the latest celebrity sex scandal?* It had to be a set up; Lucas's sick way of trying to lure her back. "Look, I can't just up and go. I have commitments. Have you forgotten that I'm about to make a film?"

Suddenly, her cell phone rang on the bureau. She snatched it up, careful not to let Lucas see the caller. It had to be Roe, she was certain.

"Hello?" She smiled when she heard the familiar voice on the other end of the line. It was Baltimore.

"Has he gotten to you yet?" Baltimore said, his voice sounding frantic.

"What? *Who?*"

"Lucas. Has he found you?"

"Yes," she said matter-of-factly, so as not to tip off Lucas, who had slithered past her and back down to the kitchen for another tea biscuit.

"Listen to me, Casey—Lucas is playing you. He is going to try to get you to sign with him again, promising a deal with some very big players in New York. Do you hear me?"

"Yes," she calmly said, keeping her voice low.

"It's legit, Case. I can tell you that. I would like you to consider this offer. Do whatever you like, but know that you don't need Lucas to get it. The people at Global want you. Do you understand? You don't owe him anything. He'll try to convince you that he spun the deal."

"I see," Casey said, her head spinning.

"Can you get on a plane tonight?"

She smiled. "Yes, I can."

"I will see you back in the States then," Baltimore said. "Be careful." Then the line went dead.

She didn't hesitate. Quickly, she bounded down the stairs,

faking tears, and declared matter-of-factly, "Well, what do you know? That was Cameron Hatch on the phone. I have just been informed that they are scrubbing the movie. It seems that the project has been shelved until further notice."

"Yes!" Lucas shouted, dribbling crumbs down his shirt and onto the floor. "Fate is a beautiful thing, wouldn't you say? You are free to move on."

Mrs. Perryman's jovial face saddened. "Oh, I'm so sorry to 'ear that, dear. So you will not be stay'n on then, I reckon?"

"I'm afraid not," Casey said, settling into the chair. She helped herself to a pancake, folding a steamy corner into her mouth, but her hand was shaking. "I guess I'm going home then." She looked at Lucas. "I'll take that flight... if you're still offering."

"Of course! See, it's all falling into place, babe. You're going to be golden."

Casey cringed. She despised him more than anyone in the world.

Lucas added, "First stop is New York City, of course, and sweet destiny. Oh, and don't forget to bring your signing pen!"

Mrs. Perryman saw him out. Casey was certain that the sweet old woman had no idea what had transpired, only that Casey would be leaving and she would be losing her latest tenant.

Casey packed quickly so as not to think too deeply about the syncretistic way that life had delivered its blow—once more giving a little something in exchange for ripping another dream from her heart.

It could never have worked with Roe, she tried to convince herself as she gathered two and a half month's worth of clothing into four suitcases and a large travel bag. It was her entire world on wheels. She wondered what Global Network would think of her if they knew how cash-poor and credit rich she was. She had a killer wardrobe, a million-dollar smile, and a body that made grown men cry, but the truth of the matter was, she was homeless. There was no place to go back to after the meeting in New York. Once again, she was flying by blind faith.

Thankfully, Baltimore warned her about Lucas or she may have just told him to go to hell. *What a slug!* How dare he follow her halfway around the world to try to get her back in his camp? She had to admit that, in a way, she was guilty of the same; for threatening to do him in as she had by blackmailing him. Maybe she and Lucas were not that different at all. They both possessed a fierce desire to get what they wanted—at any cost. Baltimore had said that Global wanted her. She could not believe her misshapen luck.

She only needed to embrace it.

Casey called Baltimore on her cell from the cab and gave him her flight information. He would be waiting for her at the gate at La Guardia. She would stay in New York prior to the meeting, which was scheduled for nine a.m. the following morning.

"Baltimore," she said and sighed, "I just want you to know, whatever happens out there, no matter what they decide, I want you to represent me. After all, this was all of your doing, wasn't it?"

He paused, and then said, "I'm flattered that you feel this way, but don't worry about any of that now. In fact, don't worry about anything. I'll do all that I can, but you're going to need expert legal representation going forward."

What was he saying? That he was abandoning her?

"I took the liberty of contacting Regina Madison. She's the best entertainment lawyer on the east coast. You'll be in great hands."

Casey paused. "I don't know how to thank you."

"No problem, kiddo. I'll see you in New York. Be prepared to stay up late. We'll be going over the players for Monday's meeting and discussing a plan going forward, okay?"

"Okay. Hey—what about Lucas? He thinks the meeting is at two p.m."

"Exactly," Baltimore said. "It should be well over by then."

Oh my God, she thought. *Lucas is going to go ballistic when he finds out that they duped him.* She loved Baltimore.

"Just be on that flight tonight, okay, superstar?"

Casey smiled. "I'm as good as there!"

CHAPTER 43

★ ★ ★

THE MEETING WAS SWIFT AND painless. Introductions were a blur to Casey. They waited a full thirty minutes for executive producer Bumpy Friedman to arrive with his entourage trailing behind him. An urgent client call or other corporate dilemma had detained them, and they were all apologies.

LeMaster, the tallest one, yanked at his tie and cleared his throat to start things off. "Thank you for coming in, Miss Singer, especially all the way from London."

Bumpy Friedman reminded Casey of a nervous bull-dog, sitting at the head of the large conference table, looking small and fidgety as he leaned forward in the massive leather chair. A diet Coke—his signature drink—was permanently affixed to his hand. Baltimore's background information on him was so thorough that she knew that Bumpy had stayed up the night before, holed up in a hotel lobby of the Sheraton, where they went over every detail of every player in the room, paying little attention to the sleep they were not getting. "You can sleep for a week after tomorrow," Baltimore had said. "Let's go over LeMaster's profile—he's really just Friedman's puppet. Stone Kendall is the one who has Friedman's ear."

A catalog of press releases and promotional photos of Casey, dating all the way back to the early days, were arranged in a file folder simply marked, SINGER, NUMBER FOUR. Her entire career—her life's résumé, was poured into that one file folder, compiled by Chase's promotional department, pitching her as the tenacious yet lovable spokeswoman of the Generation Y set; idolized in circles of young women ranging from their teens to twenties. The question being, was she compelling enough to sell it to all of America; to anchor the fourth and final seat on *The Gab*? That was the decision at hand.

Tom LeMaster, head of corporate marketing, sat next to Bumpy Friedman. Next to them was the show's director, Barry Paige, a seven-year veteran of Global Network. He had nine sit-coms to his credits and had directed two solid talk formats to Emmy glory. He was a homosexual and cared little for fussy starlets. She would need to come across as crisp and intellectual to turn around his bias against model-actresses with LA credentials.

Next to Barry was corporate accountant Mike Cross, station manager Hans Schultz, several scriptwriters, a promotions expert named Sue Lee Tan, and of course, Baltimore and Casey completing the circle.

The tension in the air could be cut with a knife. All eyes were on Casey, who sat wondering what exactly it was that they expected from her.

Bumpy Friedman had the first question for Baltimore. "Regina tells me that you launched Ms. Singer's modeling career with your agency. She attributes you as giving Casey her first break."

"Indeed we did, but make no mistake—Casey won over our client immediately. She earned a five-year contract as spokeswoman for Aussie Jeans."

"And later the face of Hot Looks cosmetics," Casey added.

Stone Kendall whispered into LeMaster's ear, and he, in turn, to Bumpy. They all nodded in unison. "And where is your current agent, Ms. Singer? Is it true that you are no longer with Lucas Morgan?" Bumpy asked. "Seems everything I've read of late has you two linked pretty tight."

"You know what they say—don't believe everything you read," Casey said slyly.

Silence befell the room. Regina stiffened, at the ready for damage control. "Uh, what she means to say—"

Casey continued. "No sir, I am not with Lucas Morgan any longer, although somebody ought to tell Lucas that."

Sue Lee, who looked like she had just bit into something sour, asked, "You have a history, let's say, shall we, of not being very reliable, Casey. How do you respond to that criticism?"

"I do my best to alleviate that now by exercising time management. I just squeeze it in between the wild parties, my Pilates class, and trips in and out of re-hab."

Sue Lee blanched. Baltimore kicked Casey sharply beneath the table and had to restrain Regina from jumping in.

Too late. Casey broke a smile and winked at Bumpy, who was already rolling with laughter. "Just kidding!" she chided. "Hey, if you can't laugh at yourself, then what have you got?"

She was marvelous. She had them. It was obvious to anyone that Casey could hold her own. She owned the room.

"Bet she could give Whoopi a run for her money," Mike Cross snickered beneath his breath.

"Really put her through the paces," Shultz added.

The day's agenda was fast-paced and furious. First, they viewed a multimedia presentation depicting the show's concept and ideas for the pilot. Set designs were already in place, and the creative for the launch was spectacular. A power point presentation followed, outlining the network's goals and the station's commitment to capturing viewership that outnumbered the competition in the mid-morning television time slot.

"We have placed the first three anchors," LeMaster said. "Of course, this is highly confidential." He outlined the other three's credentials and bios. Casey was amazed and slightly intimidated by the magnitude of talent she would be positioned to work alongside—none other than TV radio host Dr. Hannah Cortland Murphy, fashion mogul Kathryn Delacorte, and hot erotic author LaCosta Reed. The cast would be nothing short of sensational.

A series of one-on-one interviews followed, and finally, they broke for lunch at noon. Afterward, she was taken over to the studio on the ground floor to do a run through reading and camera test.

"I was so nervous about Lucas," Casey told Baltimore on the elevator ride down. "I was expecting him to burst through that door any minute. He's been texting me all morning."

"Don't you worry about him. By the time he waltzes in, this will all be over and you'll be locked into the deal of a lifetime and getting set to charm the pants off of all of America!"

His vindictive little laugh made her adore him all the more.

"I've never seen you like this, Baltimore. I never knew that you despised Lucas that much."

"I don't give a rat's ass about Lucas Morgan," he said. "I just believe in you, that's all. You deserve this, kiddo. It's yours for the taking. Not his."

She suddenly got an uneasy feeling. She wasn't often wrong about such things. "You're not going to represent me, are you?" she asked.

He shook his head. "No. That's why Regina is in the picture. She'll negotiate for you. This is her territory. You listen to her. She'll make you a very rich woman."

They called for Casey from the set. They were ready for her.

Baltimore returned to LA the next morning. Casey decided to stay on in New York. It was going to be her new home, and she would have to find a suitable apartment right away. She accompanied him to the airport to say her goodbyes. "The signing is on Thursday at eight o'clock sharp at the executive offices," he reminded her. "Regina will meet you there and walk you through it, okay? Don't be late. Show them the pro that you are. Make us all proud."

She hugged his neck. No one had ever said those words to her except for Nathan, her father, so many years ago. "Tell Connie thank you for letting me steal you away for so many days."

"I will." He smiled. "Good luck, Casey." He turned, waved goodbye, leaving her alone at the curb. She climbed into the waiting cab and dialed the UK extension. She had been putting off calling Roe and relaying the news. They had exchanged awkward e-mails a number of times, and she had texted about the pending audition. She listened as the distant line connected, sounding a million miles away. Just before he picked up, she stopped herself and hung up. She couldn't do it. She couldn't tell him the news that she had finally made it; and that it meant she wouldn't be coming back.

CHAPTER 44

★ ★ ★

ONE MONTH LATER
GLOBAL STUDIOS, NEW YORK

*S*HE COULD NOT BELIEVE THAT *it had come to this. Weeks ago, she was so certain about what she wanted; what she had worked so hard for. Either way, she would be happy. Or would she? Roe's incessant texts, pleading for her answer to his invitation to move to London to live with him seemed, itself, like a fairy tale, one of which there would never be a truer prince.*

"Ma'am?" the driver said, breaking her from her reverie. "It's time."

The photo session for the cast was scheduled for seven a.m. There was a lavish continental breakfast with lox and bagels, pastries, assorted chopped fruit, and fresh squeezed juices. Transportation was arranged for the ladies; shiny black limos in true diva style. Hair stylists and makeup artists were on hand to primp and powder them for the shoot. Bumpy Friedman spared no expense. The network photographer had run through his lighting and set adjustments and was just waiting for the entire cast to arrive.

Kathryn Delacorte, of fashion industry fame, and third cast member hired, had her own photojournalist present to snap some shots for the upcoming issue of her magazine, *High Style*. It had been arranged by the jittery junior executive in a tight pencil skirt and stilettos, who was running everyone around with directives. So much was riding on the success of both the promotional photo shoot for the network, as well as the exposé for the magazine. Ms. Delacorte's company had hired an up-and-coming photojournalist named Ellie Logan to capture the cast in a series of candid shots when they would all be officially meeting for the first time.

"This will be magic," Bumpy said, noting the time on his watch.

"If the photos of the cast are as sensational as I think they will be, we'll have our billboard and bus ads cinched for the outdoor campaign," LeMaster added.

"Are they all here?" Bumpy asked, growing more agitated than usual. It was after seven.

Somebody slammed a cell phone, fuming. "Goddamn prima donna! What does she think she's pulling?" Casey was a no-show.

The room quickly began clearing of union technicians and set decorators; one by one, lights were extinguished, and equipment shut down. Ellie started disassembling her tripods.

Bumpy's face turned fifty shades of red. He knew it! Casey was far too unpredictable to take a chance on. Clearly, she had been a risk—possibly a wrong decision all along. She was antagonistic and spoiled. Pulling this stunt so early in the game would definitely seal her fate.

"Get me legal," Bumpy said to LeMaster as he watched the room shift into chaos.

"What about the other three?" he asked.

"We'll postpone the shoot until—"

Further commotion stirred at the stage door. Everyone

turned. All eyes were on Casey, who had strolled in tragically late, but nonetheless—in the flesh. "What are you all staring at?" she said, breathless and blonde. "Let's DO this thing!"

Roe stared at the article for a full minute. His assistant, Justine, had first confiscated the celebrity magazine intended for Roe the moment she discovered it in the morning mail. She had fancied a dose of juicy entertainment gossip, along with a strong latte to get the day going. She'd noticed the bright pink post-it note tagging the featured article—an exposé on the new American talk show, *The Gab*, complete with Casey's headshot prominently gracing the glossy page with the caption:

JUST IN UNDER THE WIRE. CASEY SINGER, THE TWENTY-EIGHT-YEAR-OLD ACTRESS CHOSEN AS THE FOURTH AND FINAL DIVA OF THE NEW DAYTIME DISH-FEST.

"Aye! Isn't this that woman? Your American friend. What was she? The *actress*?" Justine had said as she handed the magazine over to Roe. "Guess she wanted to show you this."

He examined the envelope. It was Casey's handwriting, no question. His lips pressed into a light smile. *She would be brilliant*, he told himself... *brilliant*.

Then he handed the magazine back to Justine and walked out of his office, onto the empty street.

ABOUT THE AUTHOR
★ ★ ★

Jamie Collins writes larger than life women's fiction that is fun, sexy, and far from unforgettable. Her "Secrets and Stilettos" series is binge-worthy reading about the fast-track world of media and entertainment. As a former model/actress, she infuses her stories with Hollywood grit, sizzle, and heat reminiscent of the great women's fiction writers (Jackie Collins, Sidney Sheldon, and Olivia Goldsmith) of decades past on which she cut her writing chops reading and emulating their iconic styles. Collins brings a fresh, modern-day take on the throwback pocket novel tomes that defined an era of extravagance and excess in exchange for a world where women are more powerful, smart, and driven than ever. Collins' stilettos have been everywhere from nightclubs in Japan to the Playboy mansion, to dinner with a Sinatra. Her aim is to delight and entertain readers of women's fiction everywhere.

Check out Jamie Collins' website for more information about the books in her "Secrets and Stilettos" series at **www.jamiecollinsauthor.com**. Sign up to her mailing list to stay in the know and take the opportunity to join her **Stilettos Street Team** and become a part of the journey. There's nothing like a walk, in stilettos!

Follow Jamie Collins on
Twitter, Facebook, and Instagram.

Made in the USA
Middletown, DE
08 January 2021